MW00897842

THE HAPPY SHOP

AN ONI PRESS PUBLICATION

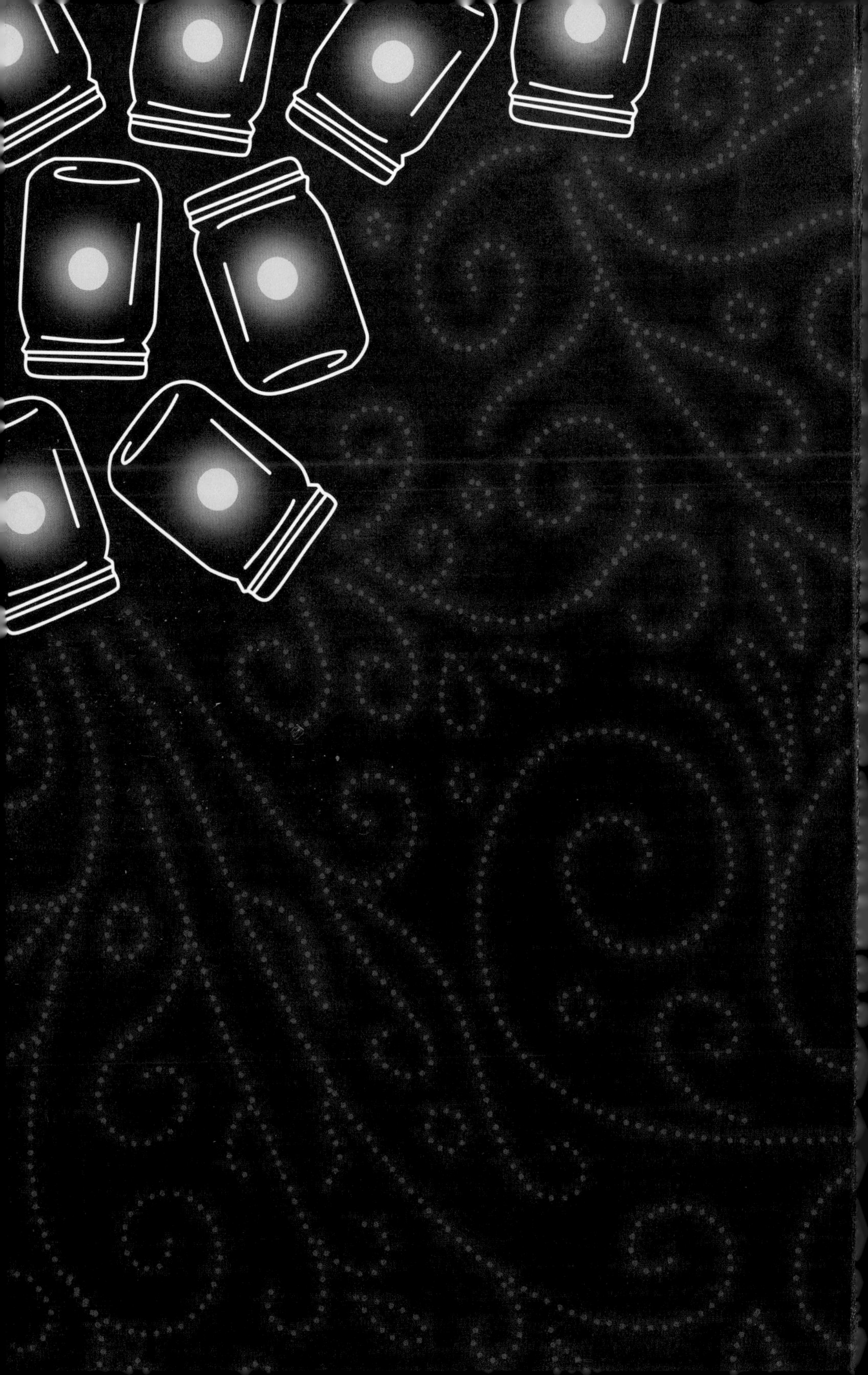

THE HAPPY SHOP

Written and Illustrated by
BRITTANY LONG OLSEN

Lettered by
CRANK!

Edited by
SHAWNA GORE and GRACE SCHEIPETER

Designed by
CAREY SOUCY

PUBLISHED BY ONI-LION FORGE PUBLISHING GROUP, LLC.
1319 SE Martin Luther King Jr. Blvd. Suite 216 Portland, OR 97214

Hunter Gorinson, president & publisher · Sierra Hahn, editor in chief · Troy Look, vp of publishing services · Angie Knowles, director of design & production Katie Sainz, director of marketing · Jeremy Colfer, director of development Chris Cerasi, managing editor · Bess Pallares, senior editor · Grace Scheipeter, senior editor · Megan Brown, editor · Gabriel Granillo, editor · Zack Soto, editor · Jung Hu Lee, assistant editor · Michael Torma, senior sales manager · Desiree Rodriguez, digital marketing manager · Andy McElliott, operations manager · Sarah Rockwell, senior graphic designer · Carey Soucy, senior graphic designer · Winston Gambro, graphic designer · Matt Harding, digital prepress technician · Sara Harding, executive coordinator · Kuian Kellum, warehouse assistant · Joe Nozemack, publisher emeritus

ONIPRESS.COM ✿ FACEBOOK.COM/ONIPRESS
✿ TWITTER.COM/ONIPRESS ✿ INSTAGRAM.COM/ONIPRESS
BRITTANY LONG OLSEN ✿✿ @BRYTNING

FIRST EDITION: FEBRUARY 2024 · ISBN: 978-1-63715-279-9 · eISBN: 978-1-63715-280-5
PRINTED IN THE USA · LIBRARY OF CONGRESS CONTROL NUMBER: 2023939193
2 3 4 5 6 7 8 9 10

THE HAPPY SHOP, February 2024. Published by Oni-Lion Forge Publishing Group, LLC., 1319 SE Martin Luther King Jr. Blvd., Suite 216, Portland, OR 97214. The Happy Shop is ™ & © 2024 Brittany Long Olsen. All rights reserved. Oni Press logo and icon are ™ & © 2024 Oni-Lion Forge Publishing Group, LLC. All rights reserved. Oni Press logo and icon artwork created by Keith A. Wood. The events, institutions, and characters presented in this book are fictional. Any resemblance to actual persons, living or dead, is purely coincidental. No portion of this publication may be reproduced, by any means, without the express written permission of the copyright holders.

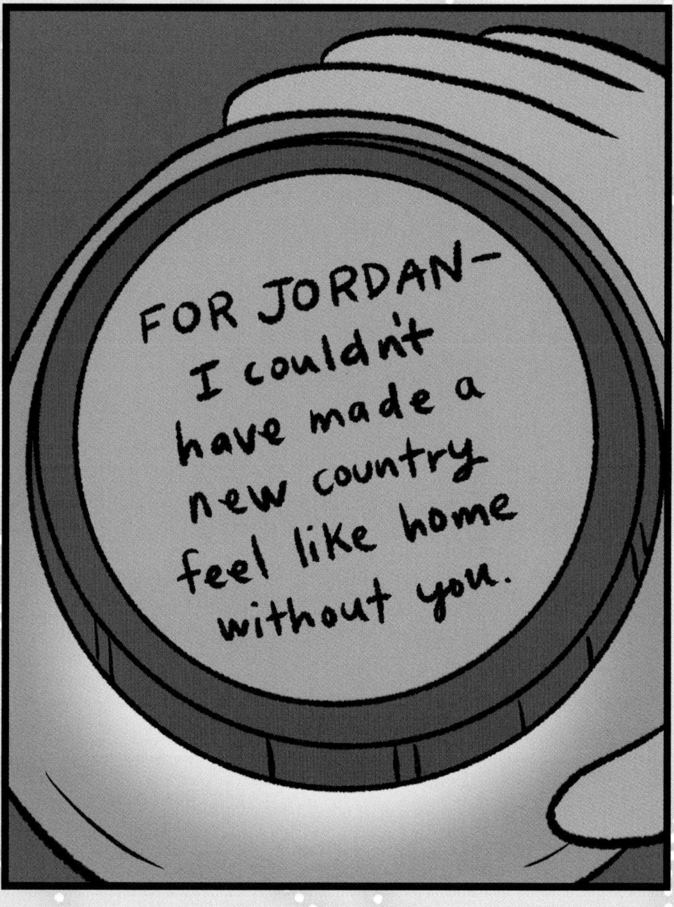
FOR JORDAN-
I couldn't
have made a
new country
feel like home
without you.

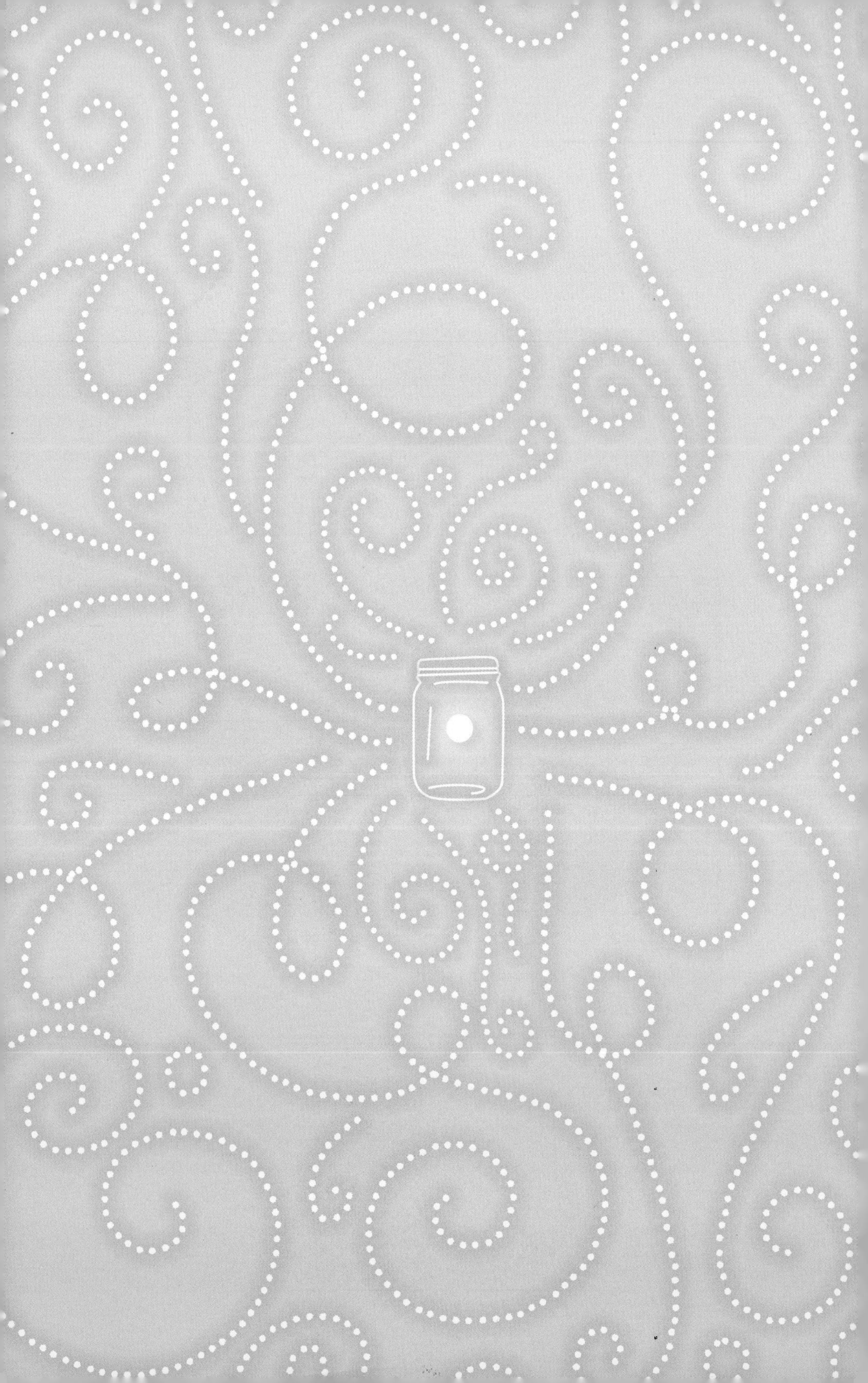

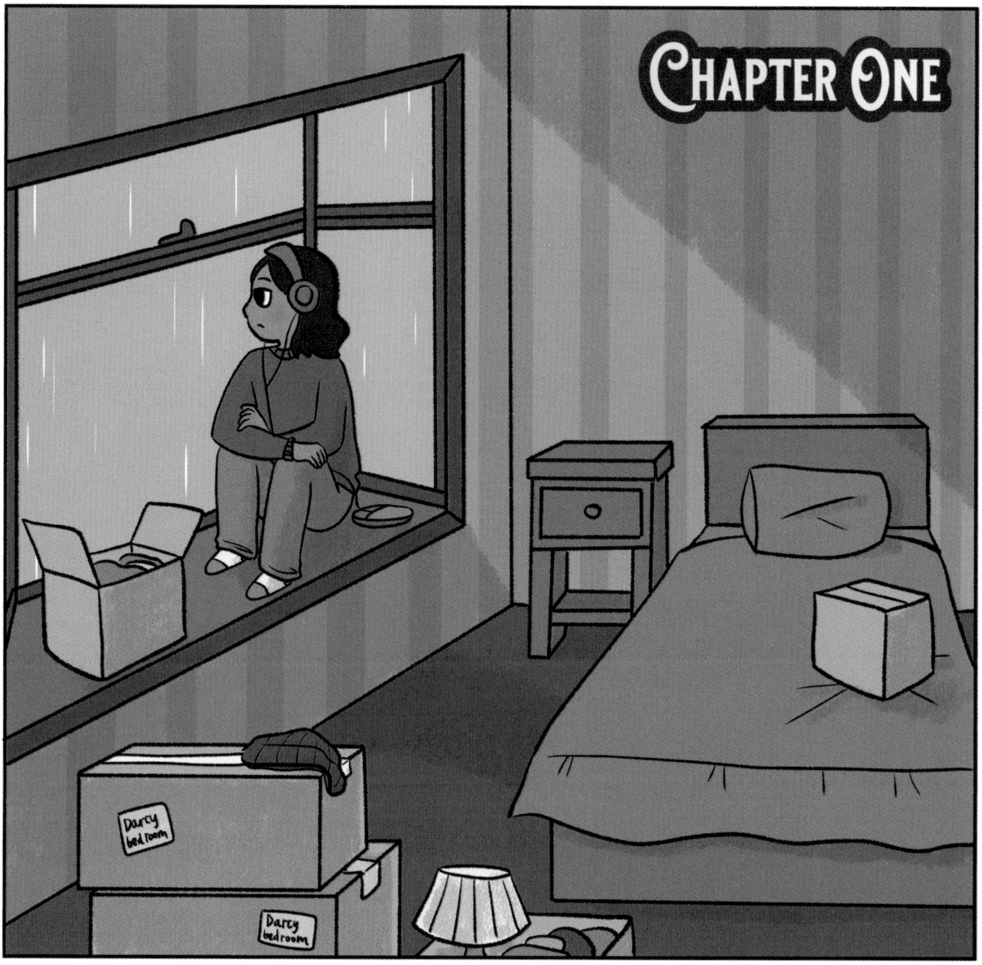
CHAPTER ONE
Darcy bedroom
Darcy bedroom

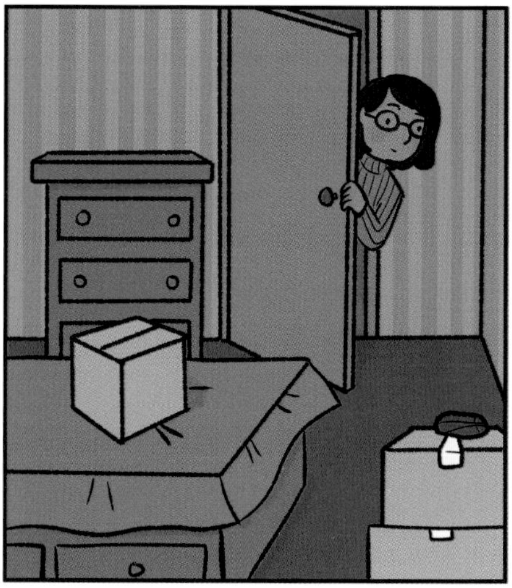

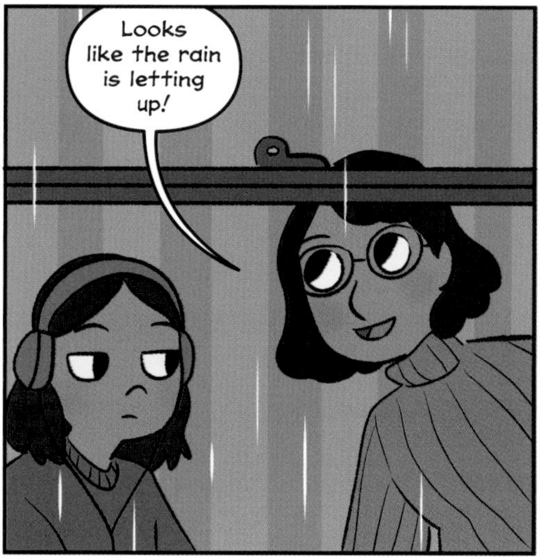
Looks like the rain is letting up!

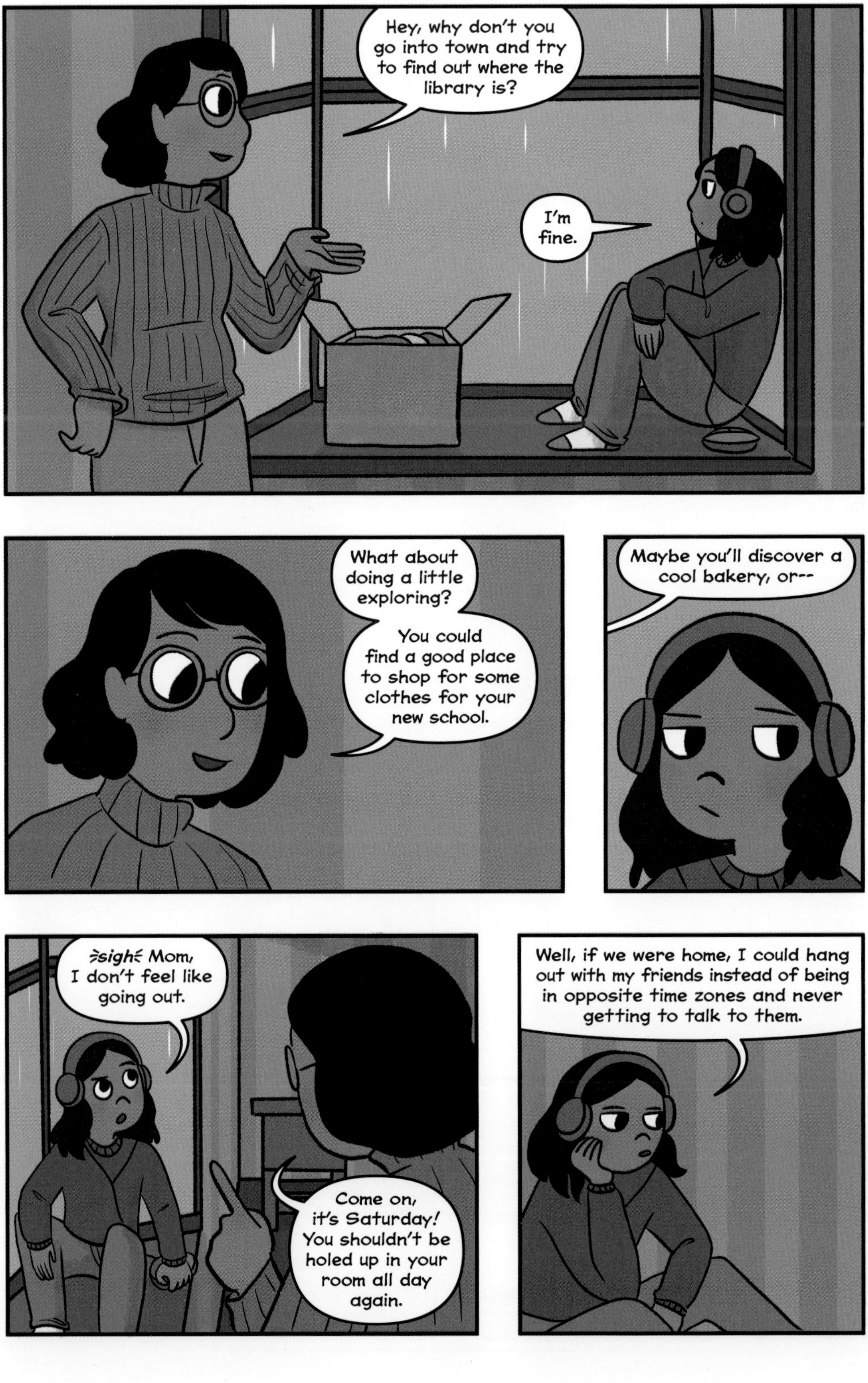
Hey, why don't you go into town and try to find out where the library is?
I'm fine.
What about doing a little exploring?
You could find a good place to shop for some clothes for your new school.
Maybe you'll discover a cool bakery, or--
sigh Mom, I don't feel like going out.
Come on, it's Saturday! You shouldn't be holed up in your room all day again.
Well, if we were home, I could hang out with my friends instead of being in opposite time zones and never getting to talk to them.

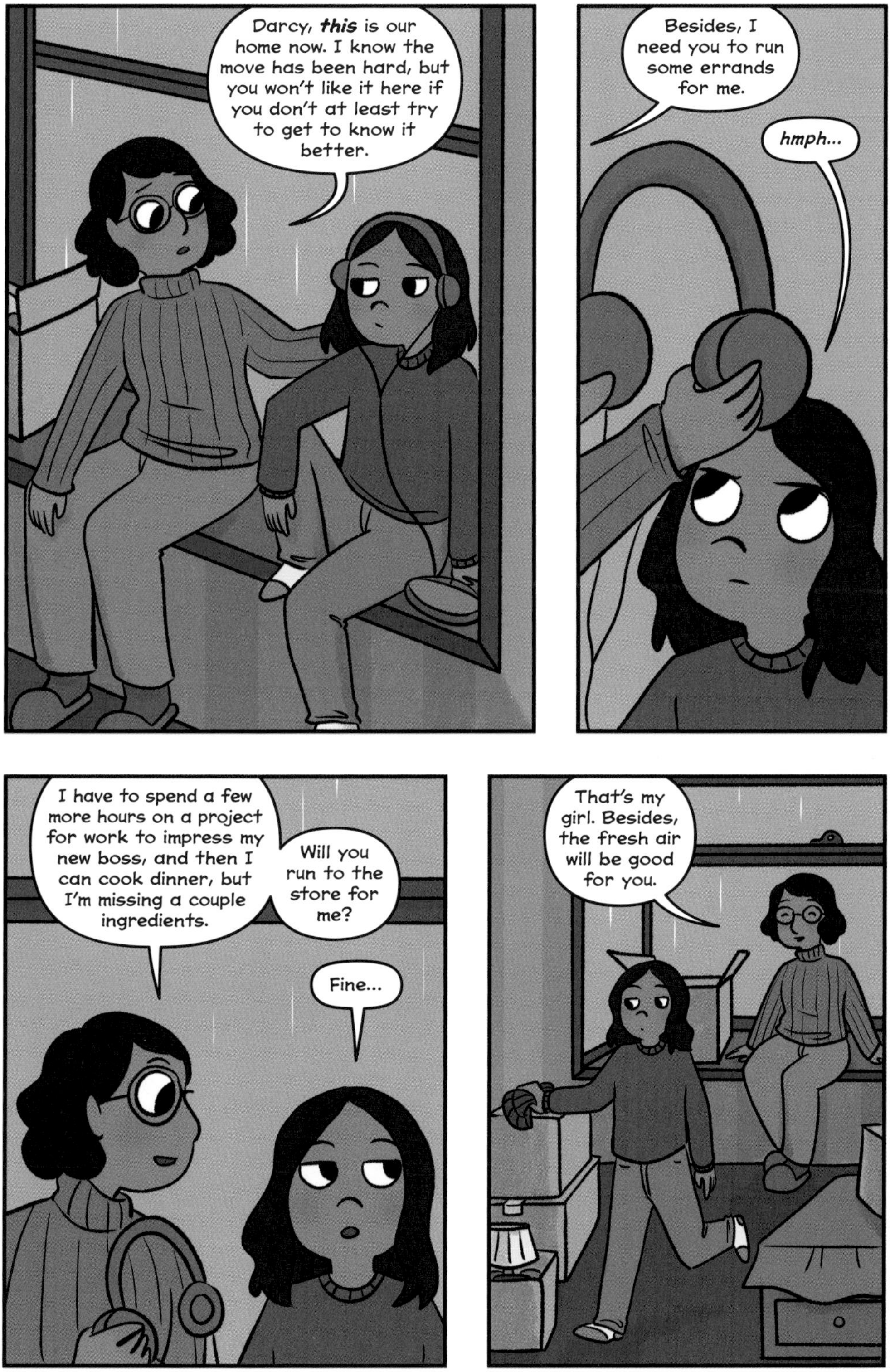
Darcy, ***this*** is our home now. I know the move has been hard, but you won't like it here if you don't at least try to get to know it better.
Besides, I need you to run some errands for me.
hmph...
I have to spend a few more hours on a project for work to impress my new boss, and then I can cook dinner, but I'm missing a couple ingredients.
Will you run to the store for me?
Fine...
That's my girl. Besides, the fresh air will be good for you.

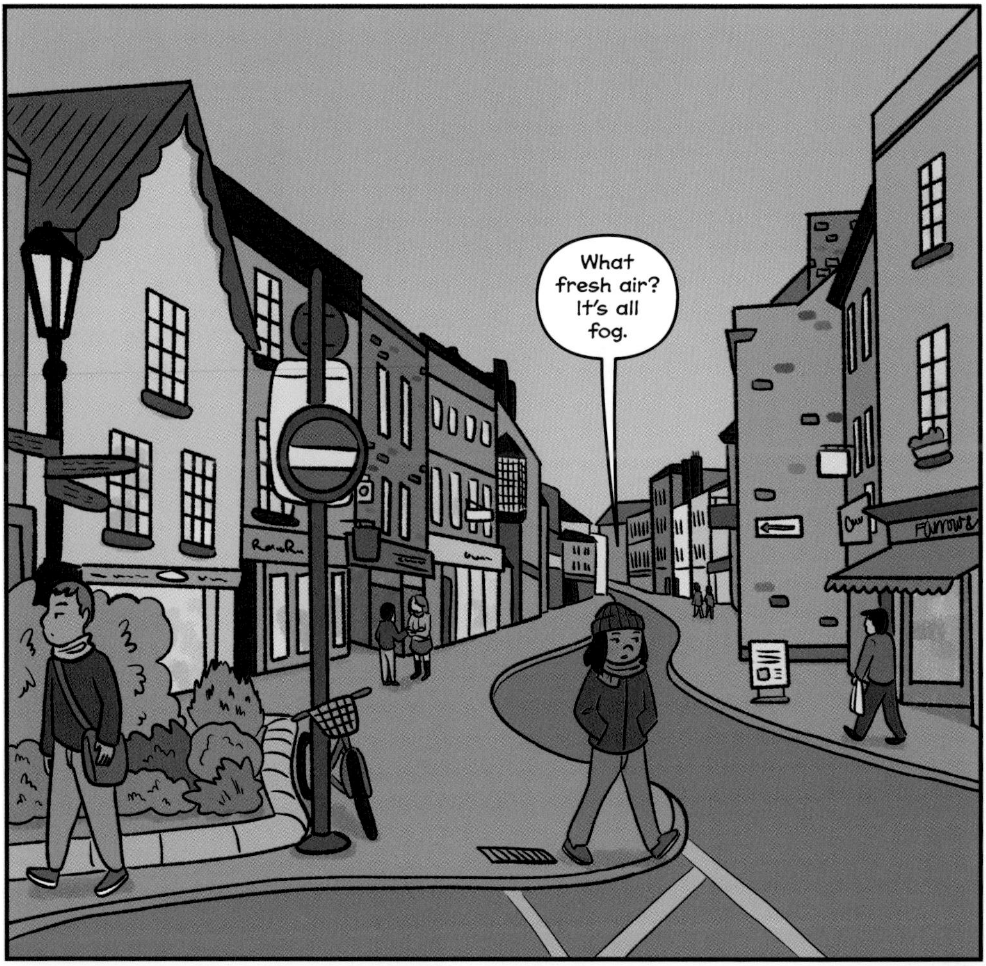
What fresh air? It's all fog.

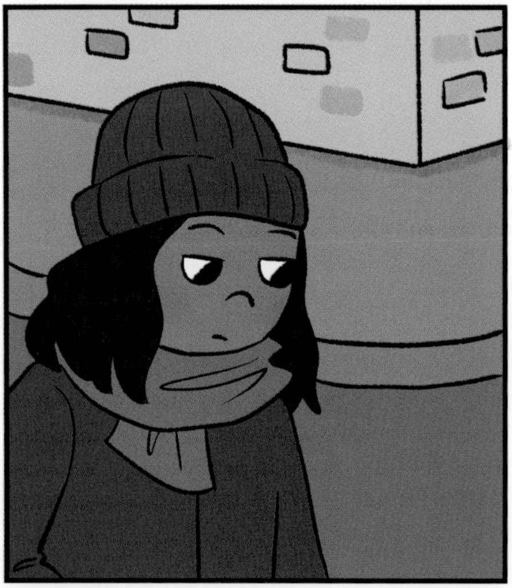

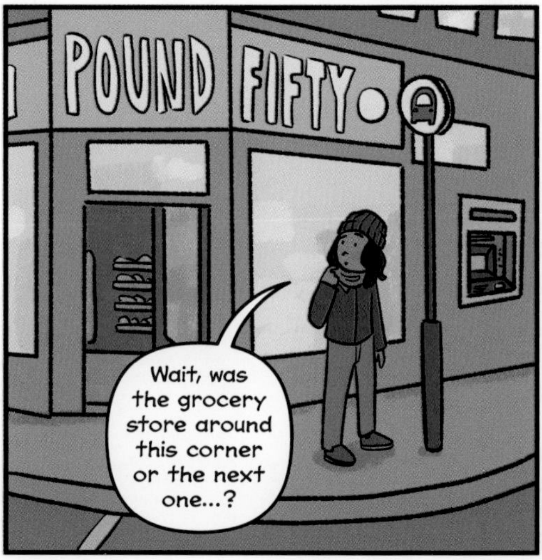
POUND FIFTY
Wait, was the grocery store around this corner or the next one...?

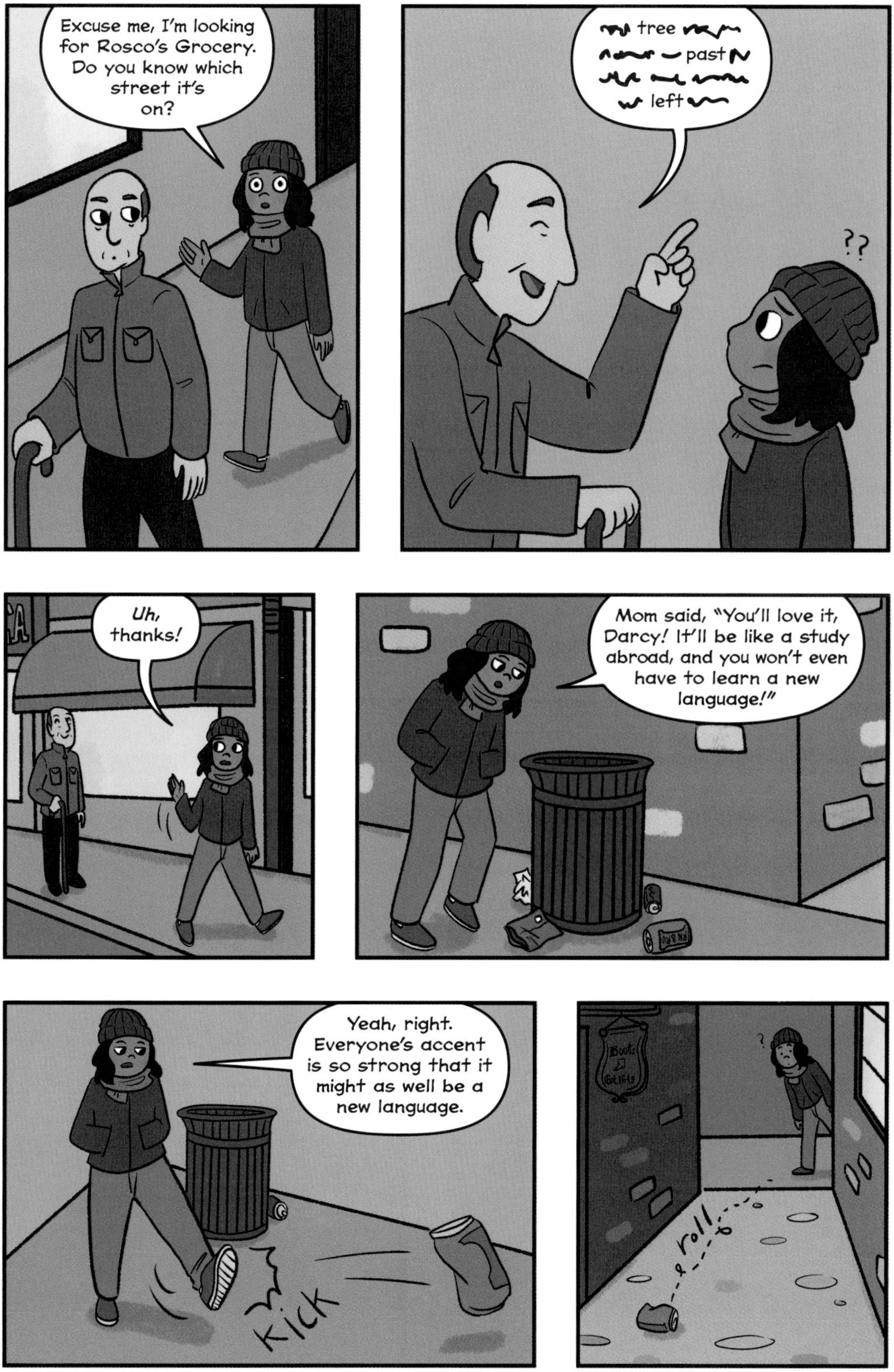
Excuse me, I'm looking for Rosco's Grocery. Do you know which street it's on?
tree
past
left
??
Uh, thanks!
Mom said, "You'll love it, Darcy! It'll be like a study abroad, and you won't even have to learn a new language!"
Yeah, right. Everyone's accent is so strong that it might as well be a new language.
KICK
roll
?

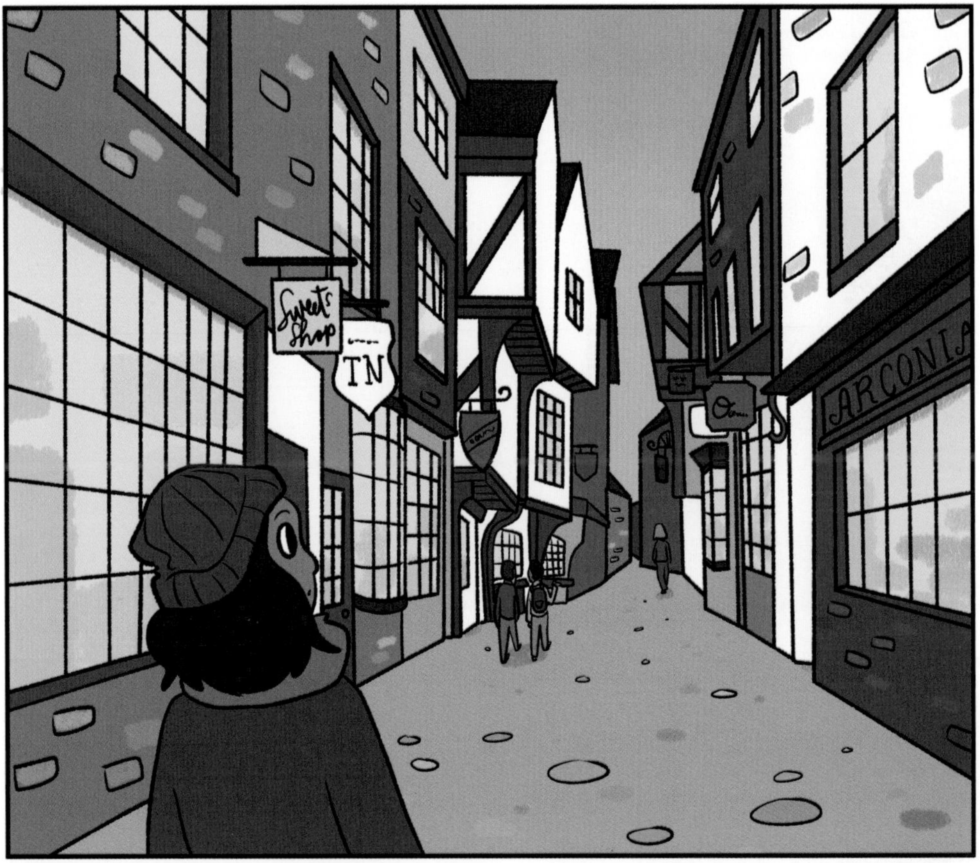
Sweets Shop
TN
ARCONIA

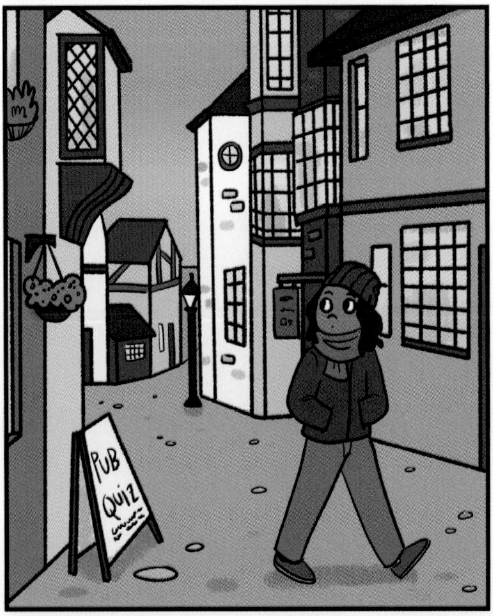
PUB QUIZ

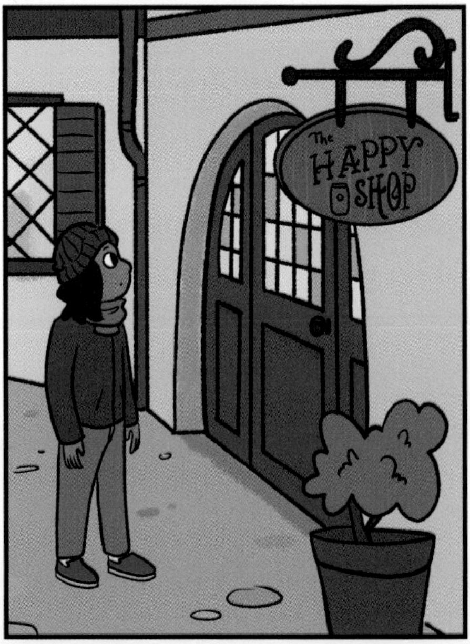
The HAPPY SHOP

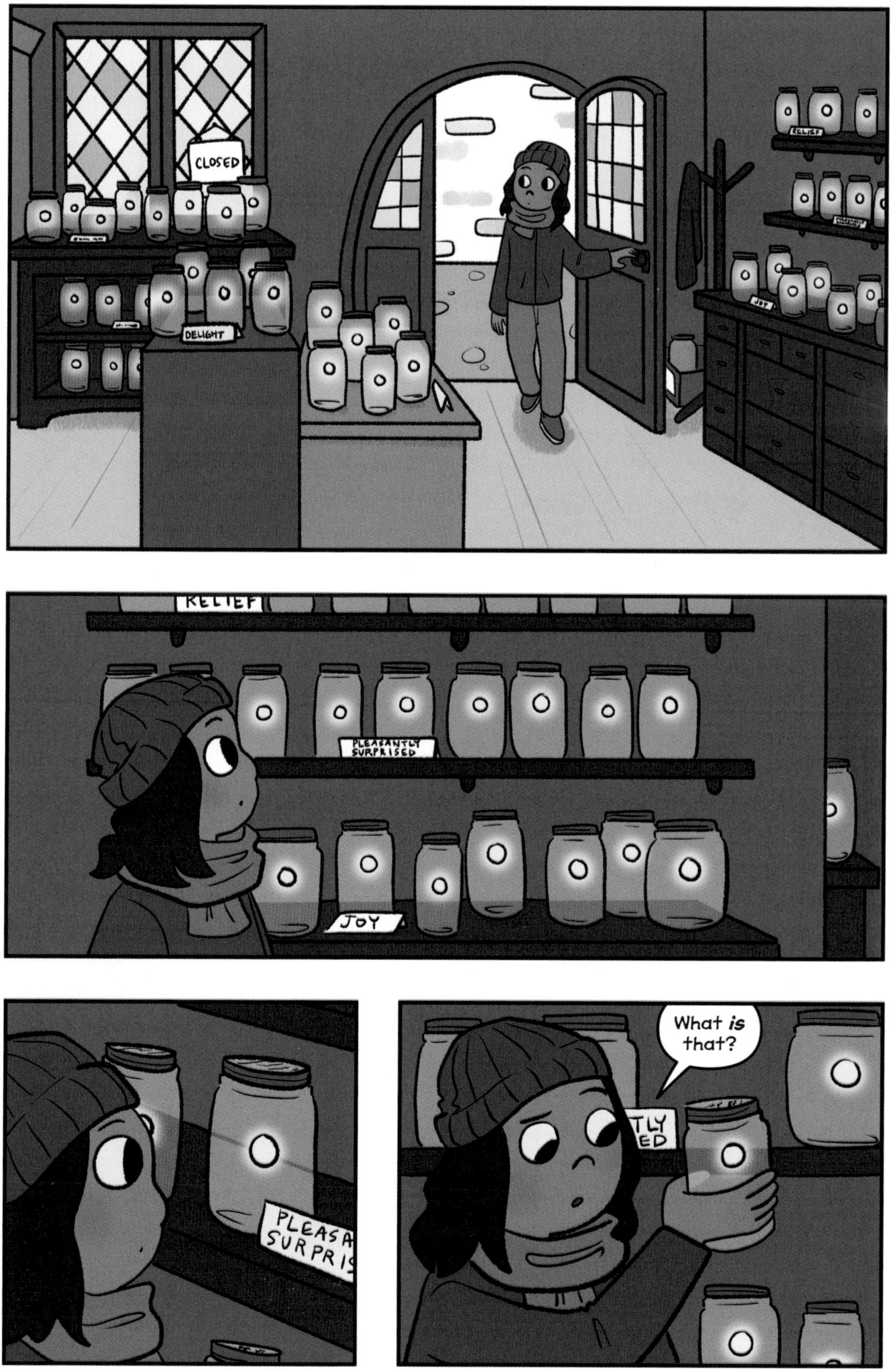
CLOSED
DELIGHT
RELIEF
PLEASANTLY SURPRISED
JOY
PLEASA
SURPRIS
What *is* that?

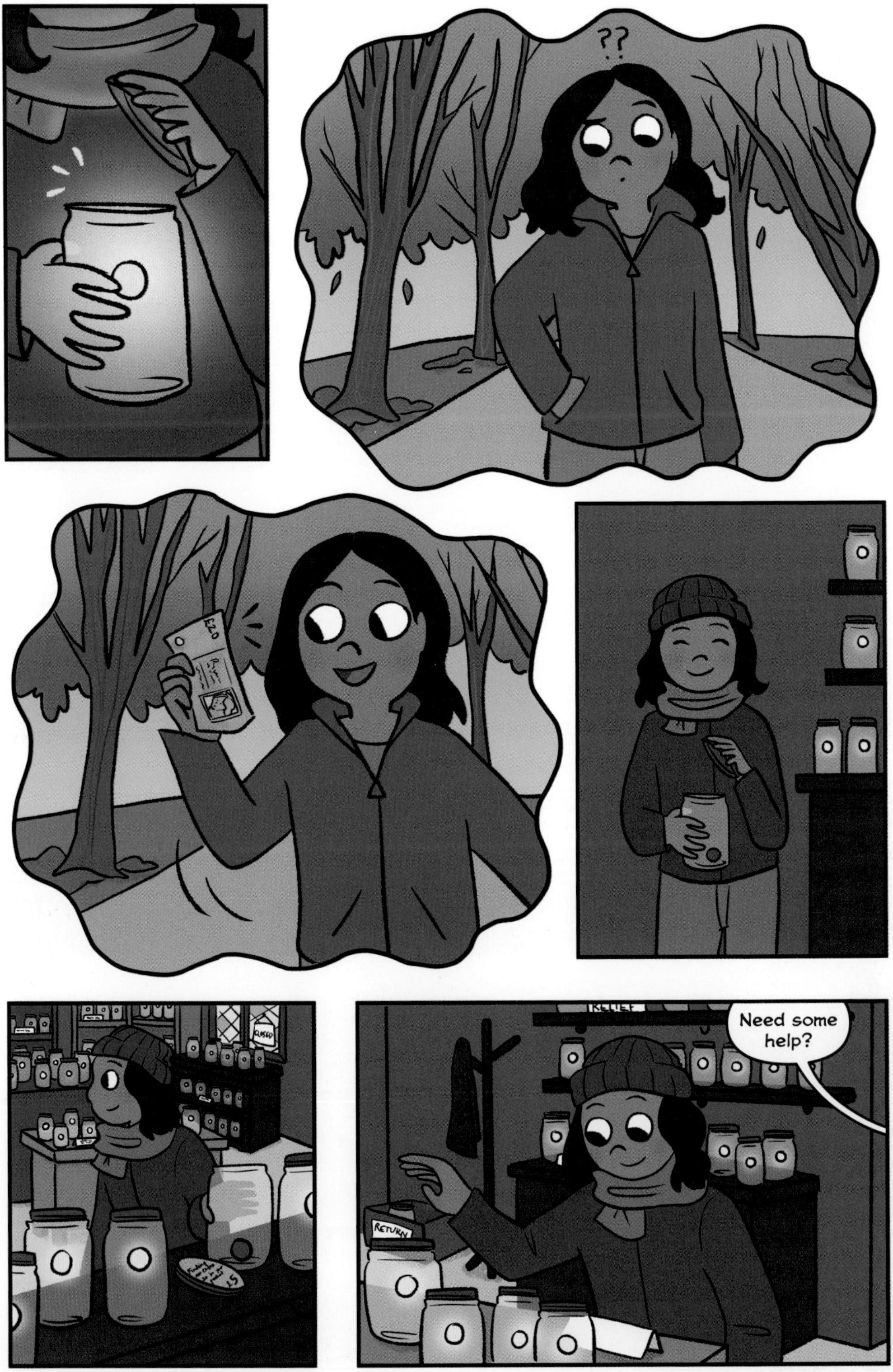
??
RETURN
Need some help?

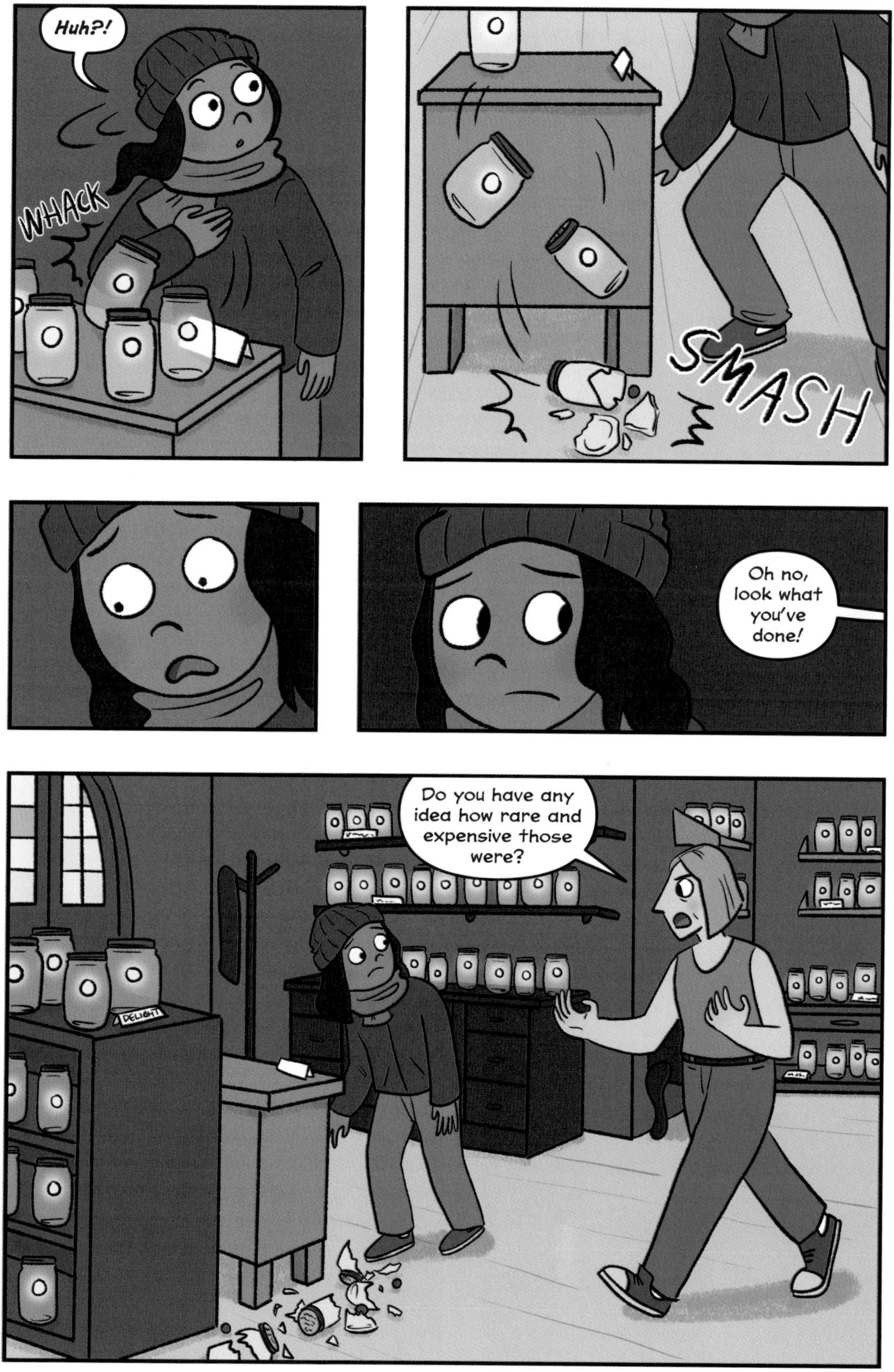
Huh?!
WHACK
SMASH
Oh no, look what you've done!
Do you have any idea how rare and expensive those were?
DELIGHT

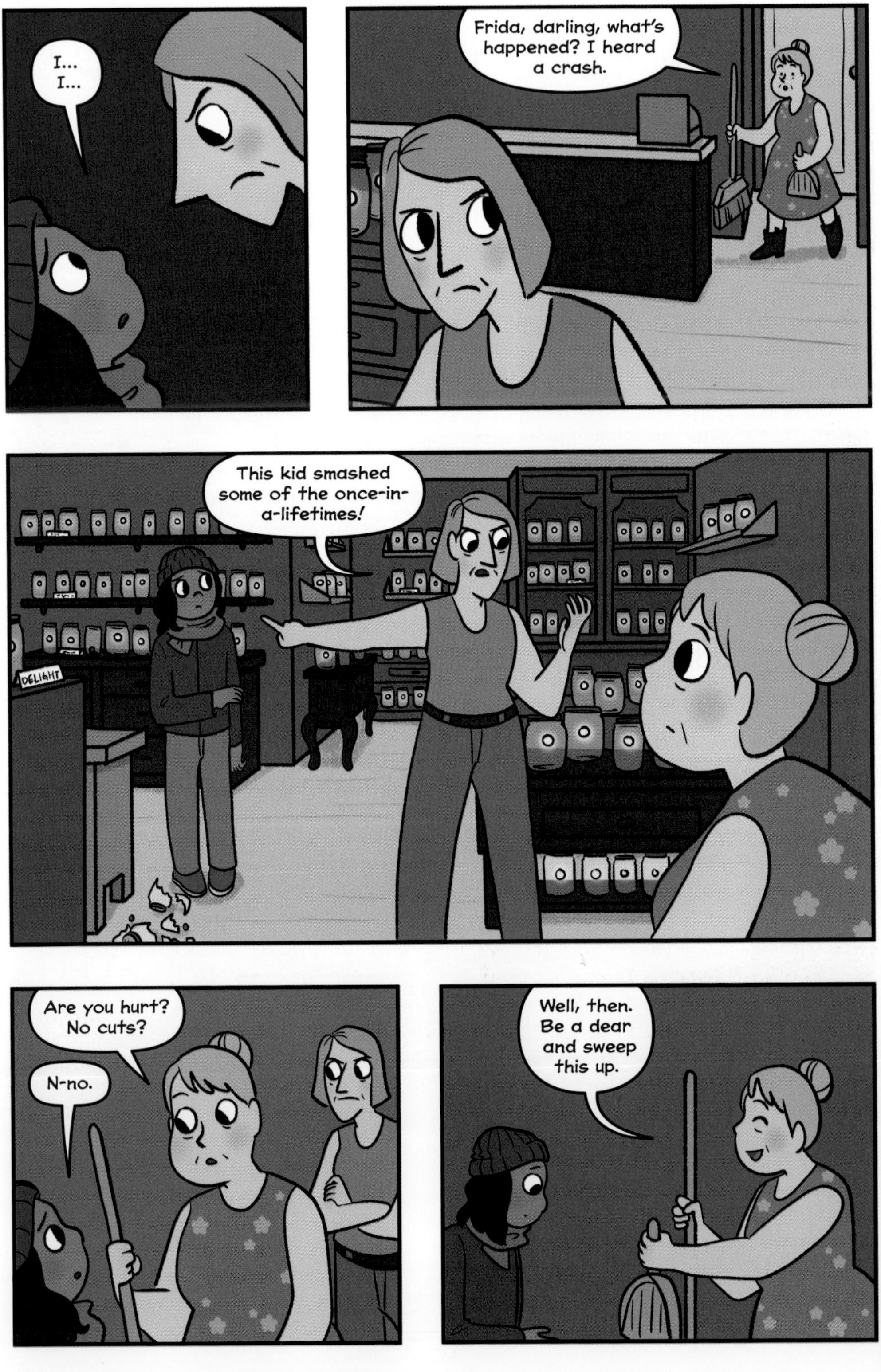
I...
I...
Frida, darling, what's happened? I heard a crash.
This kid smashed some of the once-in-a-lifetimes!
DELIGHT
Are you hurt? No cuts?
N-no.
Well, then. Be a dear and sweep this up.

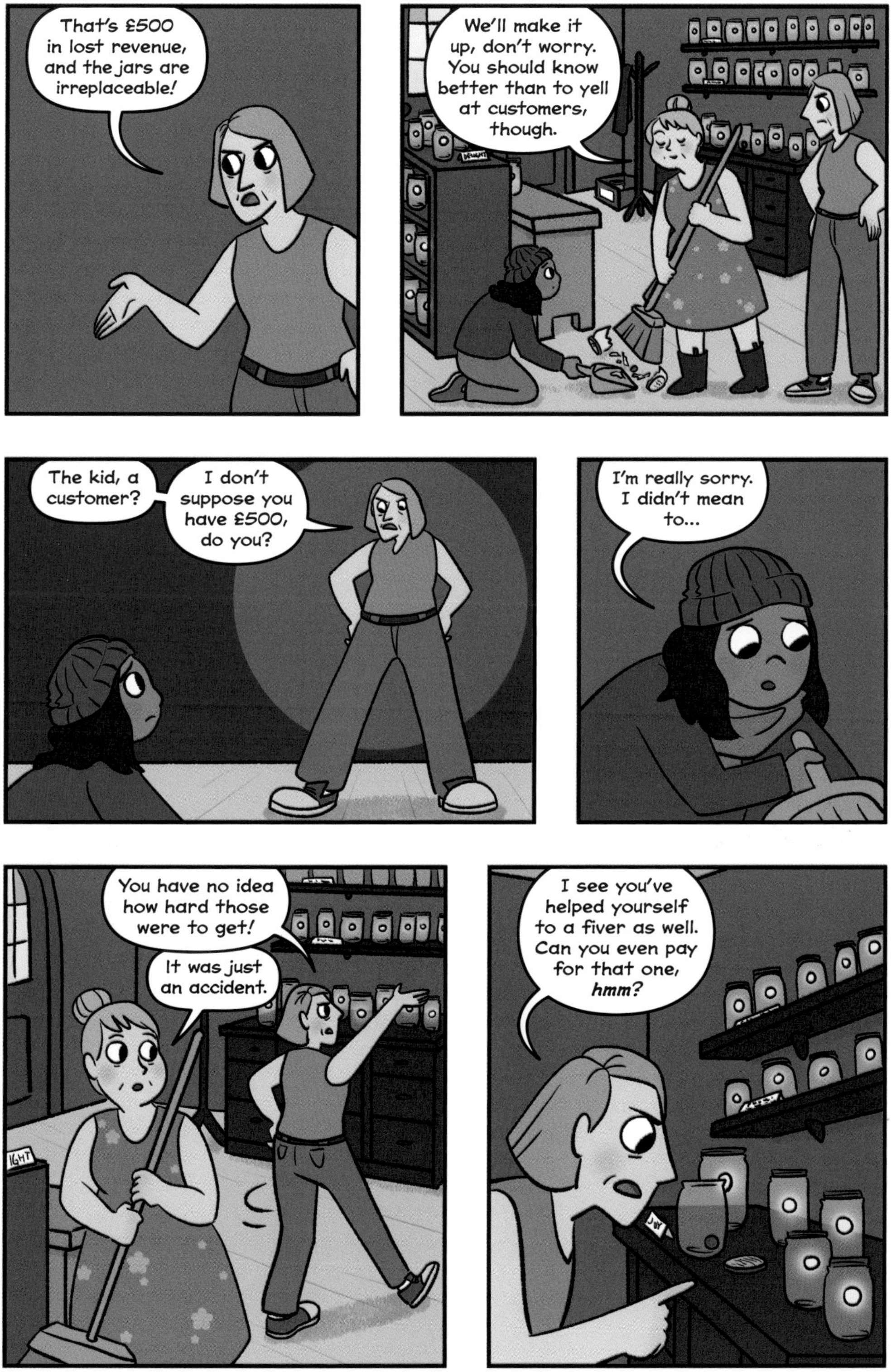
That's £500 in lost revenue, and the jars are irreplaceable!
We'll make it up, don't worry. You should know better than to yell at customers, though.
The kid, a customer?
I don't suppose you have £500, do you?
I'm really sorry. I didn't mean to...
You have no idea how hard those were to get!
It was just an accident.
I see you've helped yourself to a fiver as well. Can you even pay for that one, *hmm?*
JOY

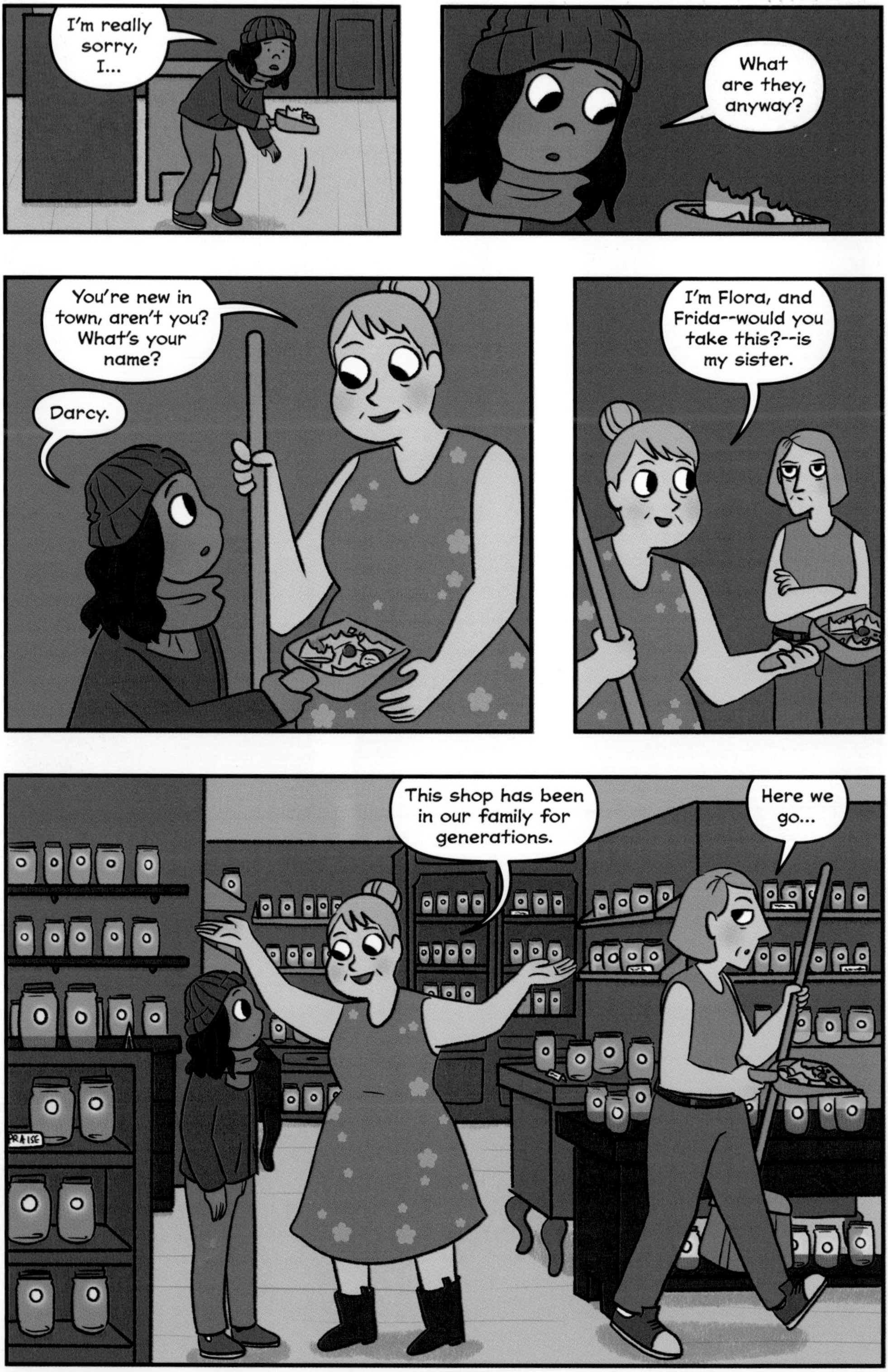
I'm really sorry, I...
What are they, anyway?
You're new in town, aren't you? What's your name?
Darcy.
I'm Flora, and Frida--would you take this?--is my sister.
This shop has been in our family for generations.
Here we go...
PRAISE

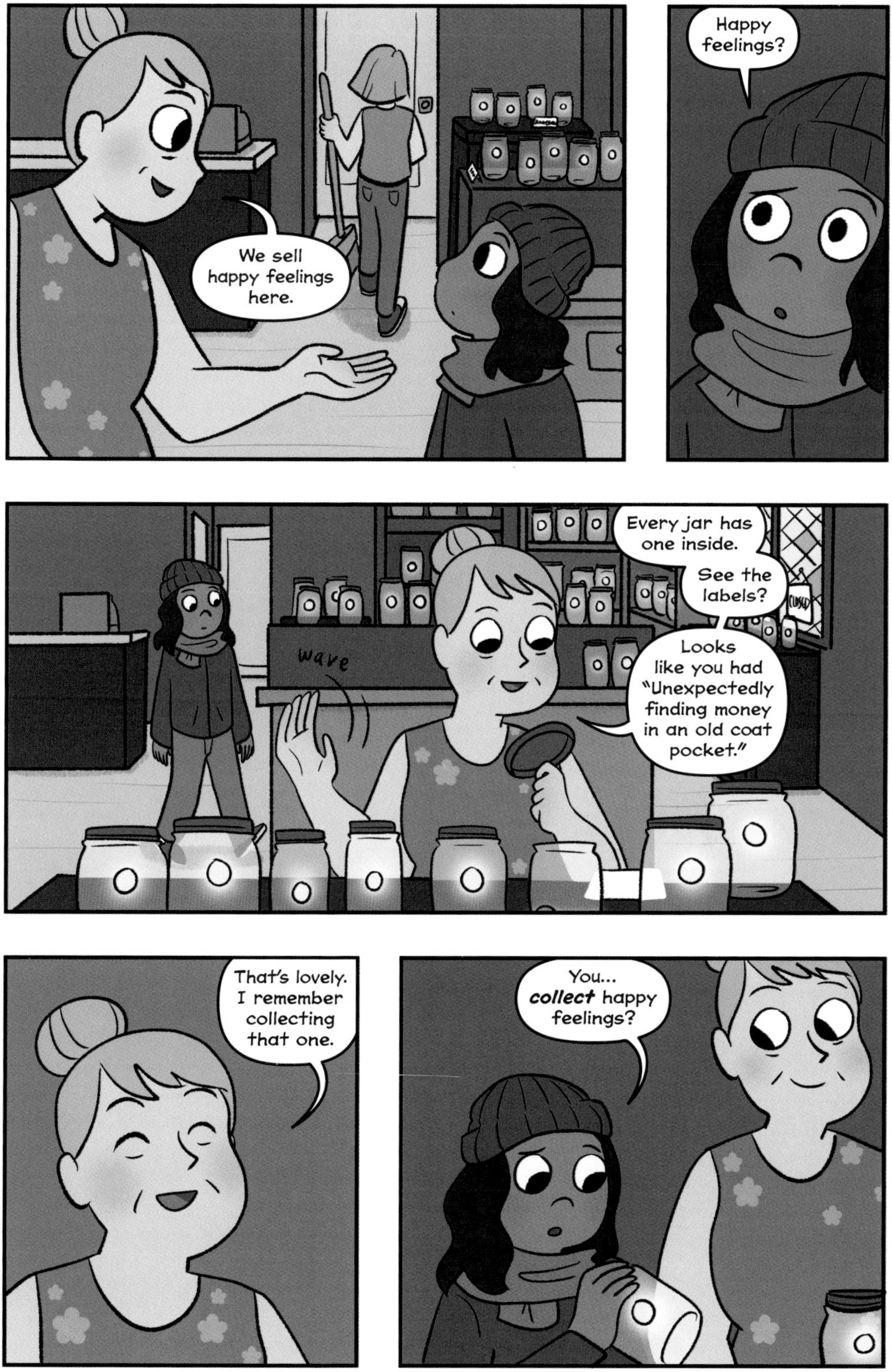
We sell happy feelings here.
Happy feelings?
Every jar has one inside.
See the labels?
wave
Looks like you had "Unexpectedly finding money in an old coat pocket."
That's lovely. I remember collecting that one.
You... ***collect*** happy feelings?

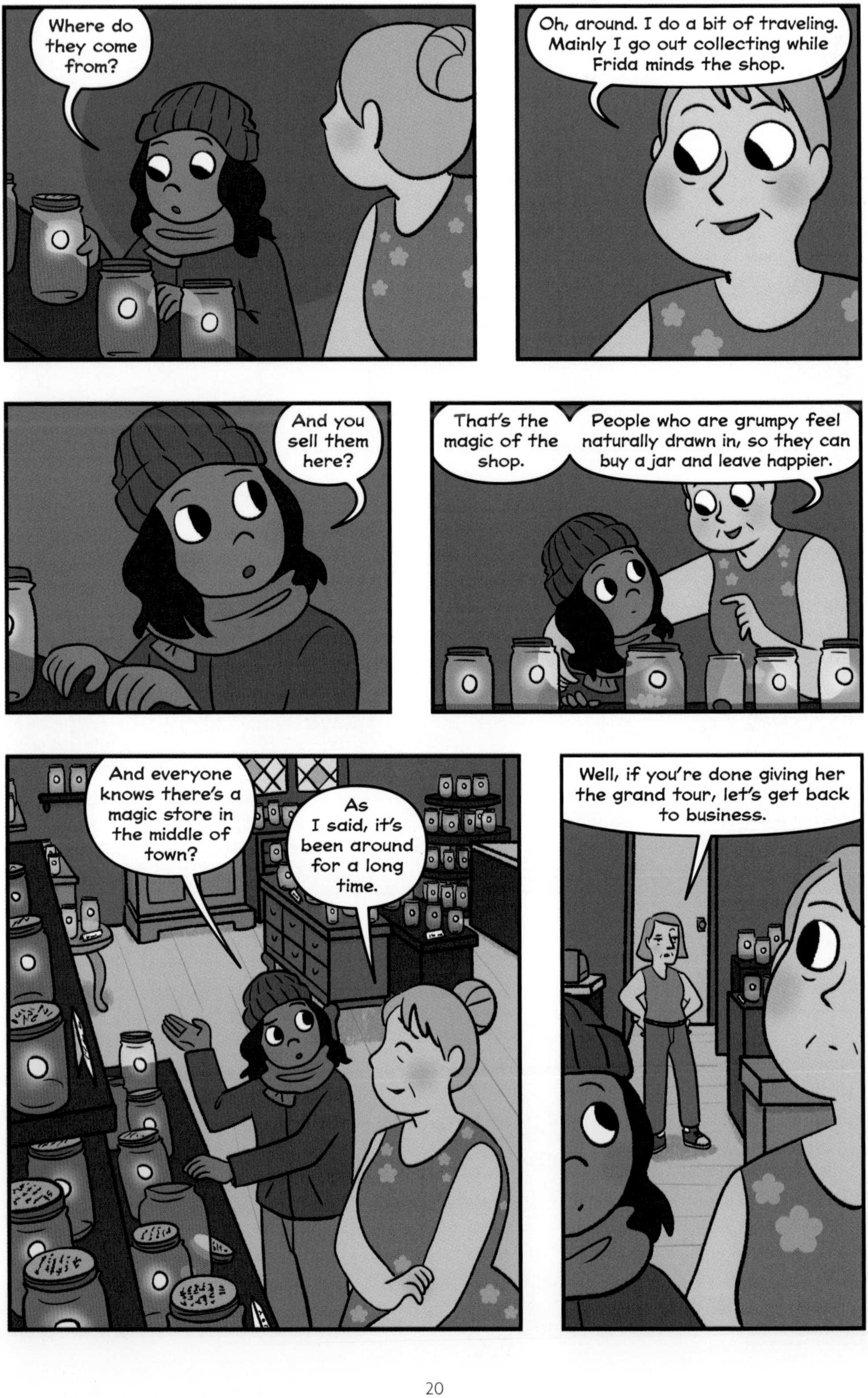
Where do they come from?
Oh, around. I do a bit of traveling. Mainly I go out collecting while Frida minds the shop.
And you sell them here?
That's the magic of the shop.
People who are grumpy feel naturally drawn in, so they can buy a jar and leave happier.
And everyone knows there's a magic store in the middle of town?
As I said, it's been around for a long time.
Well, if you're done giving her the grand tour, let's get back to business.

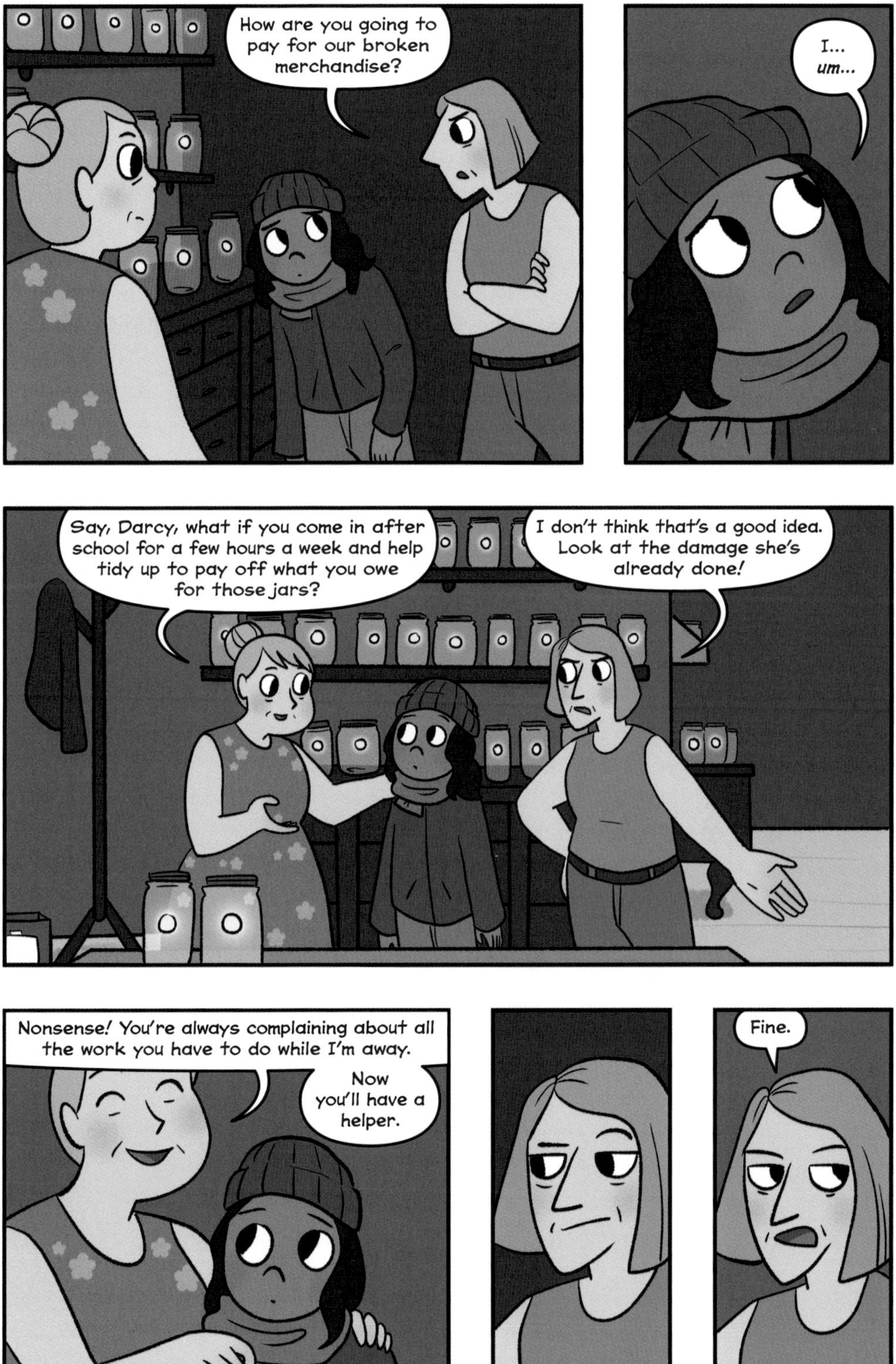
How are you going to pay for our broken merchandise?
I... um...
Say, Darcy, what if you come in after school for a few hours a week and help tidy up to pay off what you owe for those jars?
I don't think that's a good idea. Look at the damage she's already done!
Nonsense! You're always complaining about all the work you have to do while I'm away.
Now you'll have a helper.
Fine.

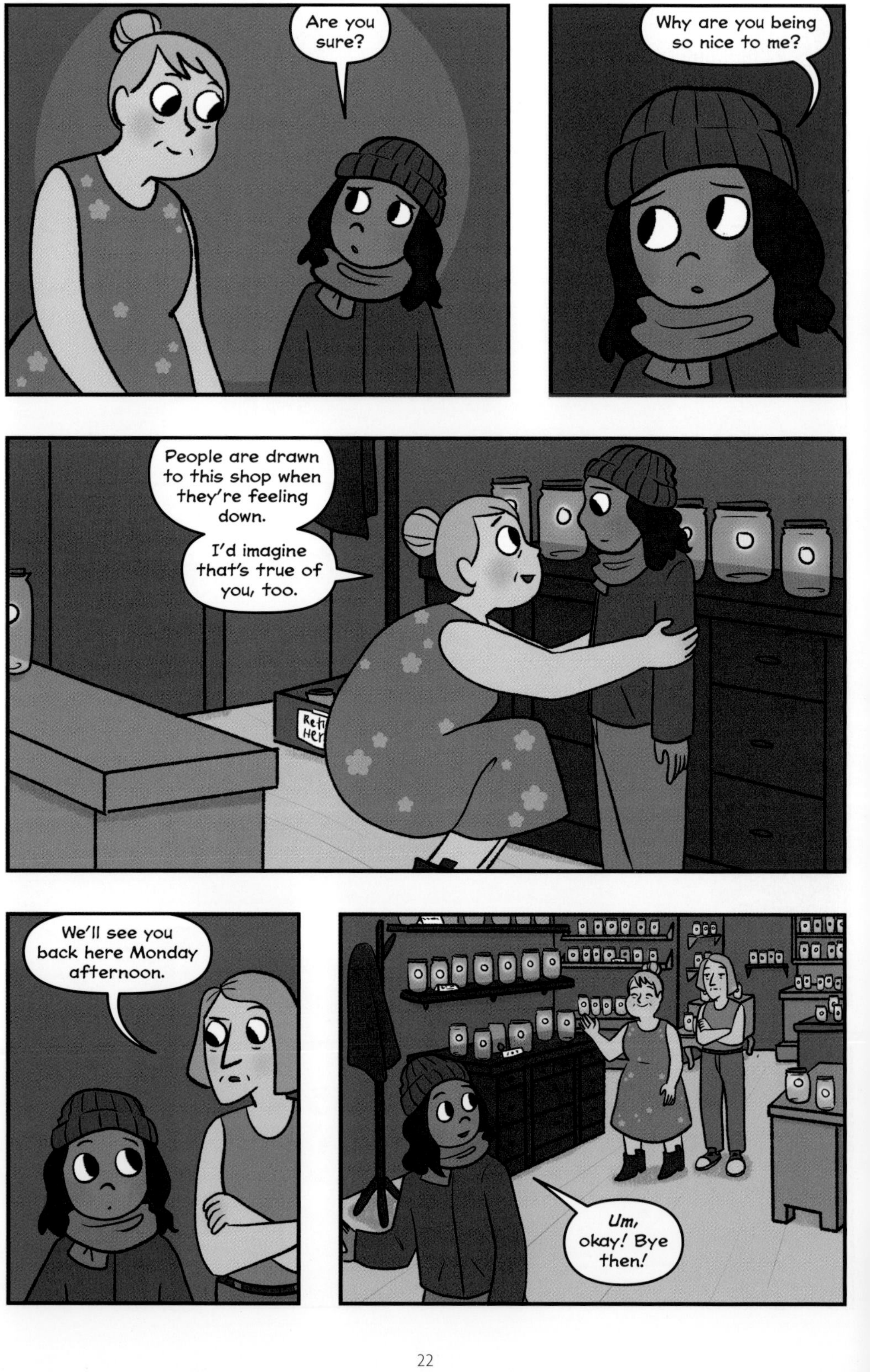
Are you sure?
Why are you being so nice to me?
People are drawn to this shop when they're feeling down.
I'd imagine that's true of you, too.
We'll see you back here Monday afternoon.
Um, okay! Bye then!

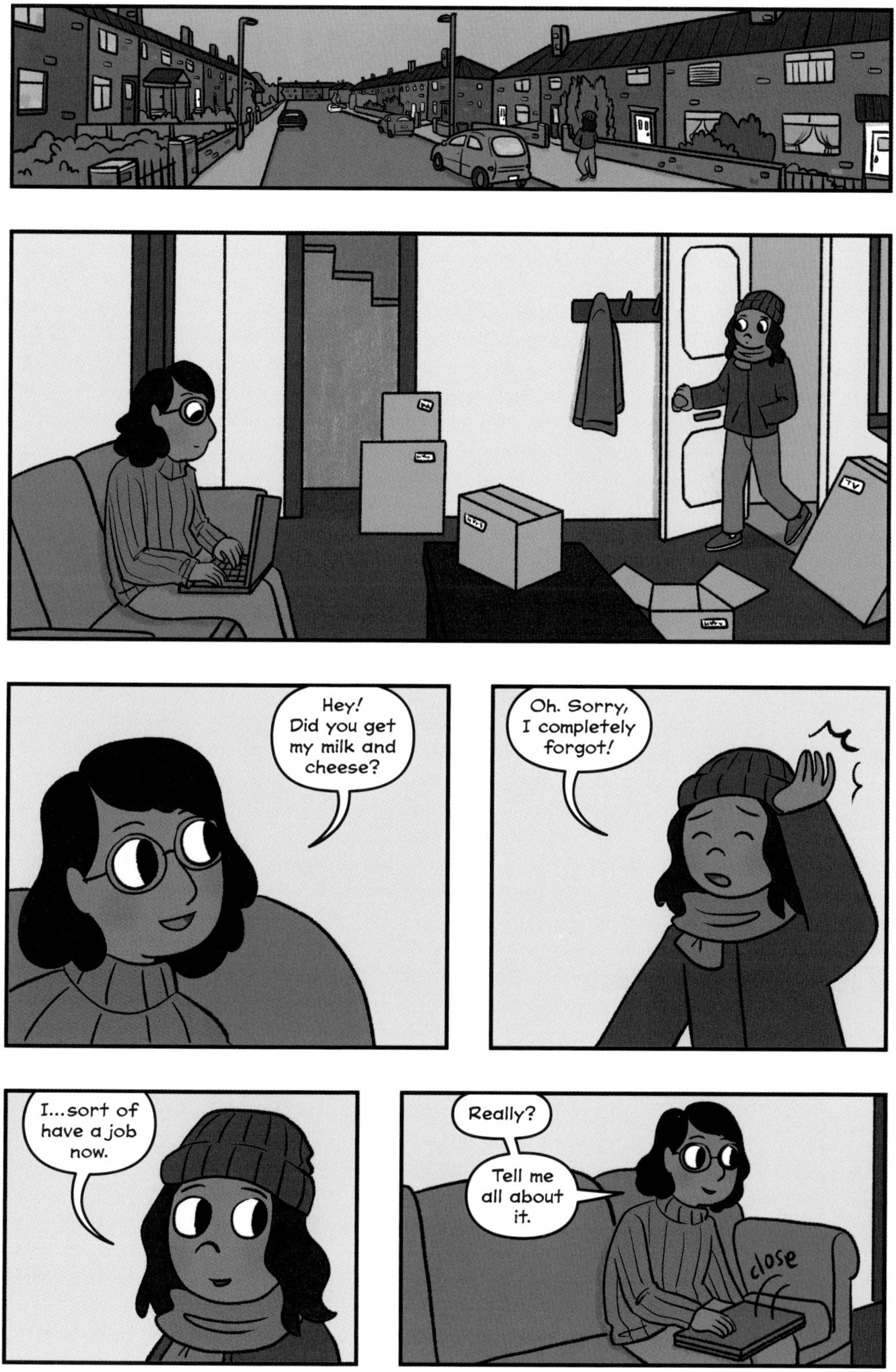
Hey! Did you get my milk and cheese?
Oh. Sorry, I completely forgot!
I...sort of have a job now.
Really?
Tell me all about it.
close

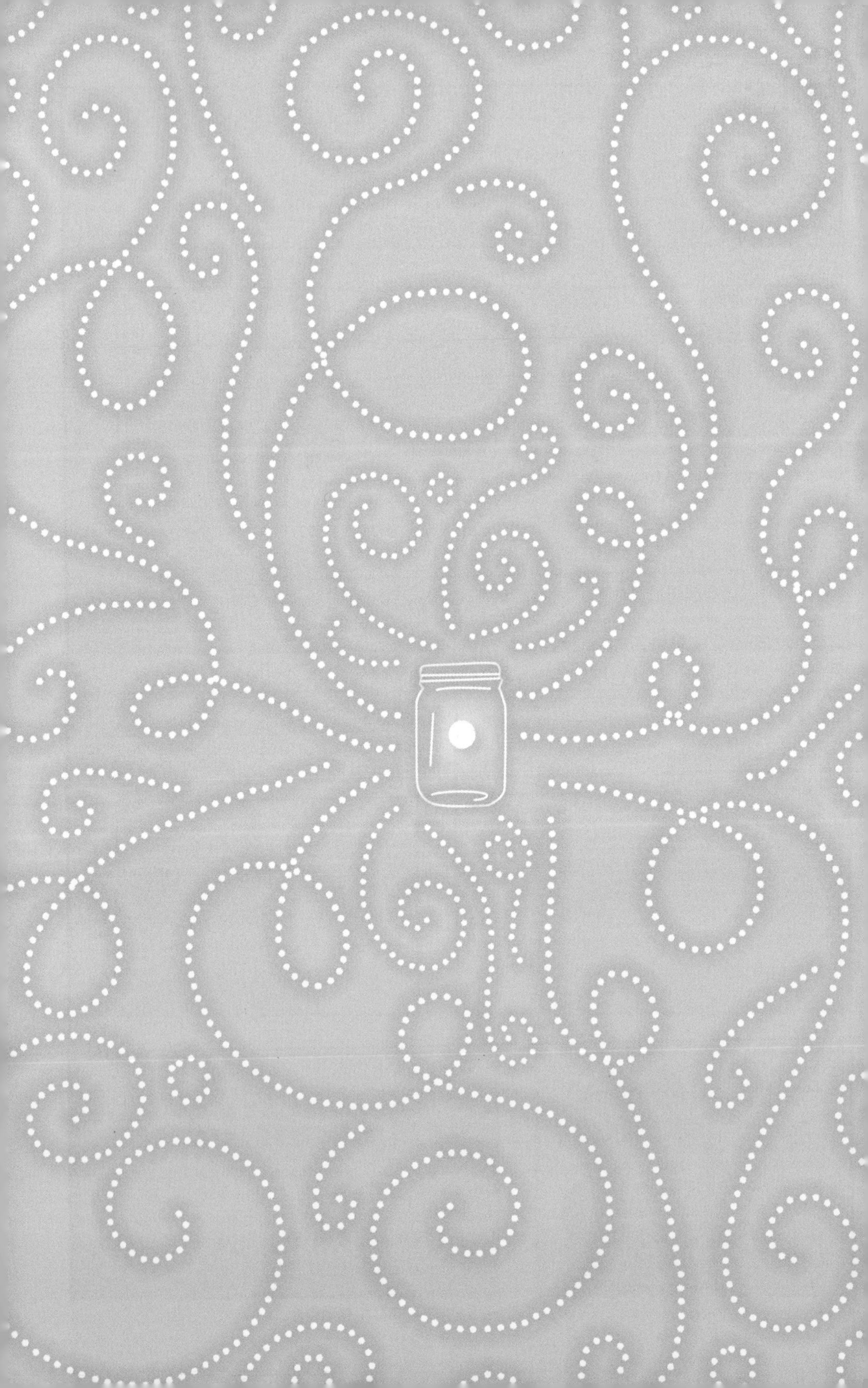

Chapter Two

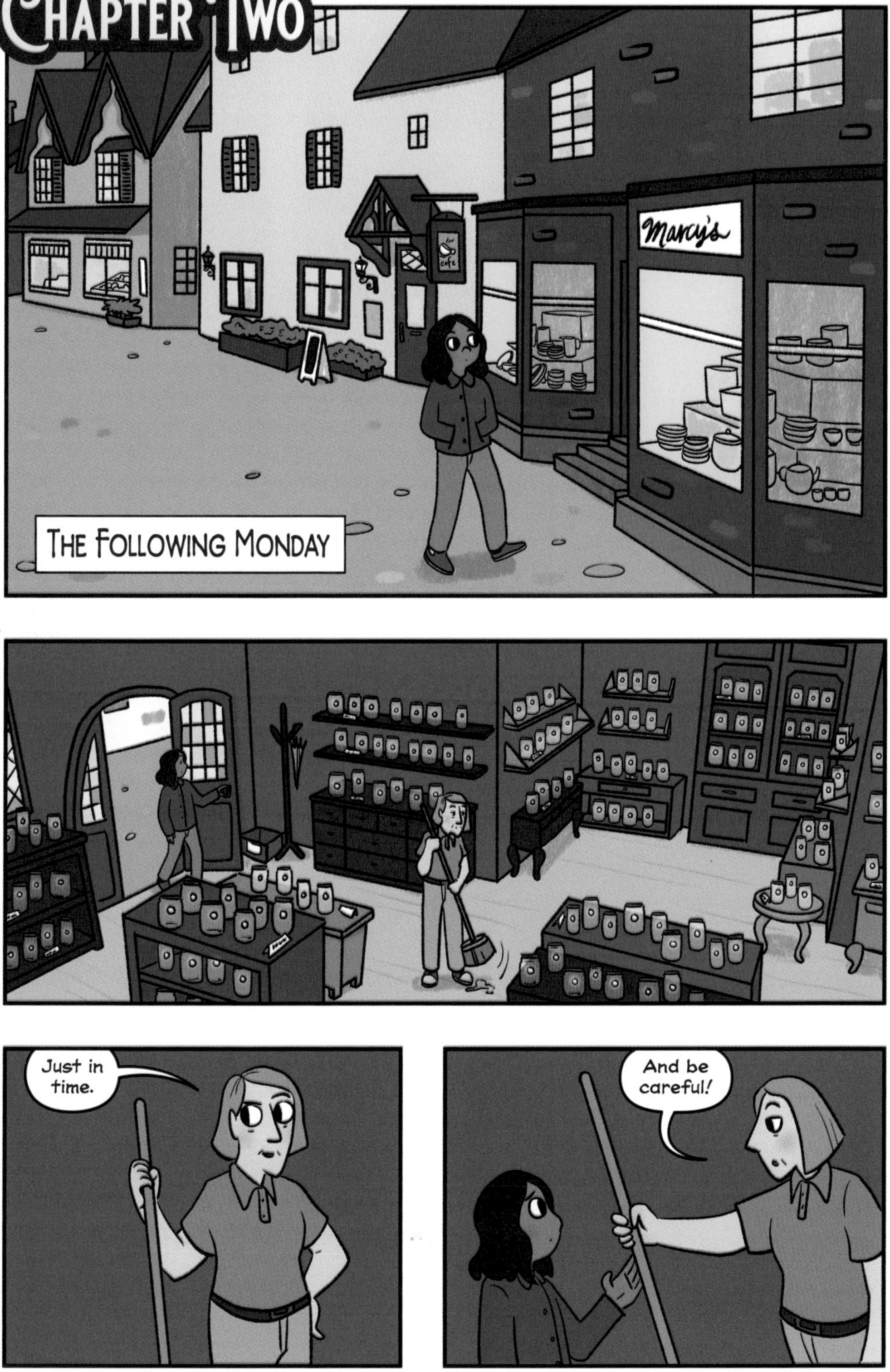
Marcy's
The Following Monday
Just in time.
And be careful!

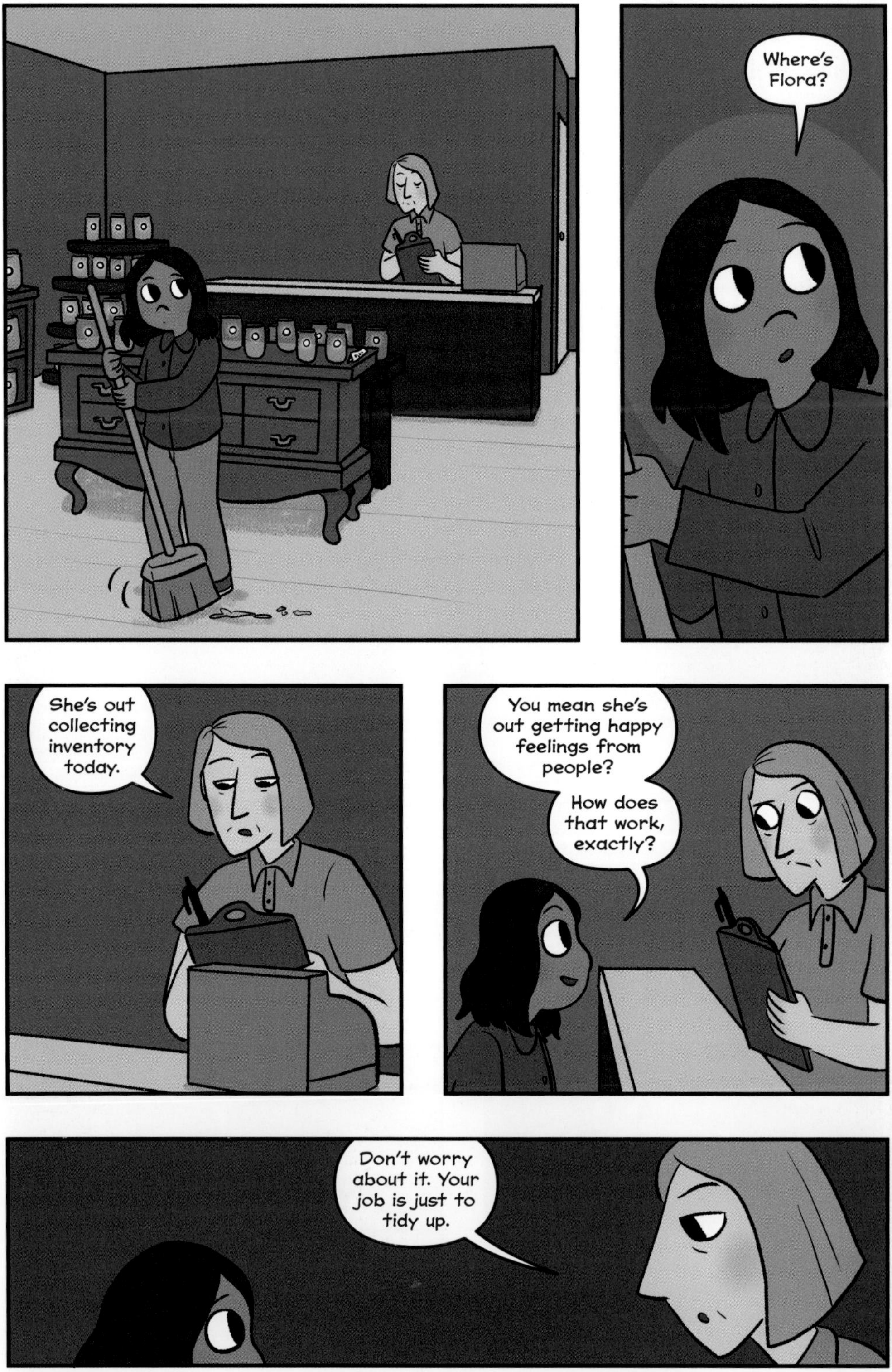
Where's Flora?
She's out collecting inventory today.
You mean she's out getting happy feelings from people?
How does that work, exactly?
Don't worry about it. Your job is just to tidy up.

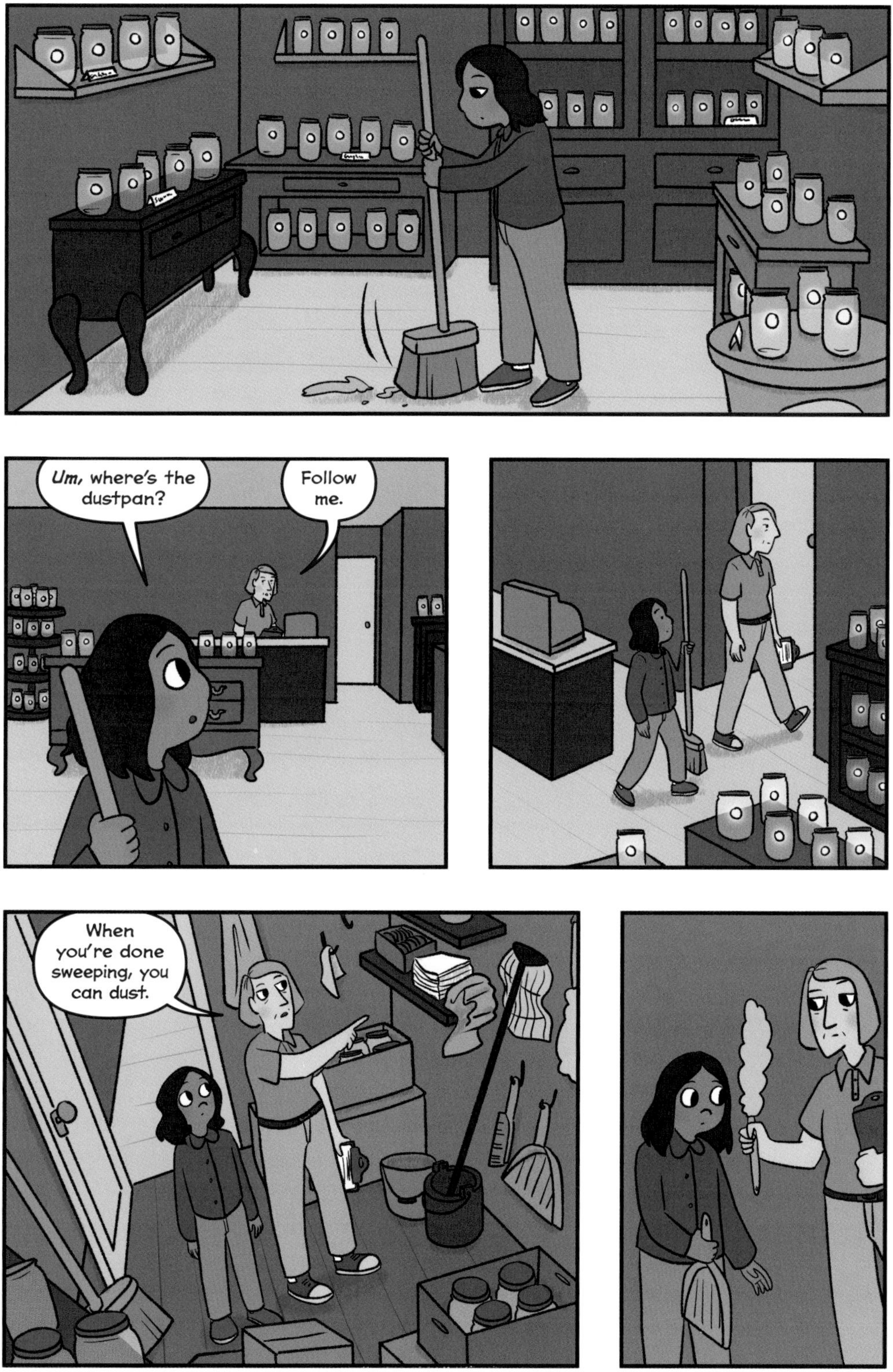
Um, where's the dustpan?
Follow me.
When you're done sweeping, you can dust.

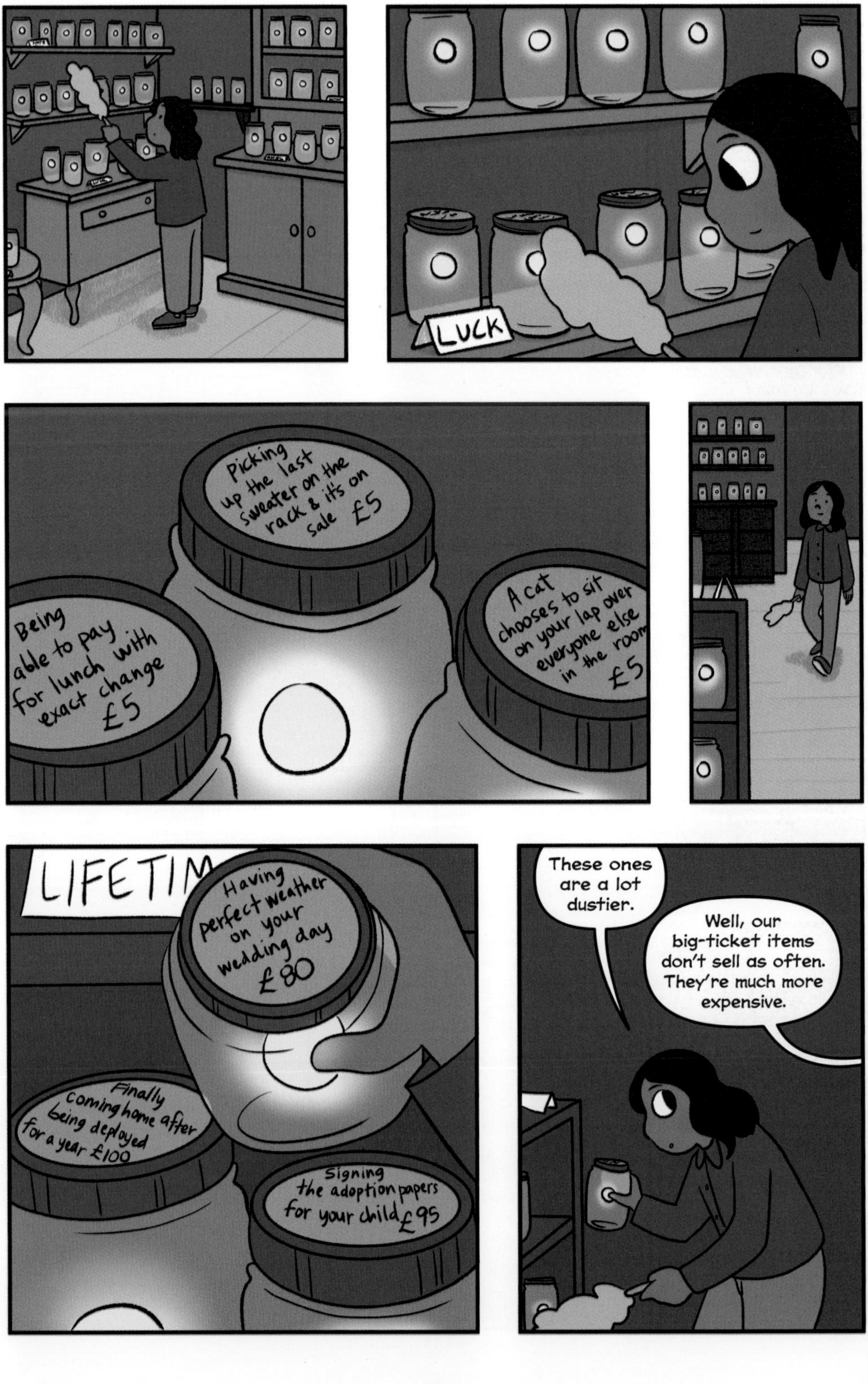
LUCK
Picking up the last sweater on the rack & it's on sale £5
Being able to pay for lunch with exact change £5
A cat chooses to sit on your lap over everyone else in the room £5
LIFETIM
Having perfect weather on your wedding day £80
Finally coming home after being deployed for a year £100
Signing the adoption papers for your child £95
These ones are a lot dustier.
Well, our big-ticket items don't sell as often. They're much more expensive.

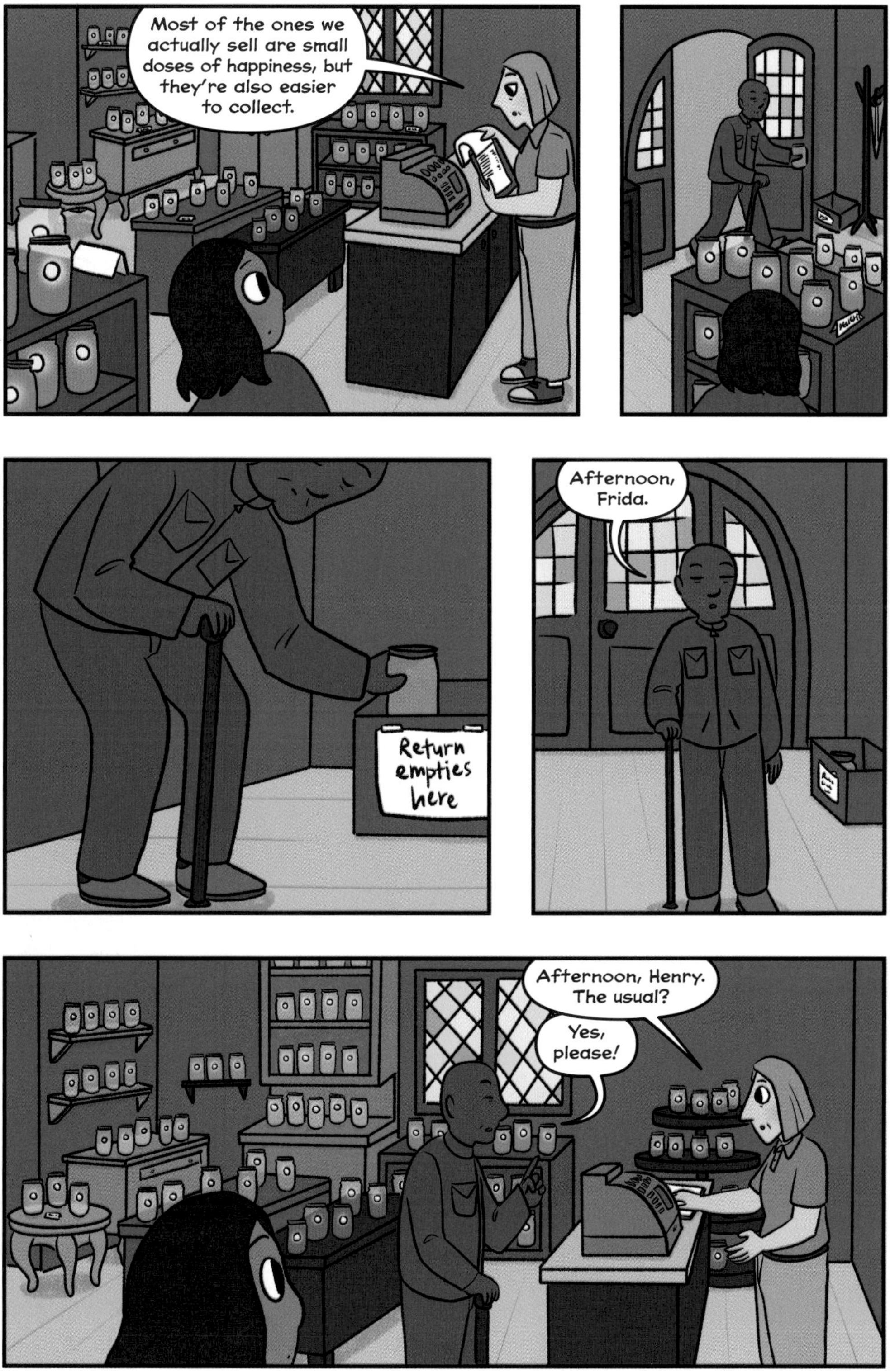
Most of the ones we actually sell are small doses of happiness, but they're also easier to collect.
Return empties here
Afternoon, Frida.
Afternoon, Henry. The usual?
Yes, please!

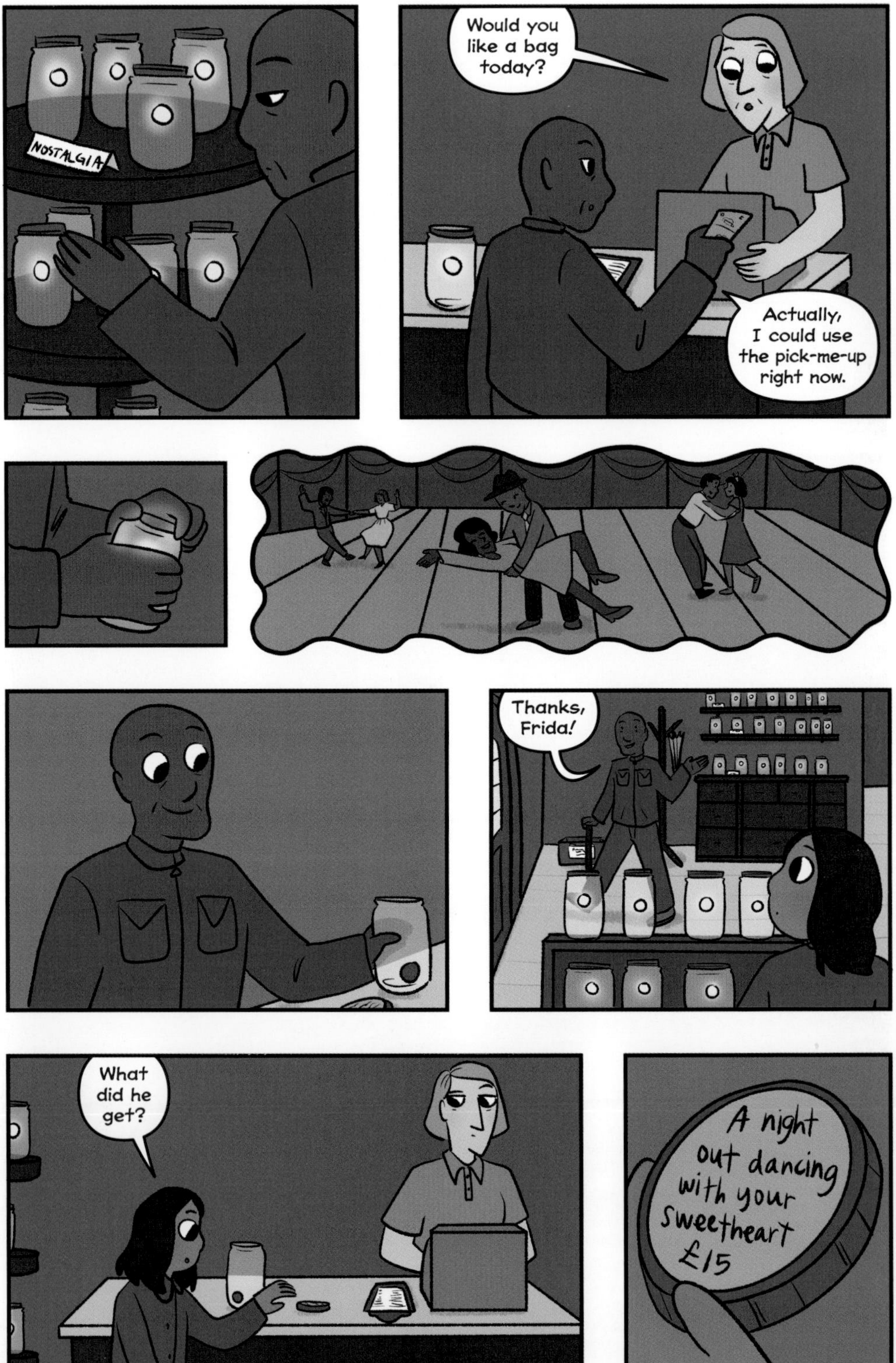
NOSTALGIA
Would you like a bag today?
Actually, I could use the pick-me-up right now.
Thanks, Frida!
What did he get?
A night out dancing with your sweetheart £15

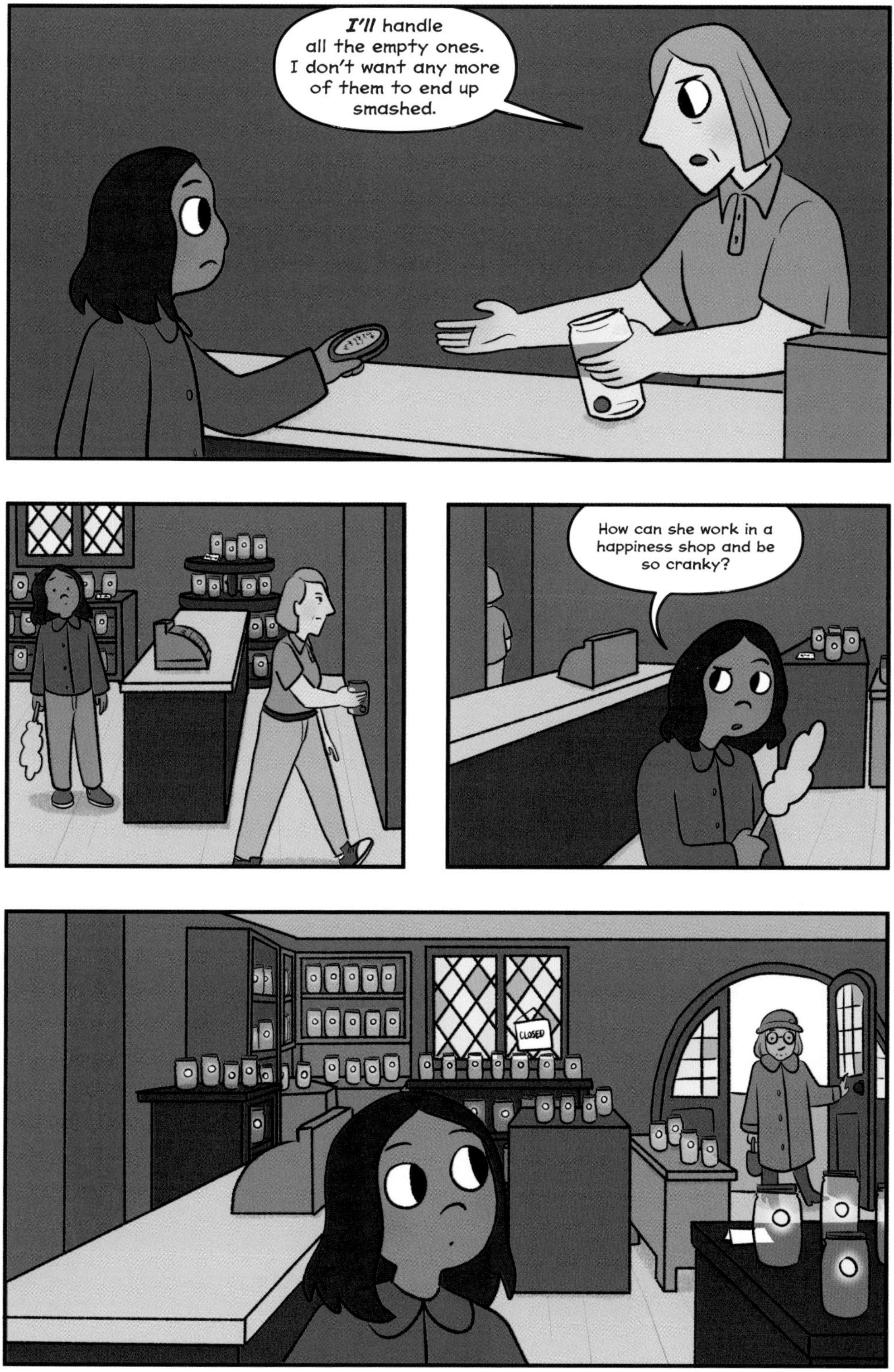
I'll handle all the empty ones. I don't want any more of them to end up smashed.
How can she work in a happiness shop and be so cranky?
CLOSED

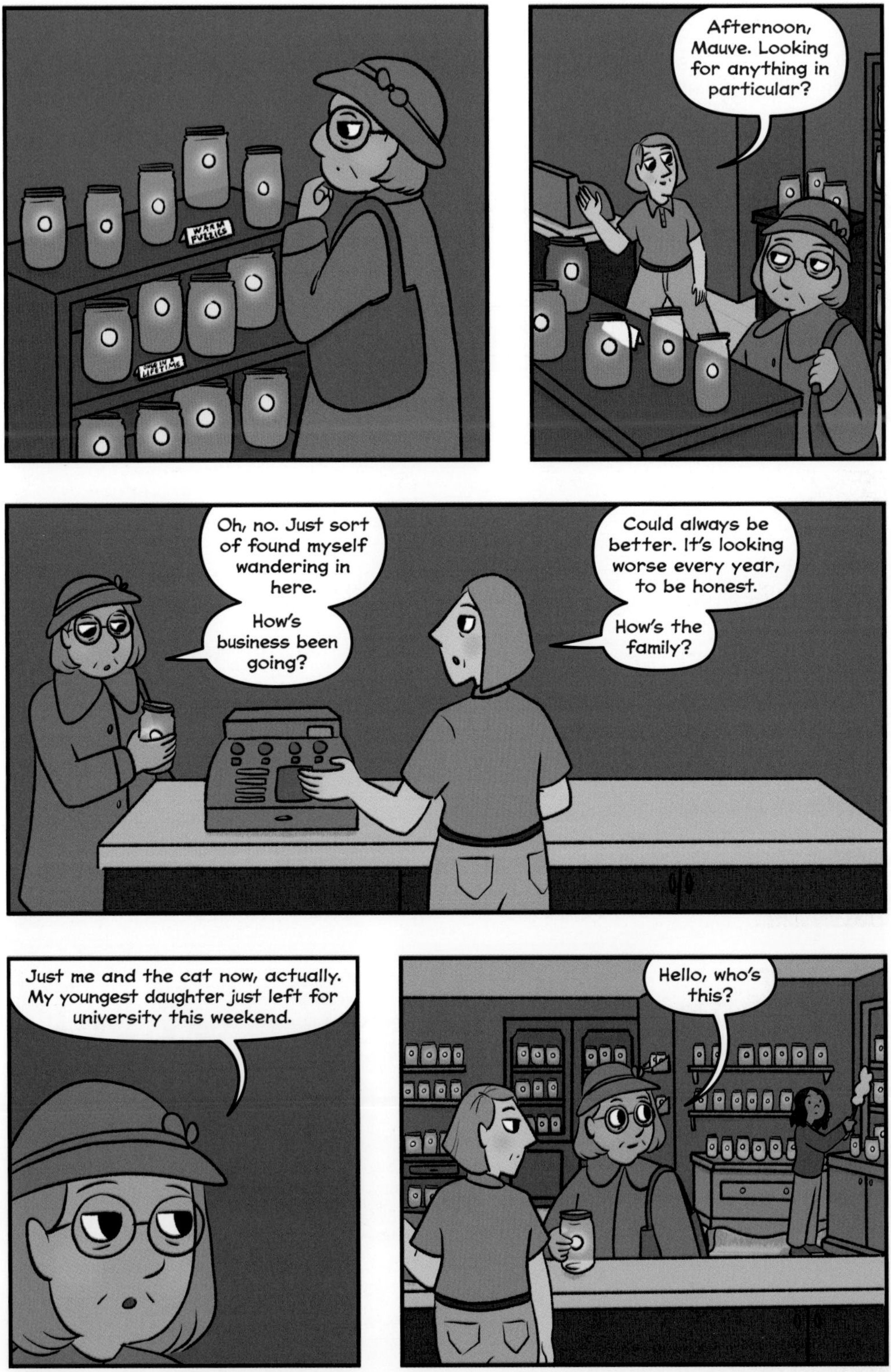

WARM FUZZIES
ONCE IN A LIFETIME
Afternoon, Mauve. Looking for anything in particular?
Oh, no. Just sort of found myself wandering in here.
How's business been going?
Could always be better. It's looking worse every year, to be honest.
How's the family?
Just me and the cat now, actually. My youngest daughter just left for university this weekend.
Hello, who's this?

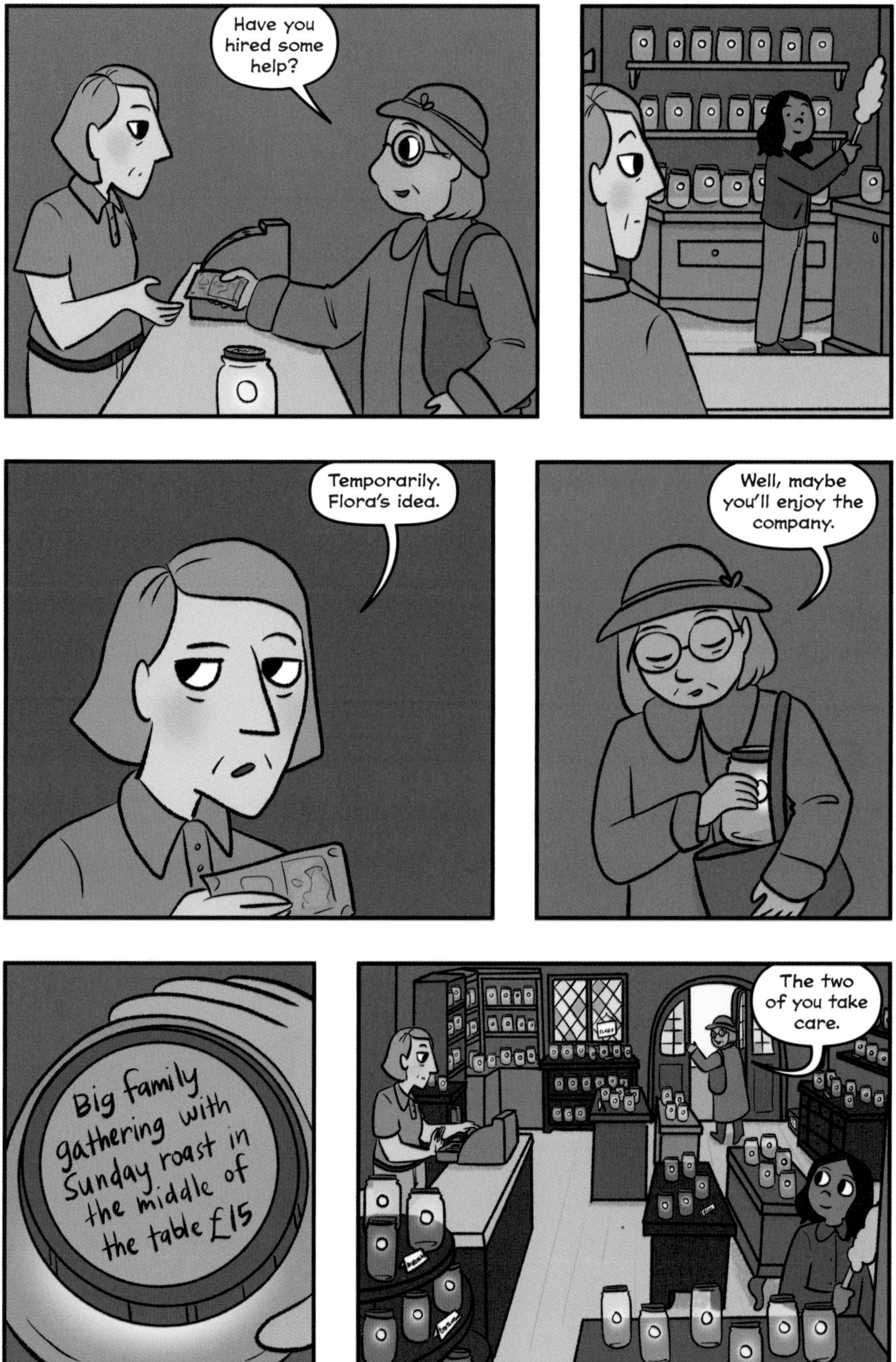
Have you hired some help?
Temporarily. Flora's idea.
Well, maybe you'll enjoy the company.
Big family gathering with Sunday roast in the middle of the table £15
The two of you take care.

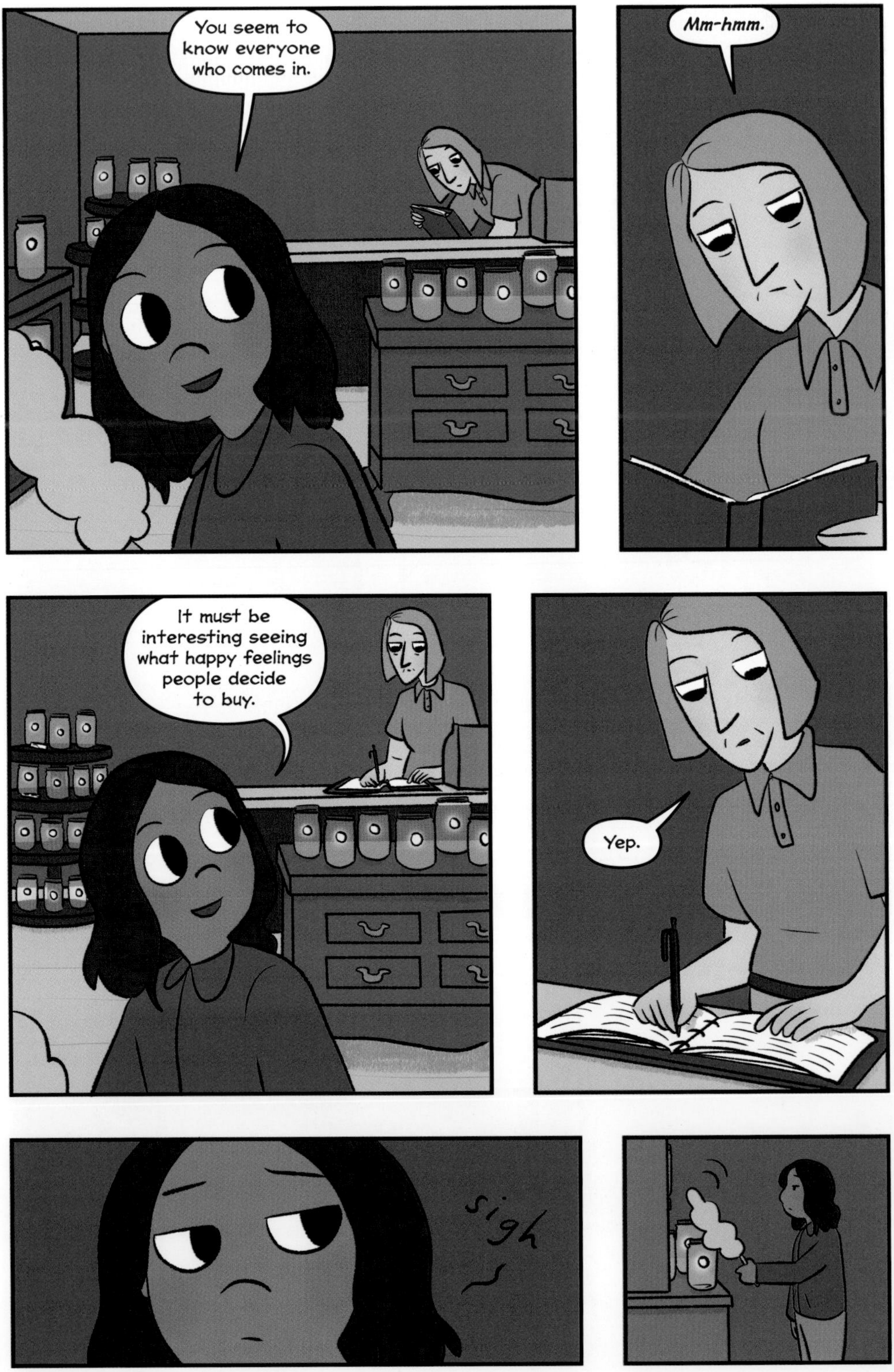
You seem to know everyone who comes in.
Mm-hmm.
It must be interesting seeing what happy feelings people decide to buy.
Yep.
sigh

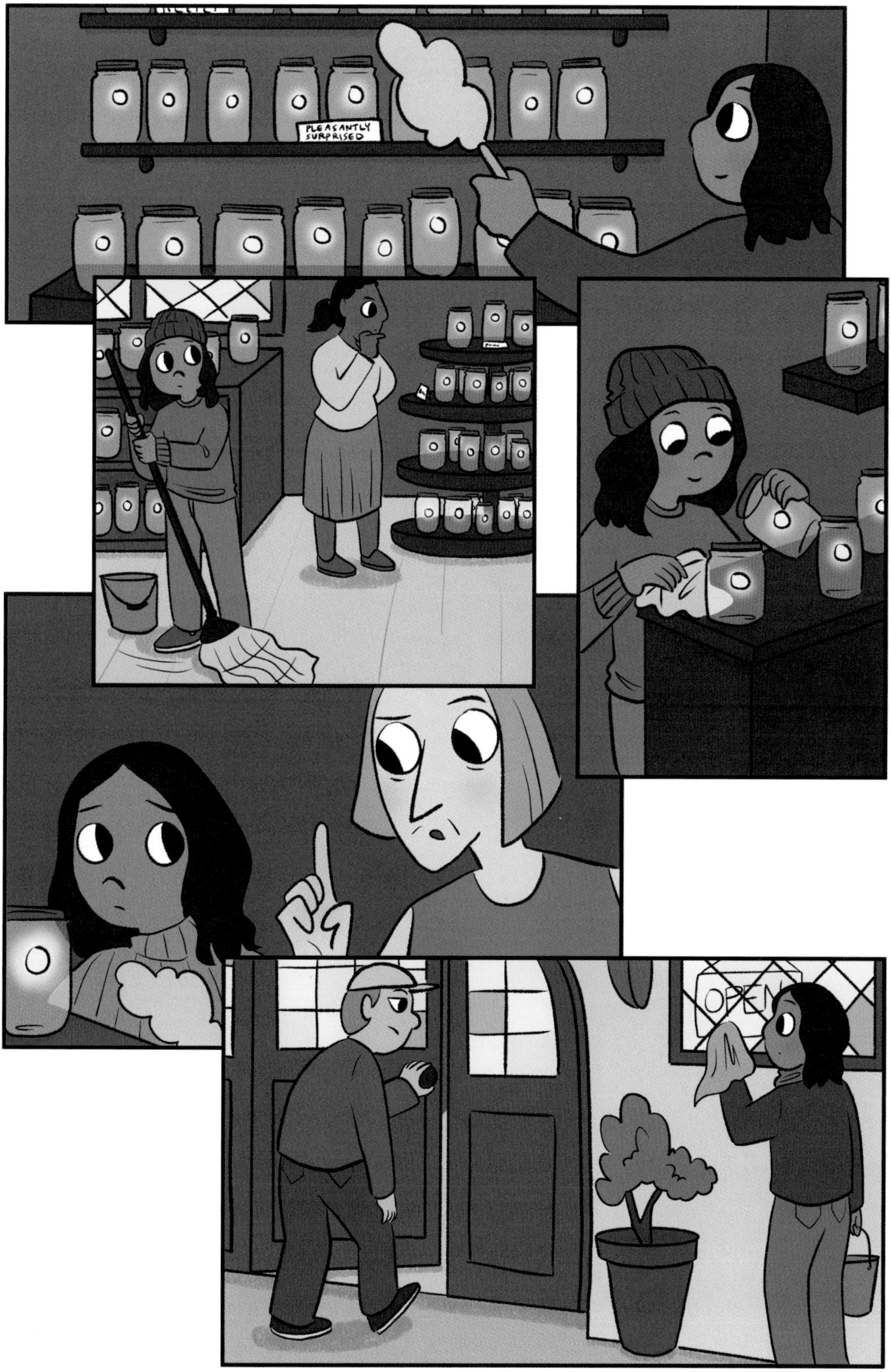
PLEASANTLY SURPRISED
OPEN

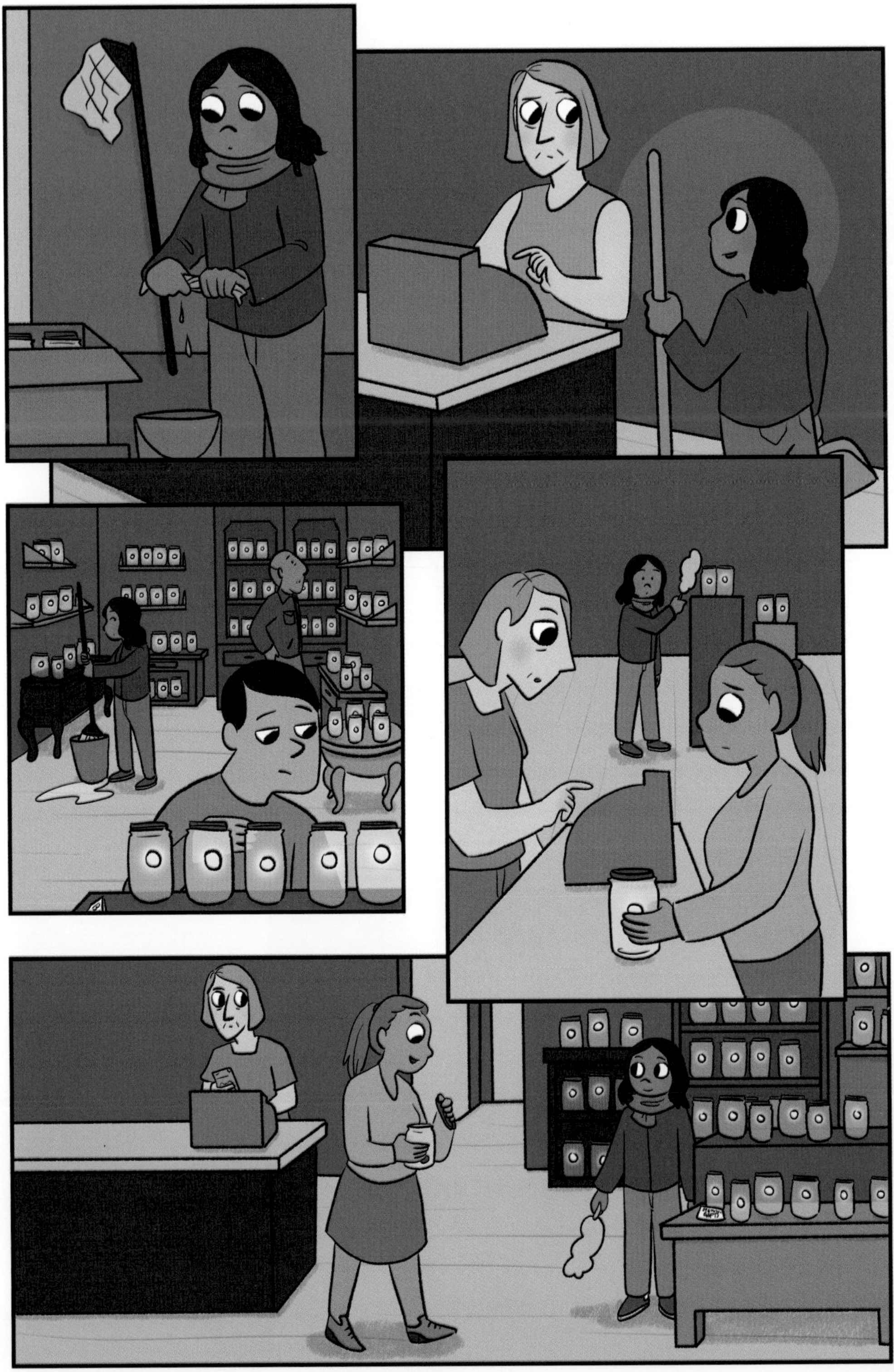

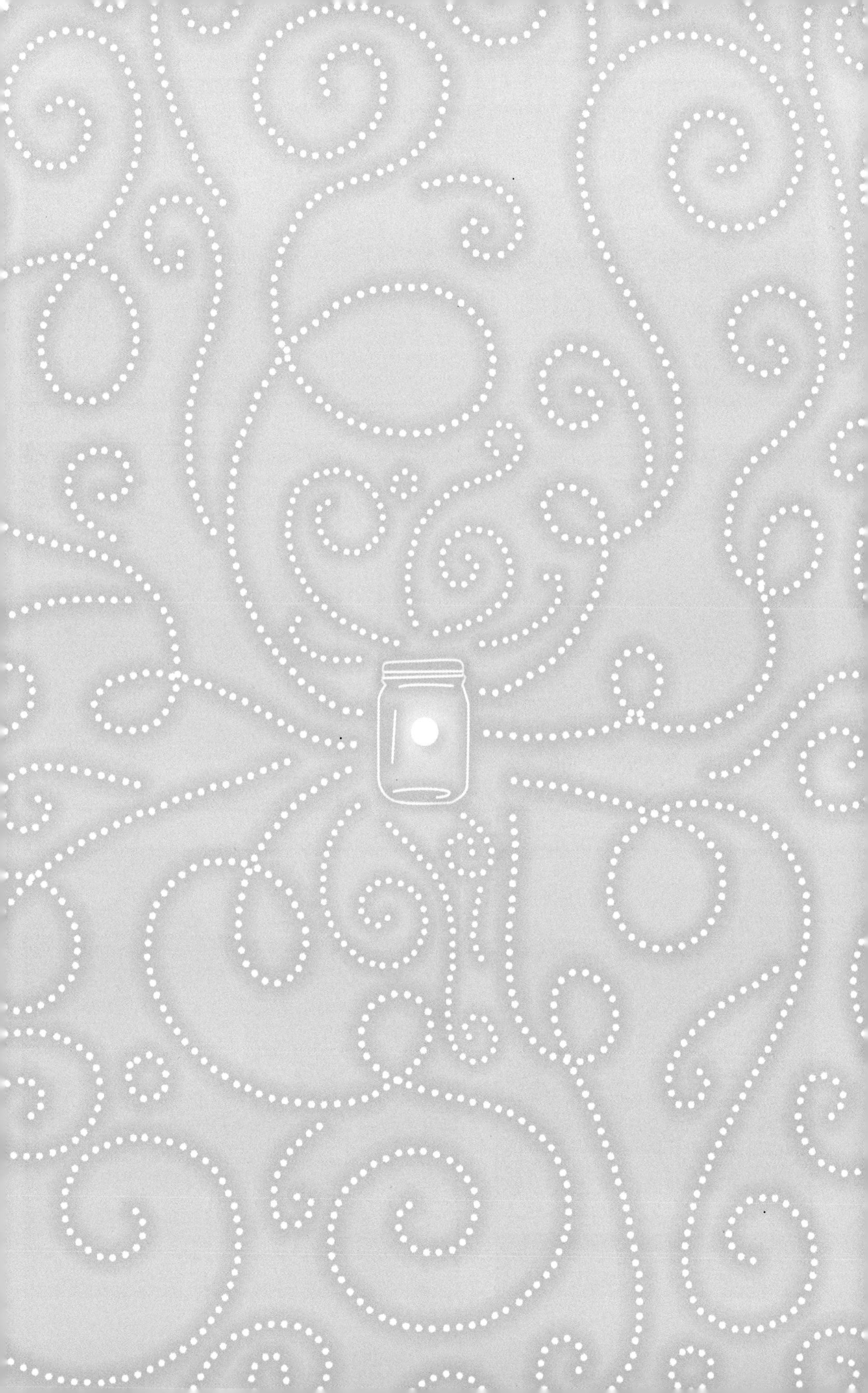

Chapter Three

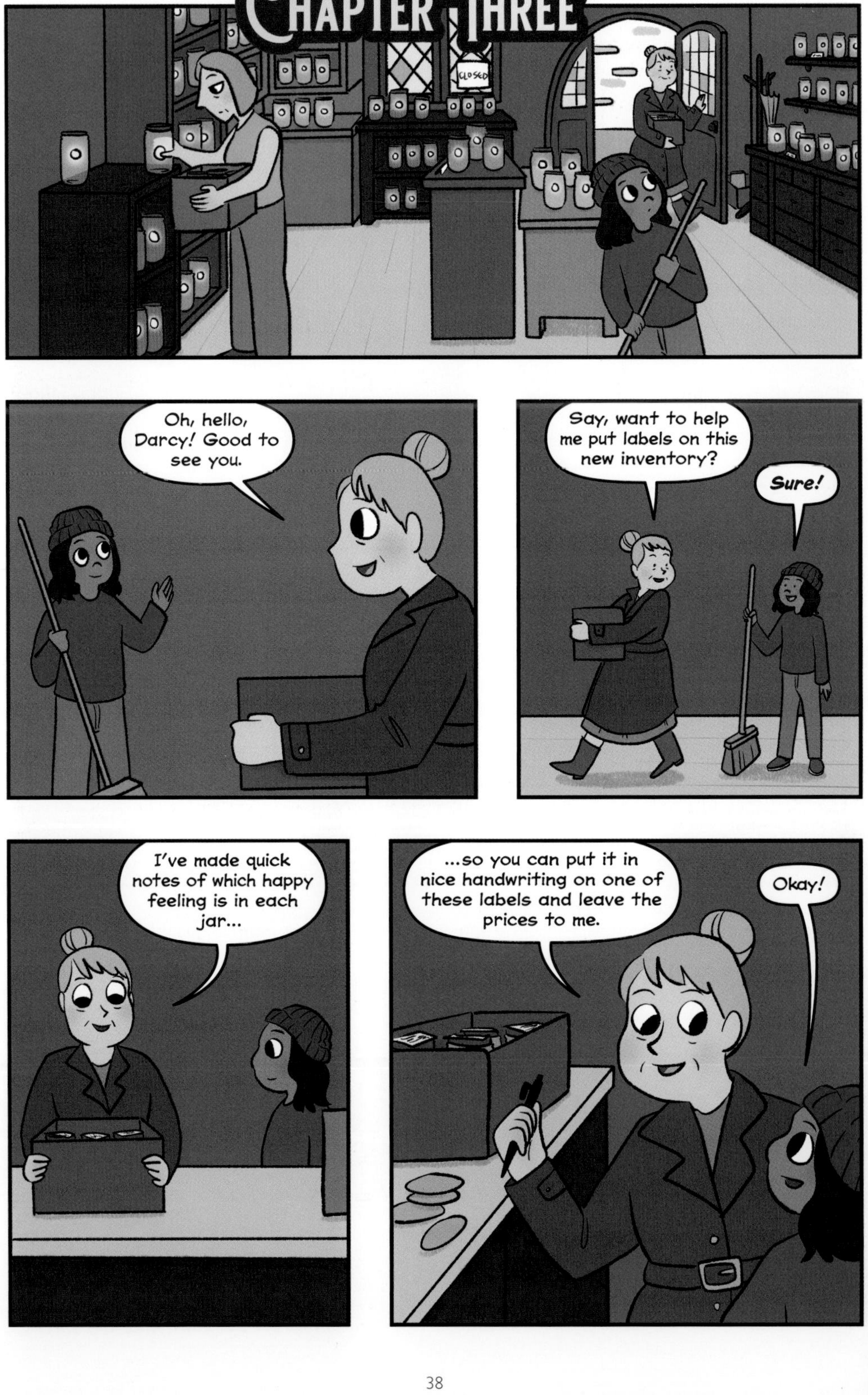
CLOSED
Oh, hello, Darcy! Good to see you.
Say, want to help me put labels on this new inventory?
Sure!
I've made quick notes of which happy feeling is in each jar...
...so you can put it in nice handwriting on one of these labels and leave the prices to me.
Okay!

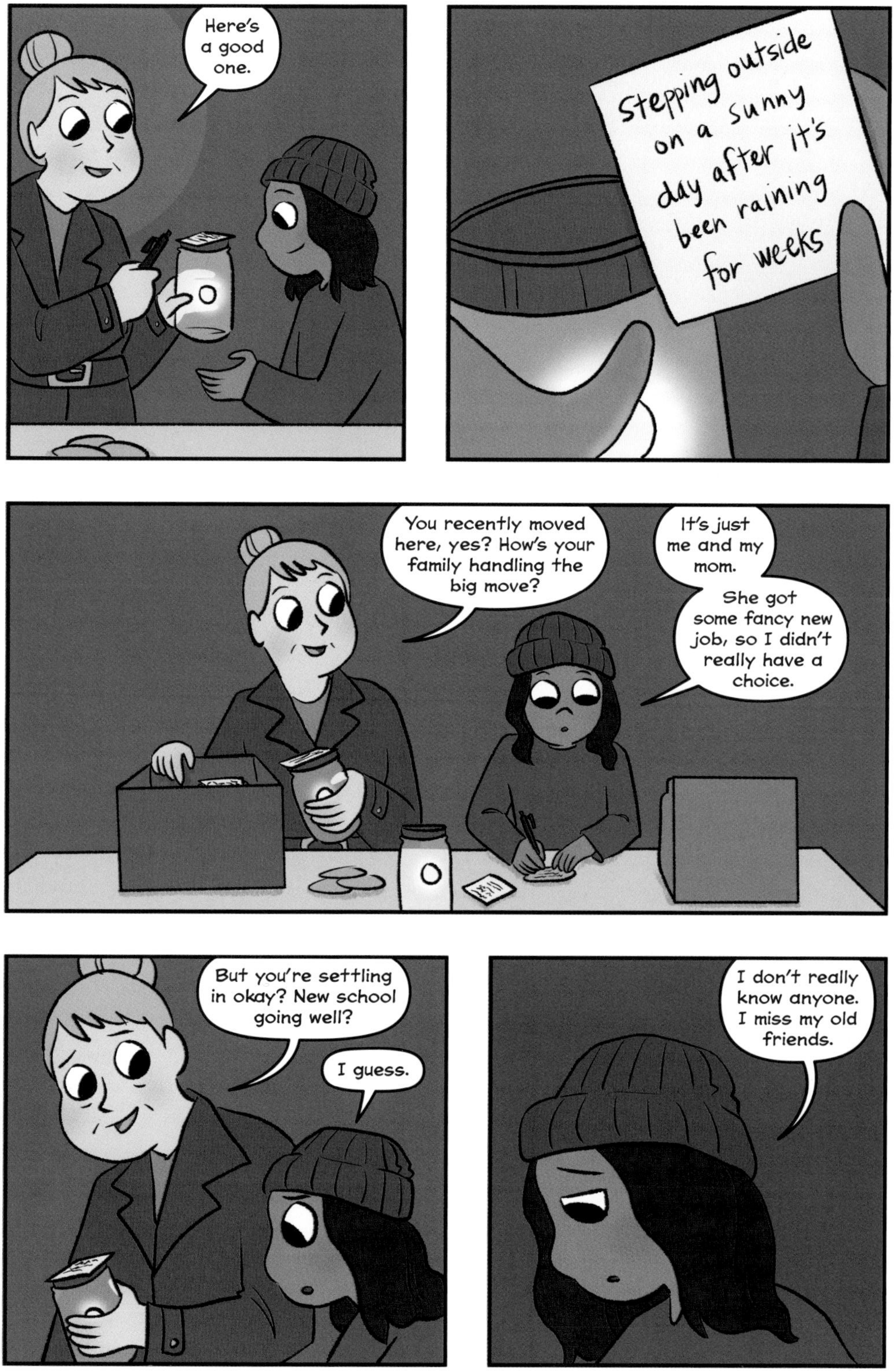
Here's a good one.
Stepping outside on a sunny day after it's been raining for weeks
You recently moved here, yes? How's your family handling the big move?
It's just me and my mom.
She got some fancy new job, so I didn't really have a choice.
But you're settling in okay? New school going well?
I guess.
I don't really know anyone. I miss my old friends.

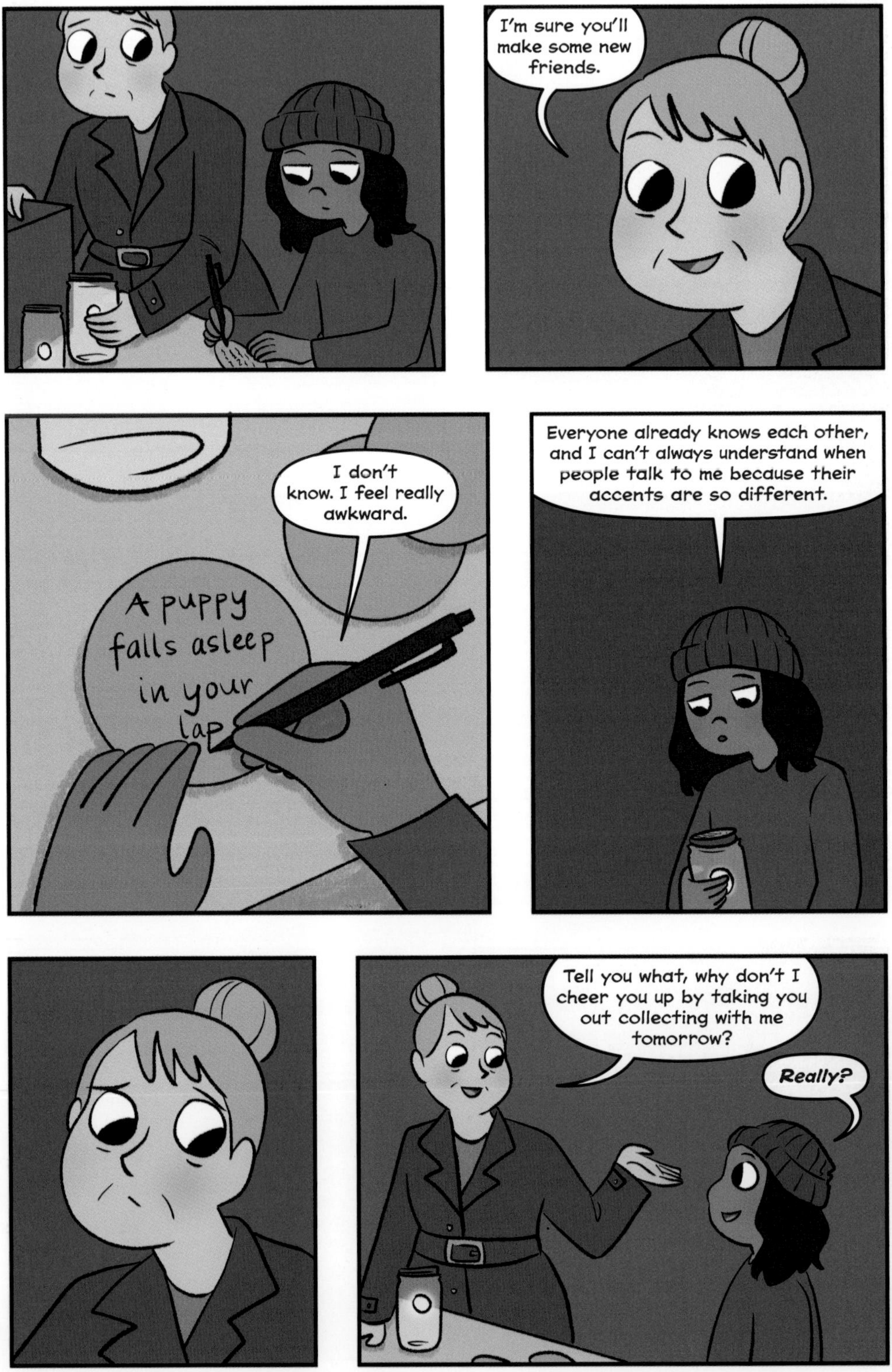
I'm sure you'll make some new friends.
I don't know. I feel really awkward.
A puppy falls asleep in your lap
Everyone already knows each other, and I can't always understand when people talk to me because their accents are so different.
Tell you what, why don't I cheer you up by taking you out collecting with me tomorrow?
Really?

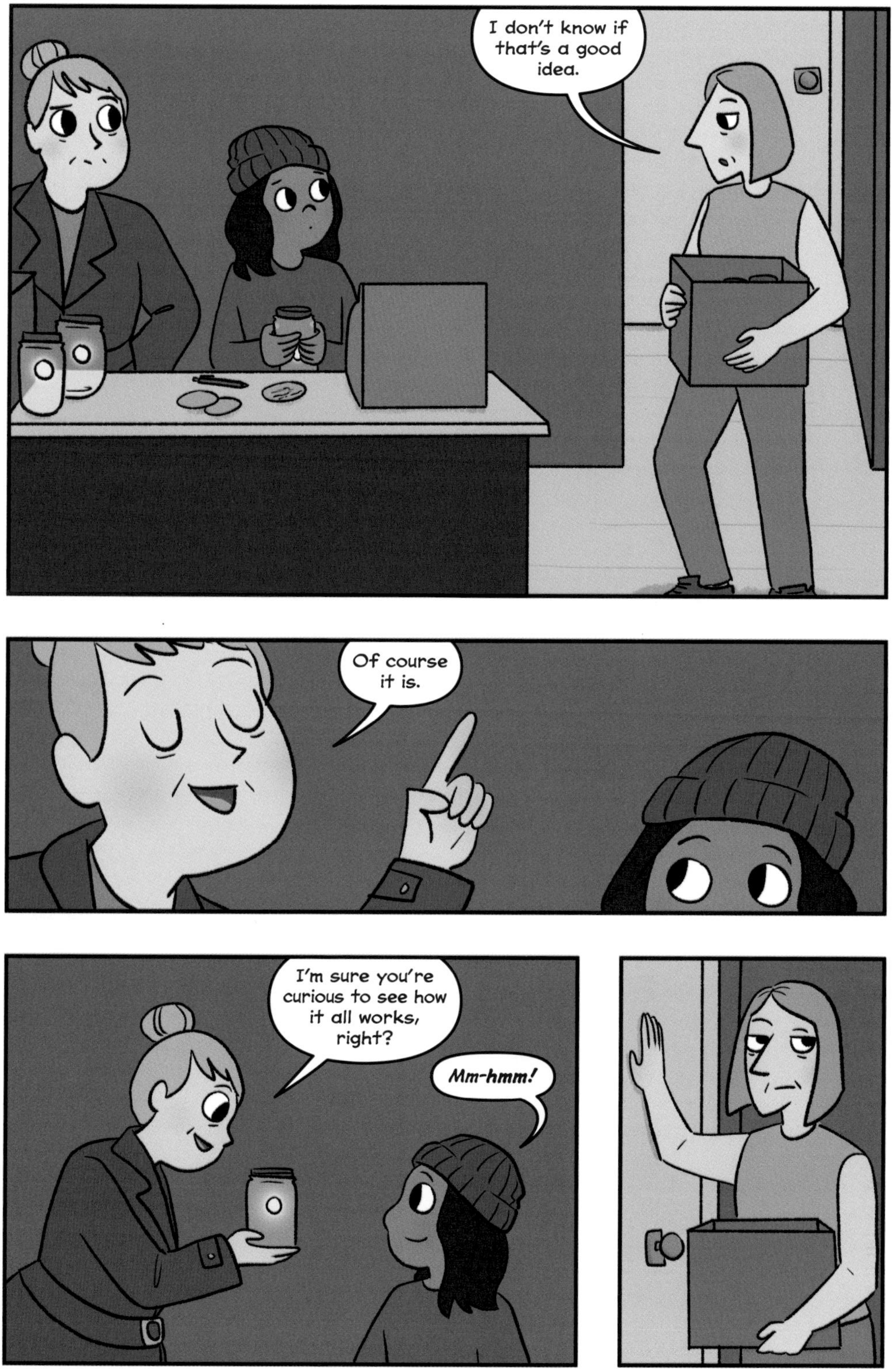
I don't know if that's a good idea.
Of course it is.
I'm sure you're curious to see how it all works, right?
Mm-hmm!

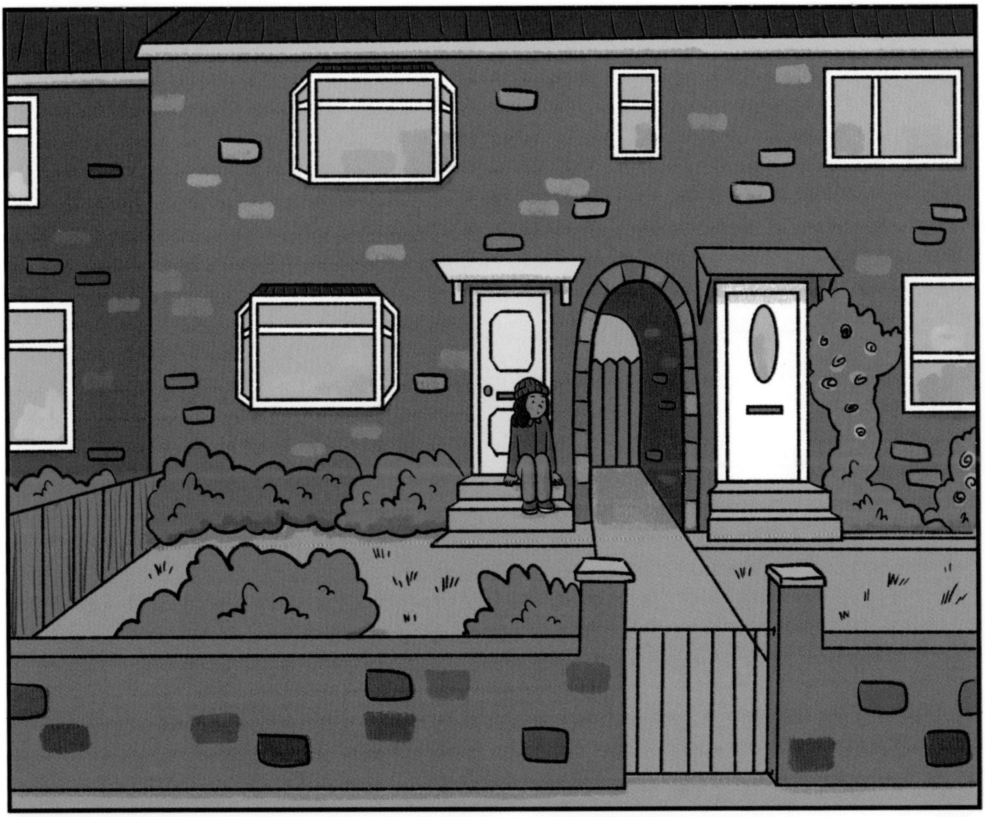

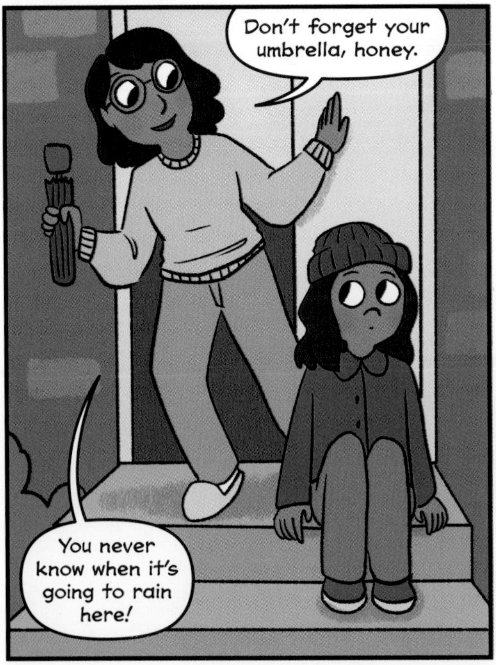
Don't forget your umbrella, honey.
You never know when it's going to rain here!

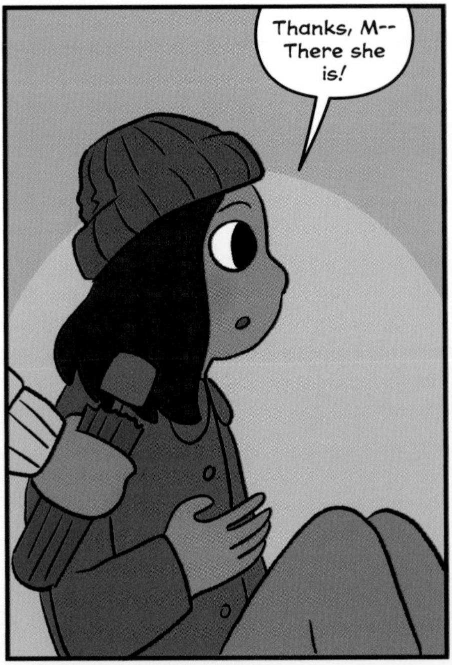
Thanks, M-- There she is!

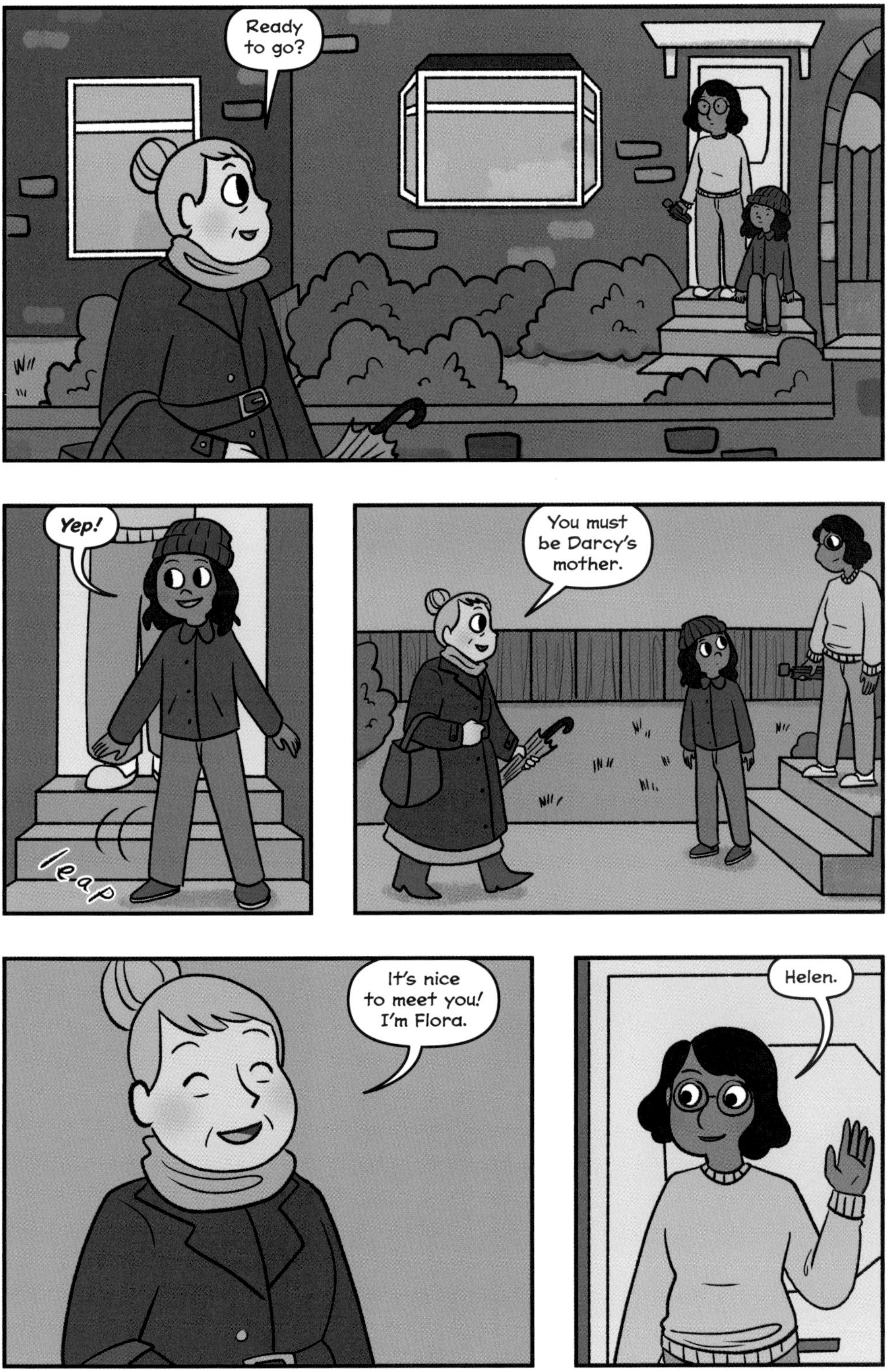
Ready to go?
Yep!
leap
You must be Darcy's mother.
It's nice to meet you! I'm Flora.
Helen.

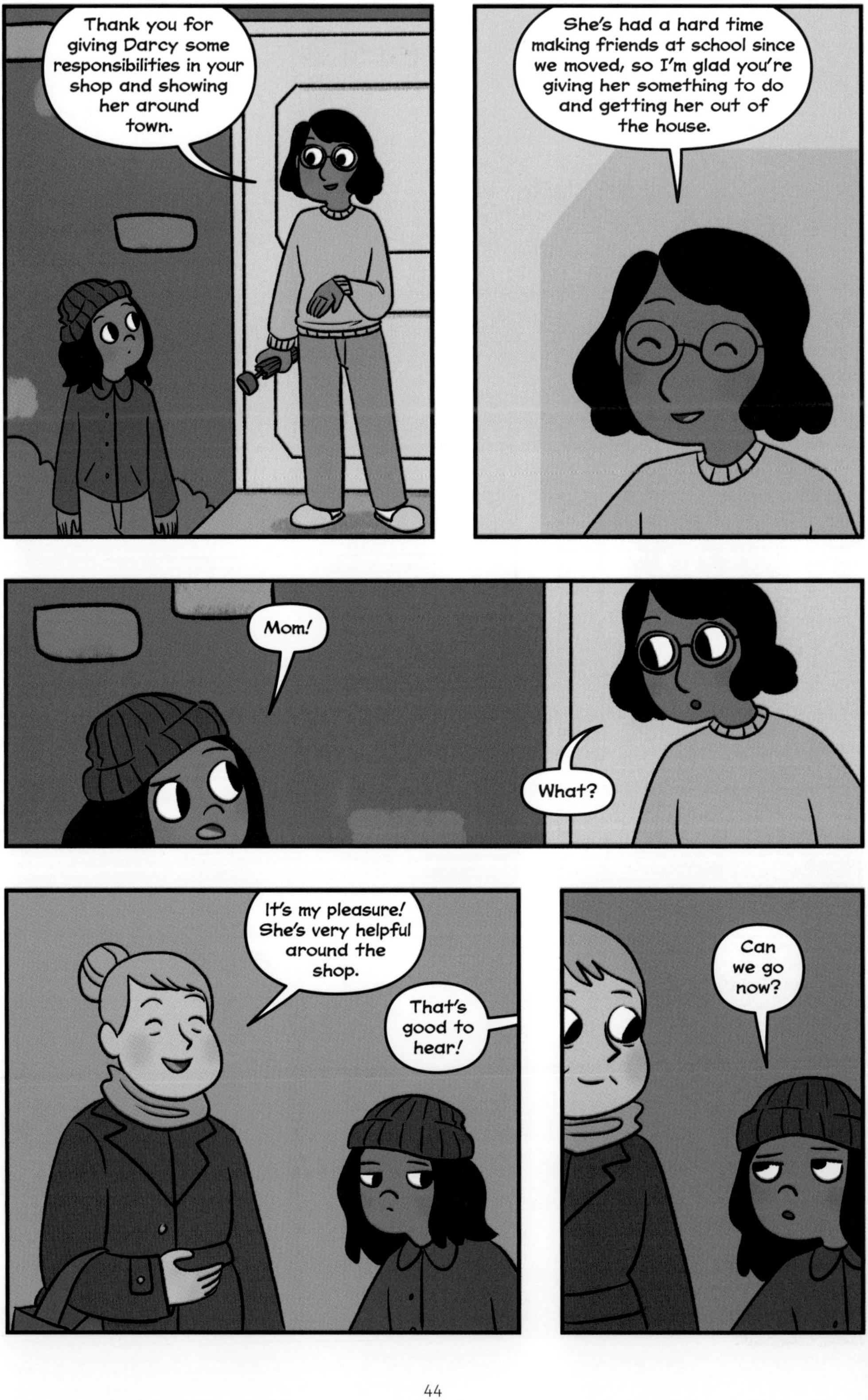

Thank you for giving Darcy some responsibilities in your shop and showing her around town.
She's had a hard time making friends at school since we moved, so I'm glad you're giving her something to do and getting her out of the house.
Mom!
What?
It's my pleasure! She's very helpful around the shop.
That's good to hear!
Can we go now?

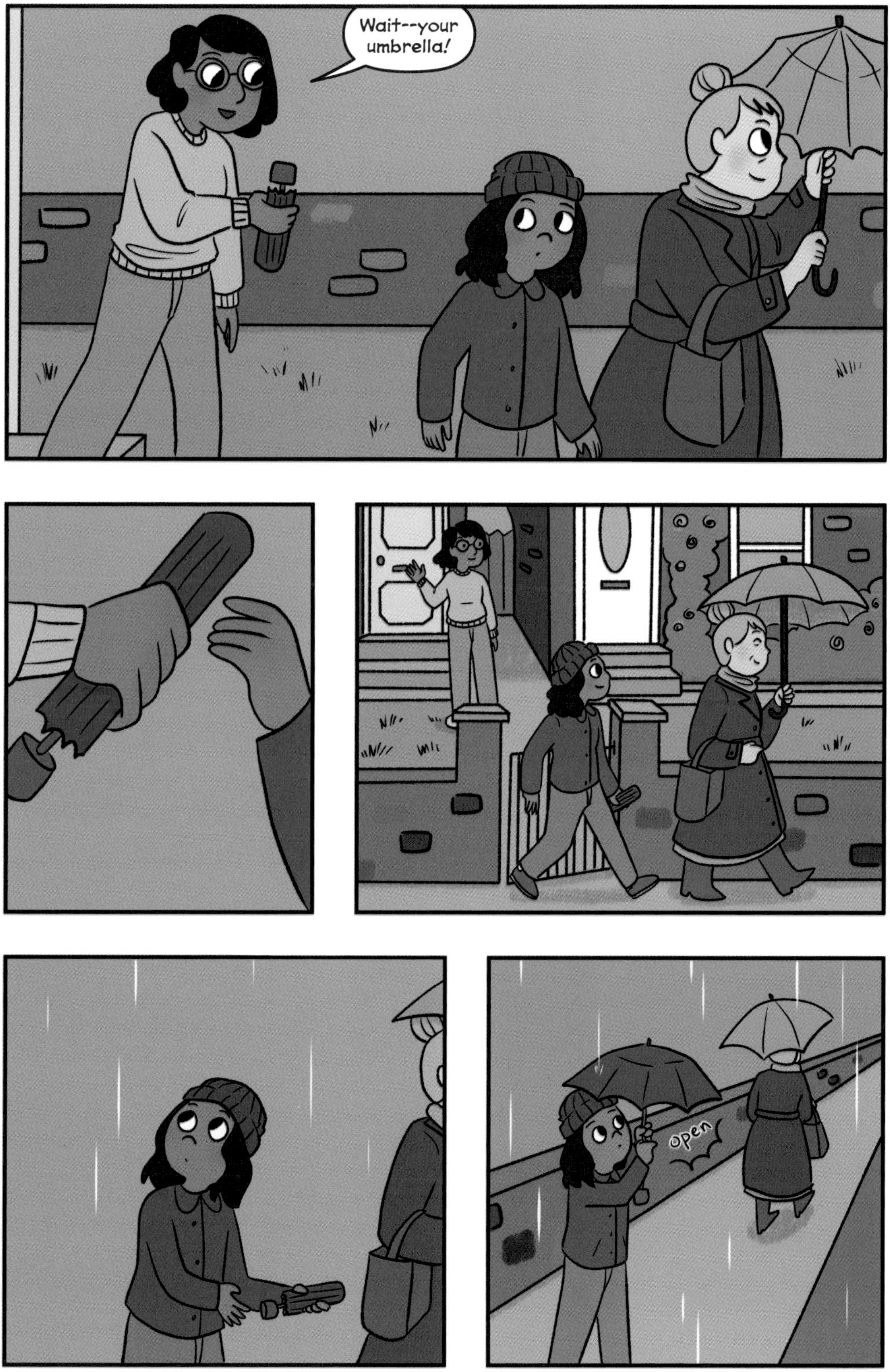
Wait--your umbrella!
open

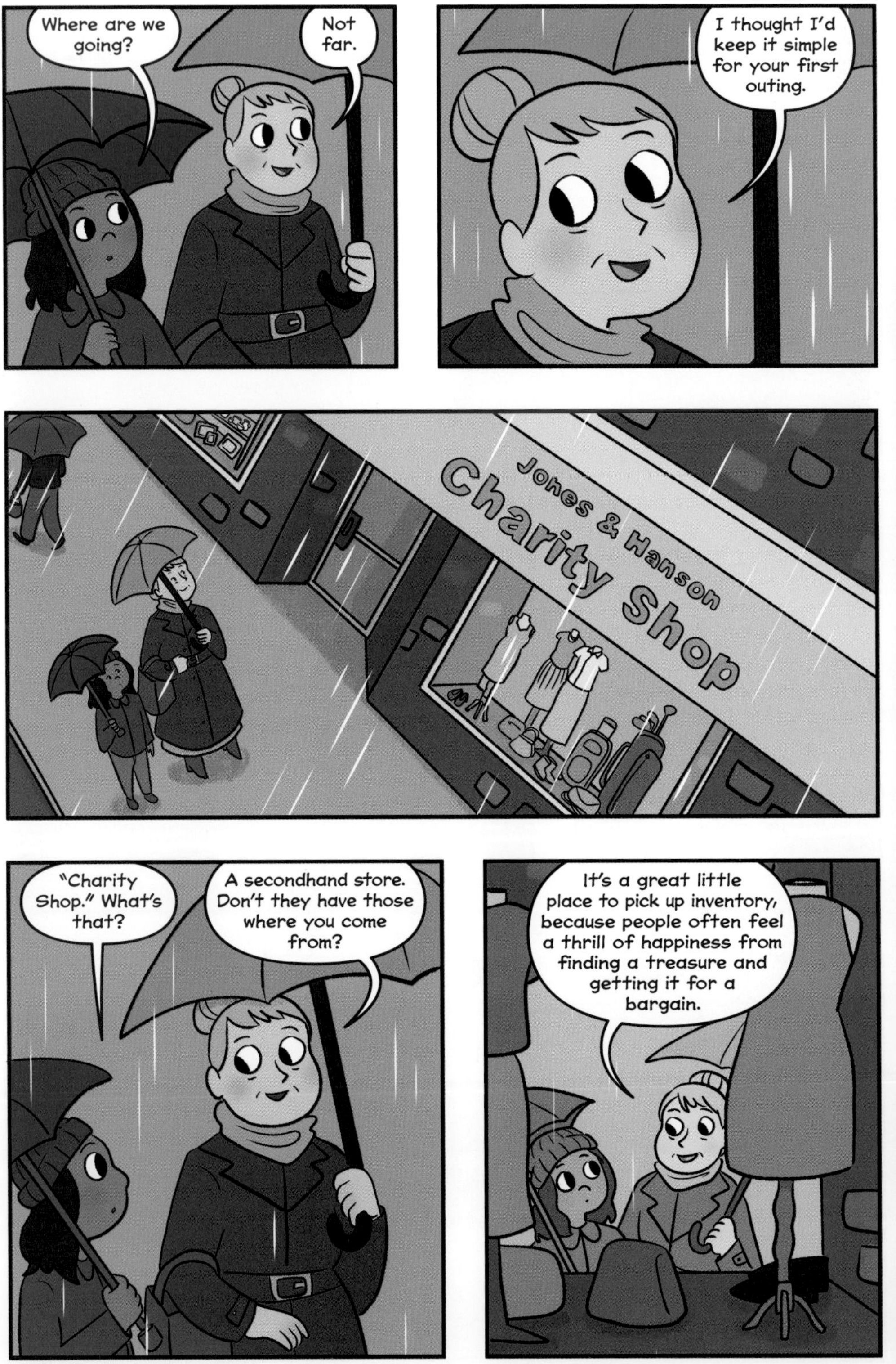
Where are we going?
Not far.
I thought I'd keep it simple for your first outing.
Jones & Hanson Charity Shop
"Charity Shop." What's that?
A secondhand store. Don't they have those where you come from?
It's a great little place to pick up inventory, because people often feel a thrill of happiness from finding a treasure and getting it for a bargain.

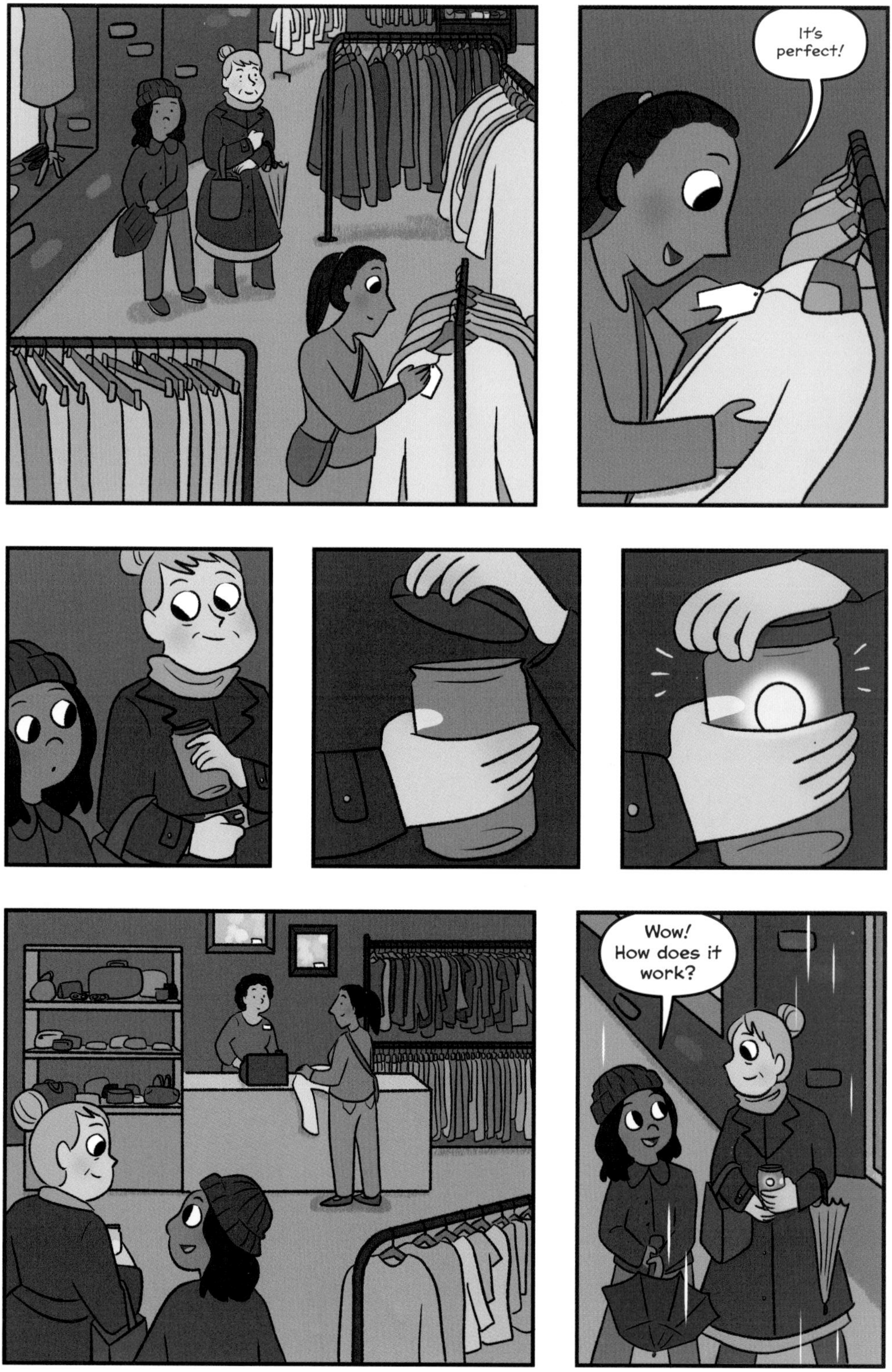
It's perfect!
Wow! How does it work?

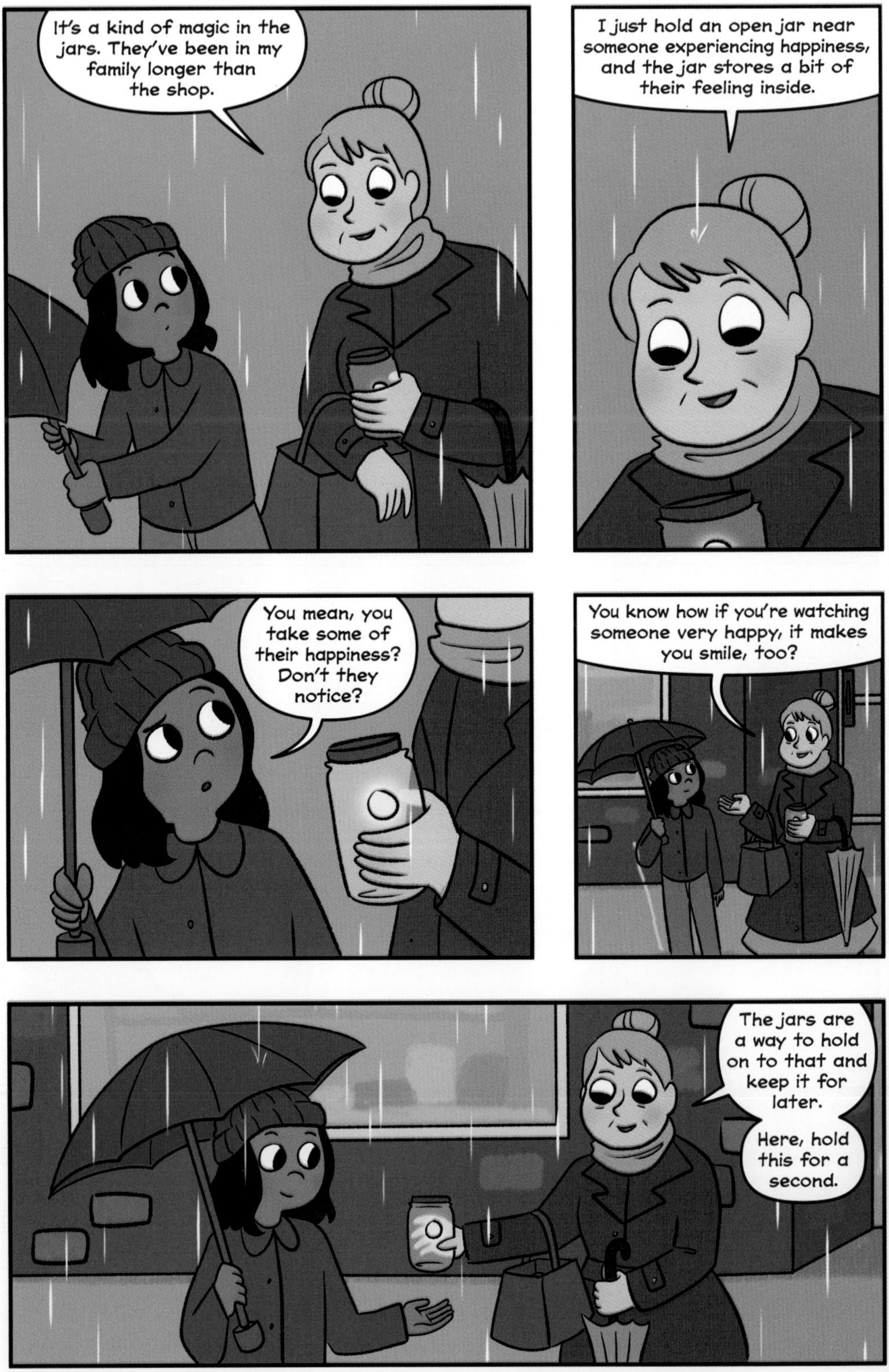

It's a kind of magic in the jars. They've been in my family longer than the shop.
I just hold an open jar near someone experiencing happiness, and the jar stores a bit of their feeling inside.
You mean, you take some of their happiness? Don't they notice?
You know how if you're watching someone very happy, it makes you smile, too?
The jars are a way to hold on to that and keep it for later.
Here, hold this for a second.

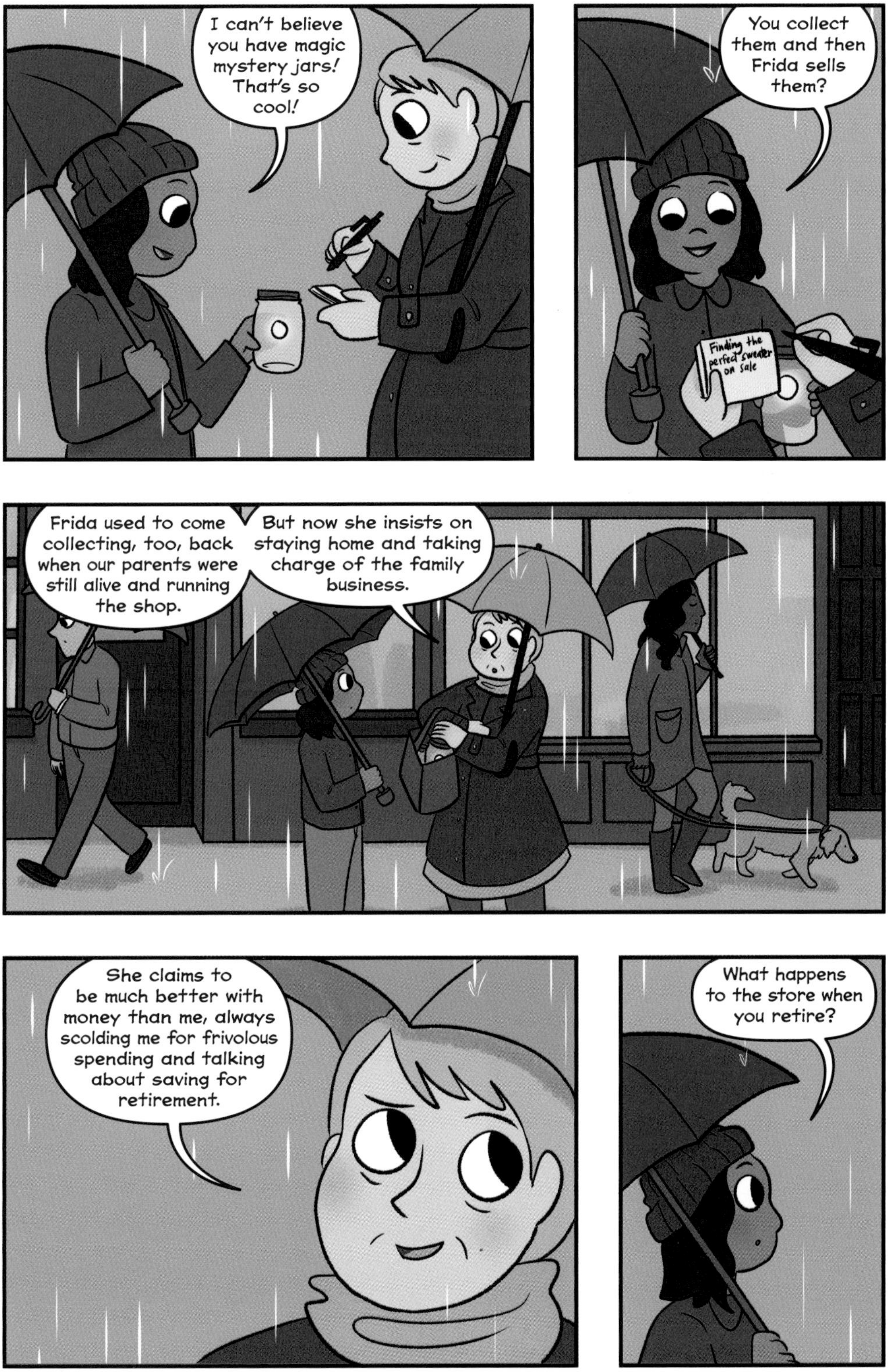
I can't believe you have magic mystery jars! That's so cool!
You collect them and then Frida sells them?
Finding the perfect sweater on sale
Frida used to come collecting, too, back when our parents were still alive and running the shop.
But now she insists on staying home and taking charge of the family business.
She claims to be much better with money than me, always scolding me for frivolous spending and talking about saving for retirement.
What happens to the store when you retire?

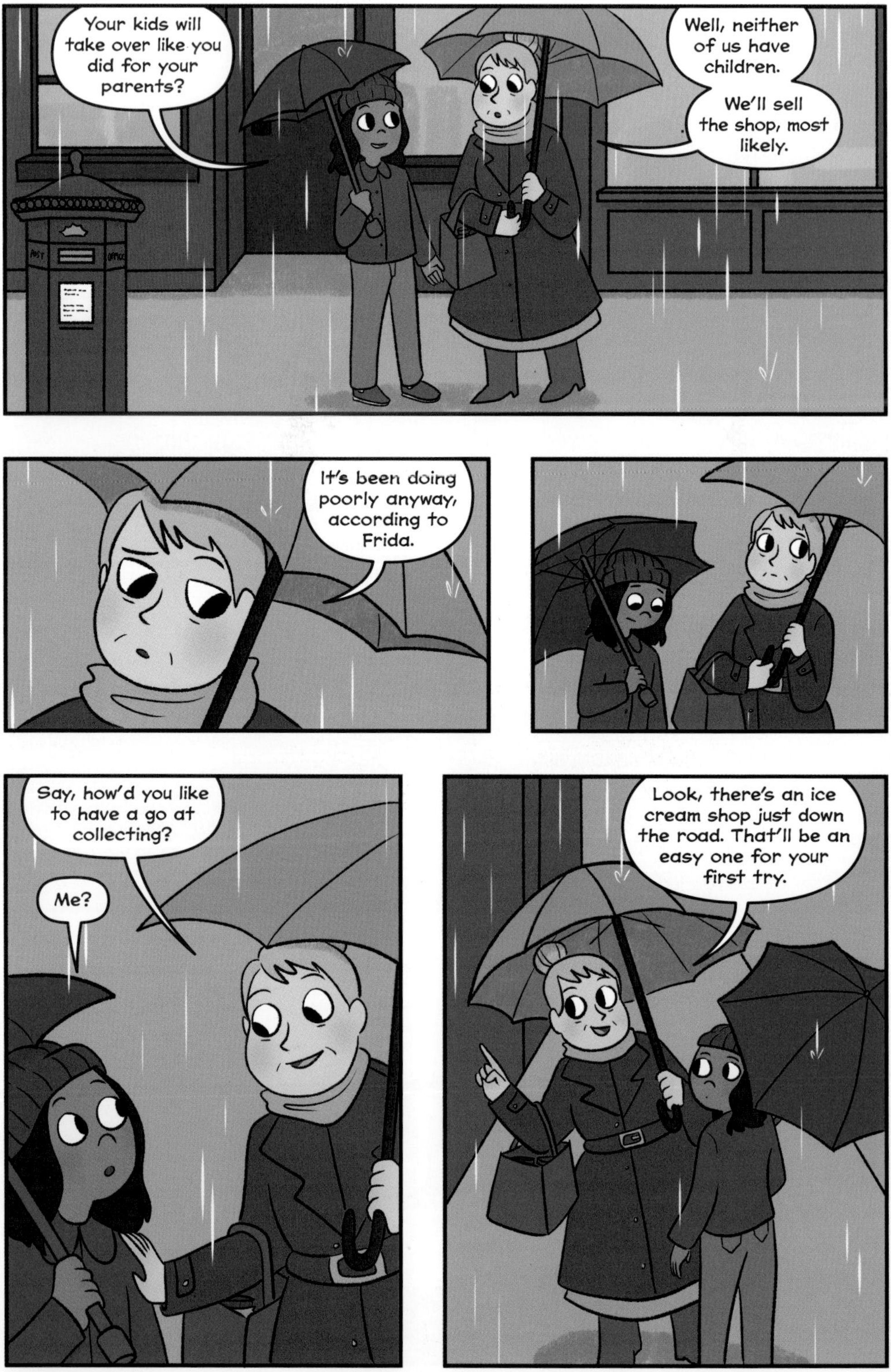
Your kids will take over like you did for your parents?
Well, neither of us have children.
We'll sell the shop, most likely.
It's been doing poorly anyway, according to Frida.
Say, how'd you like to have a go at collecting?
Me?
Look, there's an ice cream shop just down the road. That'll be an easy one for your first try.

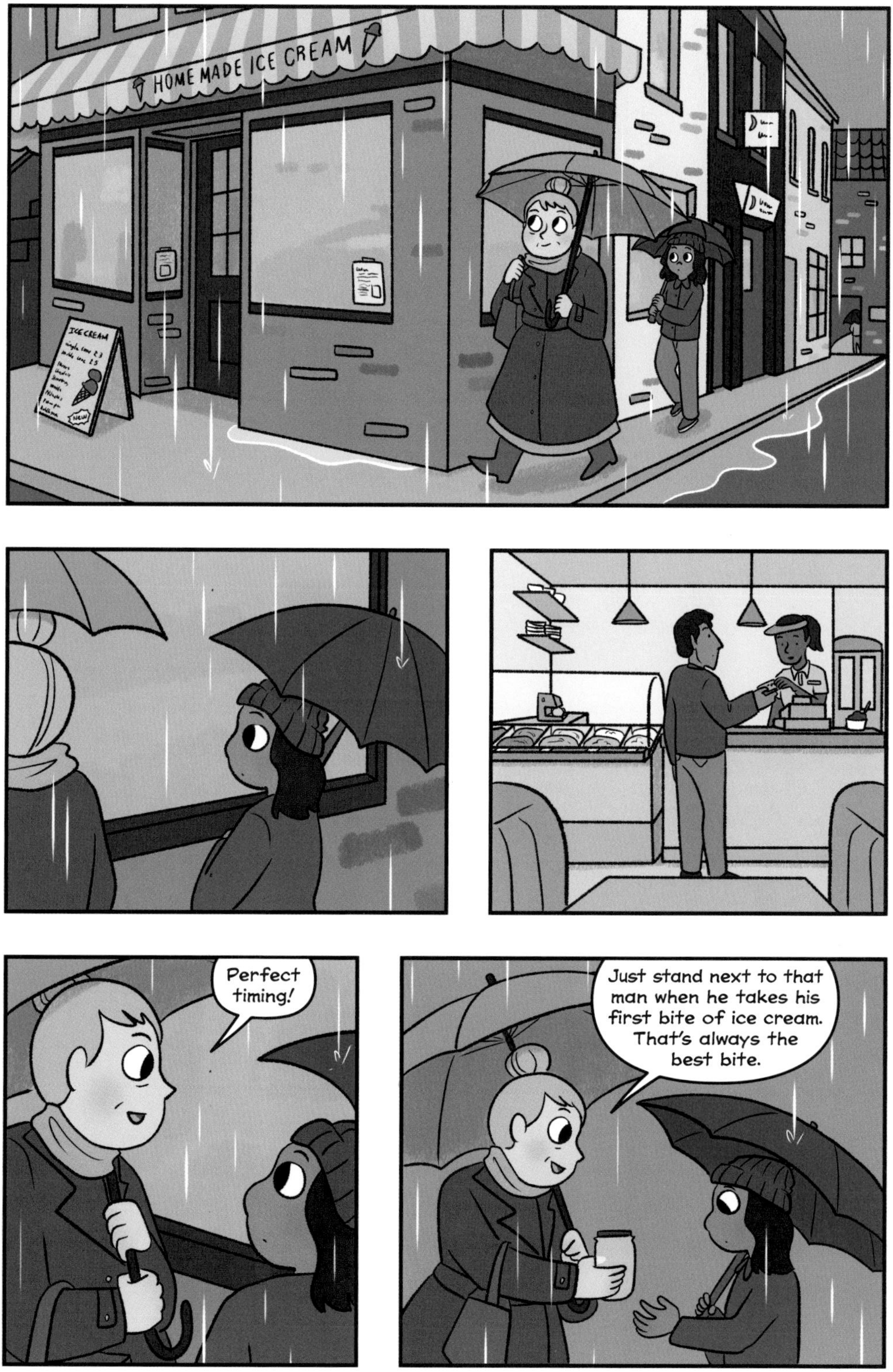
HOME MADE ICE CREAM
ICE CREAM
NEW
Perfect timing!
Just stand next to that man when he takes his first bite of ice cream. That's always the best bite.

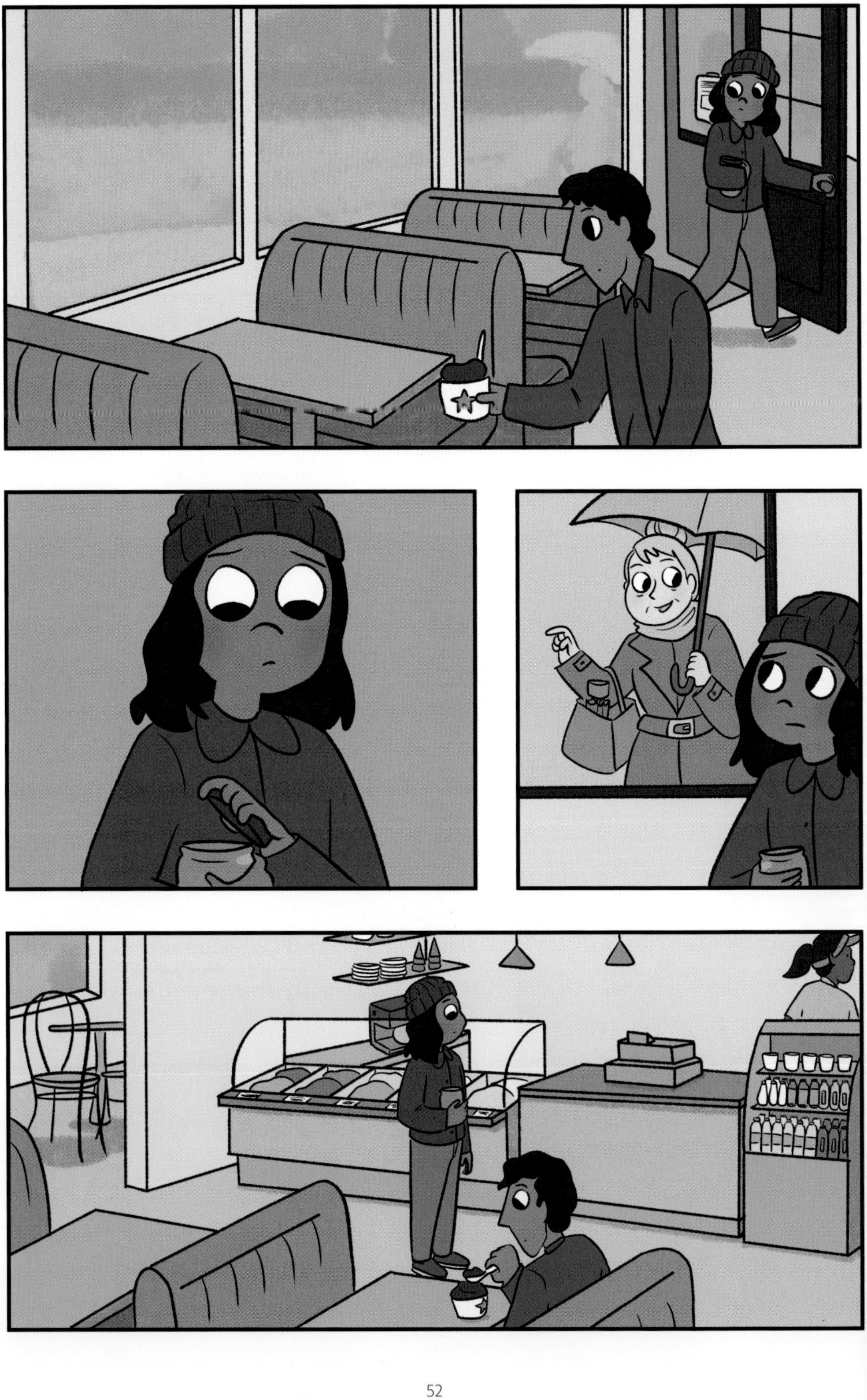

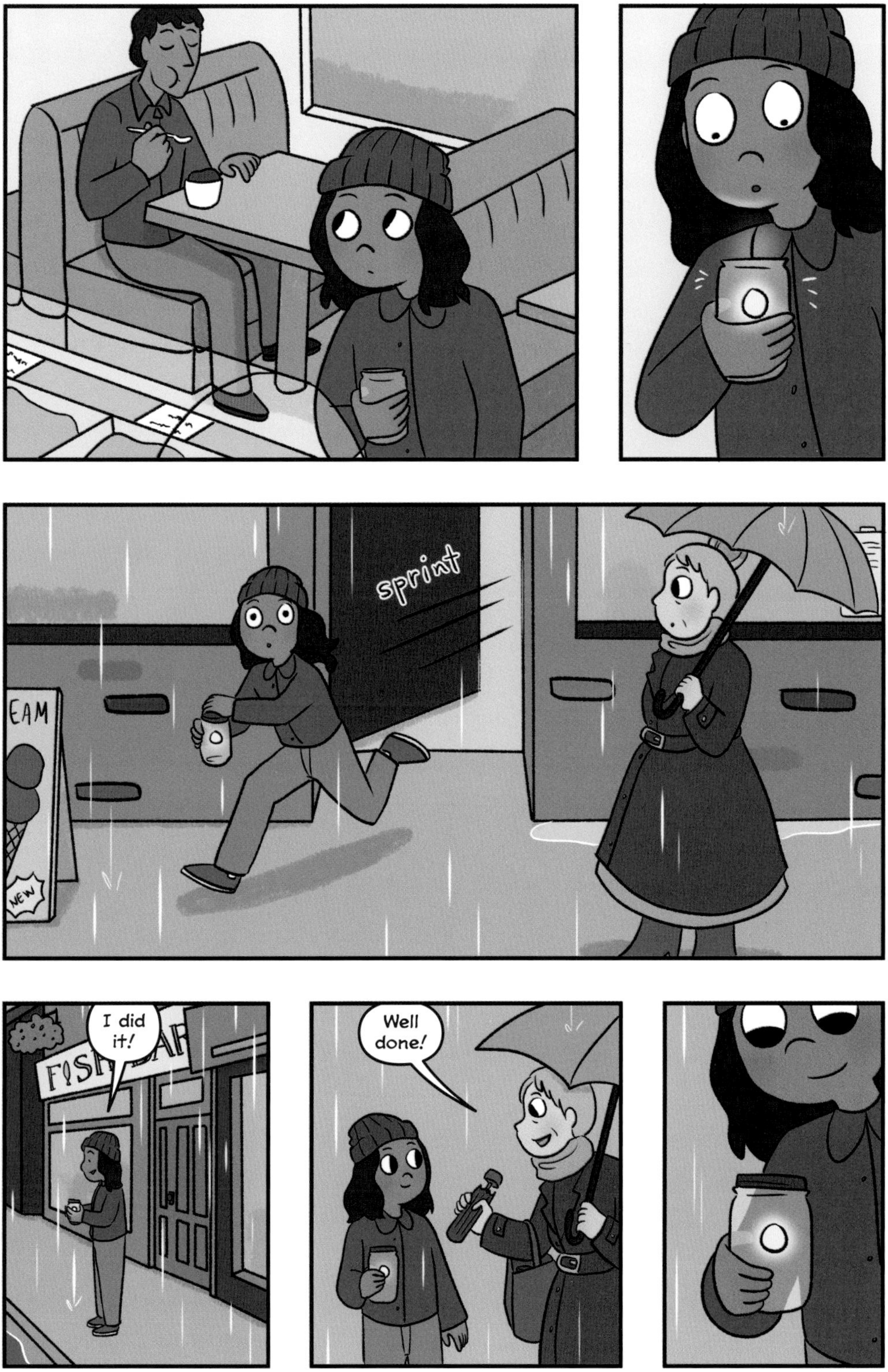
sprint
EAM
NEW
I did it!
FISH BAR
Well done!

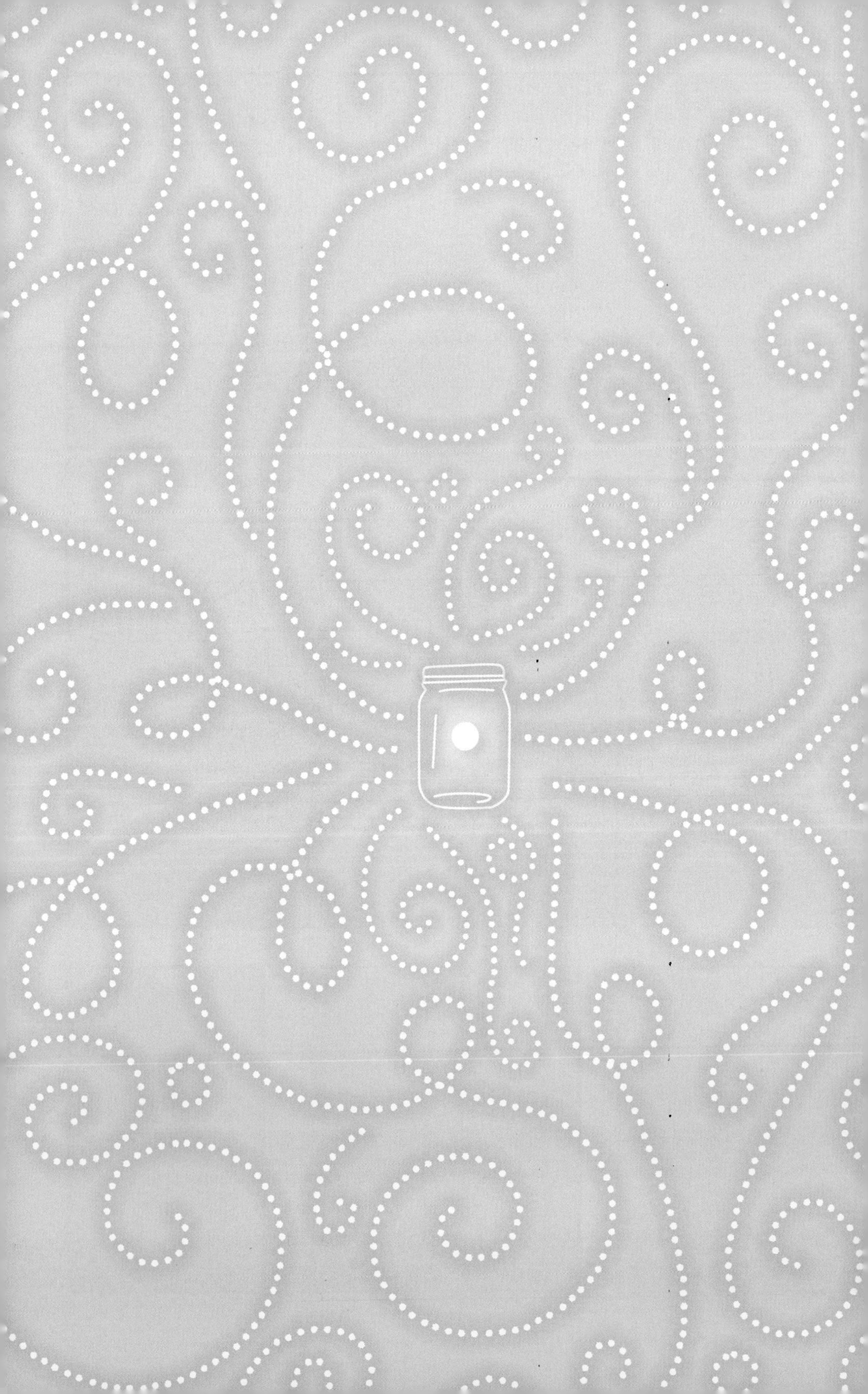

Chapter Four

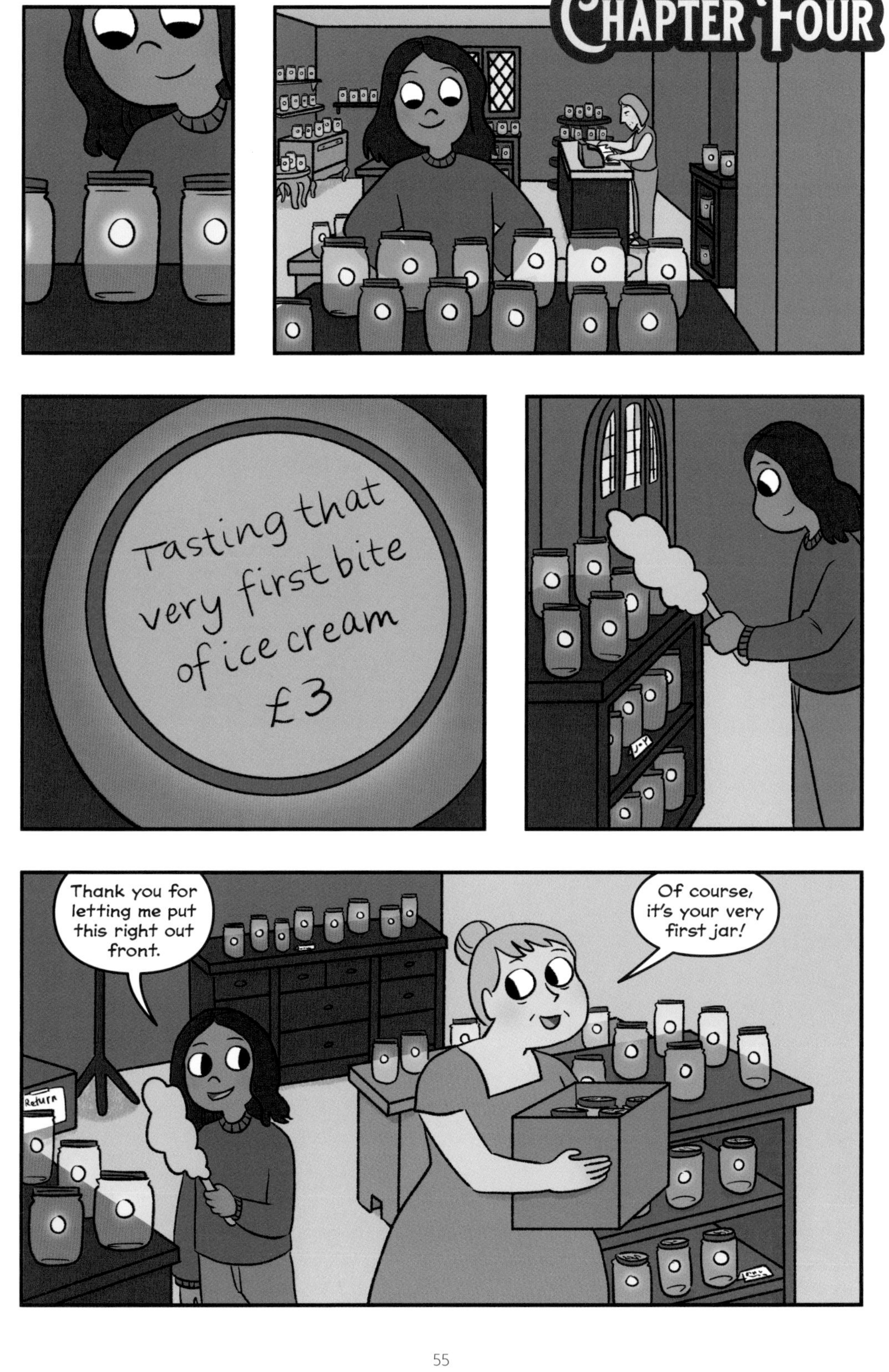
Tasting that very first bite of ice cream £3
Thank you for letting me put this right out front.
Of course, it's your very first jar!

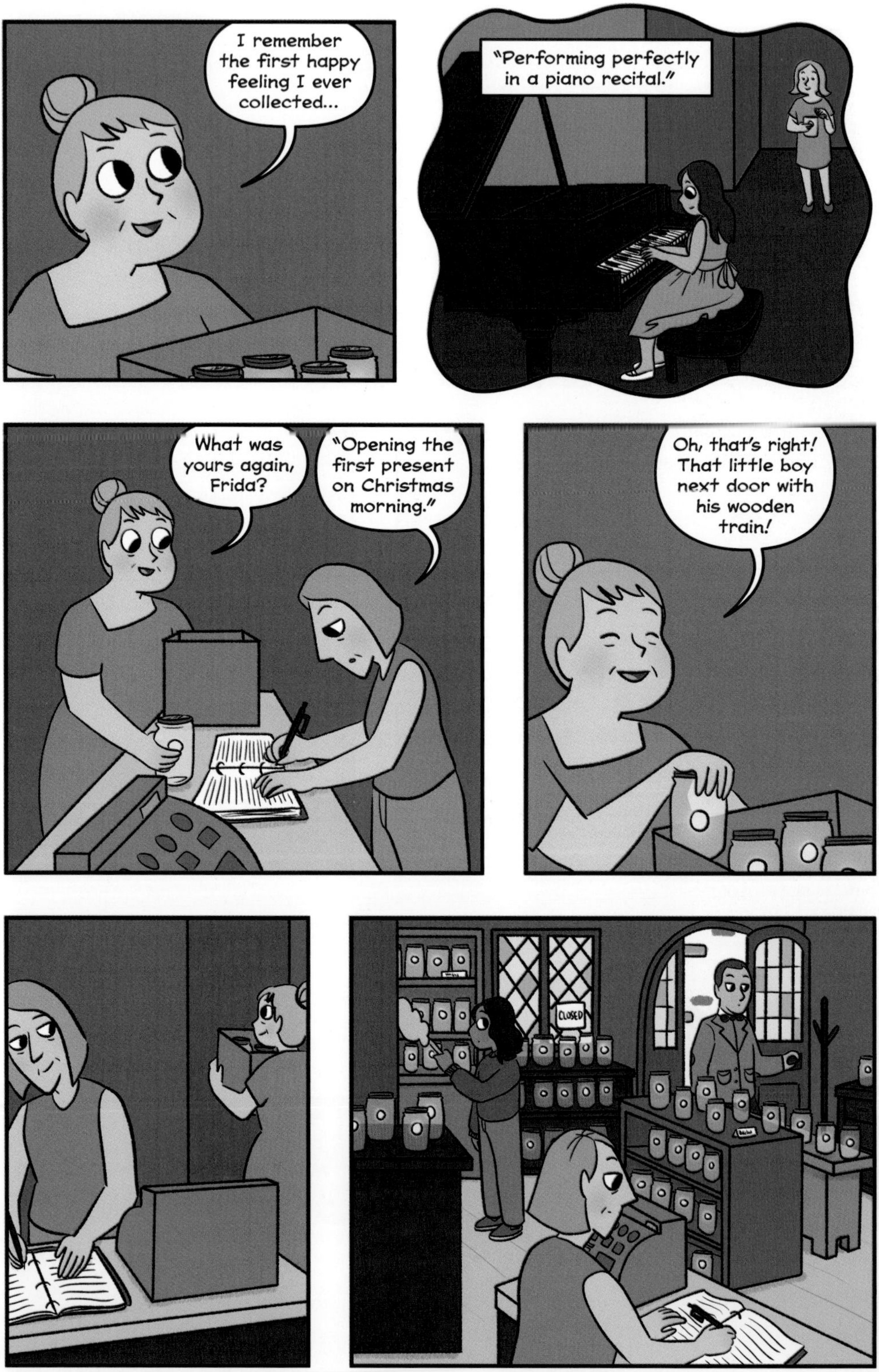
I remember the first happy feeling I ever collected...
"Performing perfectly in a piano recital."
What was yours again, Frida?
"Opening the first present on Christmas morning."
Oh, that's right! That little boy next door with his wooden train!
CLOSED

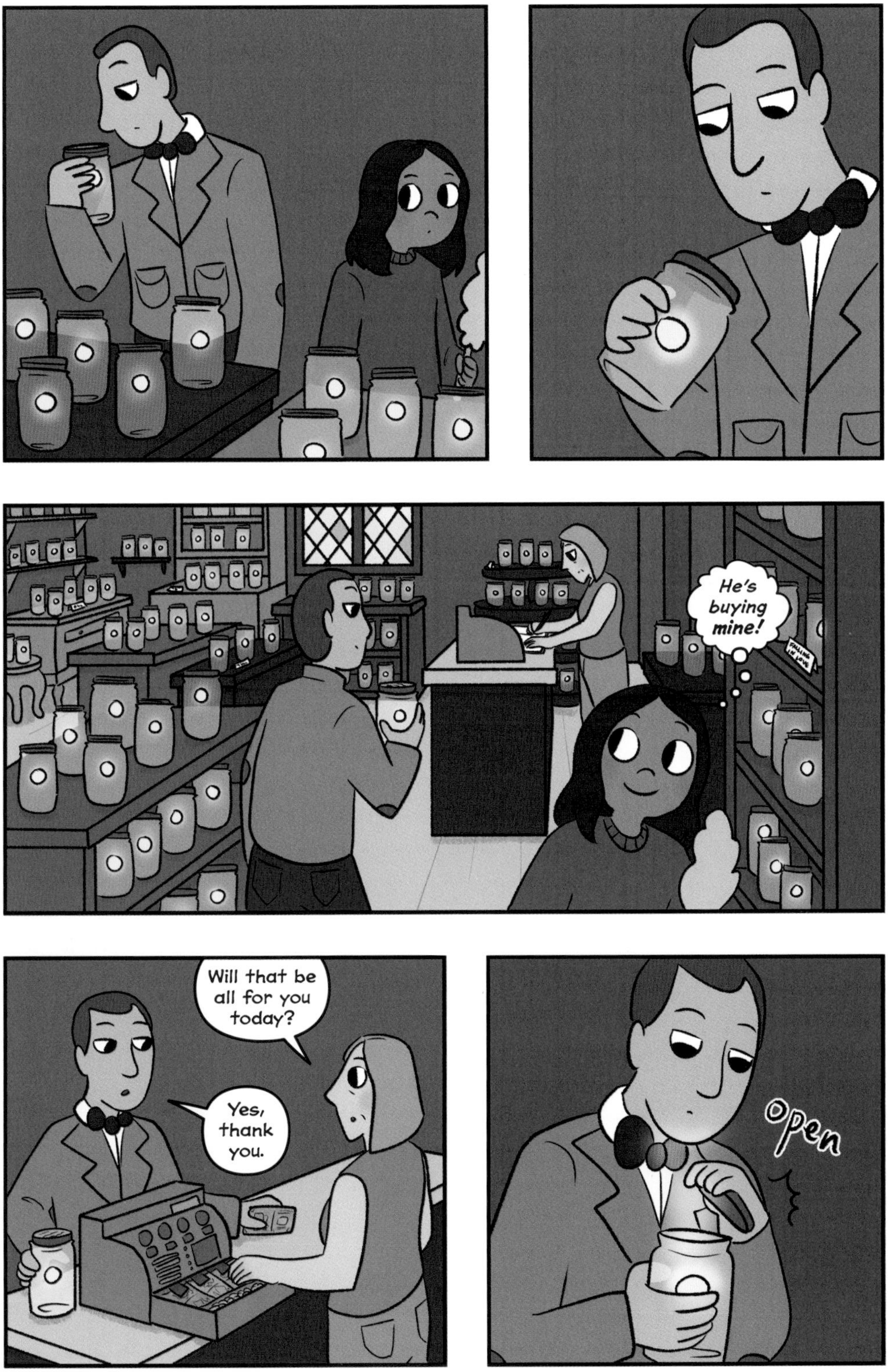
He's buying mine!
Will that be all for you today?
Yes, thank you.
Open

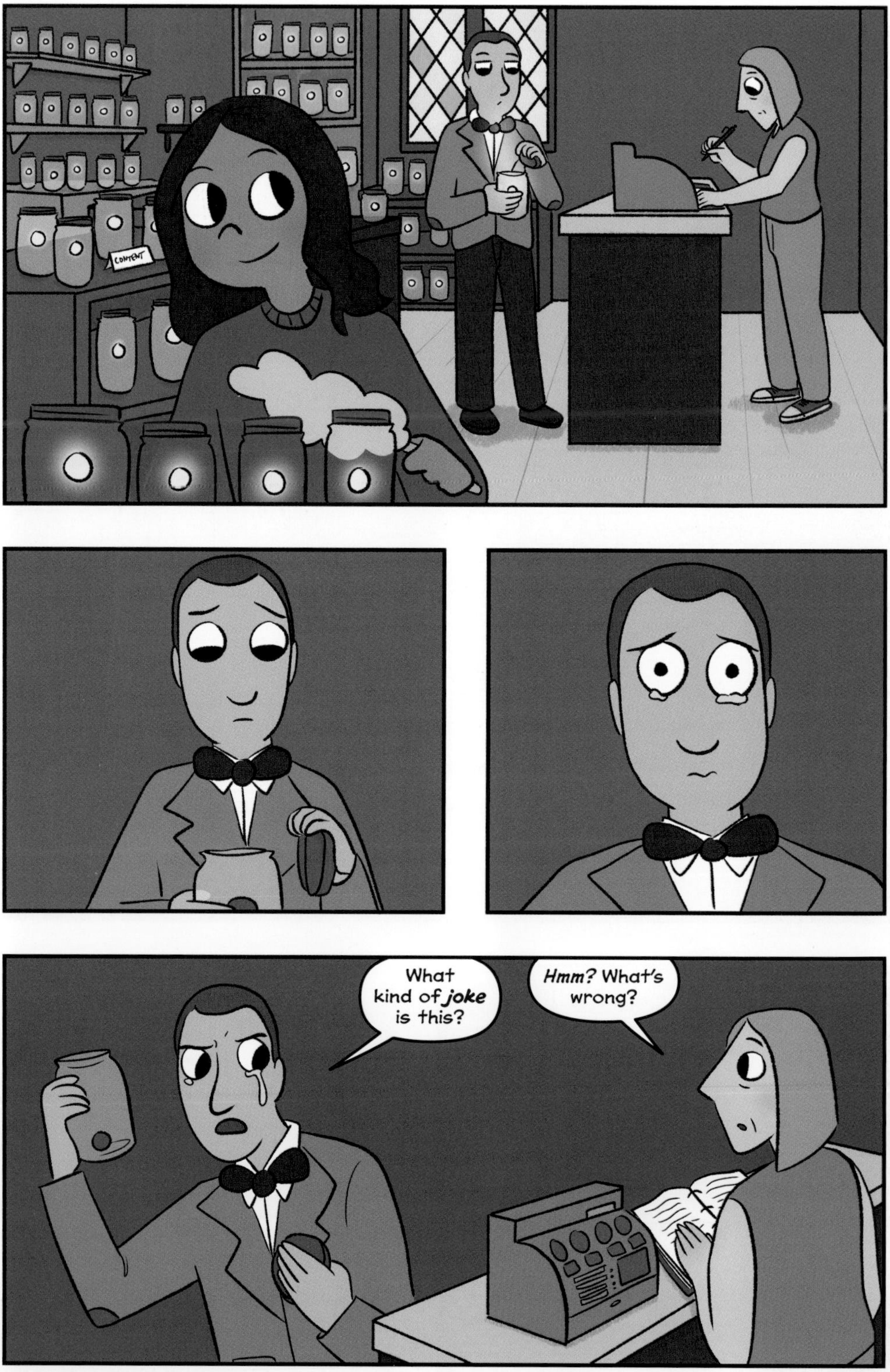
CONTENT
What kind of *joke* is this?
Hmm? What's wrong?

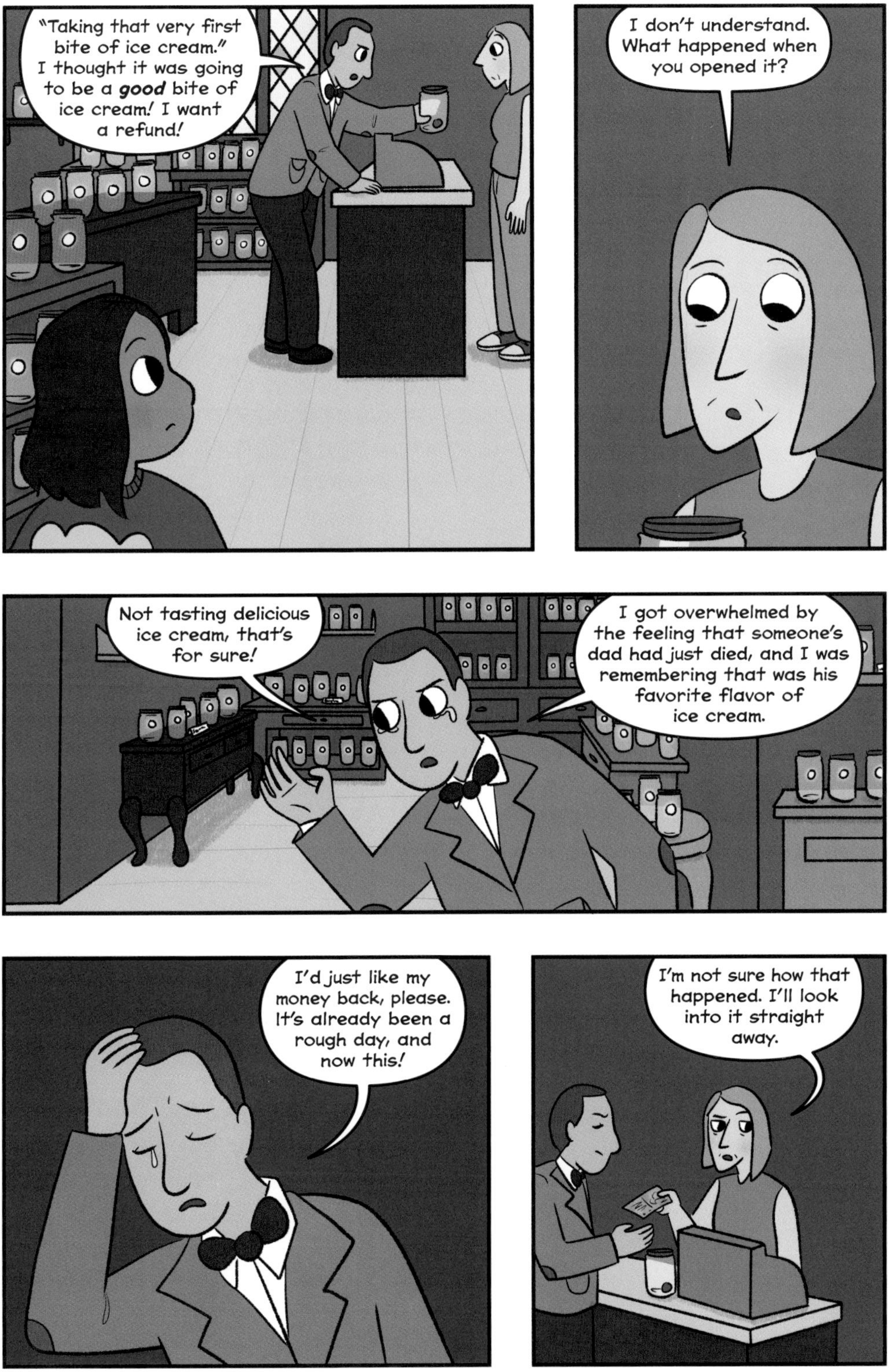
"Taking that very first bite of ice cream." I thought it was going to be a good bite of ice cream! I want a refund!
I don't understand. What happened when you opened it?
Not tasting delicious ice cream, that's for sure!
I got overwhelmed by the feeling that someone's dad had just died, and I was remembering that was his favorite flavor of ice cream.
I'd just like my money back, please. It's already been a rough day, and now this!
I'm not sure how that happened. I'll look into it straight away.

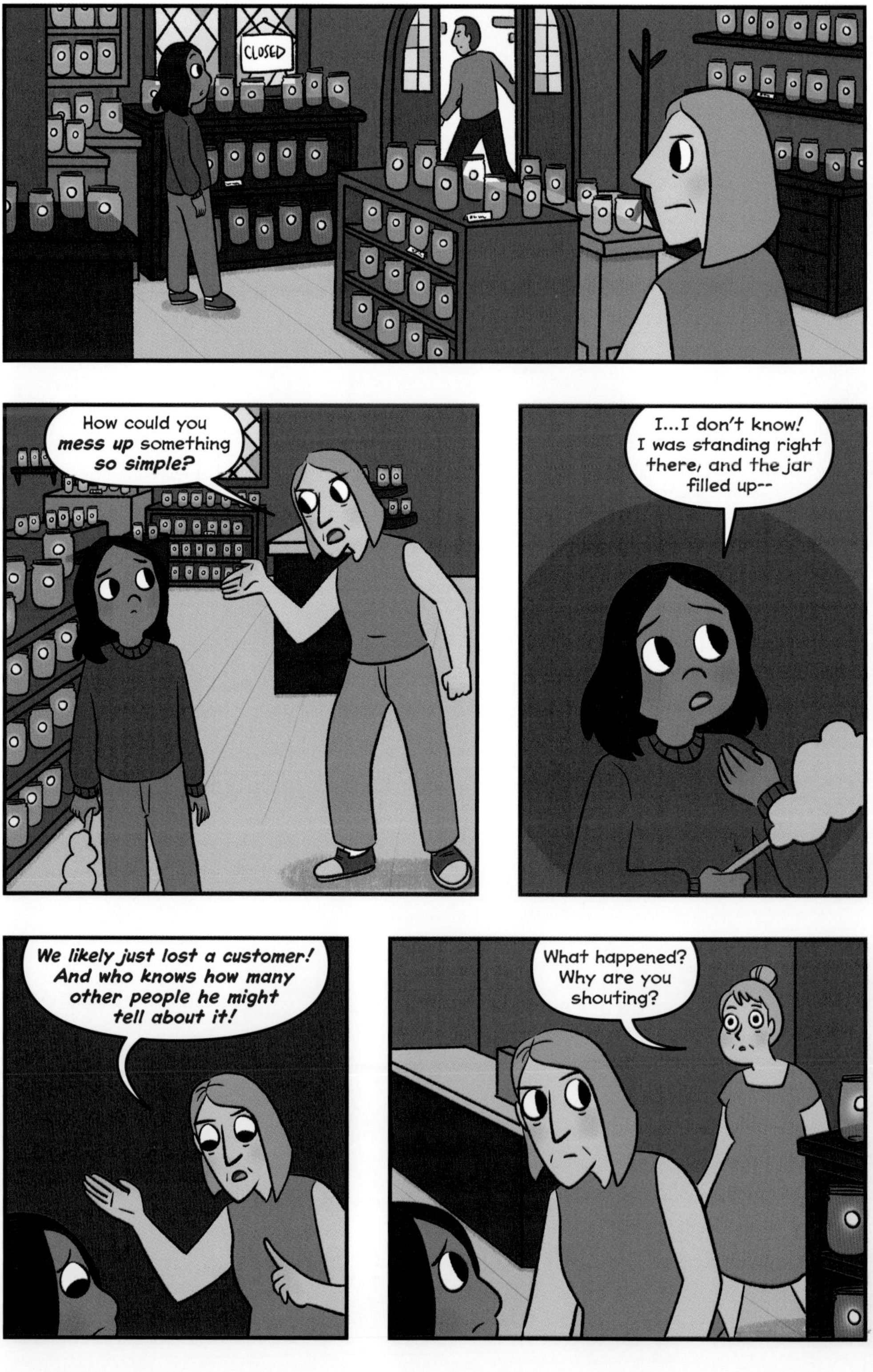
CLOSED
How could you *mess up* something *so simple?*
I...I don't know! I was standing right there, and the jar filled up--
We likely just lost a customer! And who knows how many other people he might tell about it!
What happened? Why are you shouting?

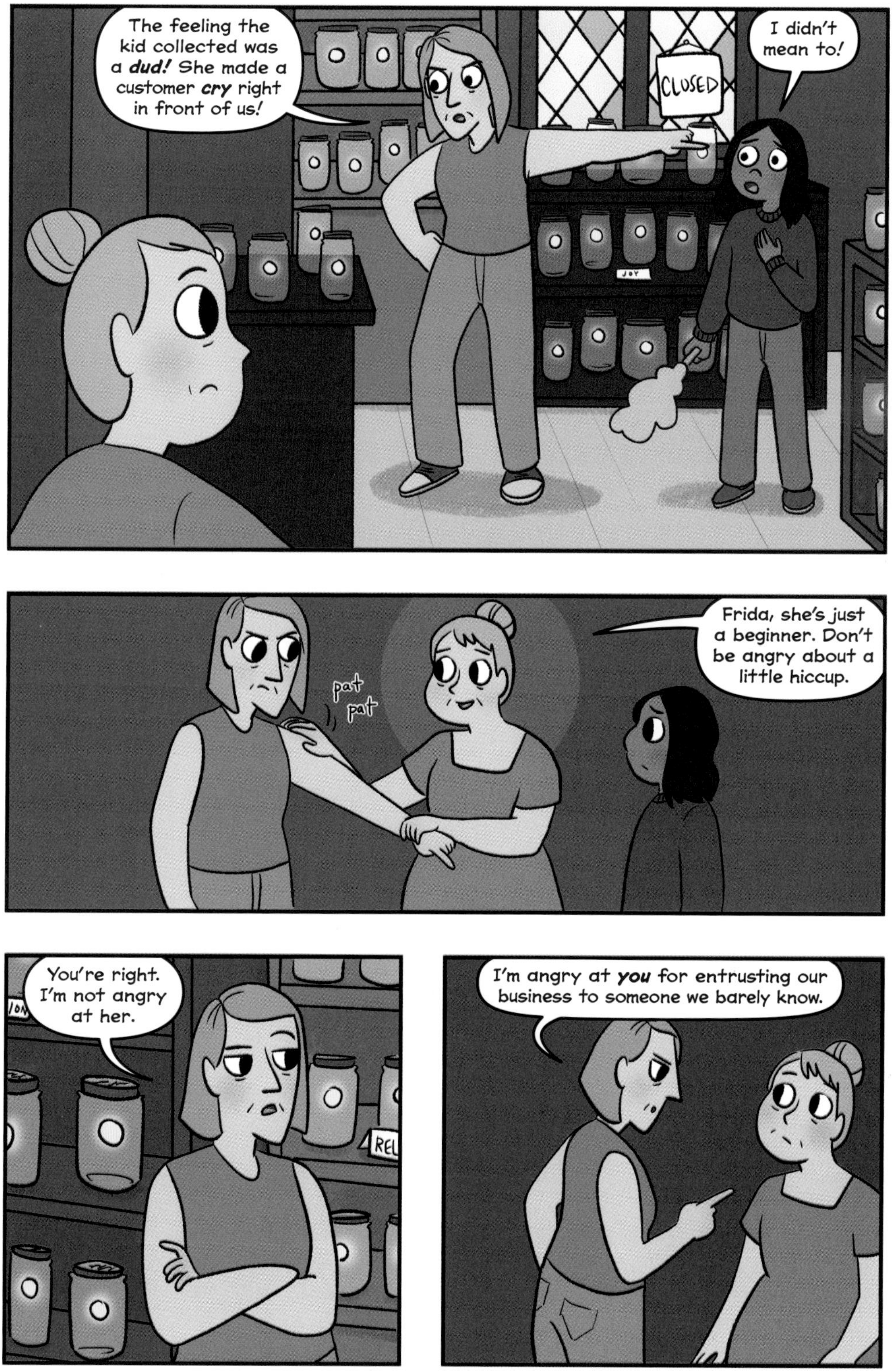
The feeling the kid collected was a *dud!* She made a customer *cry* right in front of us!
CLOSED
I didn't mean to!
JOY
pat pat
Frida, she's just a beginner. Don't be angry about a little hiccup.
You're right. I'm not angry at her.
I'm angry at *you* for entrusting our business to someone we barely know.

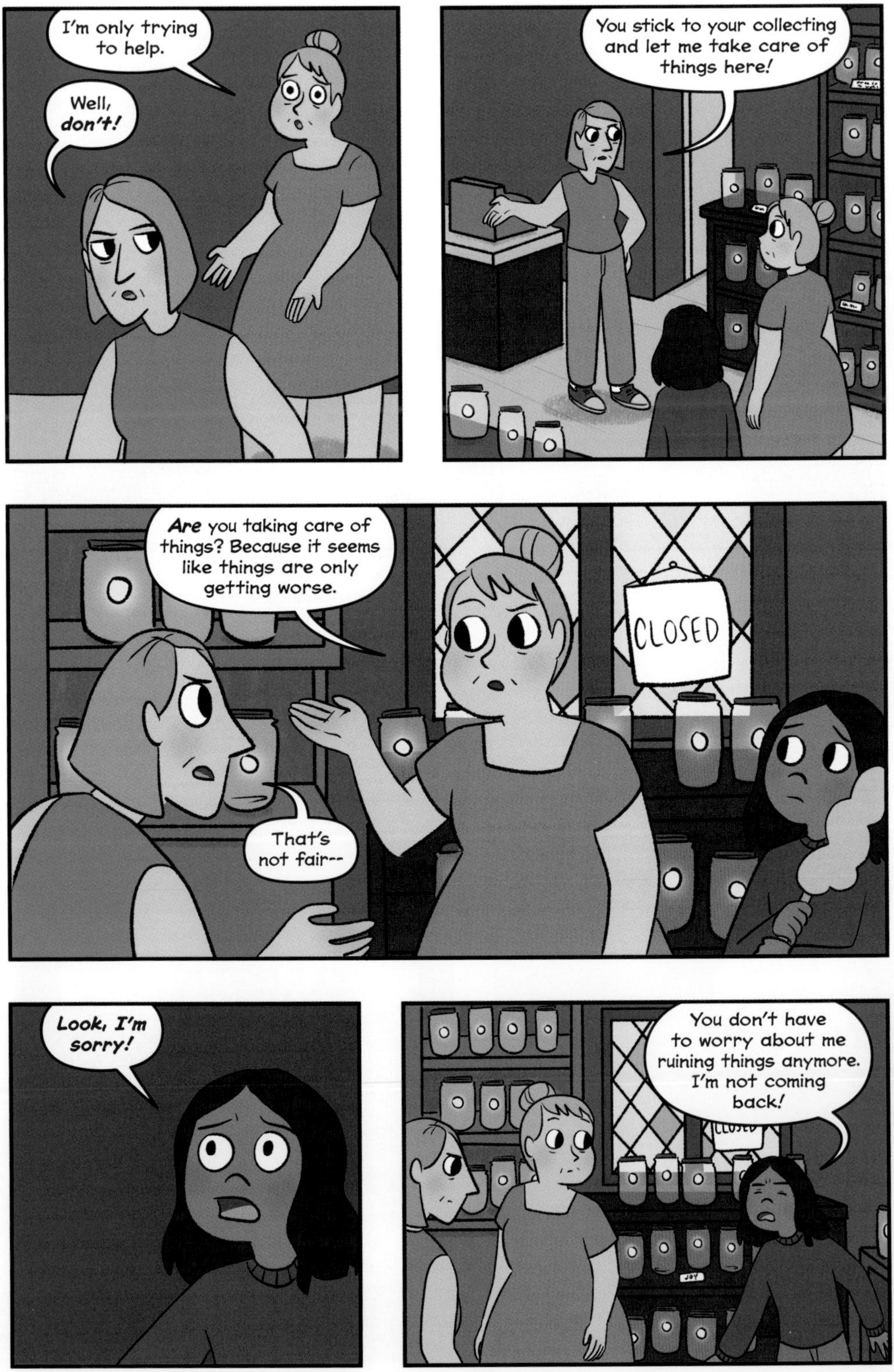
I'm only trying to help.
Well, ***don't!***
You stick to your collecting and let me take care of things here!
Are you taking care of things? Because it seems like things are only getting worse.
CLOSED
That's not fair--
Look, I'm sorry!
You don't have to worry about me ruining things anymore. I'm not coming back!

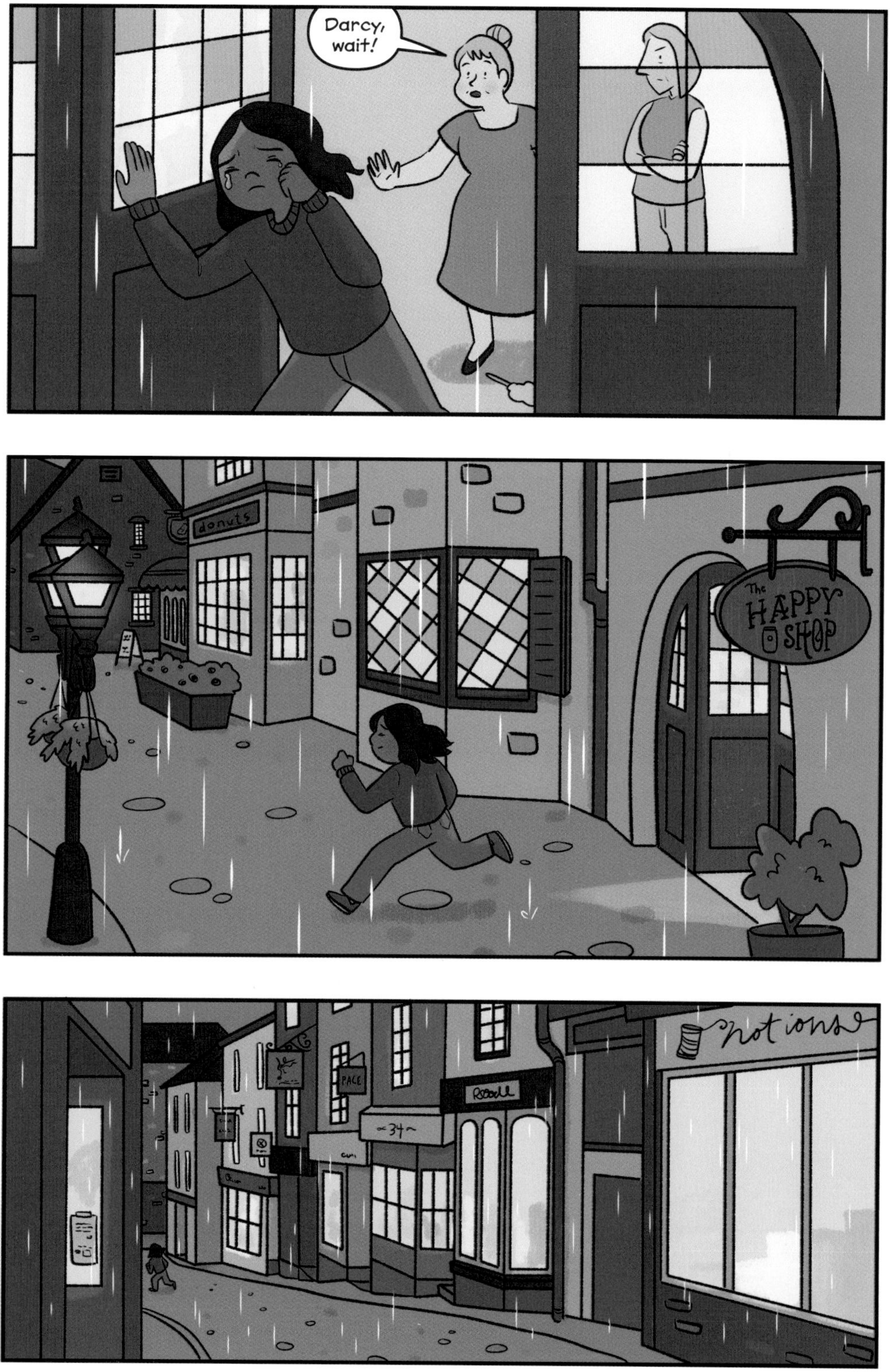
Darcy, wait!
donuts
The HAPPY SHOP
notions

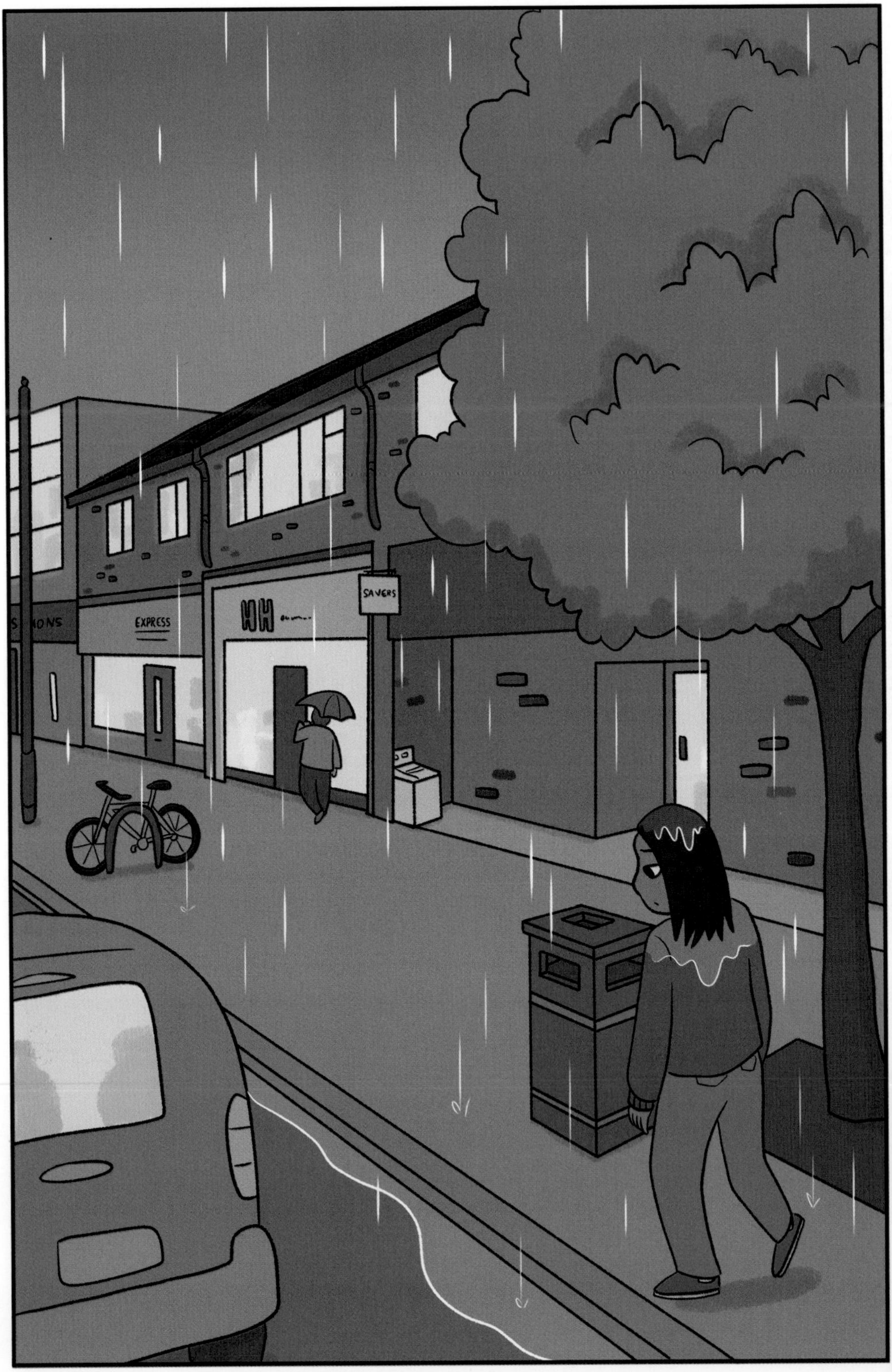
EXPRESS
HH
SAVERS

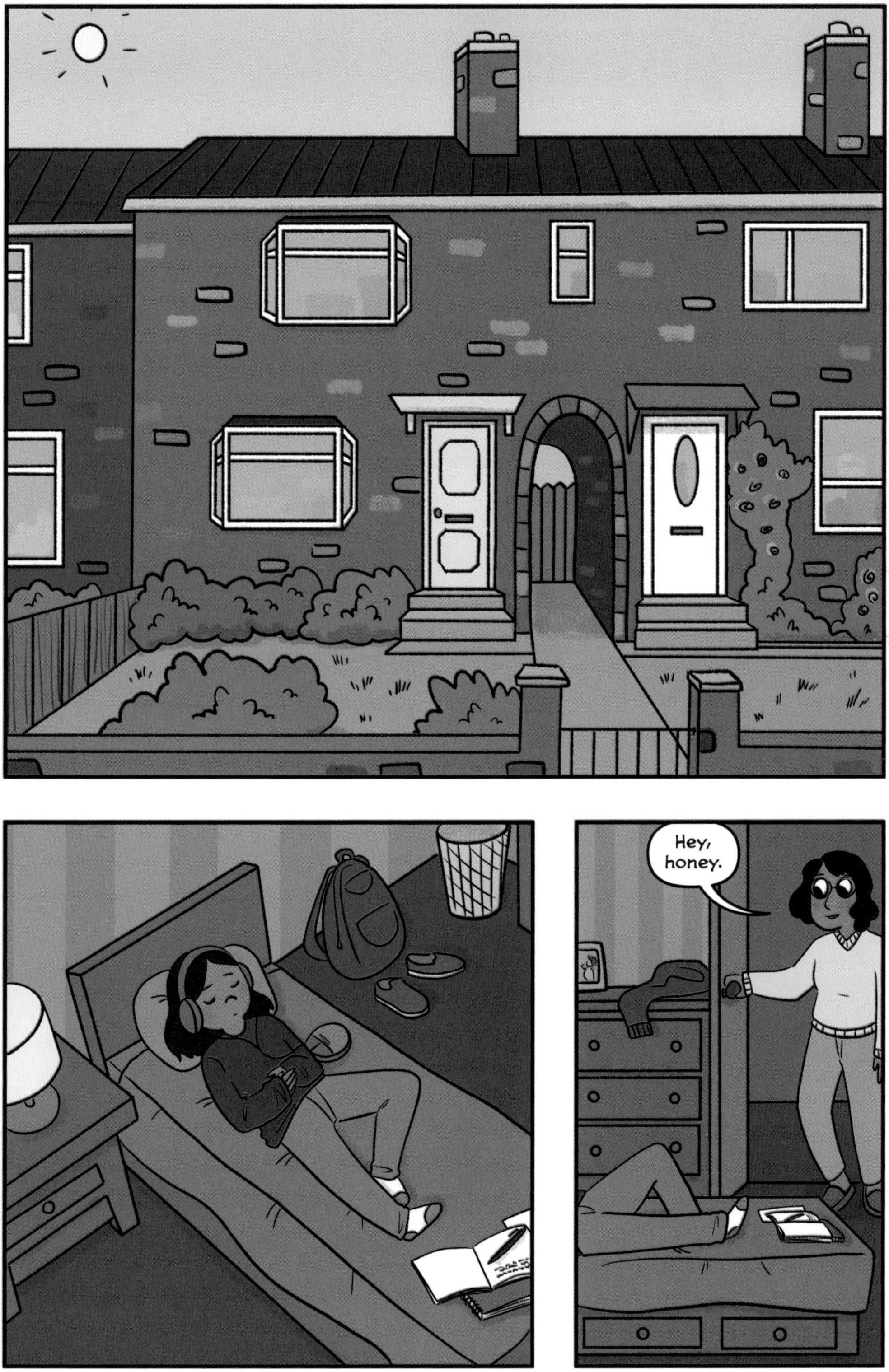
Hey, honey.

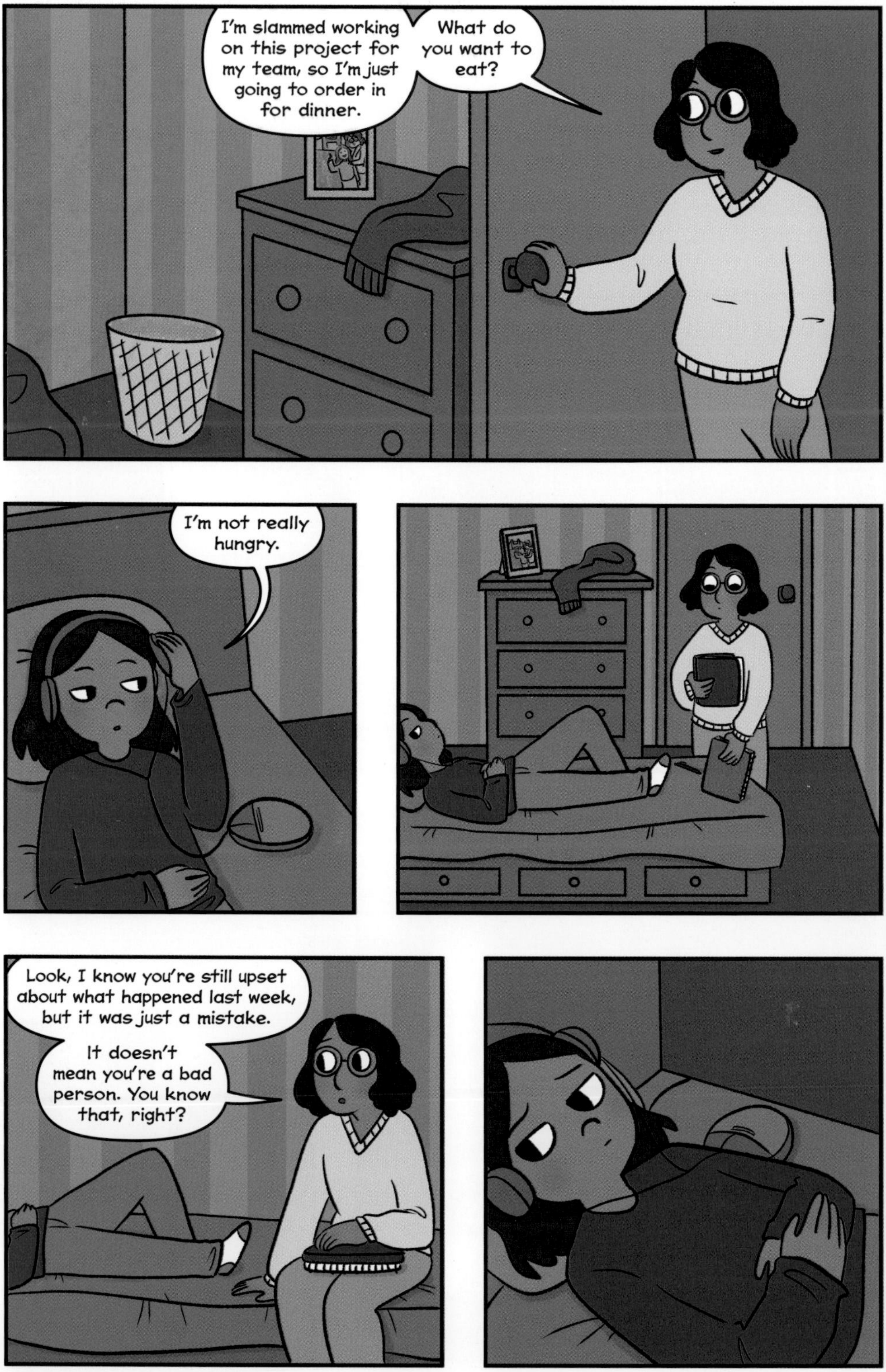

I'm slammed working on this project for my team, so I'm just going to order in for dinner.
What do you want to eat?
I'm not really hungry.
Look, I know you're still upset about what happened last week, but it was just a mistake.
It doesn't mean you're a bad person. You know that, right?

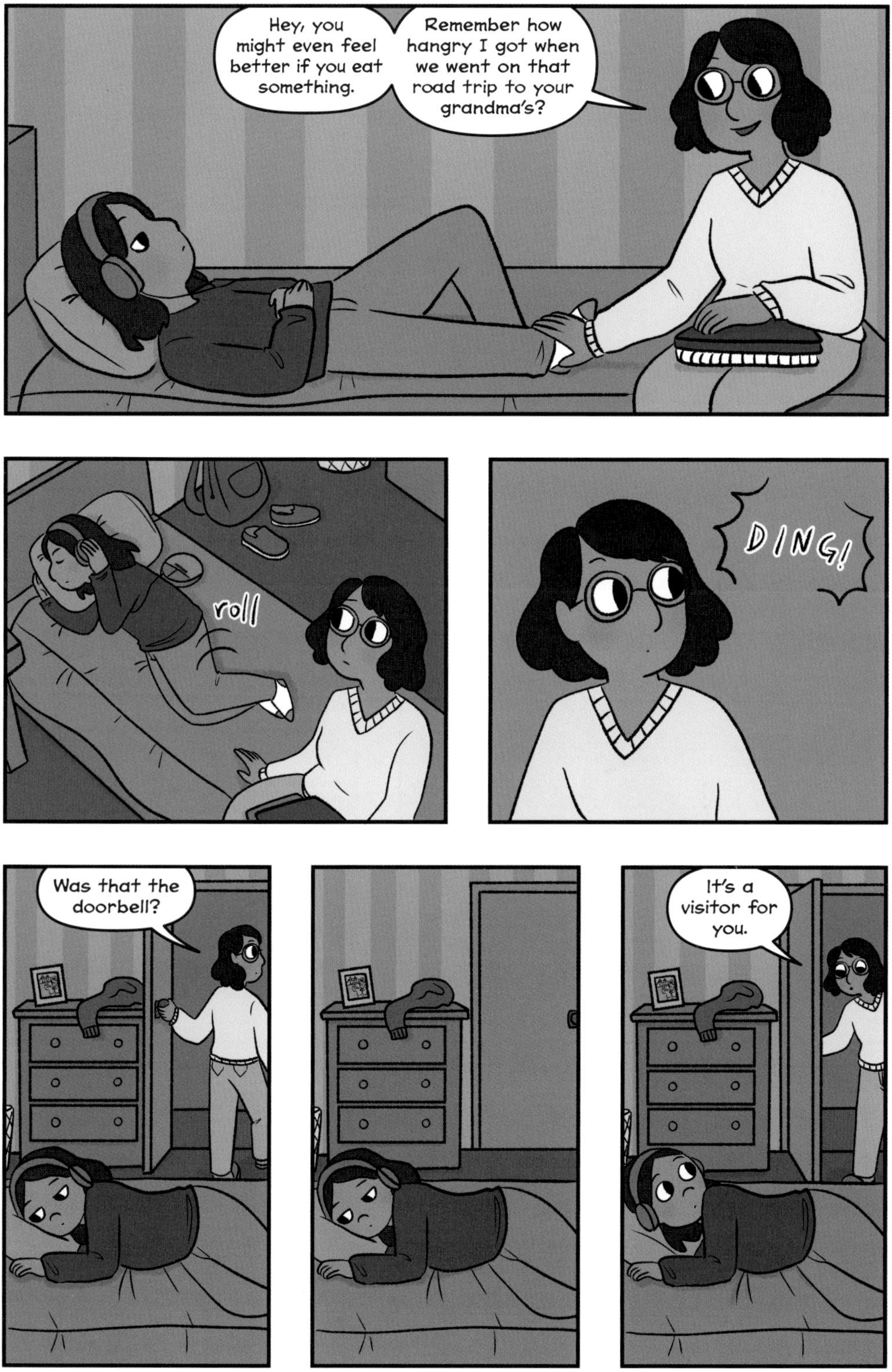

Hey, you might even feel better if you eat something.
Remember how hangry I got when we went on that road trip to your grandma's?
roll
DING!
Was that the doorbell?
It's a visitor for you.

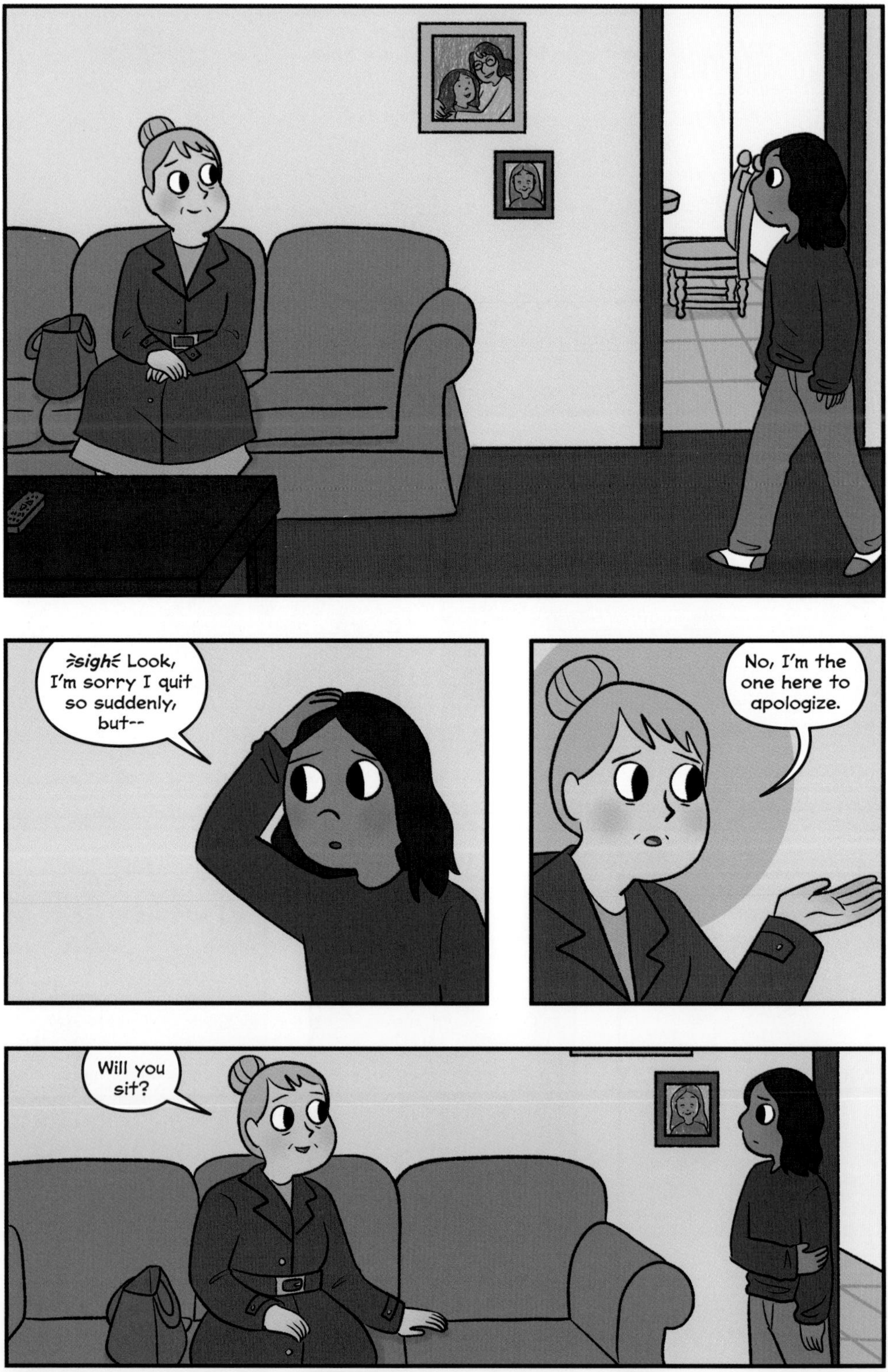

sigh Look, I'm sorry I quit so suddenly, but--
No, I'm the one here to apologize.
Will you sit?

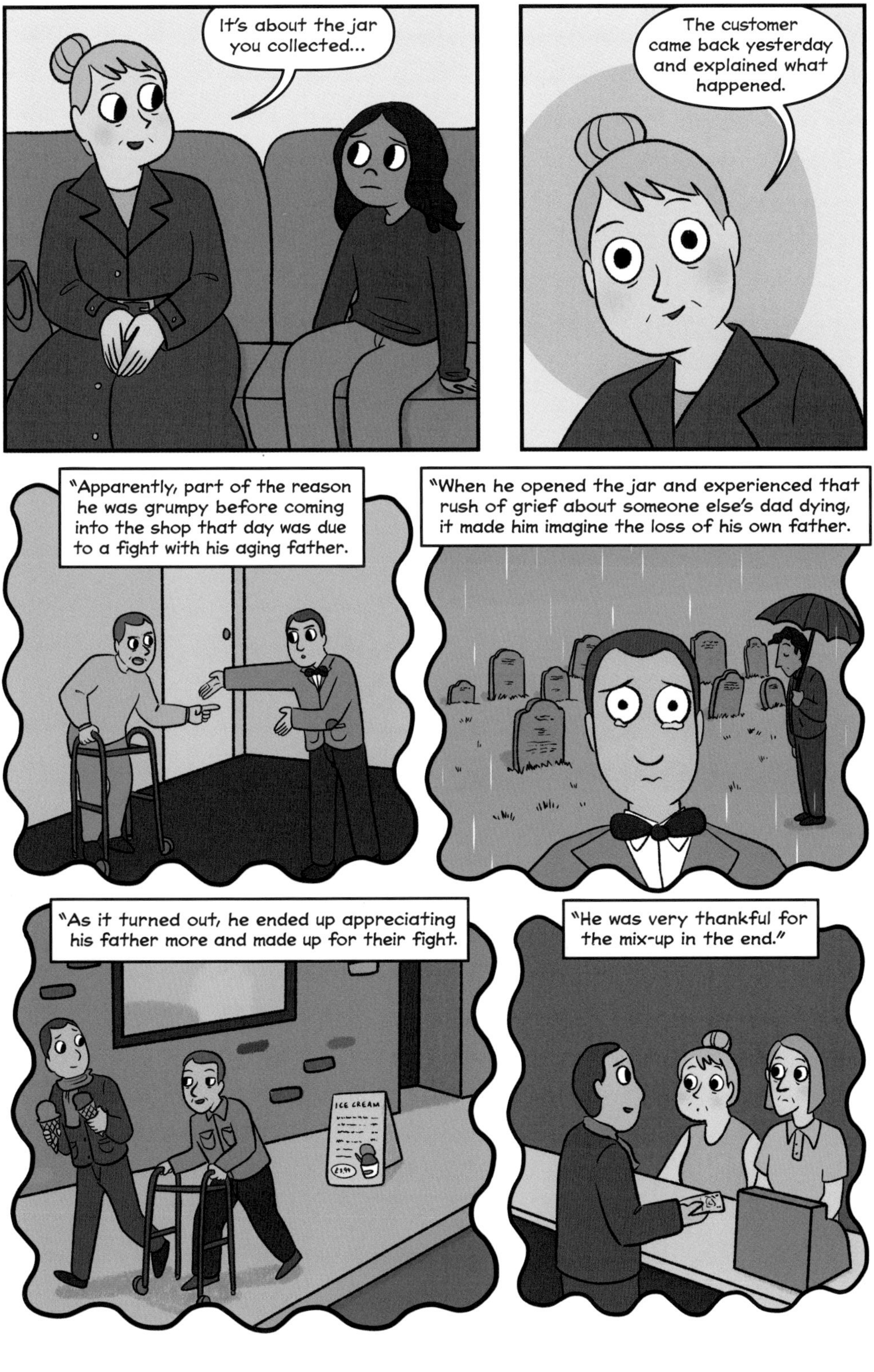
It's about the jar you collected...
The customer came back yesterday and explained what happened.
"Apparently, part of the reason he was grumpy before coming into the shop that day was due to a fight with his aging father.
"When he opened the jar and experienced that rush of grief about someone else's dad dying, it made him imagine the loss of his own father.
"As it turned out, he ended up appreciating his father more and made up for their fight.
ICE CREAM
"He was very thankful for the mix-up in the end."

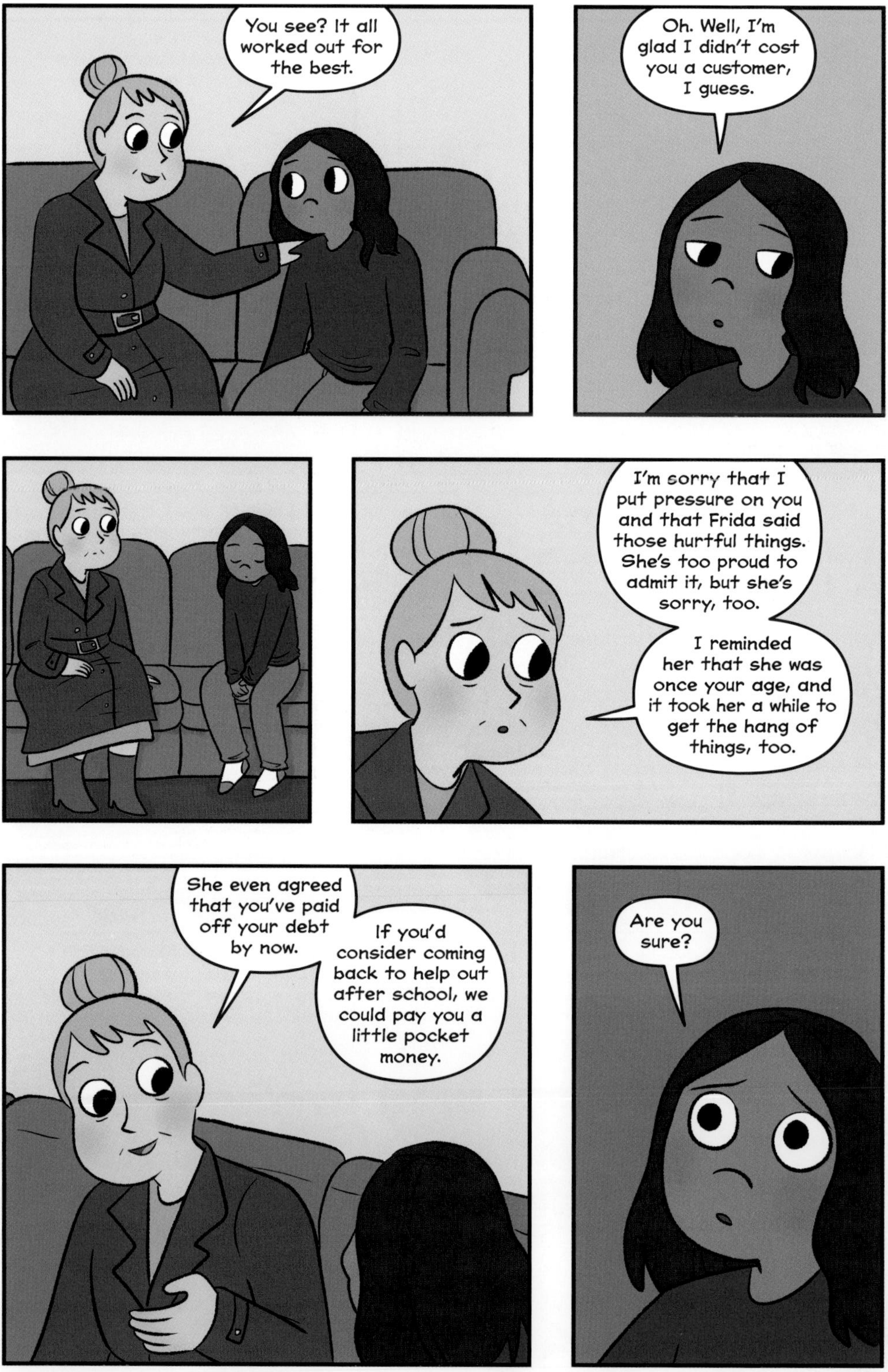

You see? It all worked out for the best.
Oh. Well, I'm glad I didn't cost you a customer, I guess.
I'm sorry that I put pressure on you and that Frida said those hurtful things. She's too proud to admit it, but she's sorry, too.
I reminded her that she was once your age, and it took her a while to get the hang of things, too.
She even agreed that you've paid off your debt by now.
If you'd consider coming back to help out after school, we could pay you a little pocket money.
Are you sure?

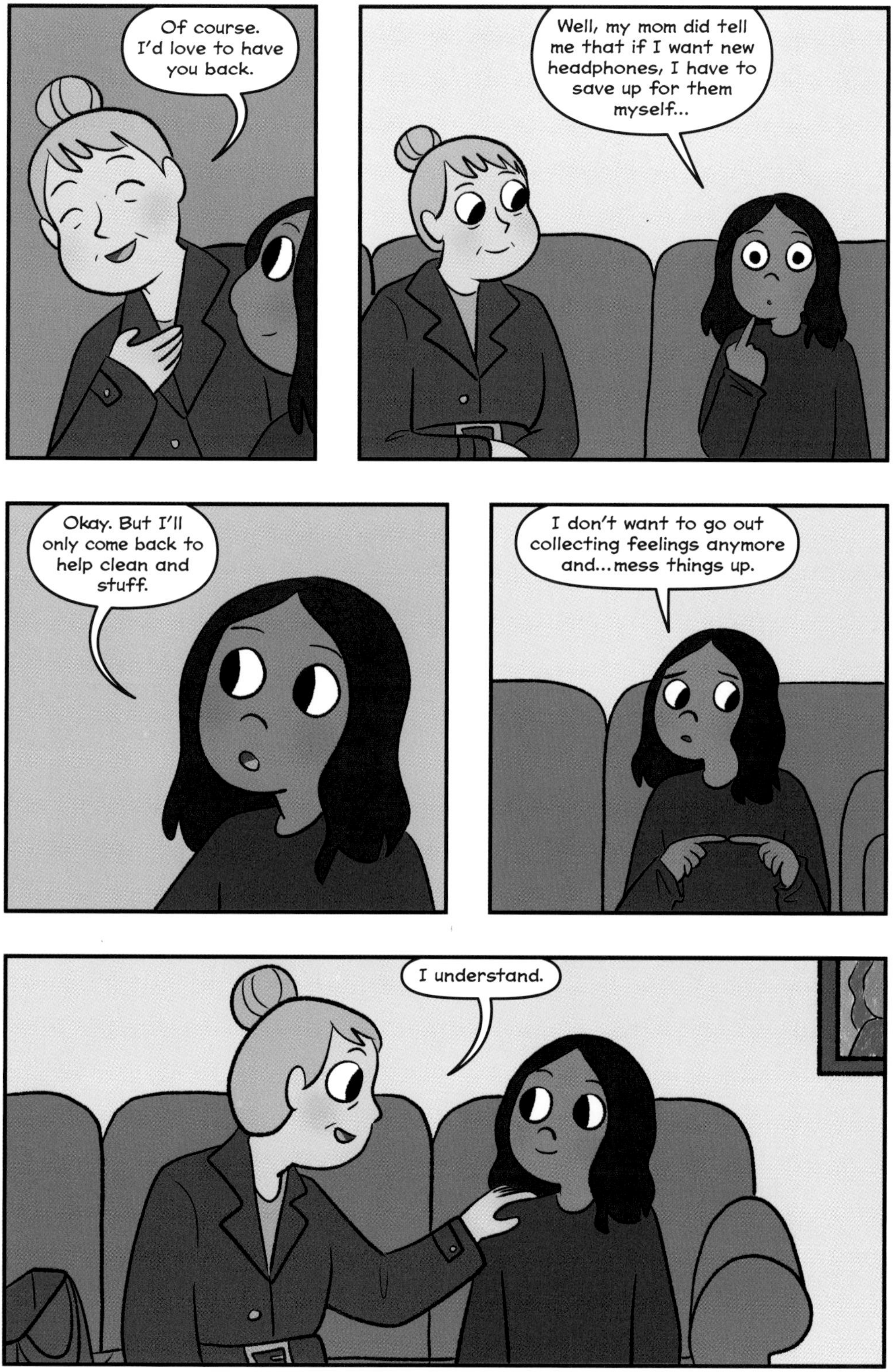
Of course. I'd love to have you back.
Well, my mom did tell me that if I want new headphones, I have to save up for them myself...
Okay. But I'll only come back to help clean and stuff.
I don't want to go out collecting feelings anymore and...mess things up.
I understand.

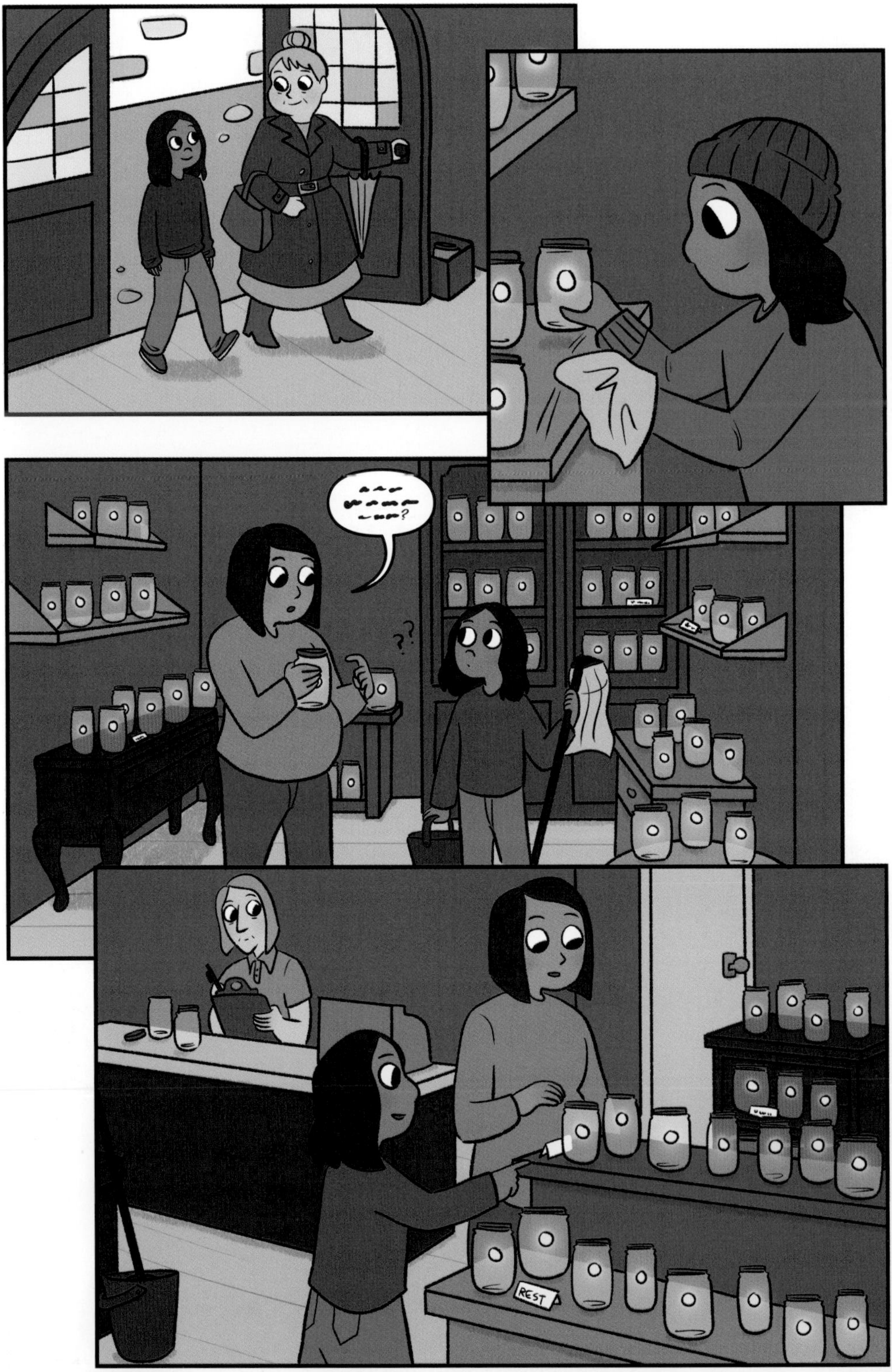
REST

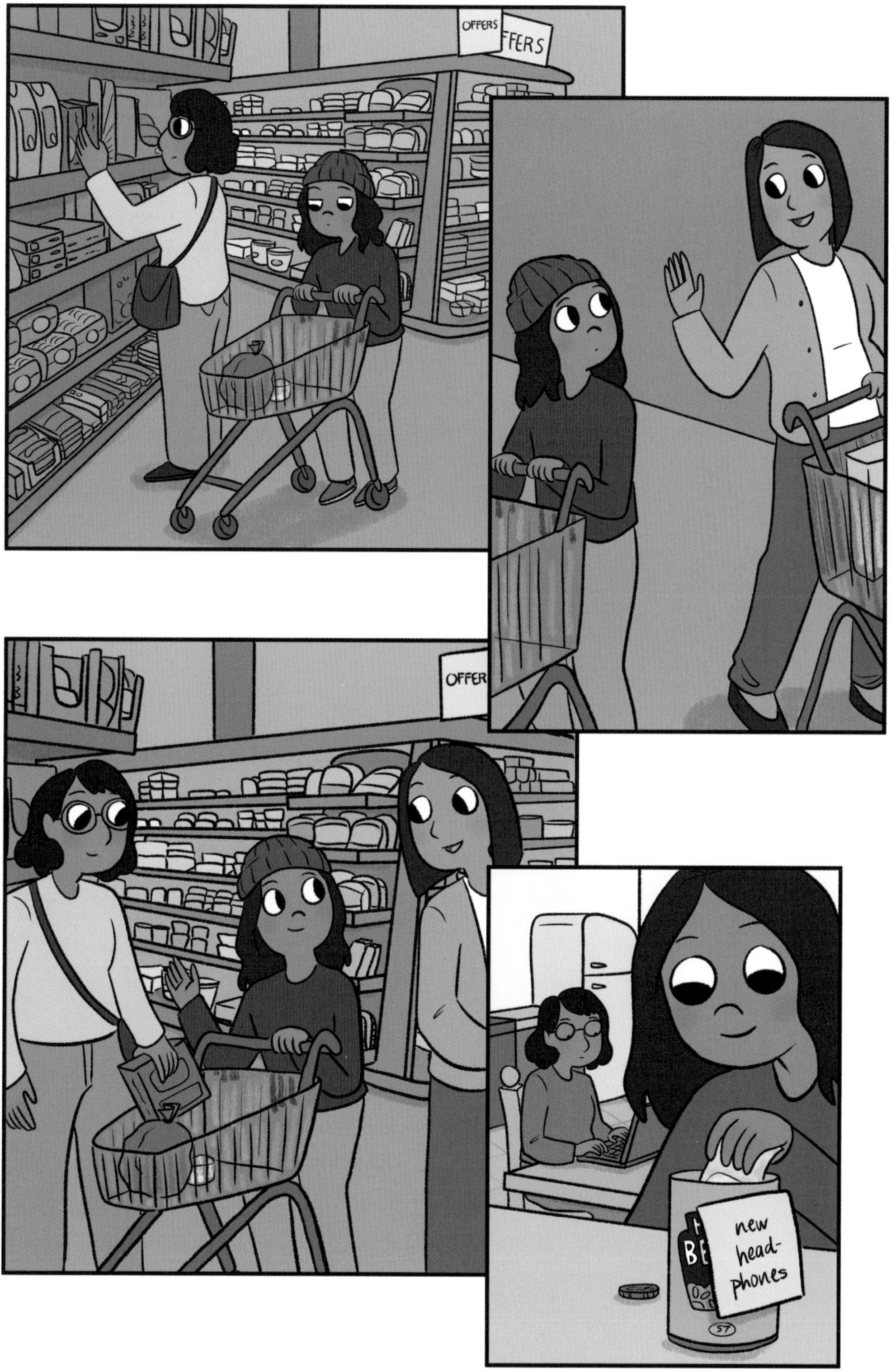
OFFERS
FFERS
OFFER
new head- phones
57

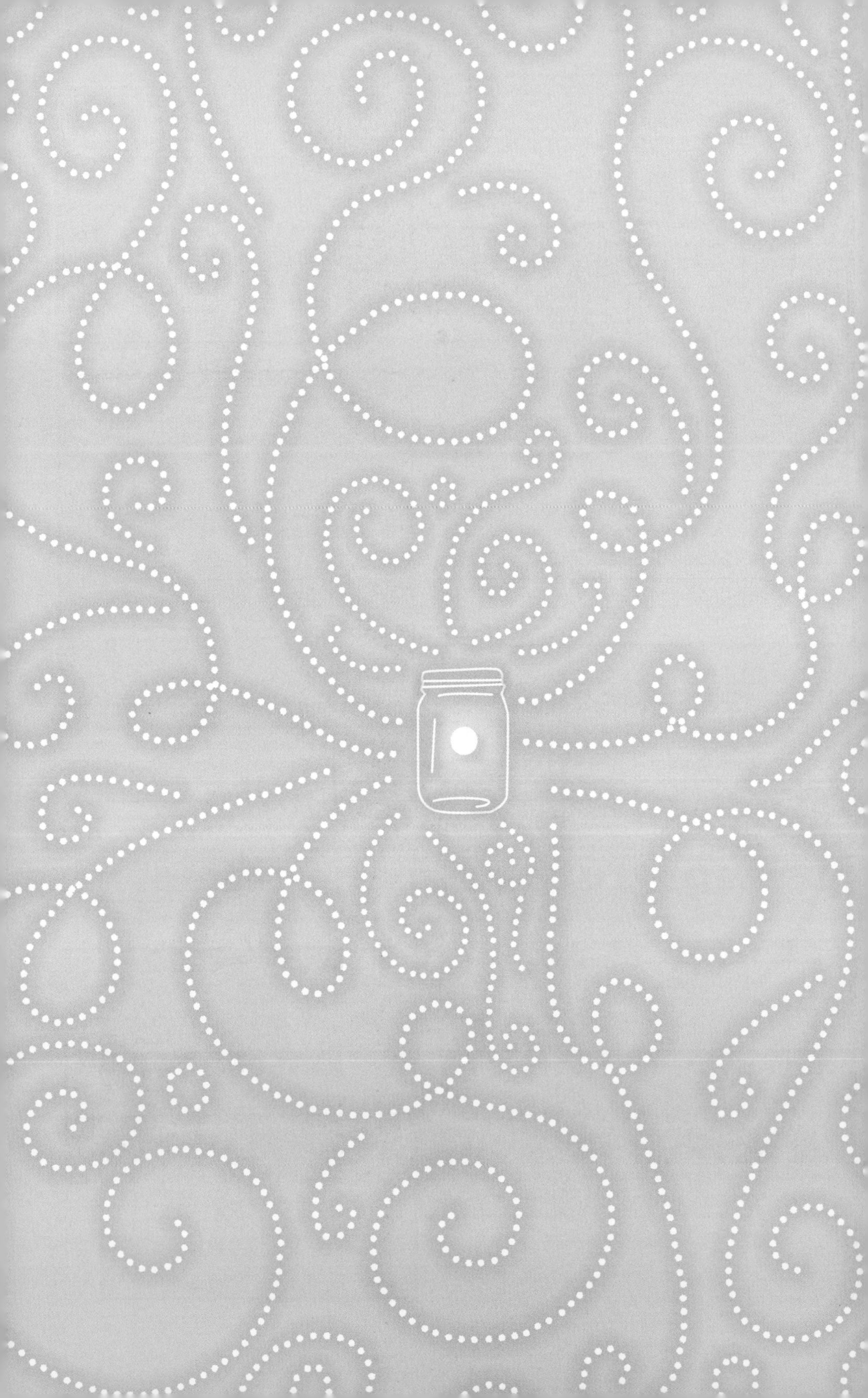

CHAPTER FIVE

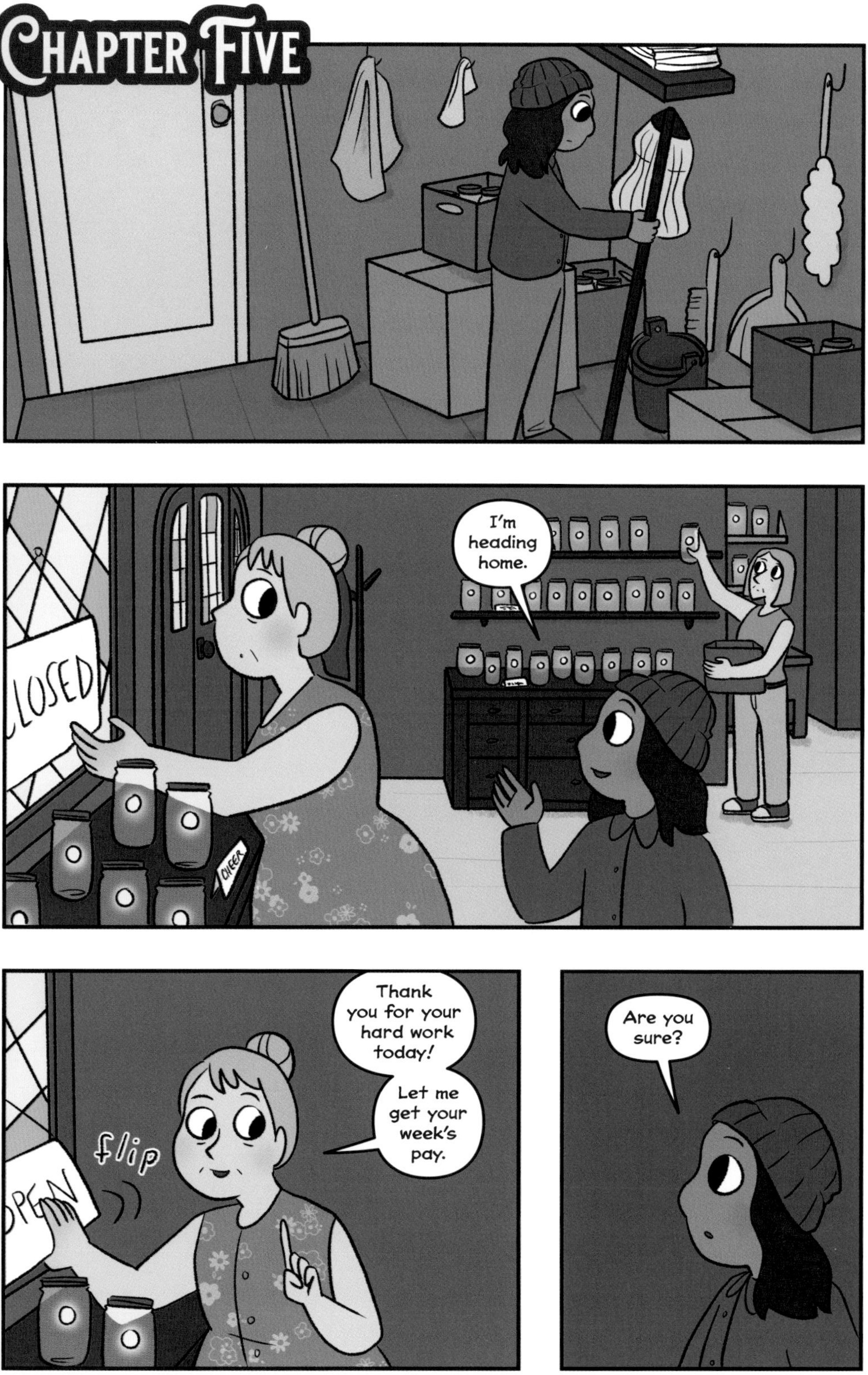
I'm heading home.
CHEER
Thank you for your hard work today!
Let me get your week's pay.
flip
Are you sure?

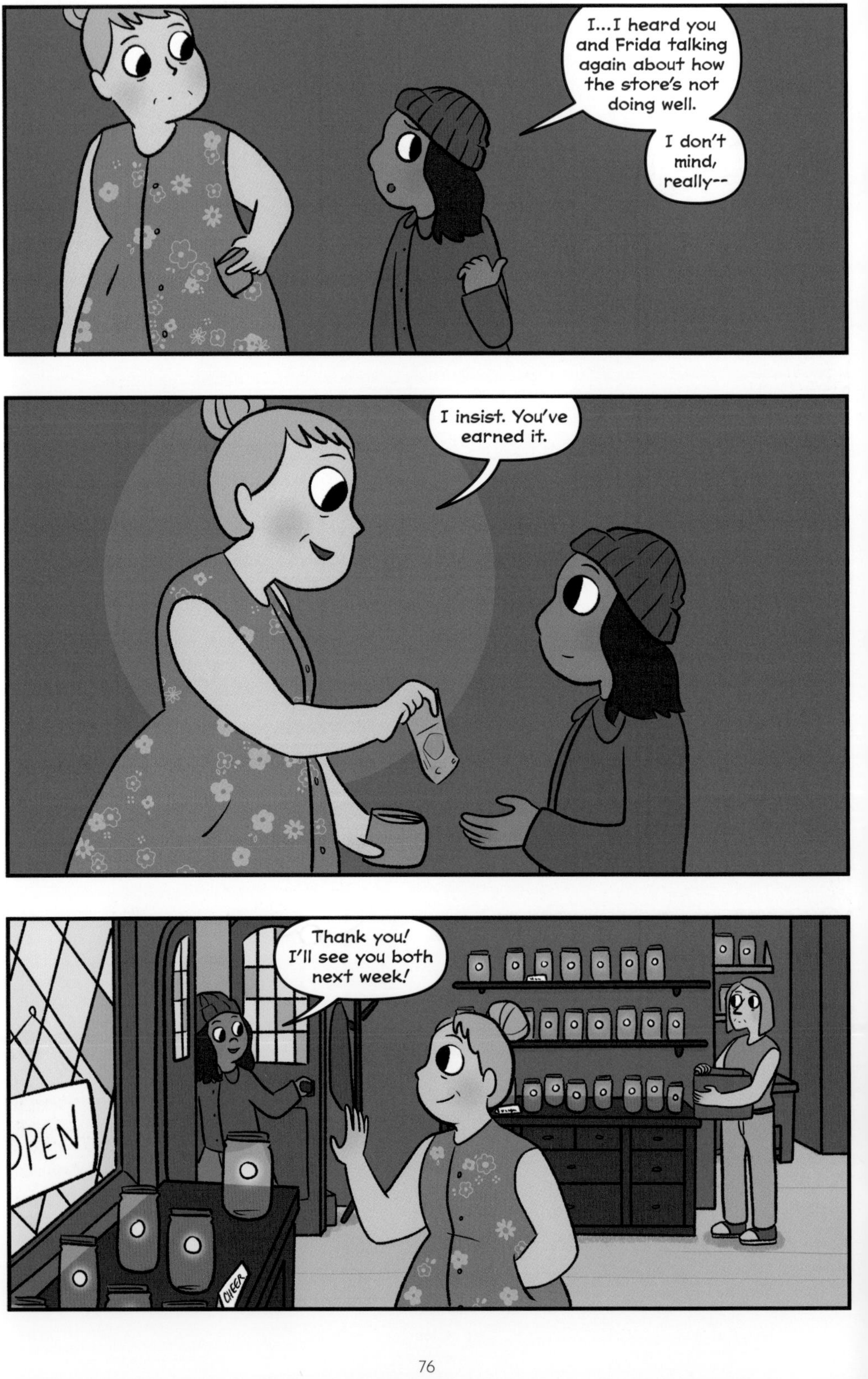
I...I heard you and Frida talking again about how the store's not doing well.
I don't mind, really--
I insist. You've earned it.
Thank you! I'll see you both next week!
OPEN
CHEER

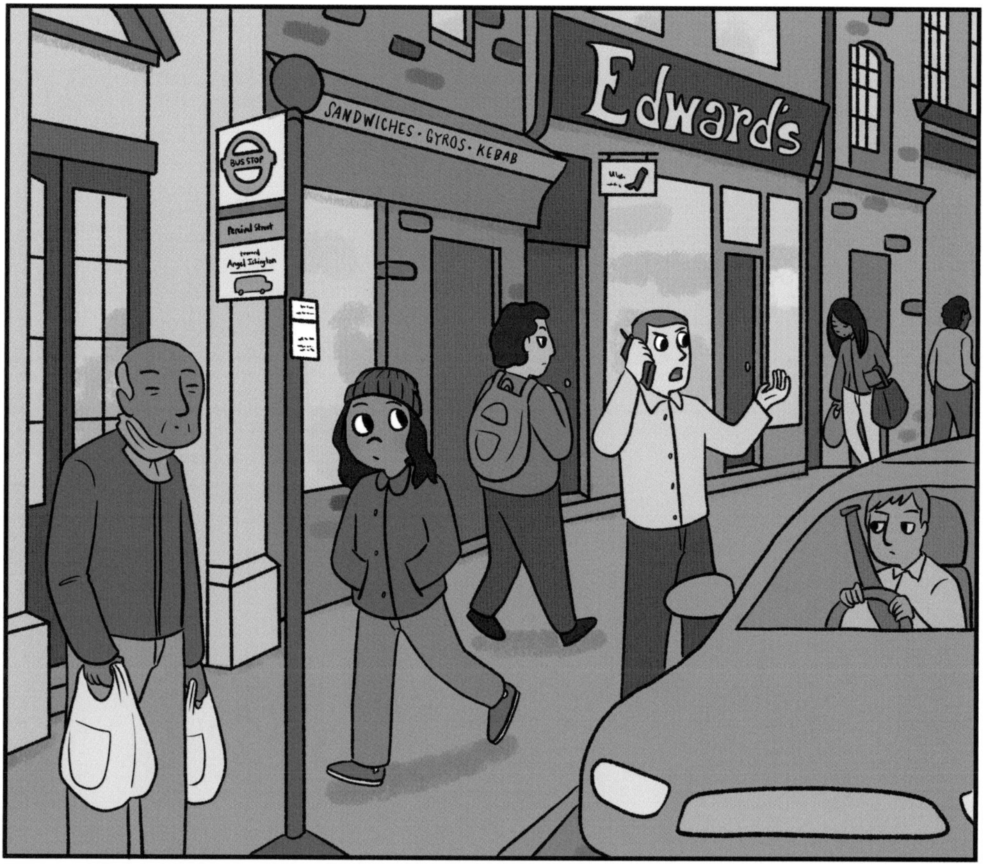
SANDWICHES • GYROS • KEBAB
BUS STOP
Percival Street
Angel Islington
Edward's

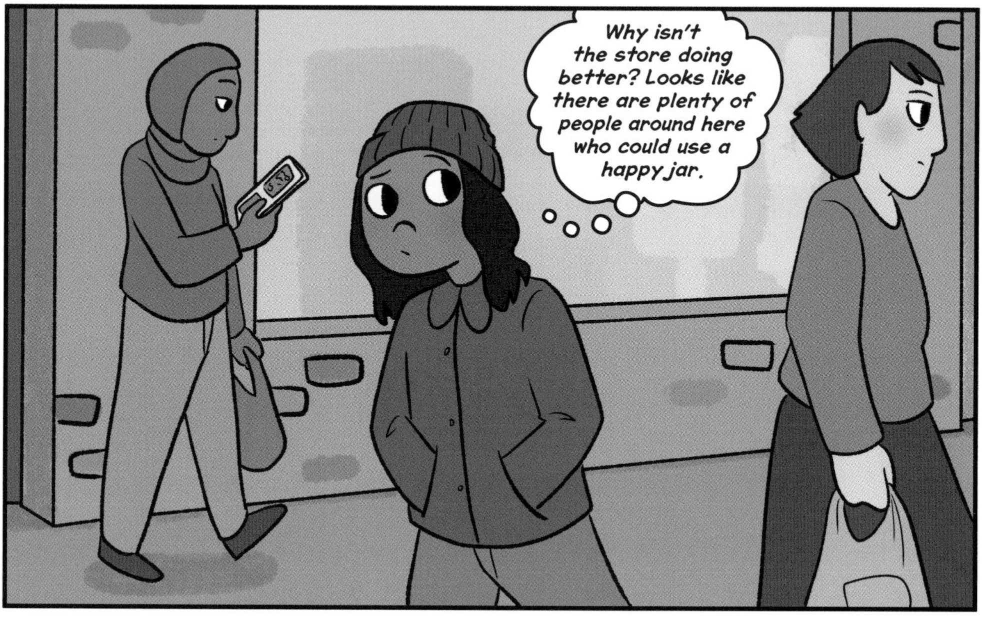
Why isn't the store doing better? Looks like there are plenty of people around here who could use a happy jar.

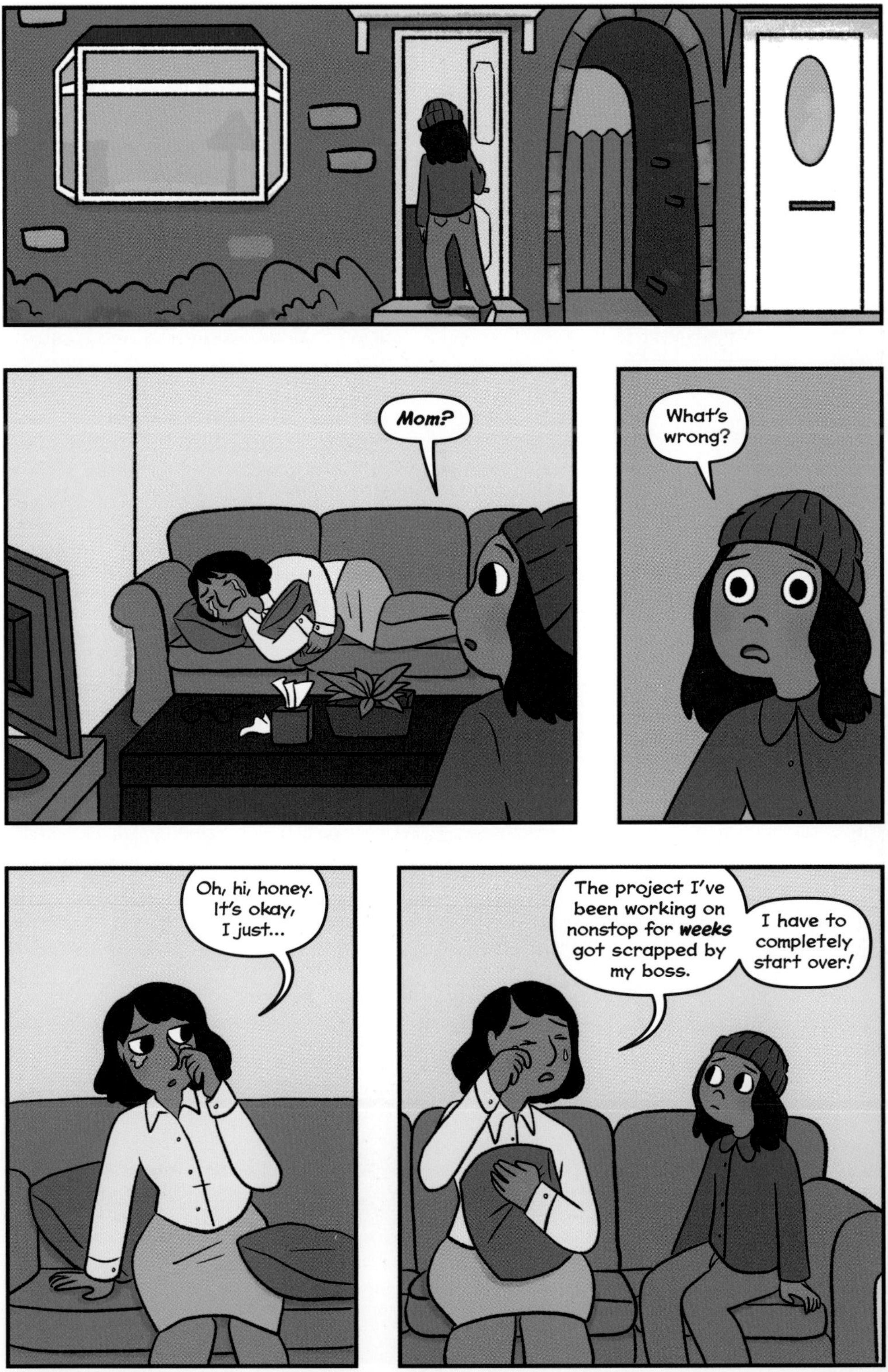
Mom?
What's wrong?
Oh, hi, honey. It's okay, I just...
The project I've been working on nonstop for *weeks* got scrapped by my boss.
I have to completely start over!

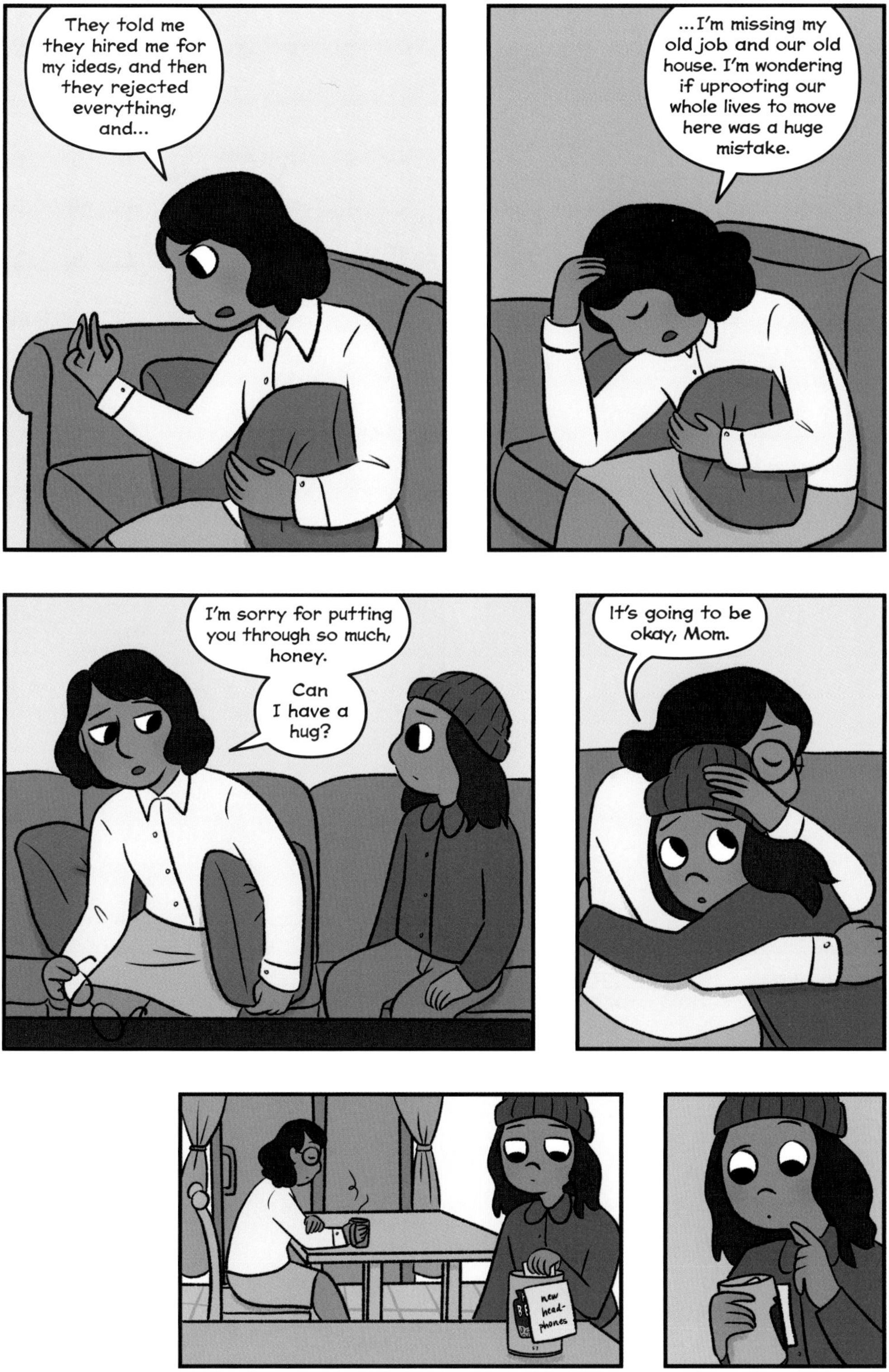
They told me they hired me for my ideas, and then they rejected everything, and...
...I'm missing my old job and our old house. I'm wondering if uprooting our whole lives to move here was a huge mistake.
I'm sorry for putting you through so much, honey.
Can I have a hug?
It's going to be okay, Mom.
new head-phones

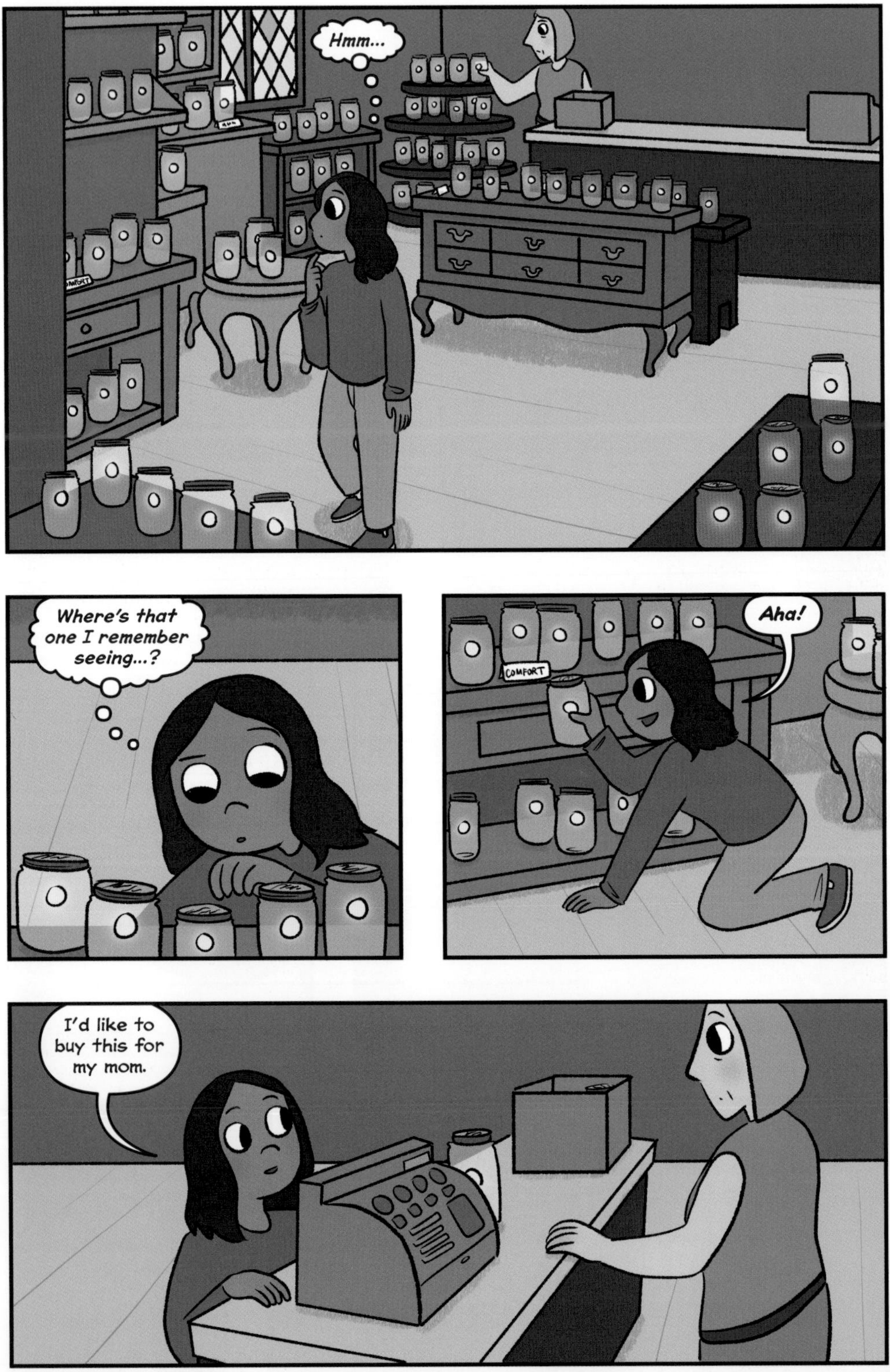
Hmm...
Where's that one I remember seeing...?
COMFORT
Aha!
I'd like to buy this for my mom.

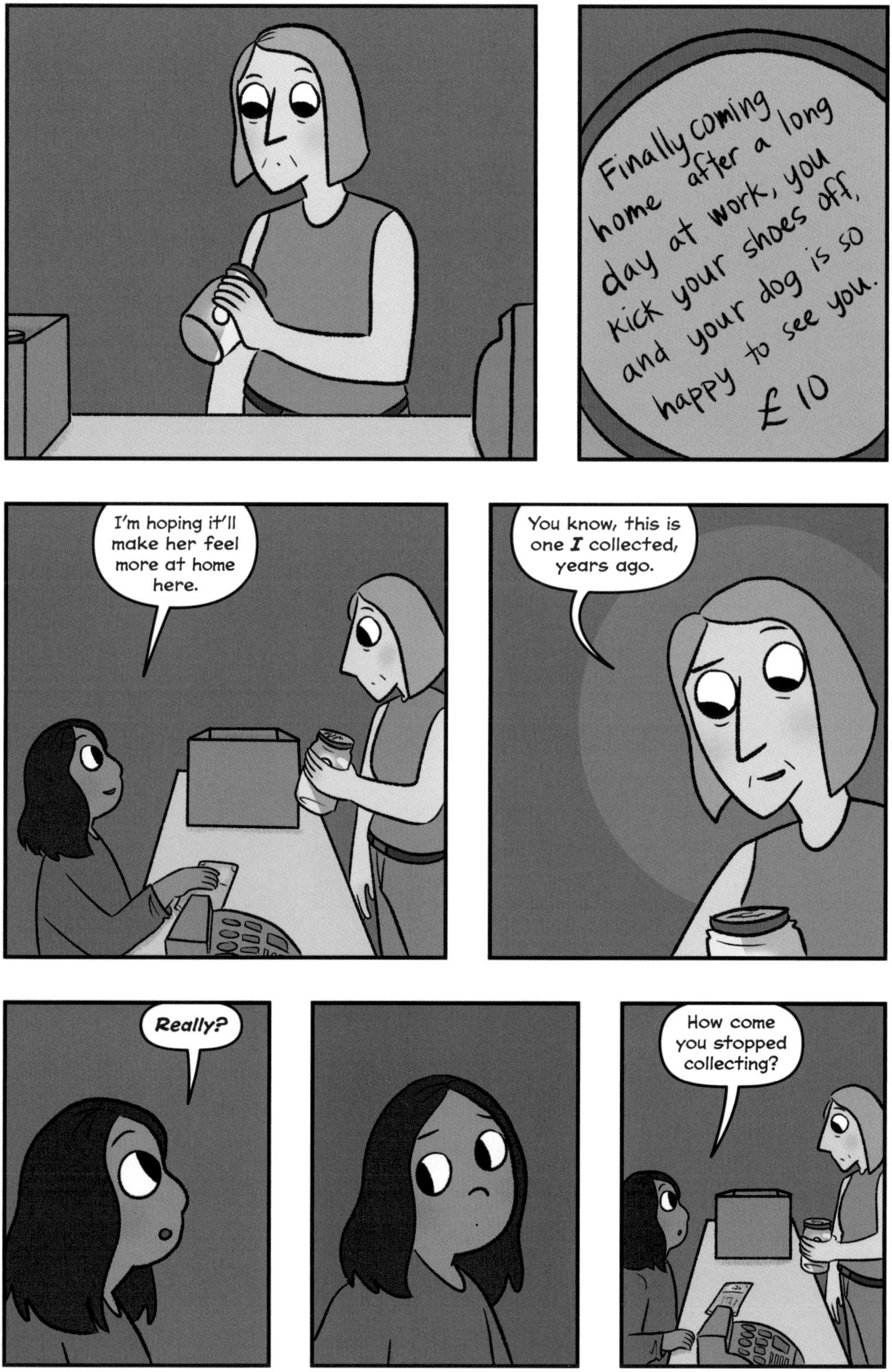
Finally coming home after a long day at work, you kick your shoes off, and your dog is so happy to see you.
£10
I'm hoping it'll make her feel more at home here.
You know, this is one *I* collected, years ago.
Really?
How come you stopped collecting?

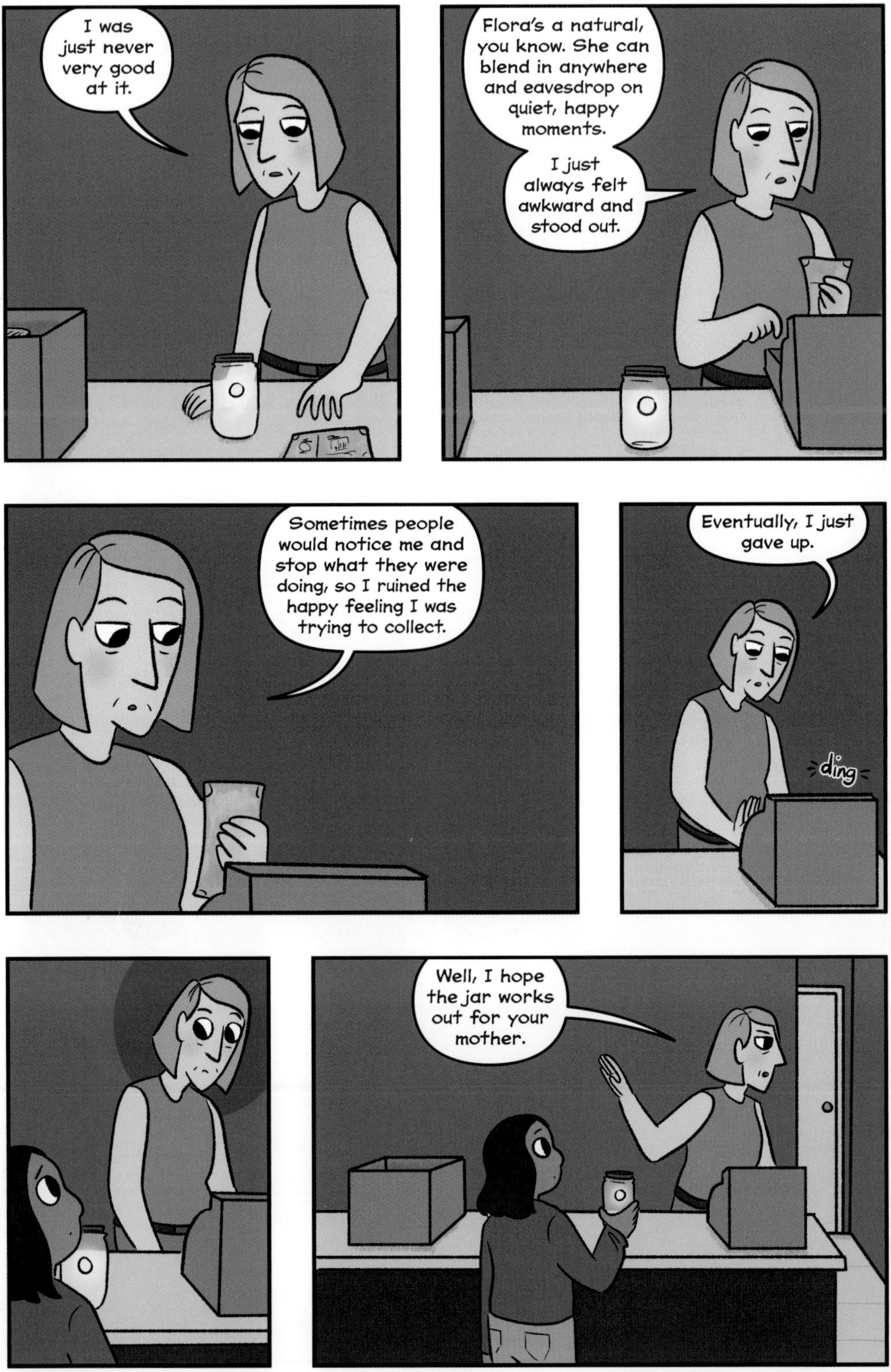
I was just never very good at it.
Flora's a natural, you know. She can blend in anywhere and eavesdrop on quiet, happy moments.
I just always felt awkward and stood out.
Sometimes people would notice me and stop what they were doing, so I ruined the happy feeling I was trying to collect.
Eventually, I just gave up.
ding
Well, I hope the jar works out for your mother.

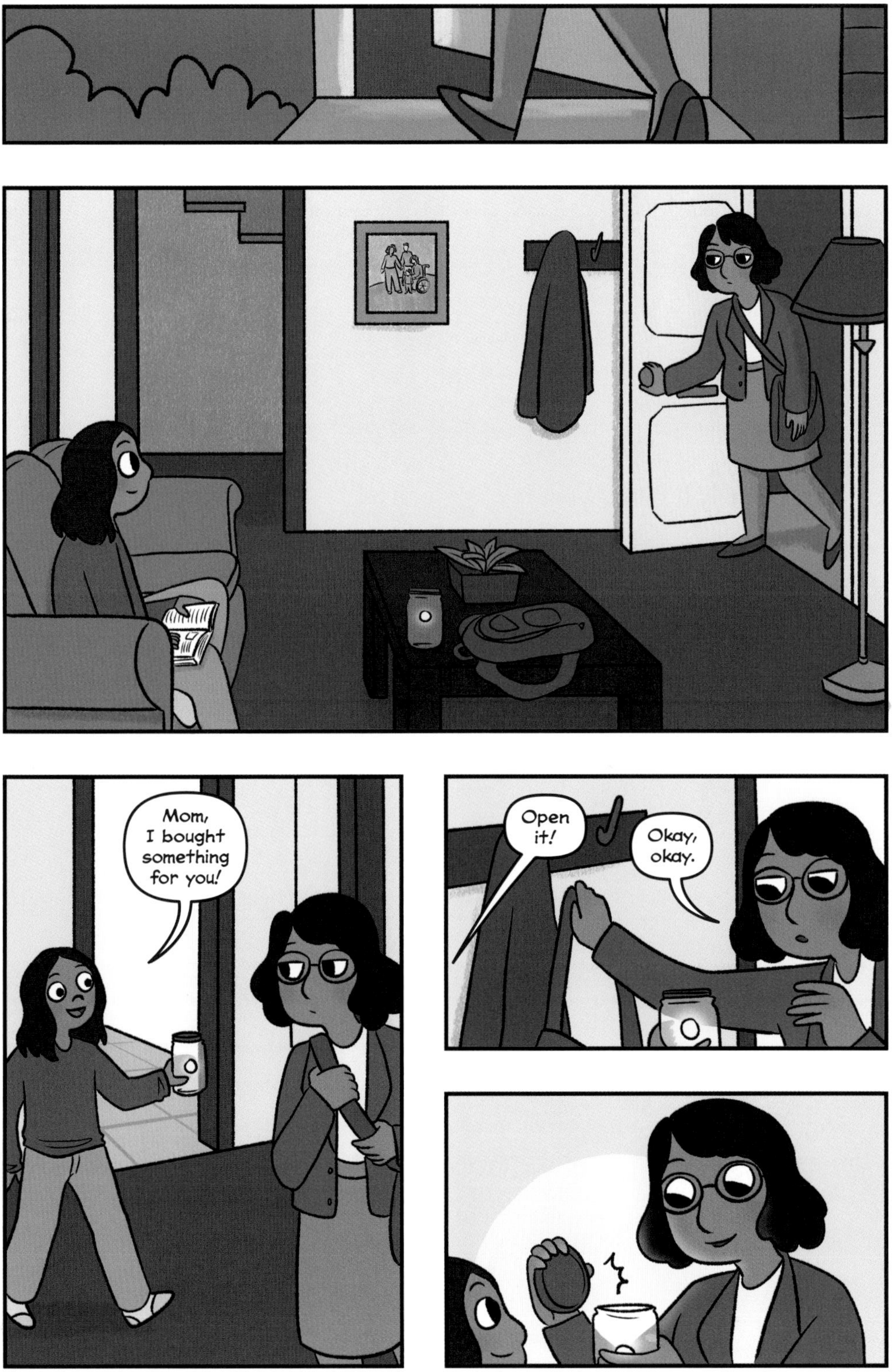
Mom, I bought something for you!
Open it!
Okay, okay.

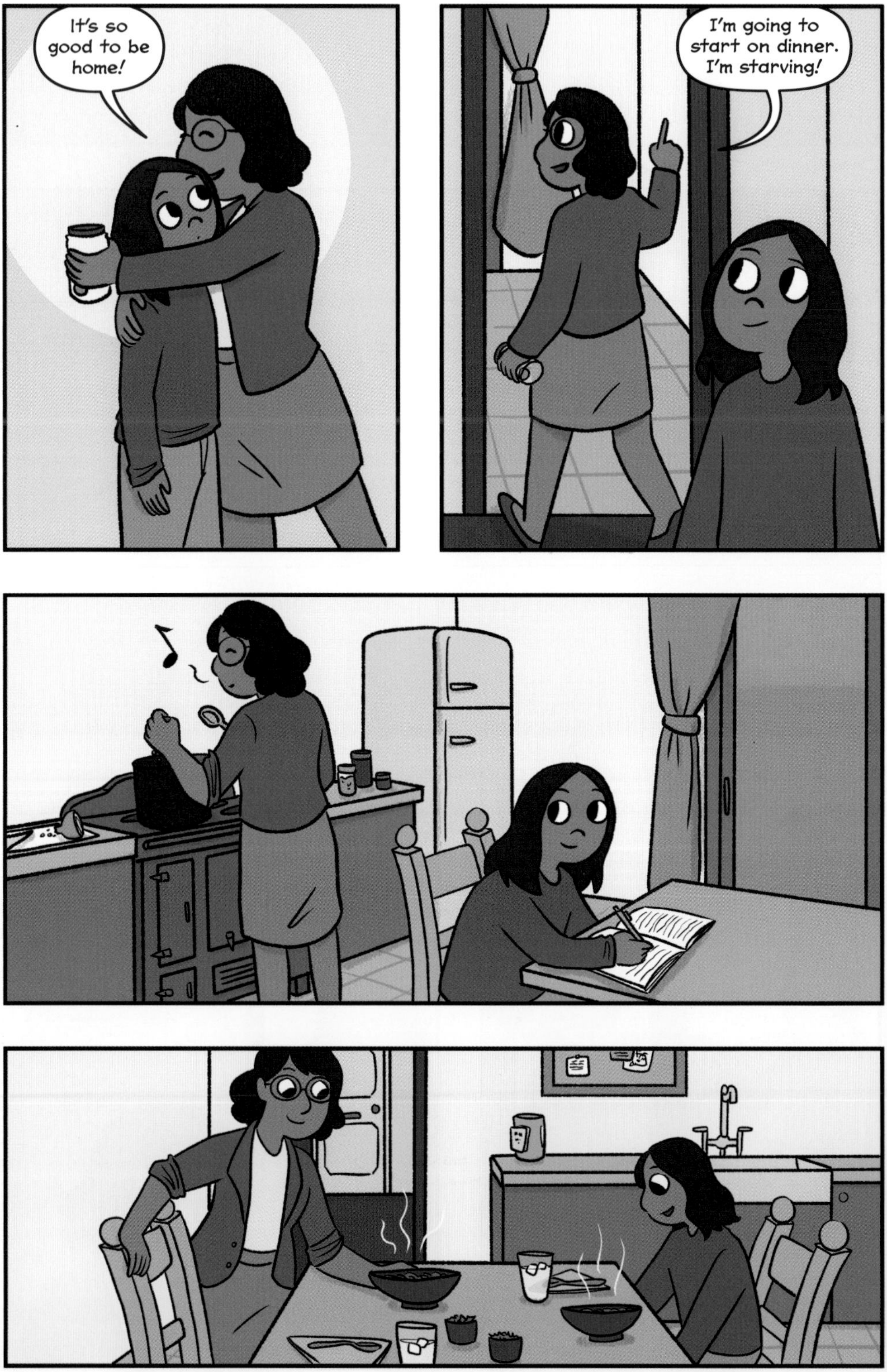

It's so good to be home!
I'm going to start on dinner. I'm starving!

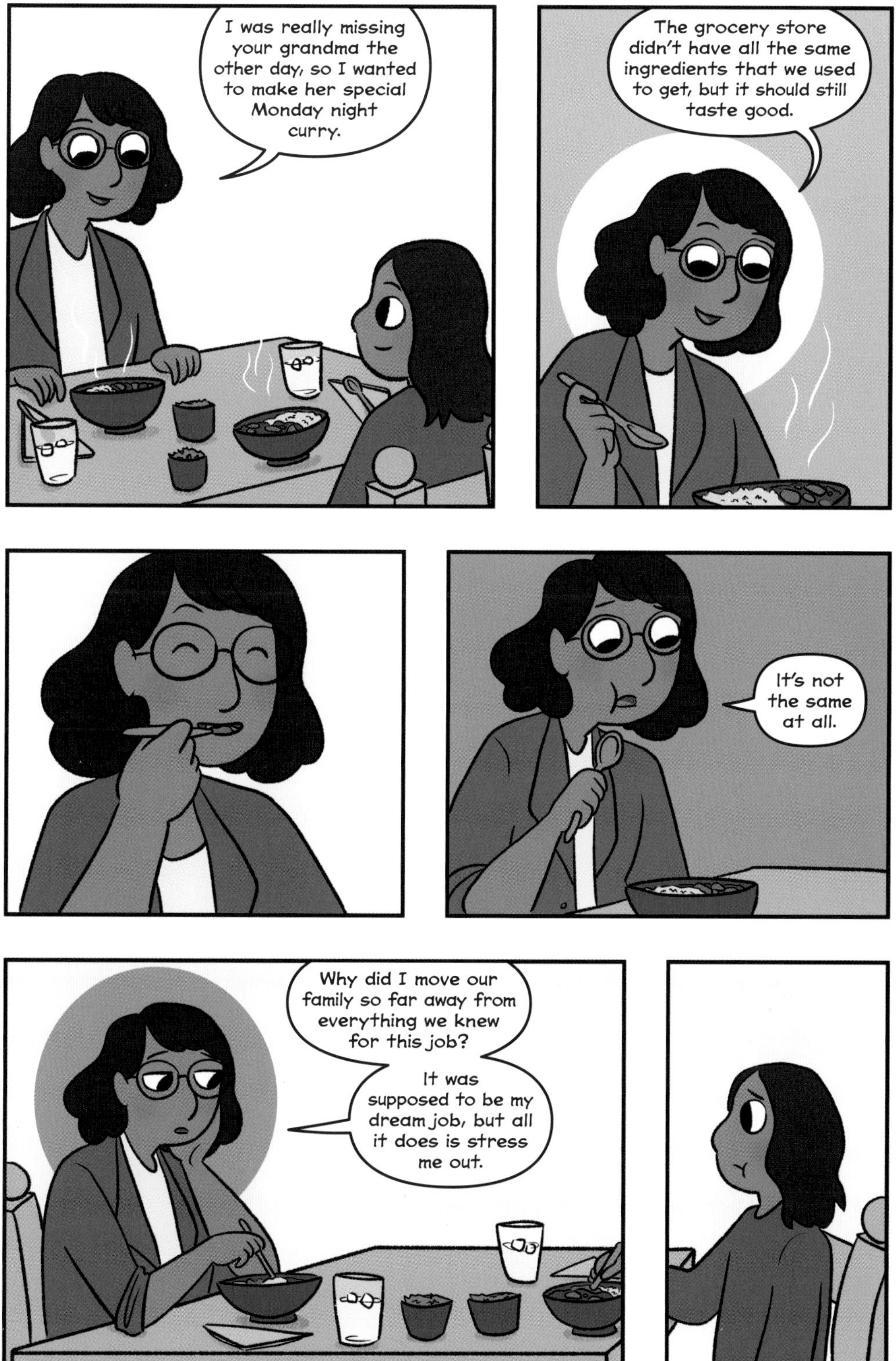
I was really missing your grandma the other day, so I wanted to make her special Monday night curry.
The grocery store didn't have all the same ingredients that we used to get, but it should still taste good.
It's not the same at all.
Why did I move our family so far away from everything we knew for this job?
It was supposed to be my dream job, but all it does is stress me out.

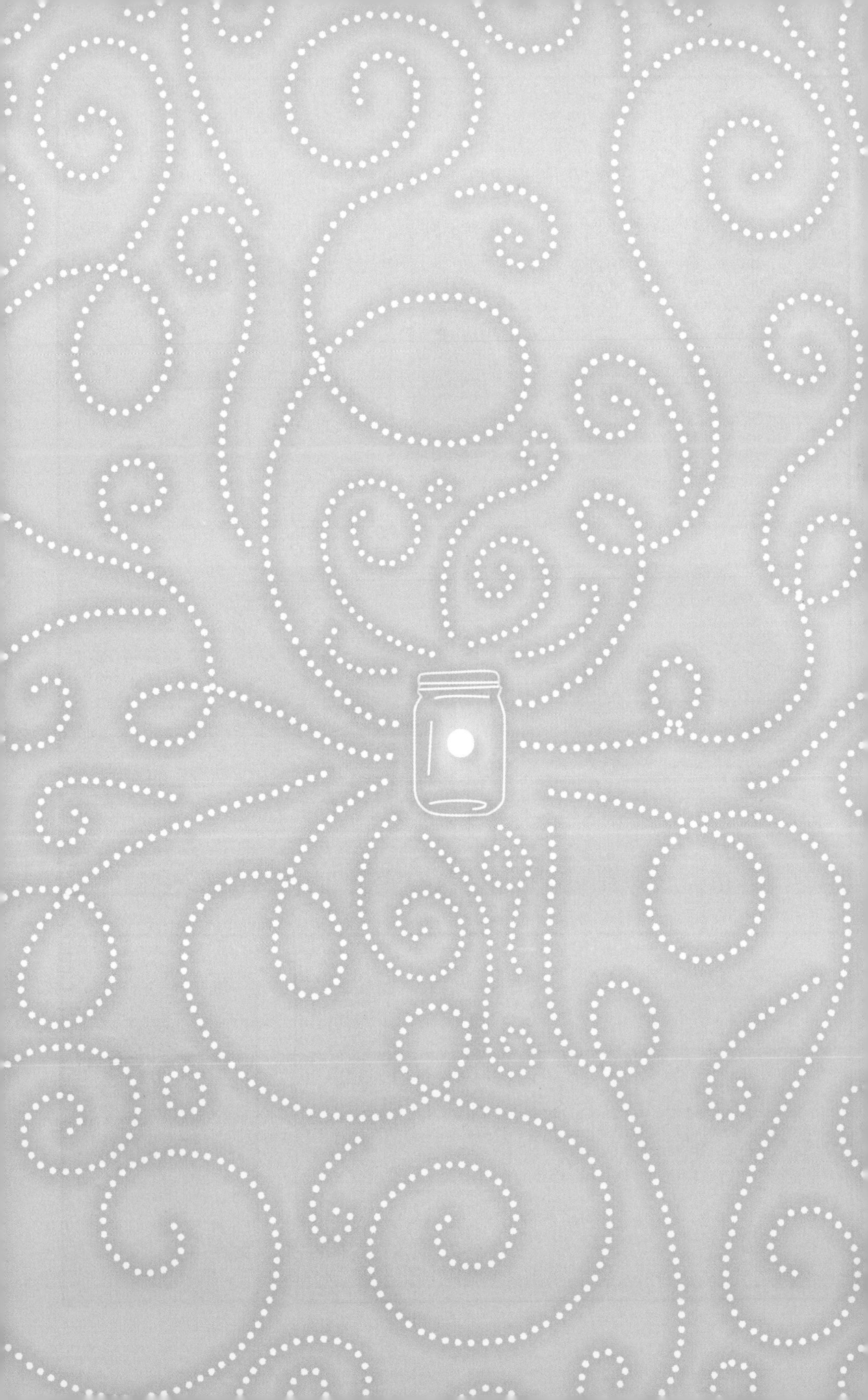

Chapter Six

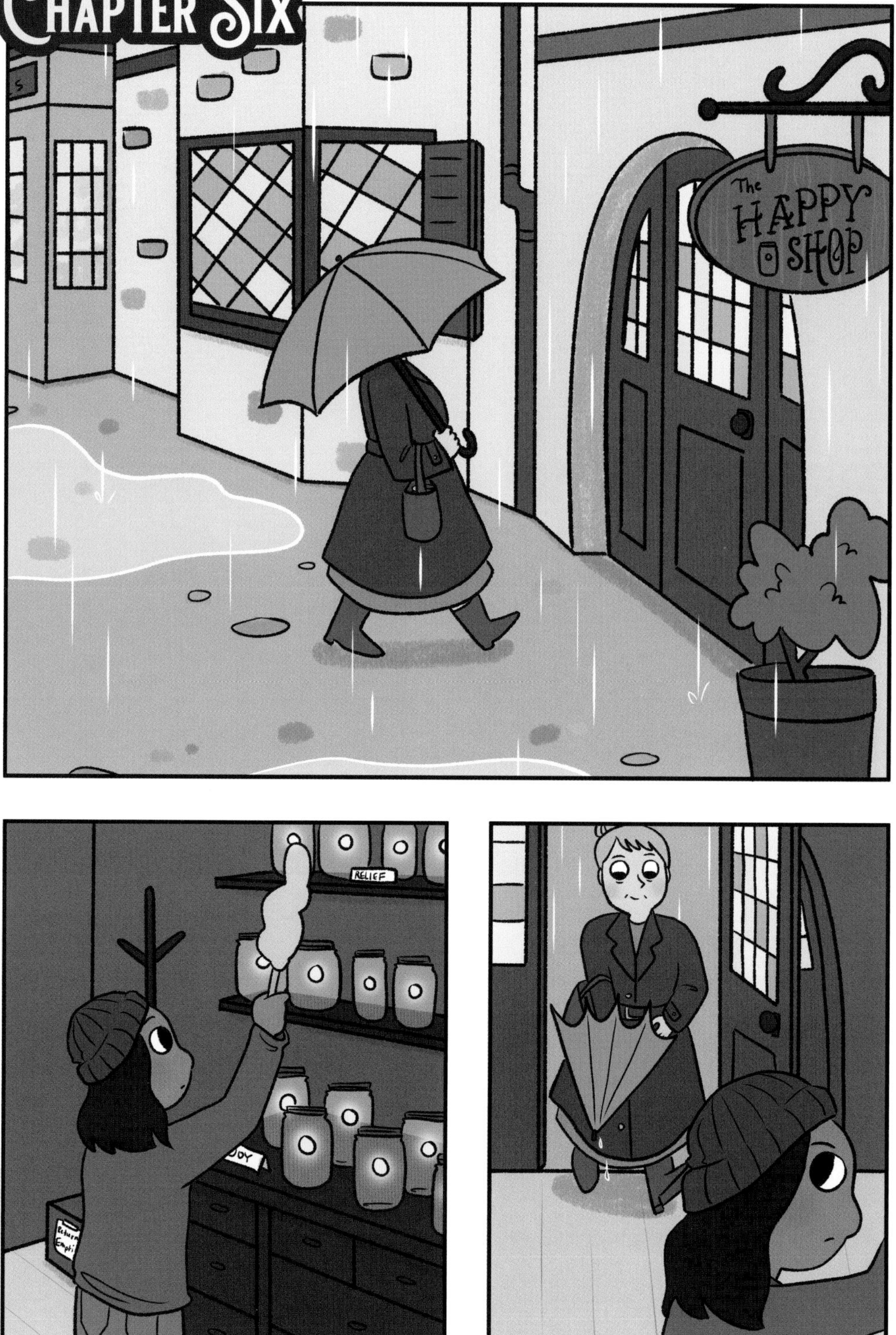
The HAPPY SHOP
RELIEF
JOY

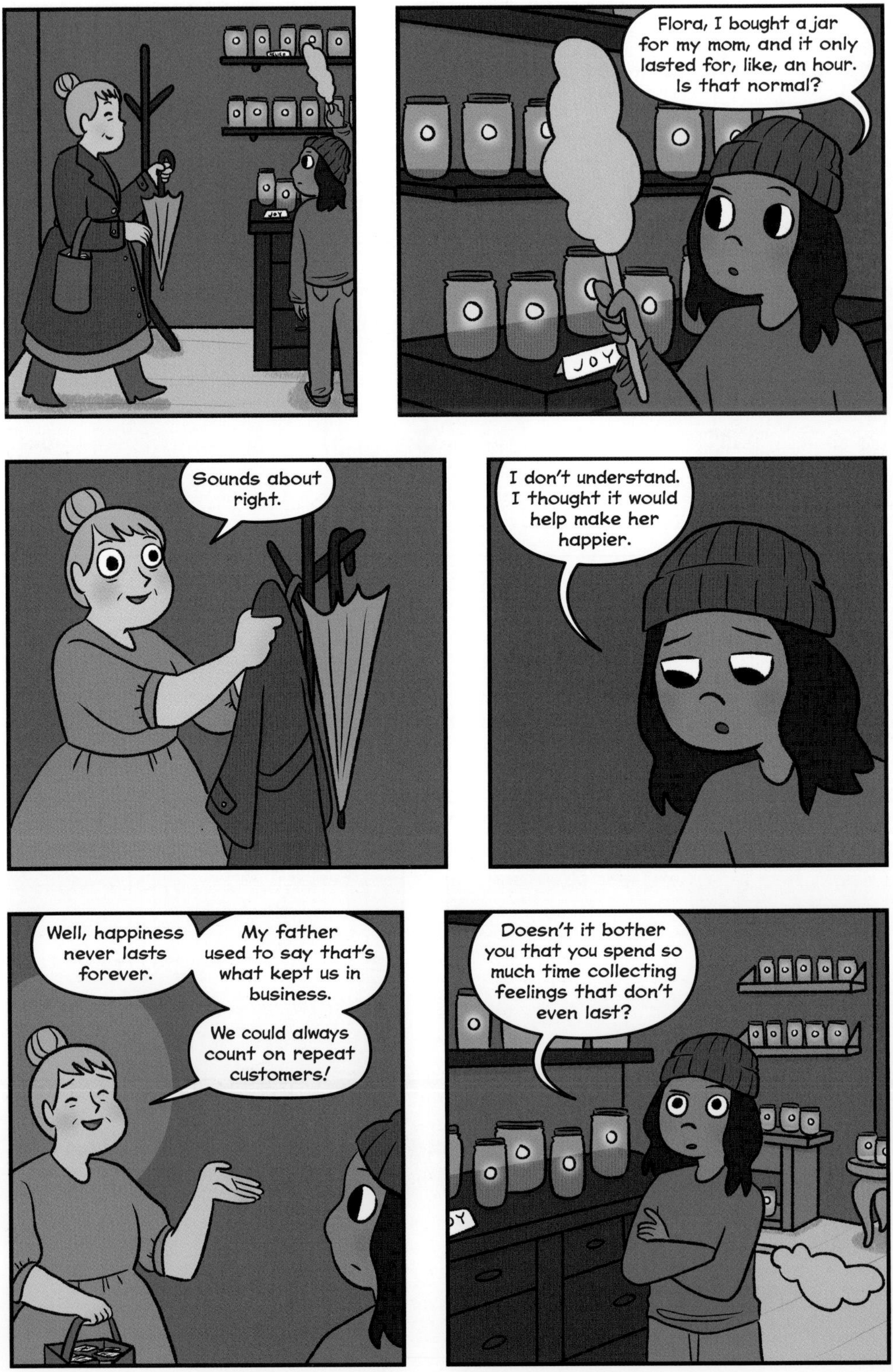
Flora, I bought a jar for my mom, and it only lasted for, like, an hour. Is that normal?
JOY
Sounds about right.
I don't understand. I thought it would help make her happier.
Well, happiness never lasts forever.
My father used to say that's what kept us in business.
We could always count on repeat customers!
Doesn't it bother you that you spend so much time collecting feelings that don't even last?

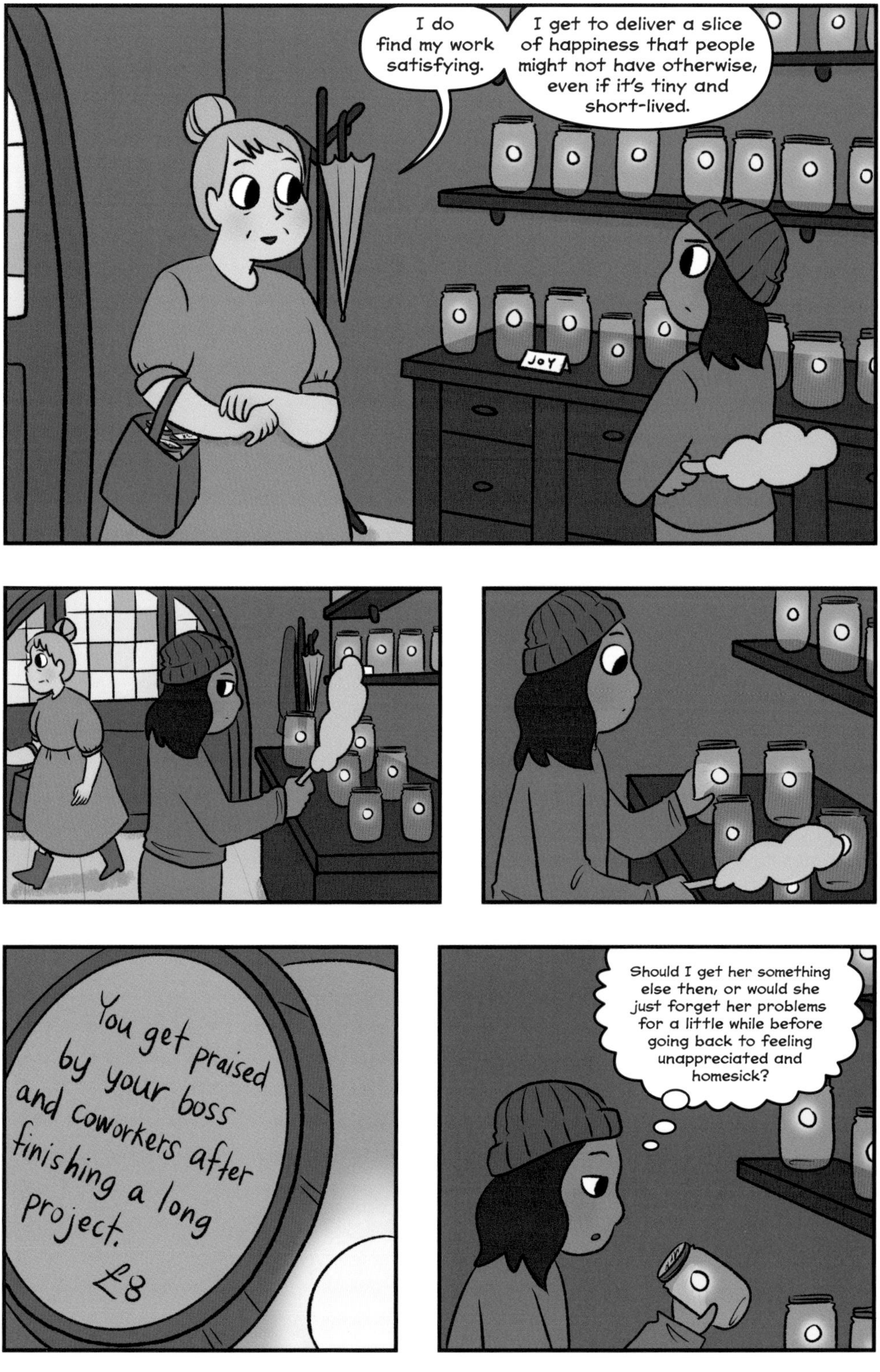
I do find my work satisfying.
I get to deliver a slice of happiness that people might not have otherwise, even if it's tiny and short-lived.
JOY
You get praised by your boss and coworkers after finishing a long project. £8
Should I get her something else then, or would she just forget her problems for a little while before going back to feeling unappreciated and homesick?

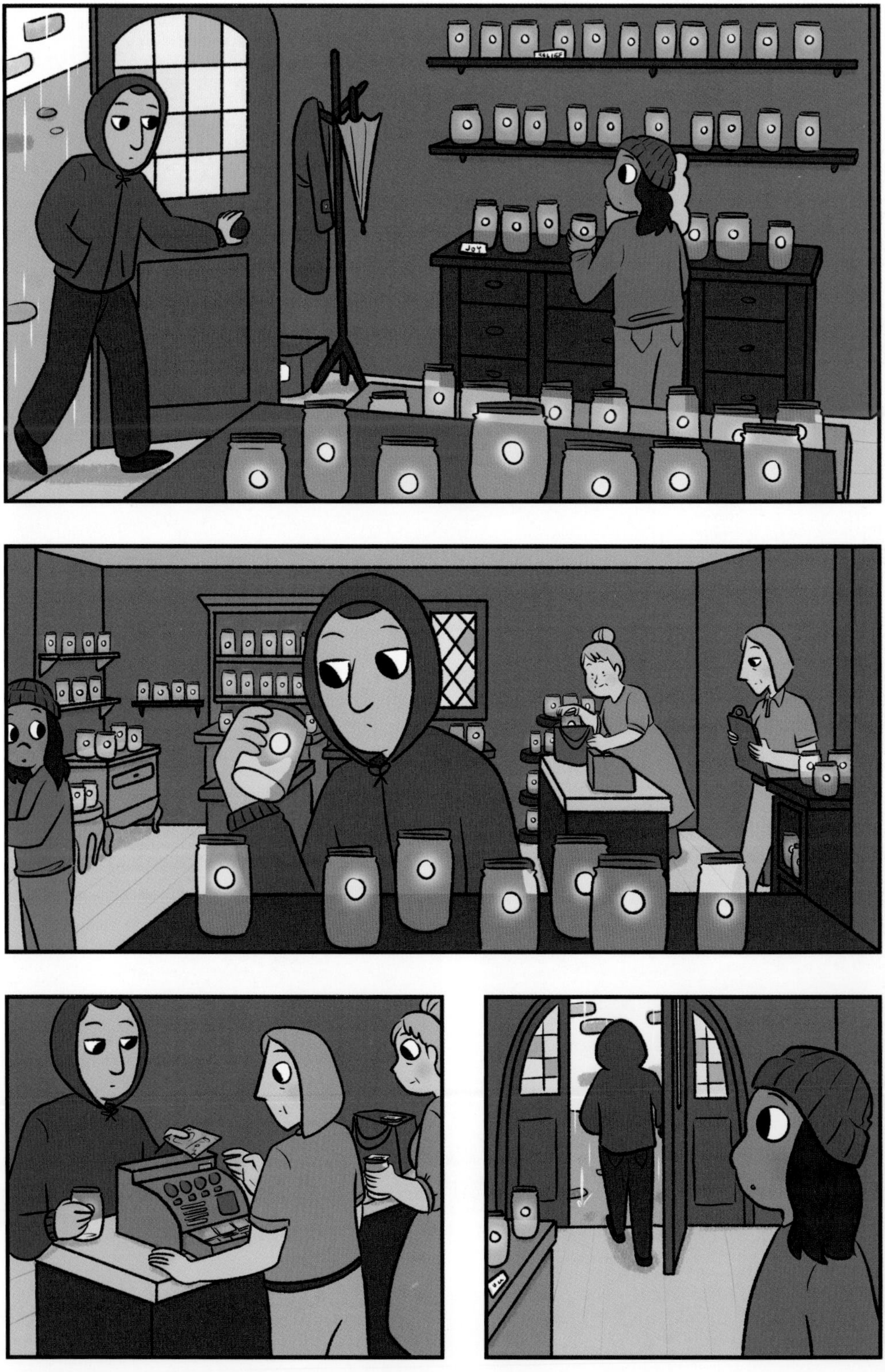
JOY

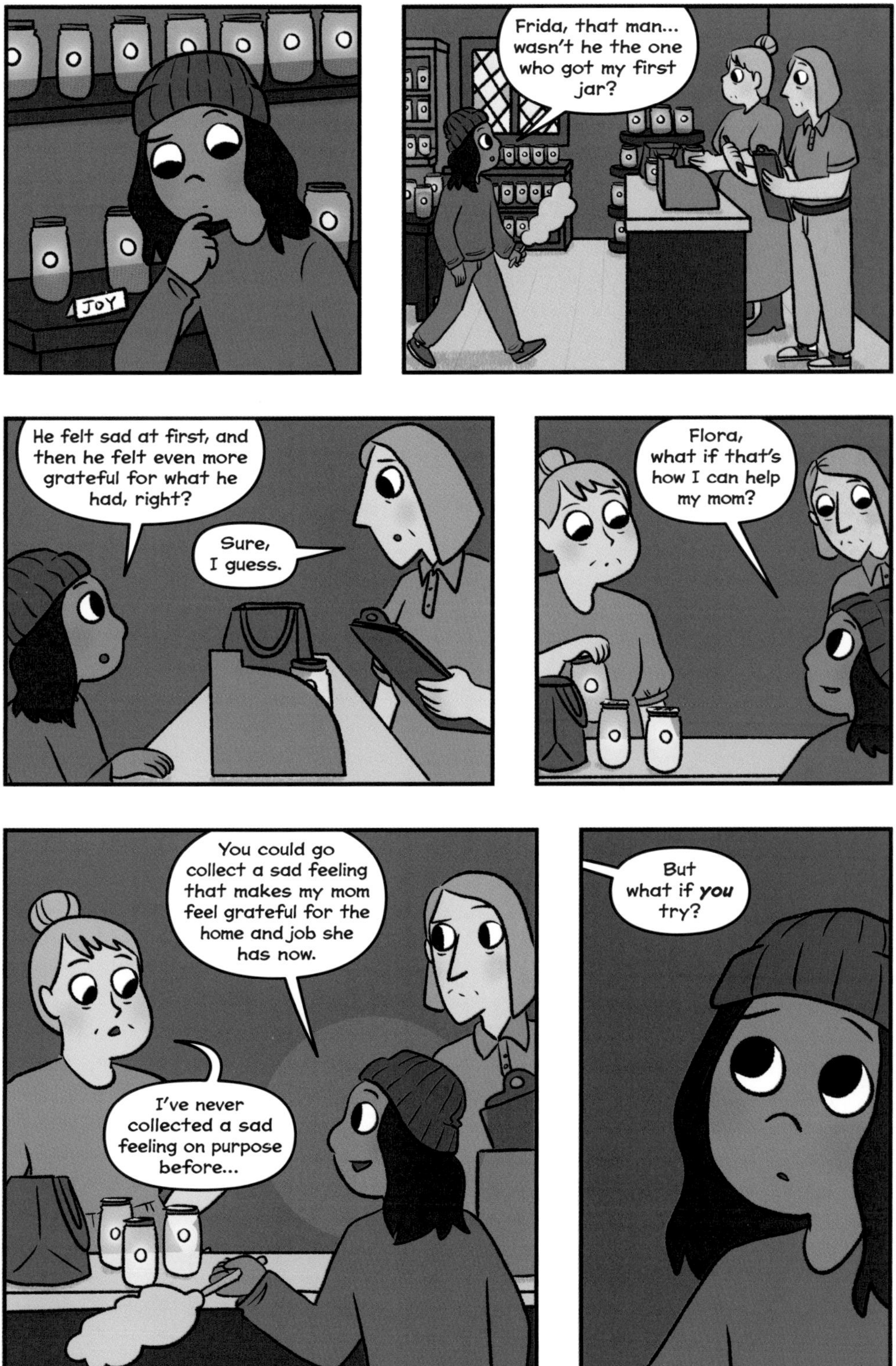
JOY
Frida, that man... wasn't he the one who got my first jar?
He felt sad at first, and then he felt even more grateful for what he had, right?
Sure, I guess.
Flora, what if that's how I can help my mom?
You could go collect a sad feeling that makes my mom feel grateful for the home and job she has now.
I've never collected a sad feeling on purpose before...
But what if *you* try?

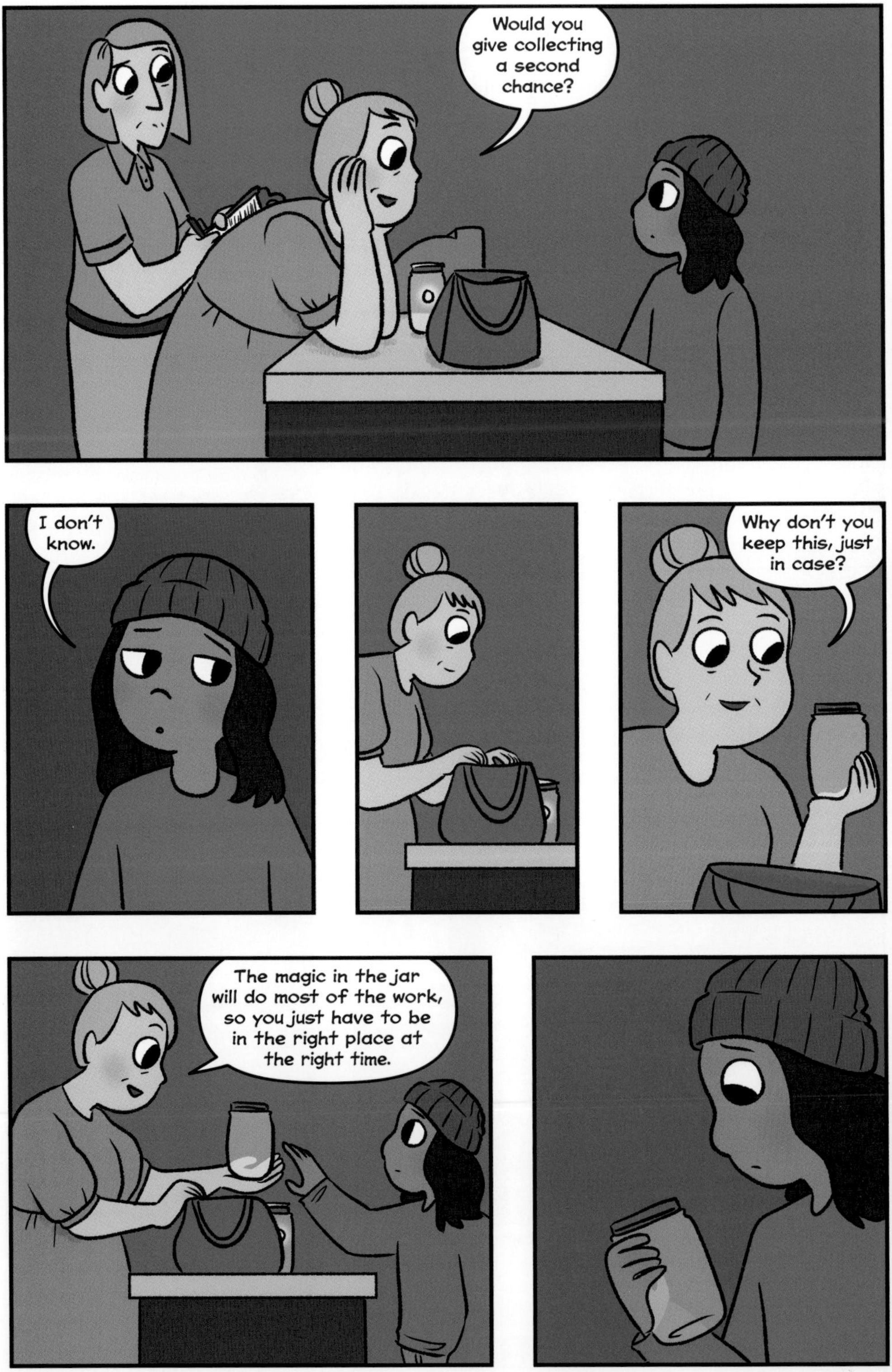
Would you give collecting a second chance?
I don't know.
Why don't you keep this, just in case?
The magic in the jar will do most of the work, so you just have to be in the right place at the right time.

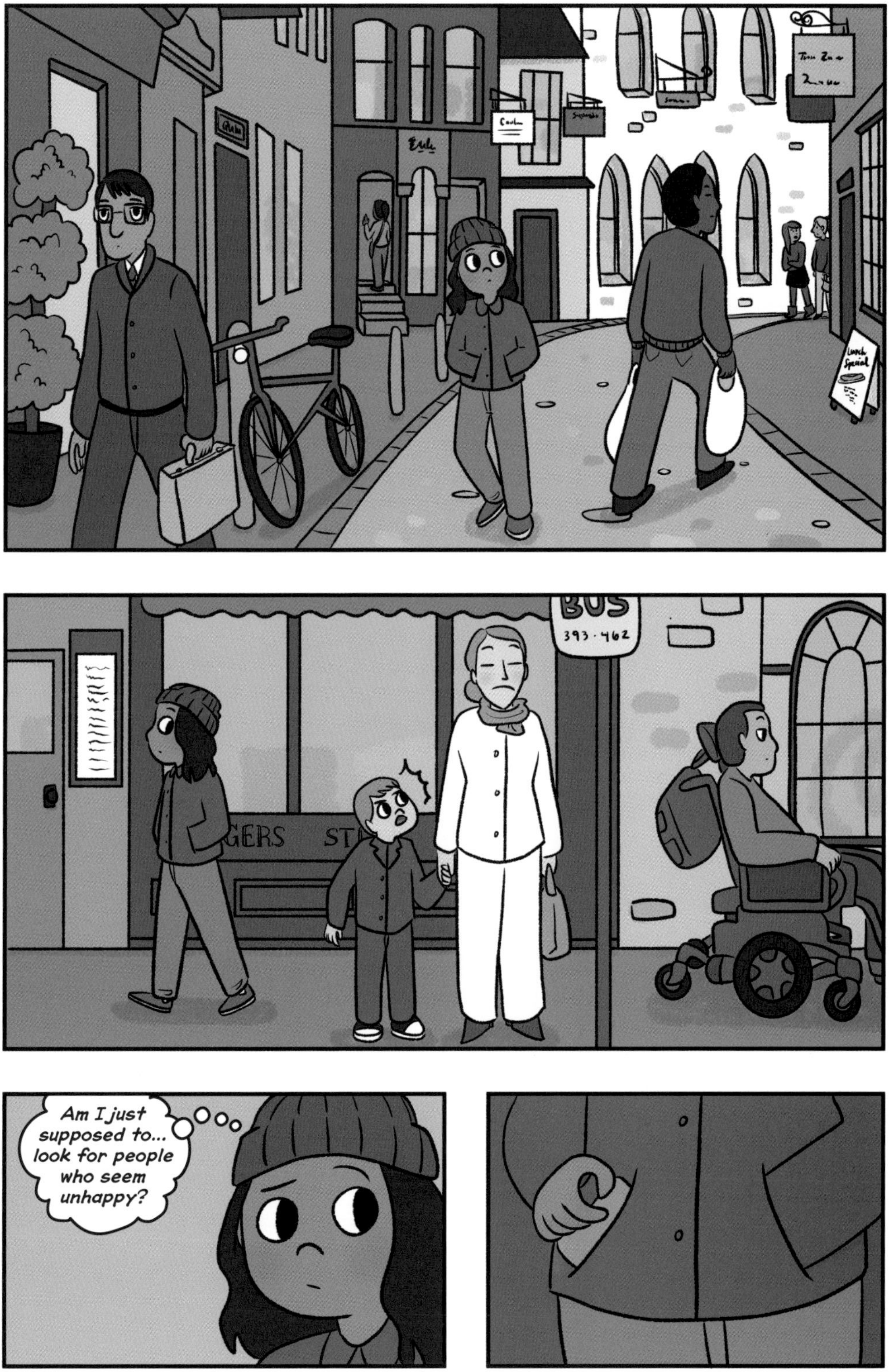
Lunch Special
BUS
393·462
Am I just supposed to... look for people who seem unhappy?

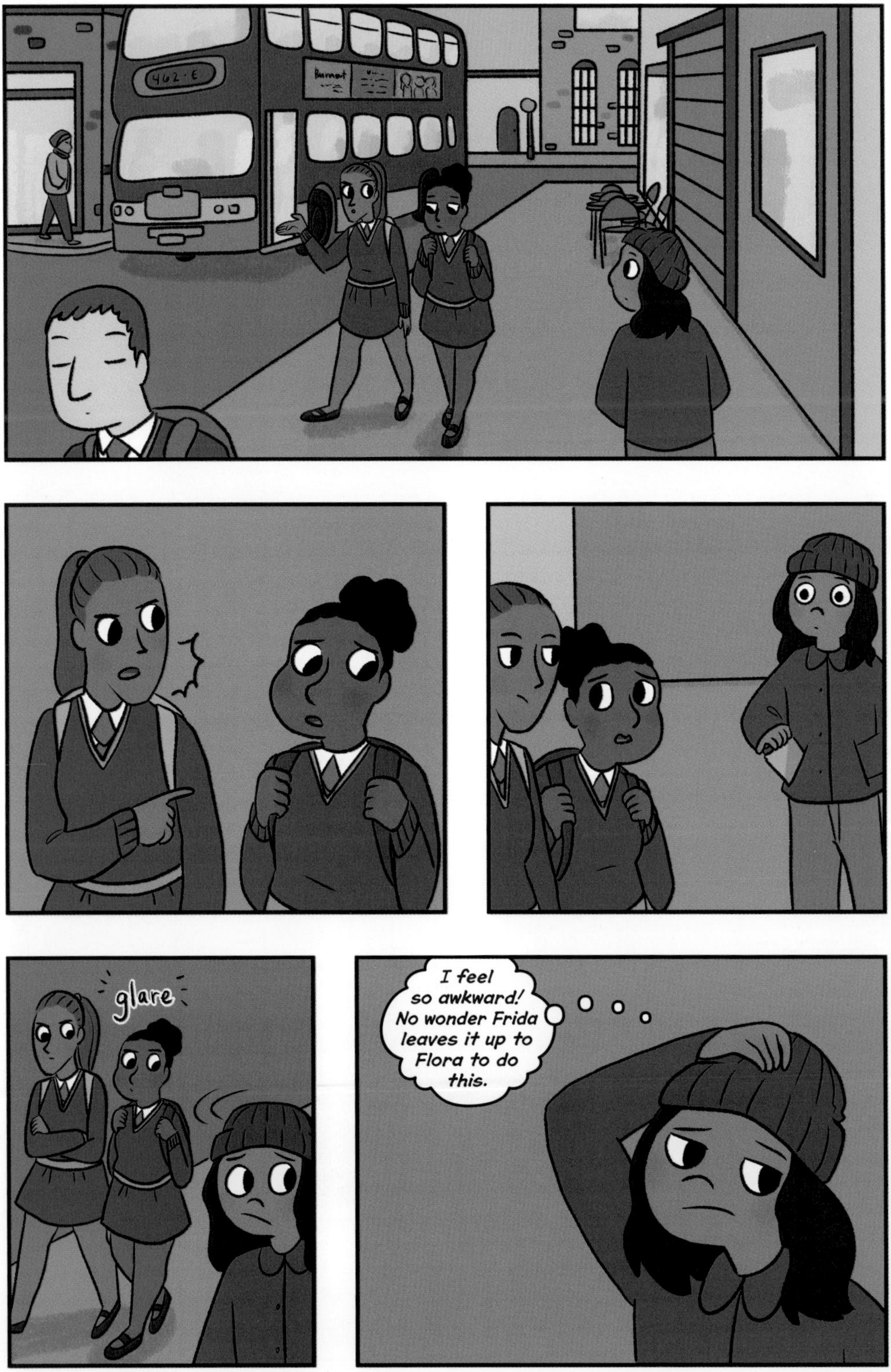
glare
I feel so awkward! No wonder Frida leaves it up to Flora to do this.

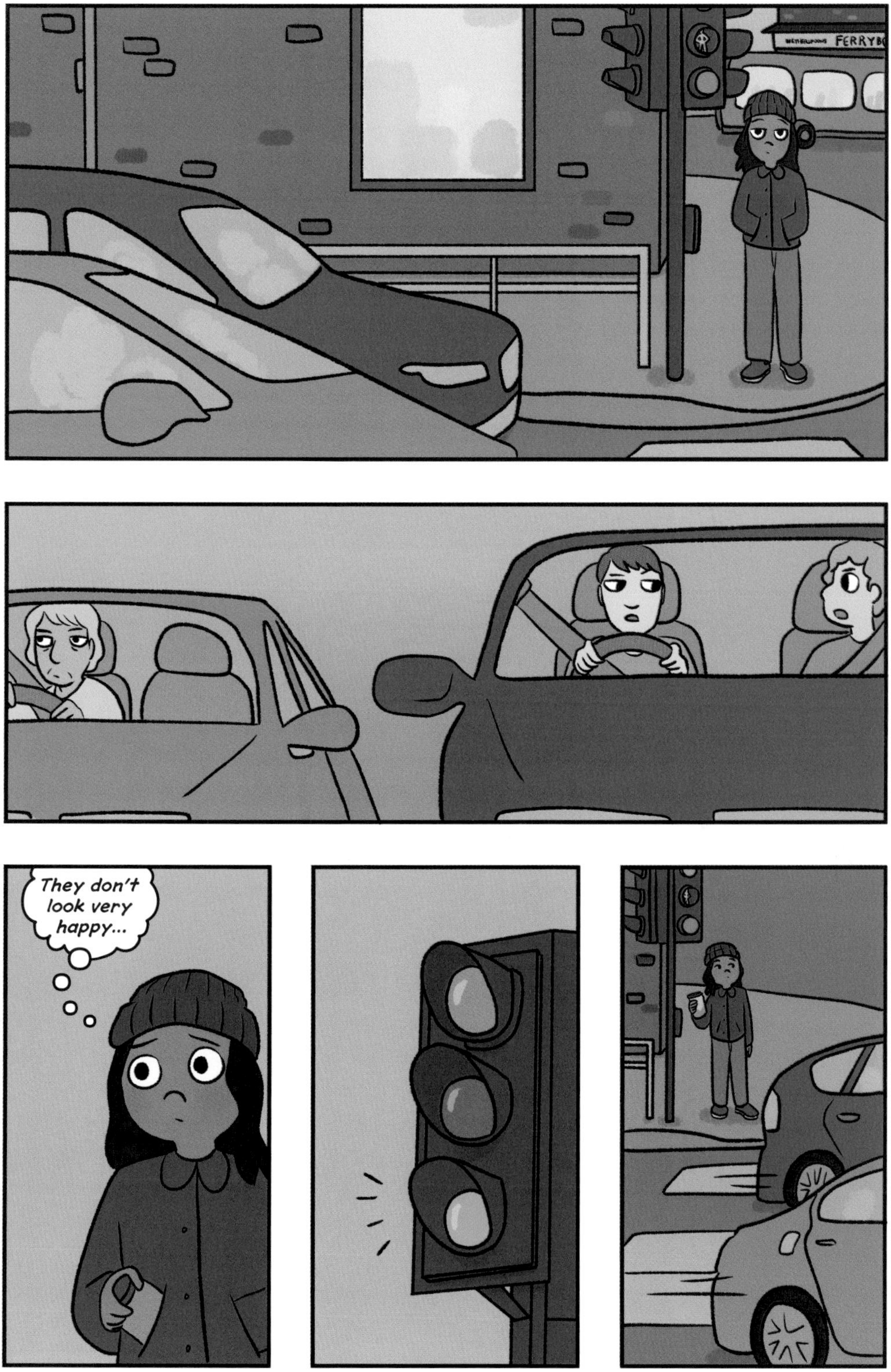
They don't look very happy...

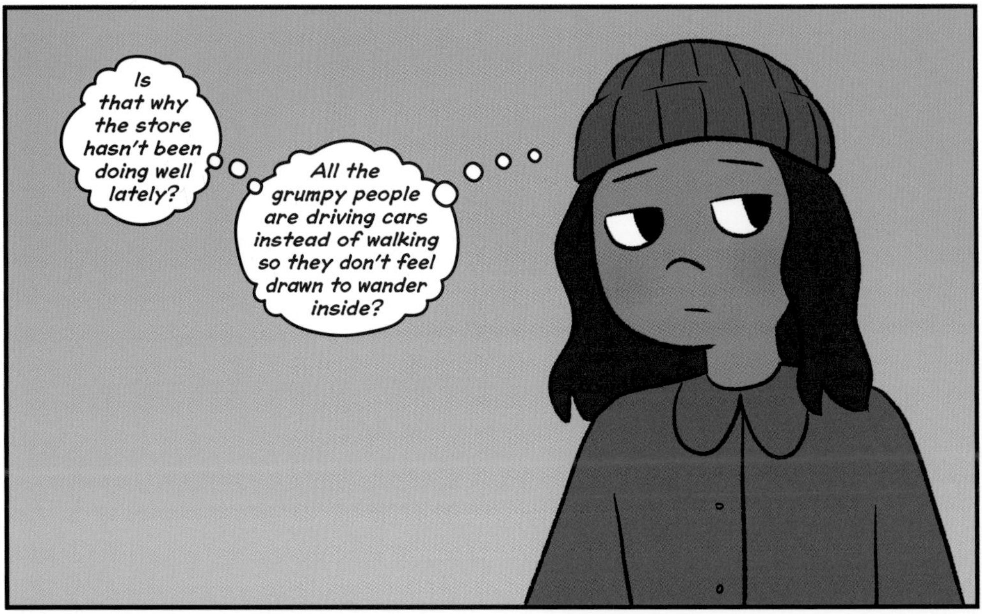
Is that why the store hasn't been doing well lately?
All the grumpy people are driving cars instead of walking so they don't feel drawn to wander inside?

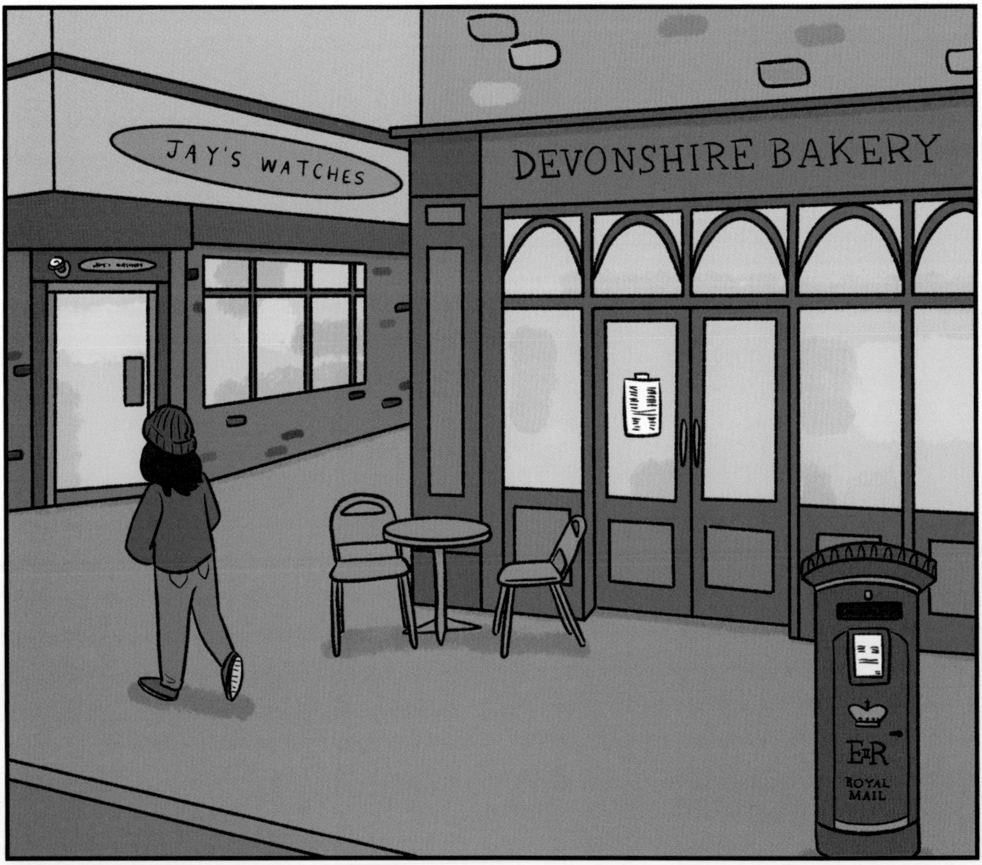
JAY'S WATCHES
DEVONSHIRE BAKERY
ER
ROYAL MAIL

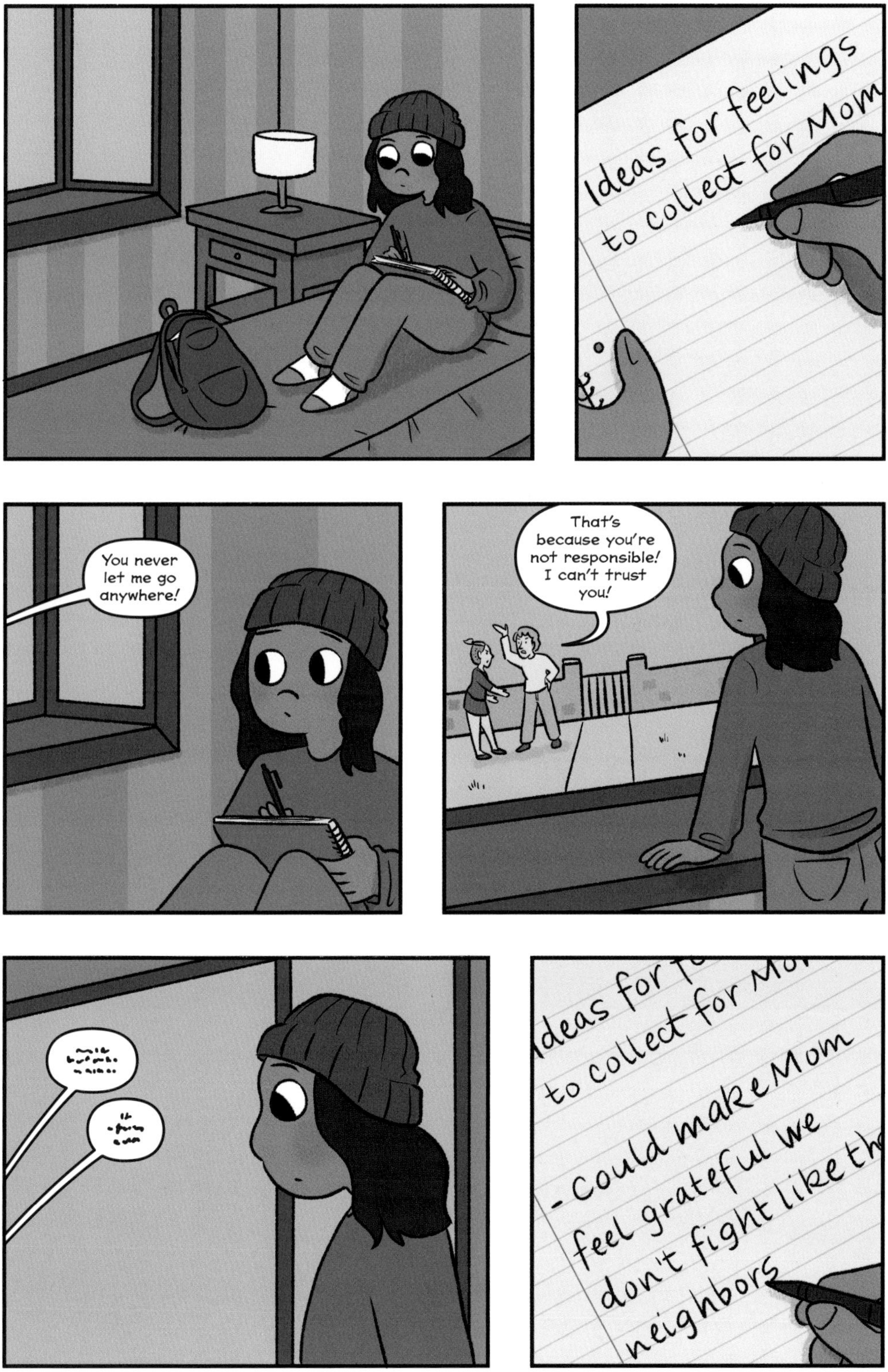
Ideas for feelings
to collect for Mom
You never let me go anywhere!
That's because you're not responsible! I can't trust you!
to collect for Mo
- could make Mom
feel grateful we
don't fight like th
neighbors

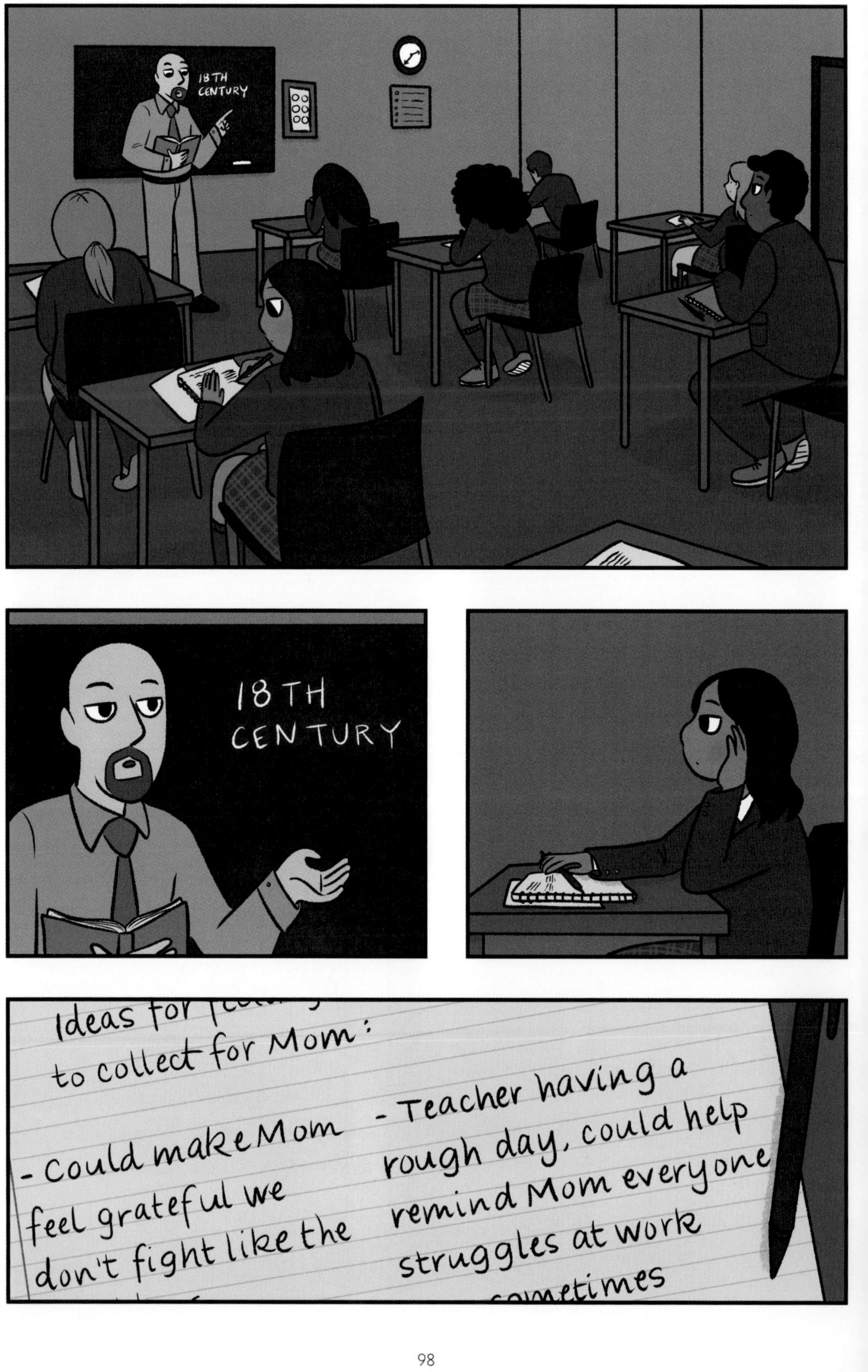
18TH CENTURY
18TH CENTURY
Ideas for
to collect for Mom:
- Could make Mom feel grateful we don't fight like the
- Teacher having a rough day, could help remind Mom everyone struggles at work

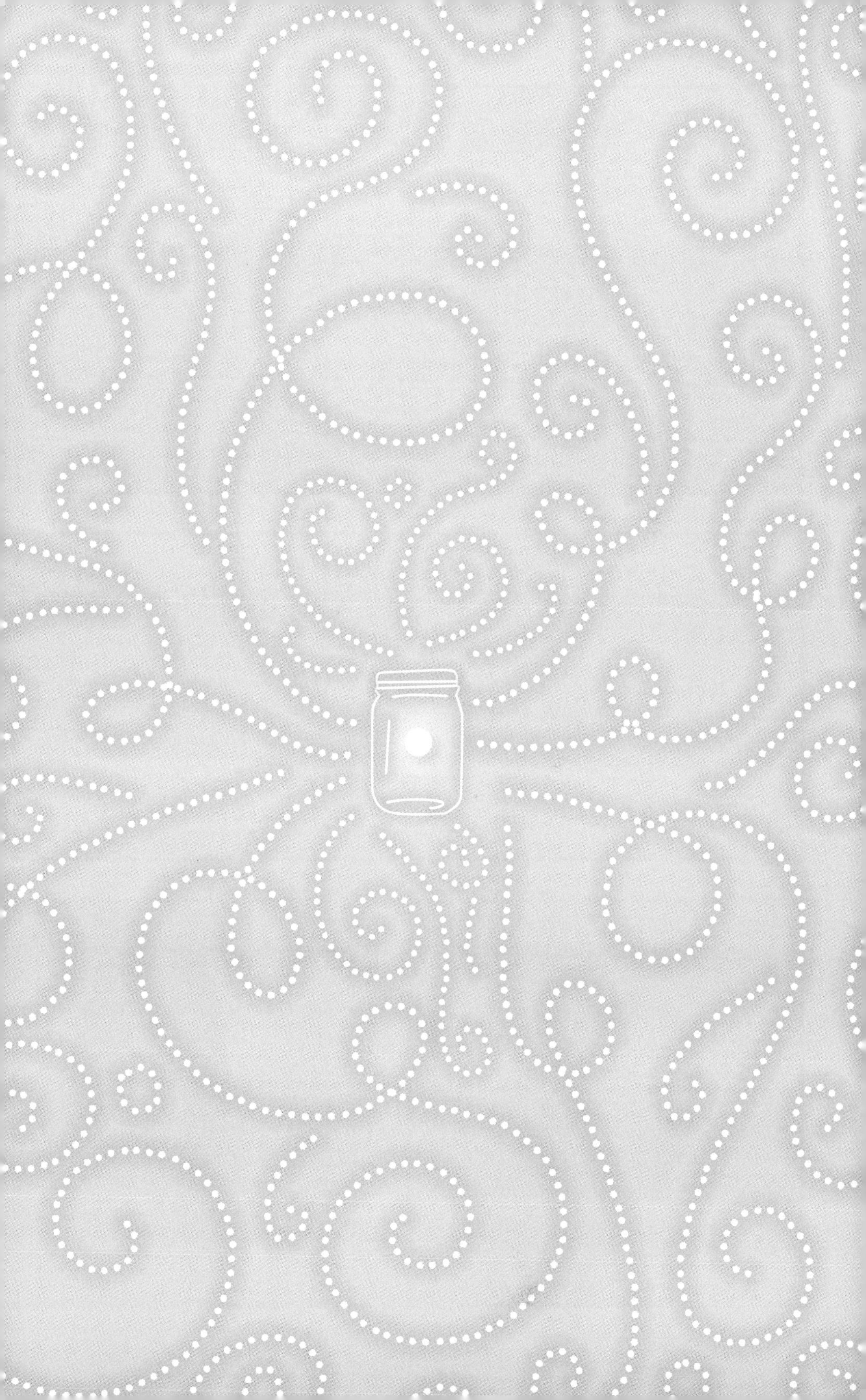

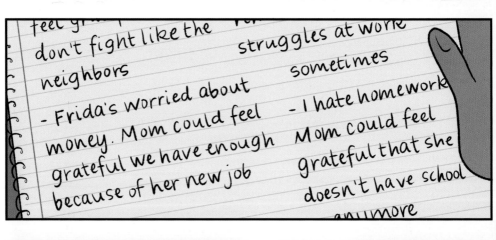

feel gr...
don't fight like the ...
neighbors

struggles at work
sometimes

- Frida's worried about
money. Mom could feel
grateful we have enough
because of her new job

- I hate homework
Mom could feel
grateful that she
doesn't have school
anymore

Oh no, I forgot my umbrella!

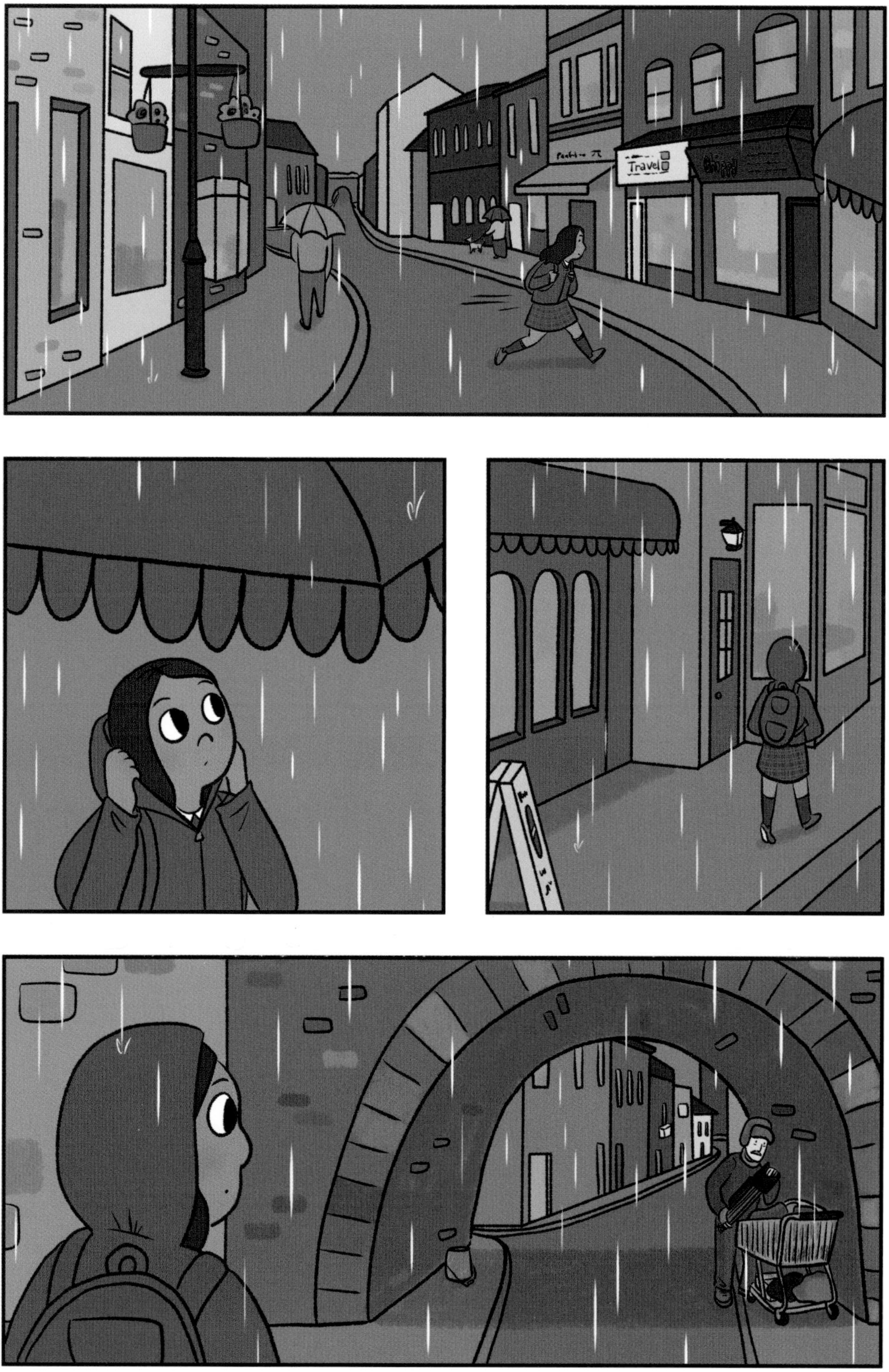
Travel

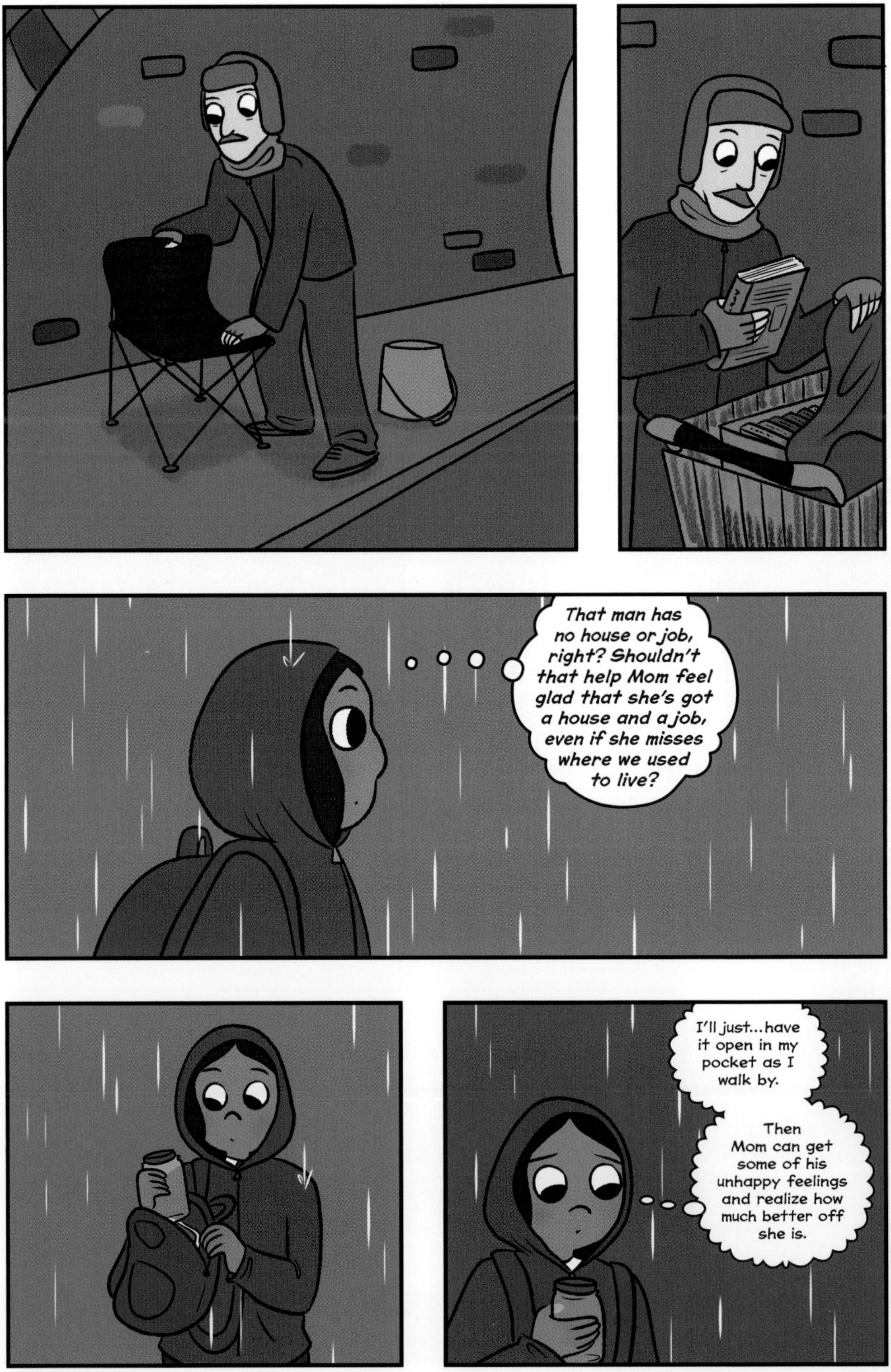
That man has no house or job, right? Shouldn't that help Mom feel glad that she's got a house and a job, even if she misses where we used to live?
I'll just...have it open in my pocket as I walk by.
Then Mom can get some of his unhappy feelings and realize how much better off she is.

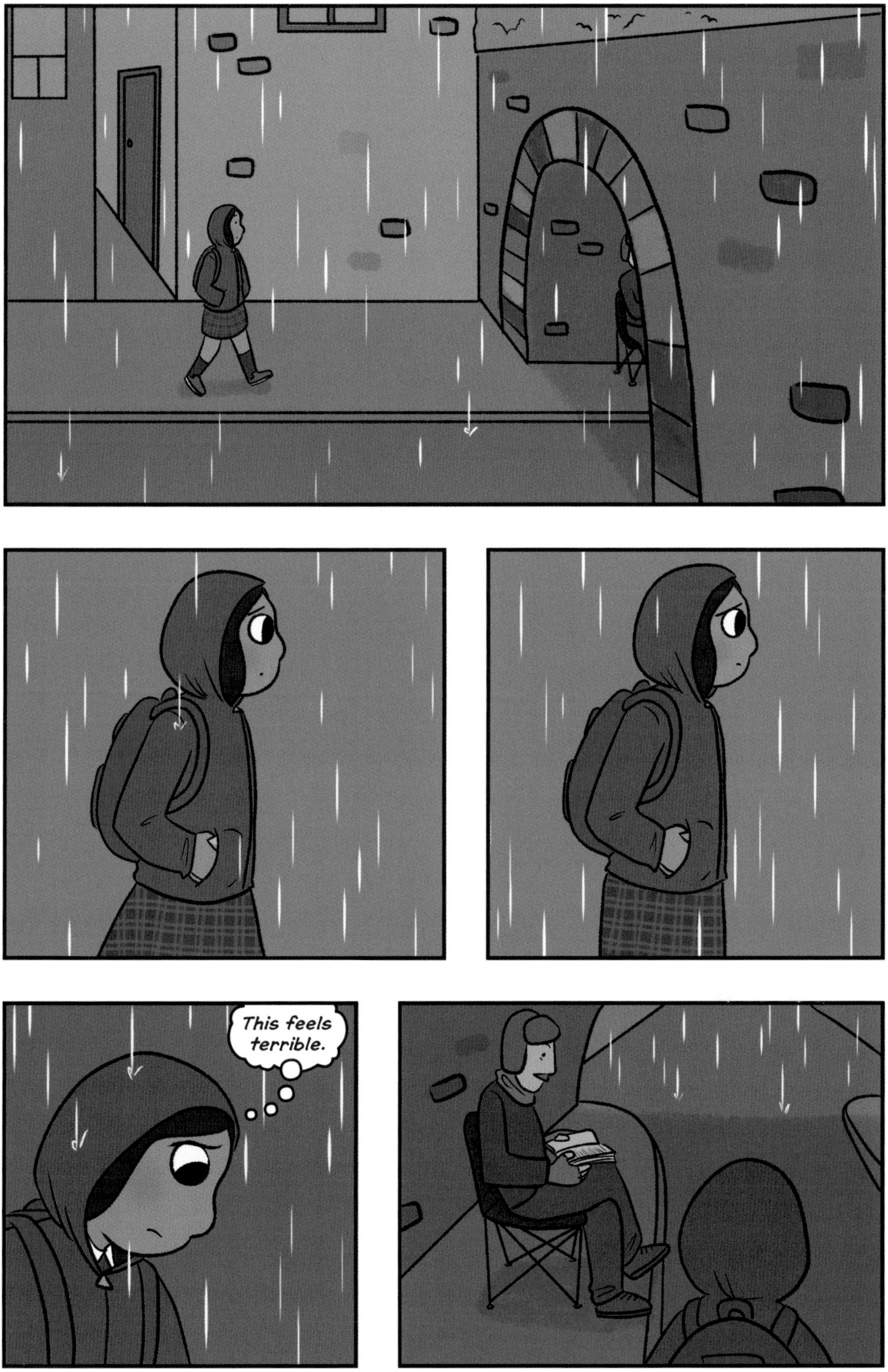
This feels terrible.

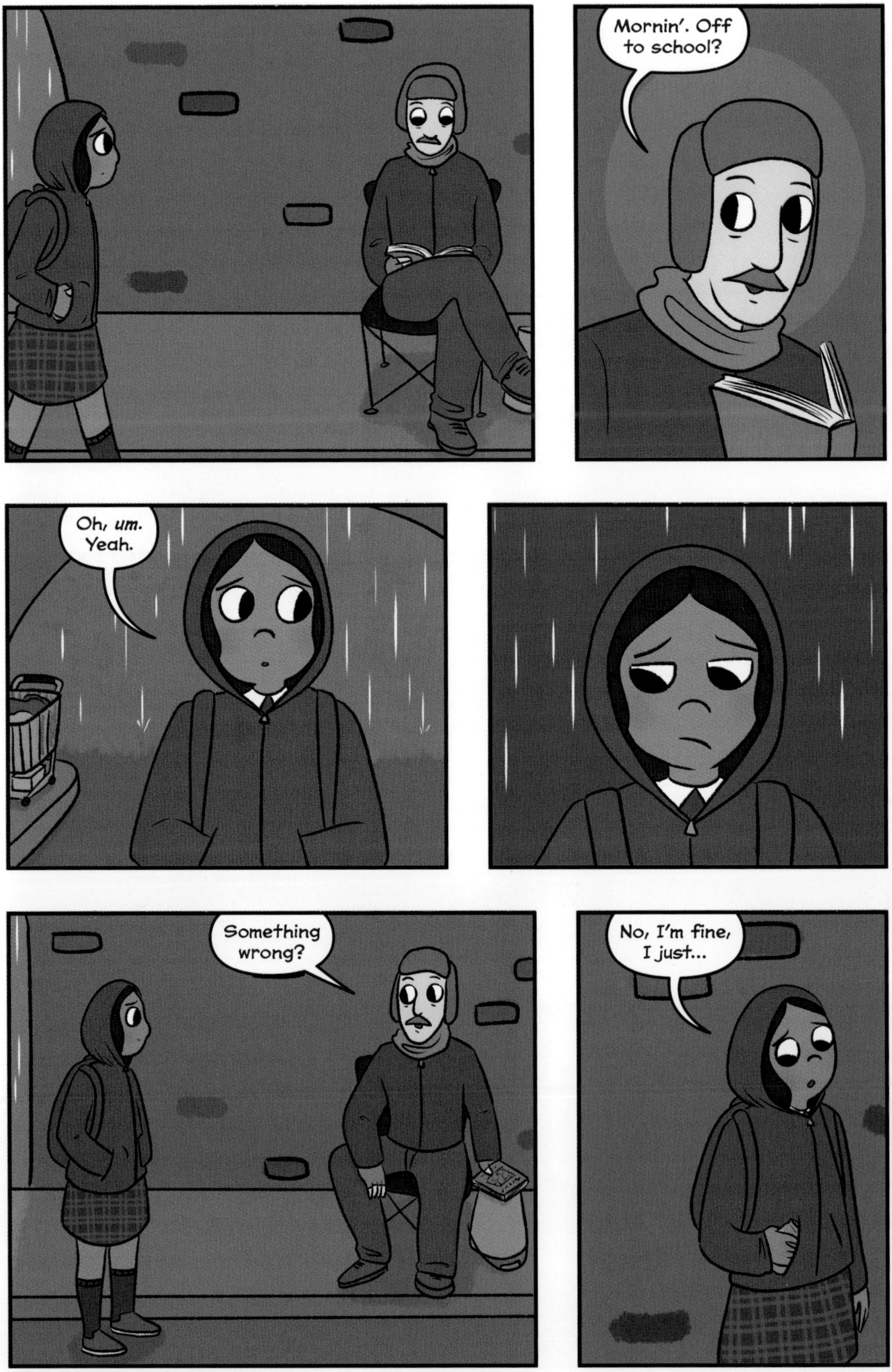
Mornin'. Off to school?
Oh, *um*. Yeah.
Something wrong?
No, I'm fine, I just...

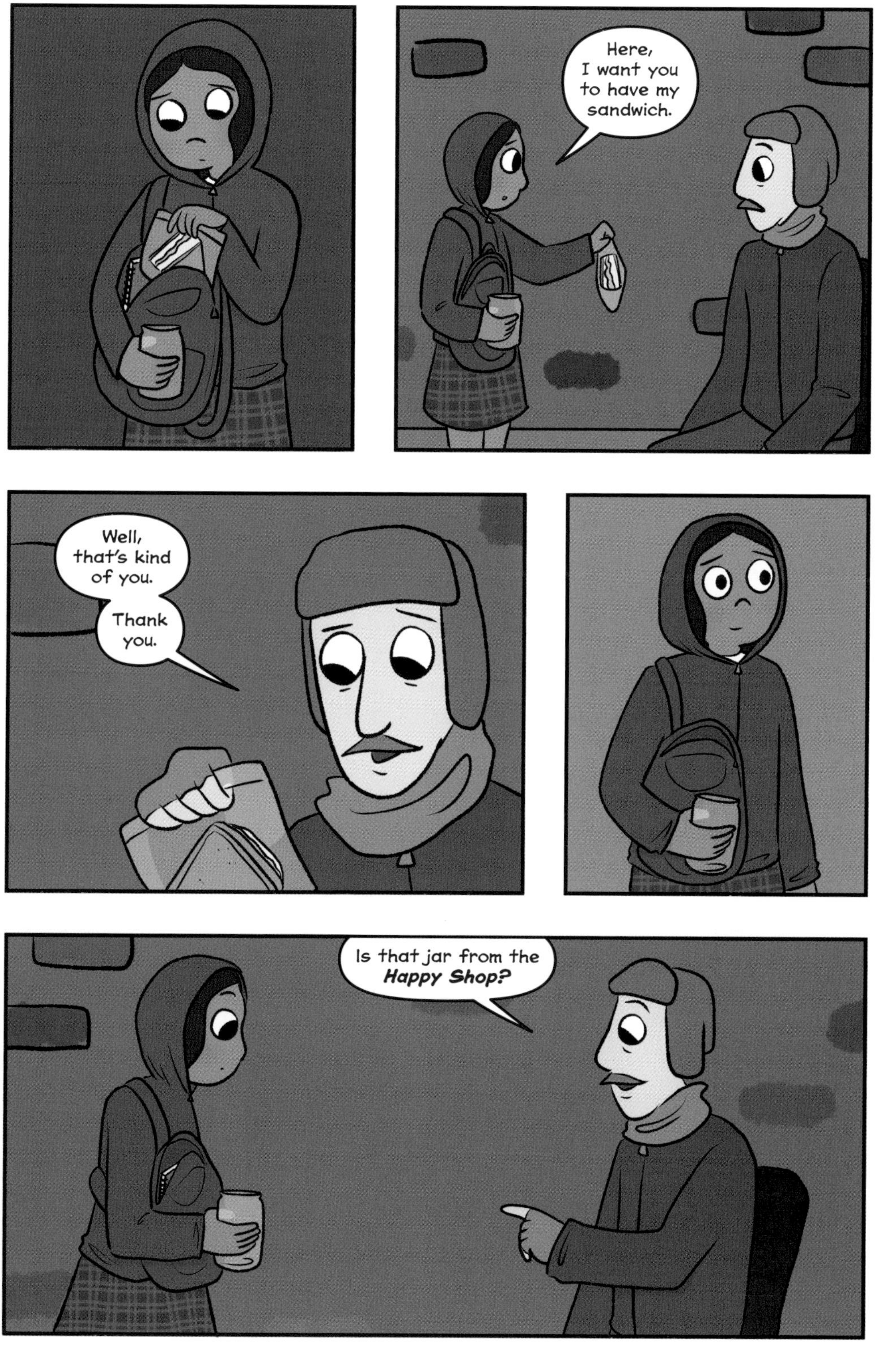
Here, I want you to have my sandwich.
Well, that's kind of you.
Thank you.
Is that jar from the *Happy Shop?*

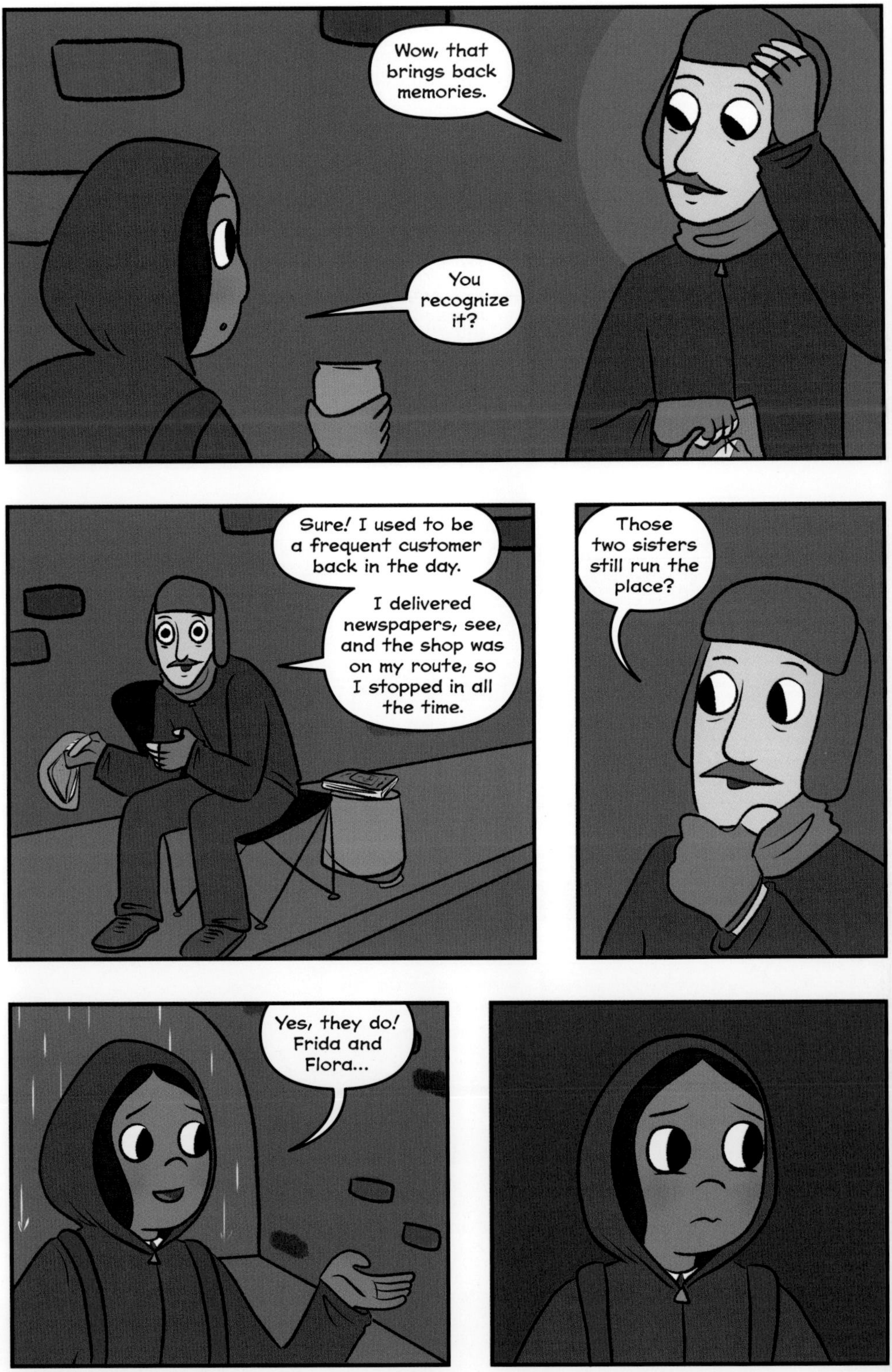

Wow, that brings back memories.
You recognize it?
Sure! I used to be a frequent customer back in the day.
I delivered newspapers, see, and the shop was on my route, so I stopped in all the time.
Those two sisters still run the place?
Yes, they do! Frida and Flora...

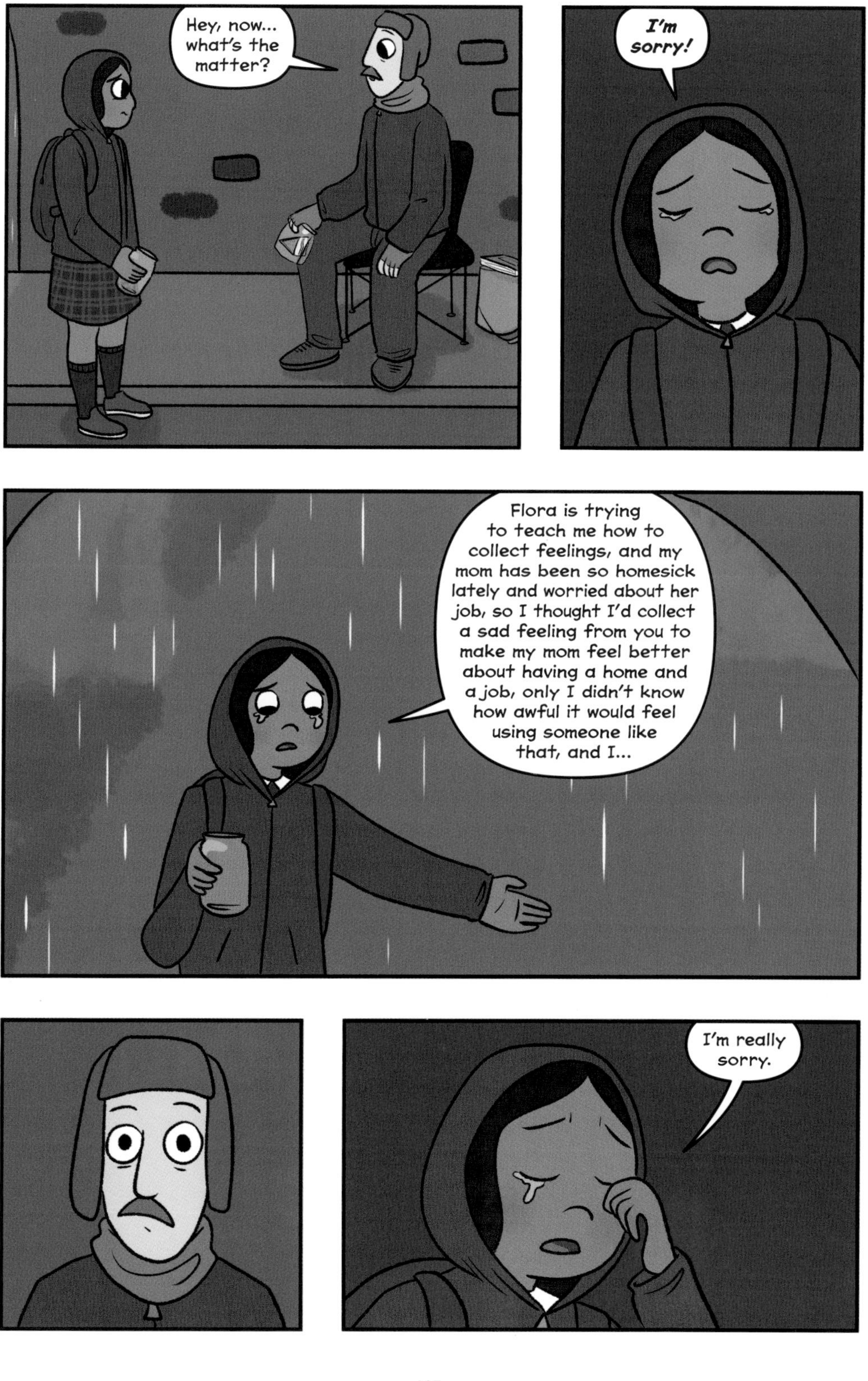

Hey, now... what's the matter?
I'm sorry!
Flora is trying to teach me how to collect feelings, and my mom has been so homesick lately and worried about her job, so I thought I'd collect a sad feeling from you to make my mom feel better about having a home and a job, only I didn't know how awful it would feel using someone like that, and I...
I'm really sorry.

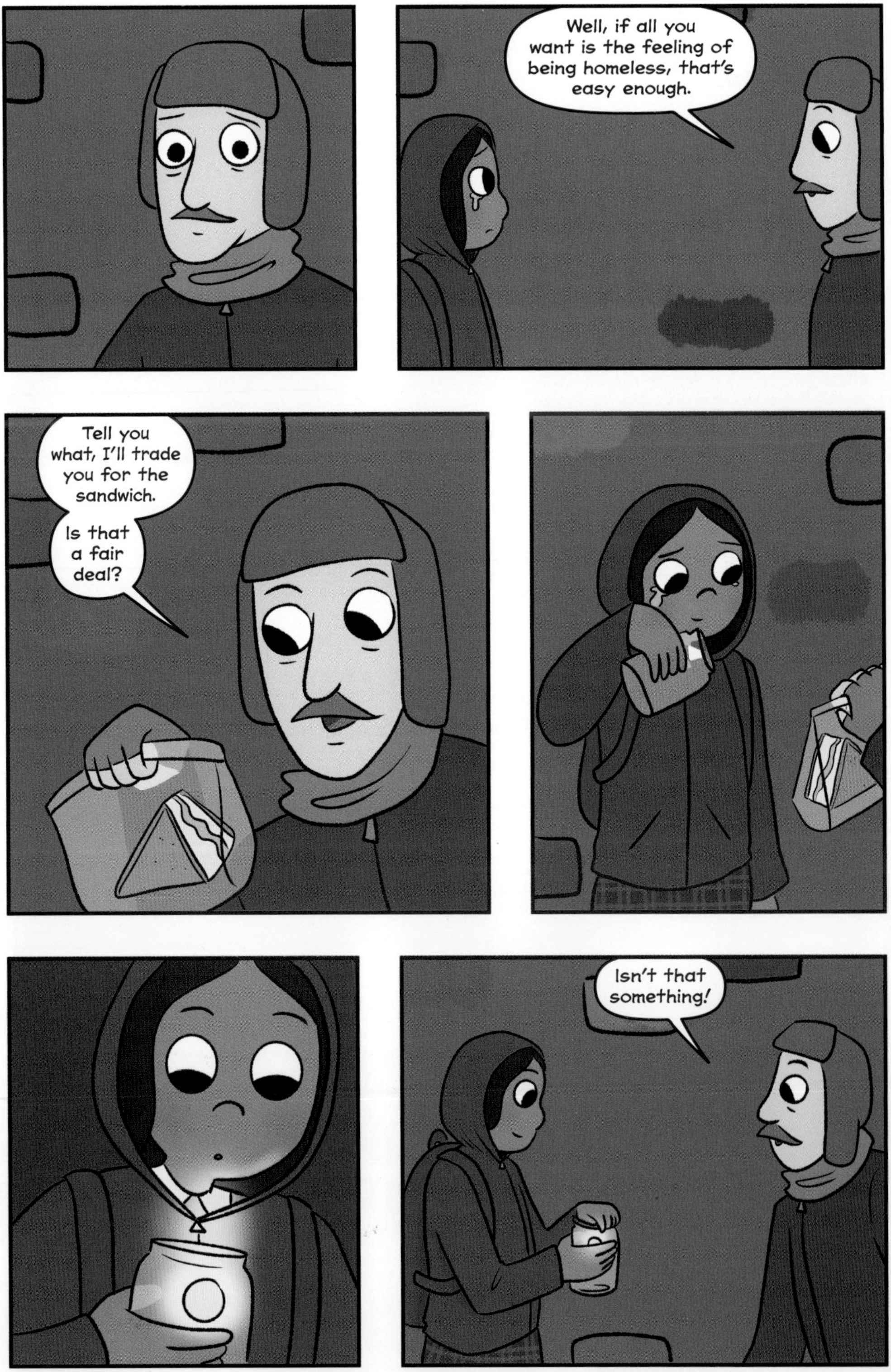

Well, if all you want is the feeling of being homeless, that's easy enough.
Tell you what, I'll trade you for the sandwich.
Is that a fair deal?
Isn't that something!

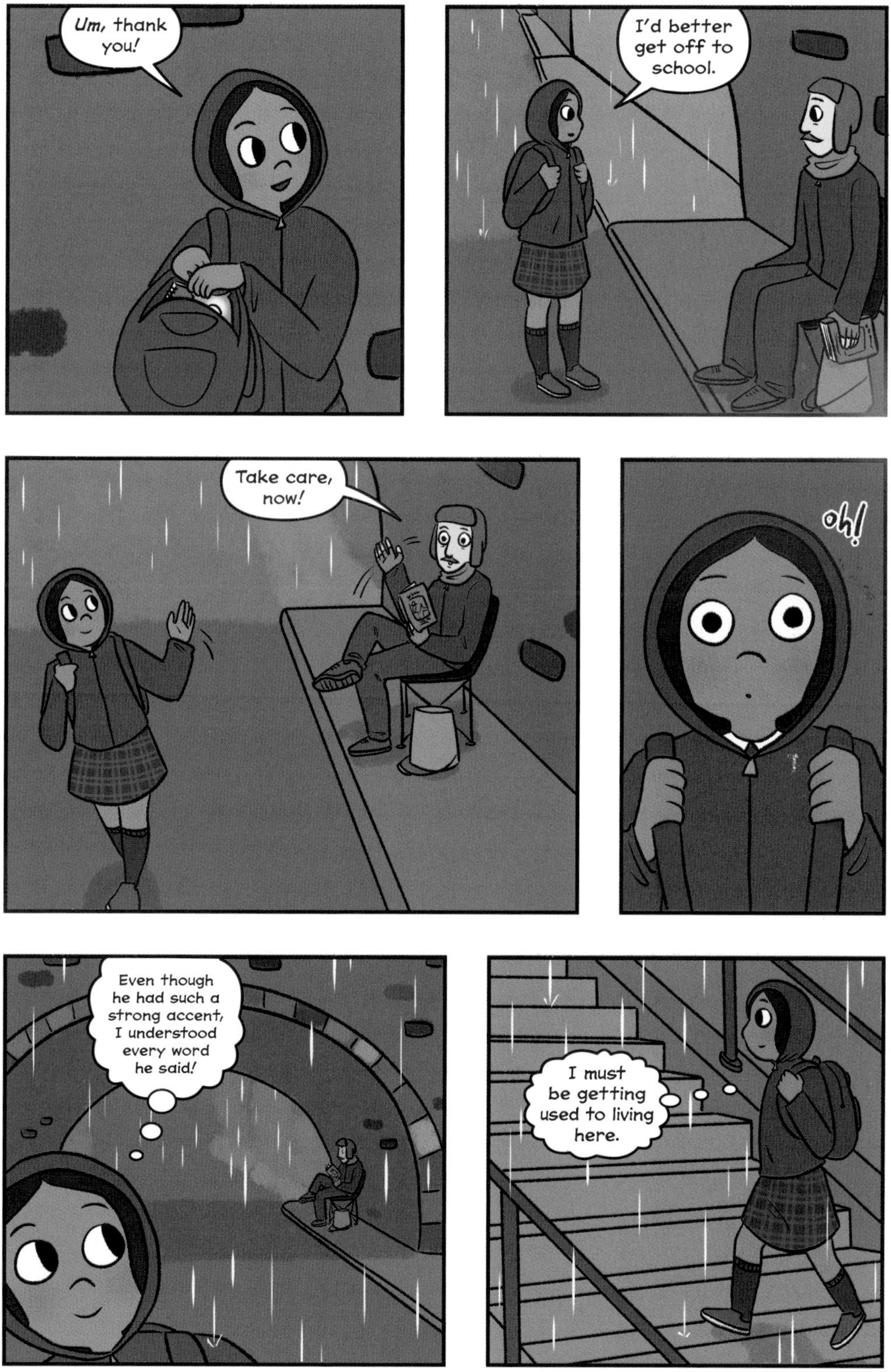
Um, thank you!
I'd better get off to school.
Take care, now!
oh!
Even though he had such a strong accent, I understood every word he said!
I must be getting used to living here.

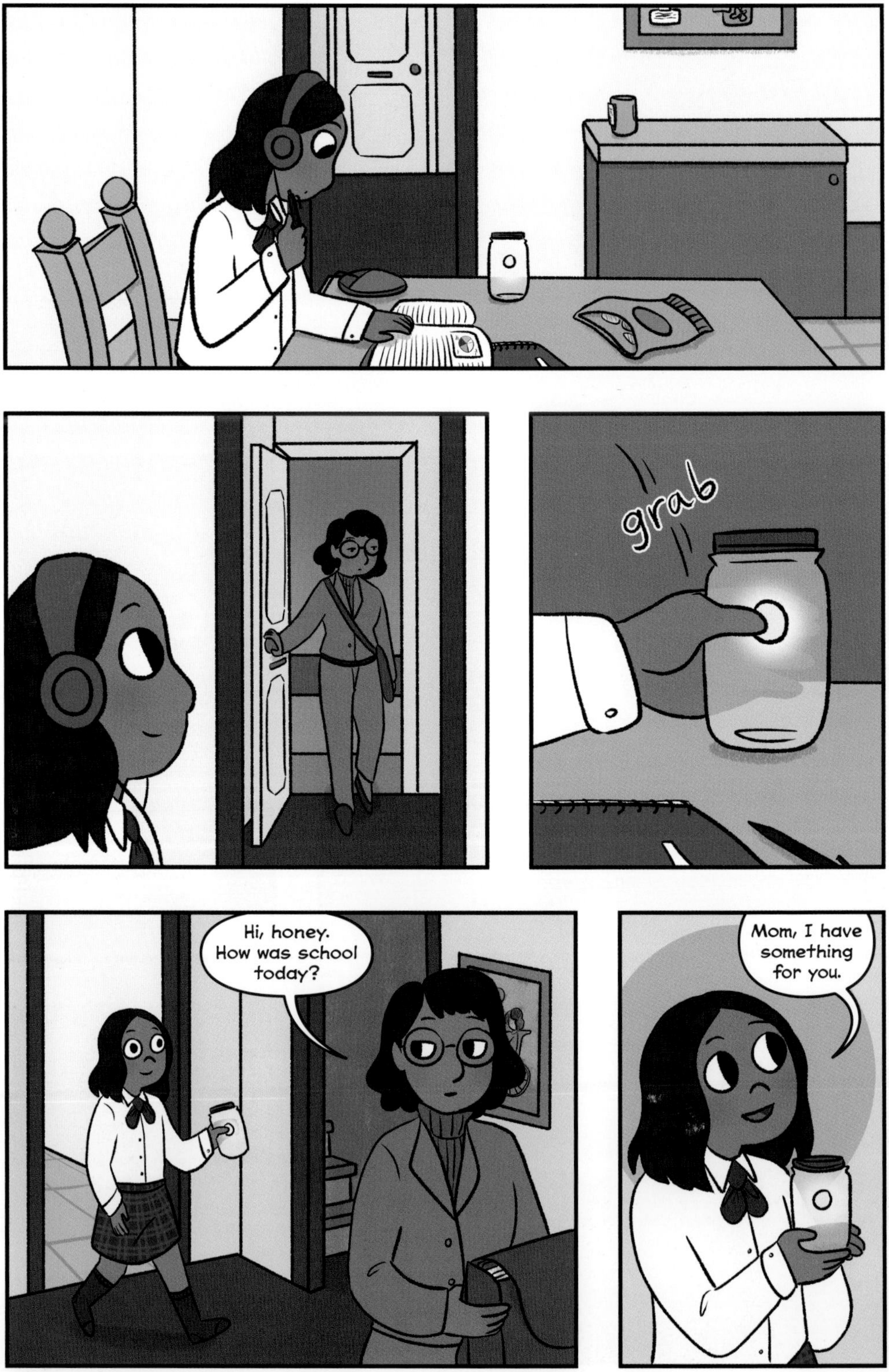
grab
Hi, honey. How was school today?
Mom, I have something for you.

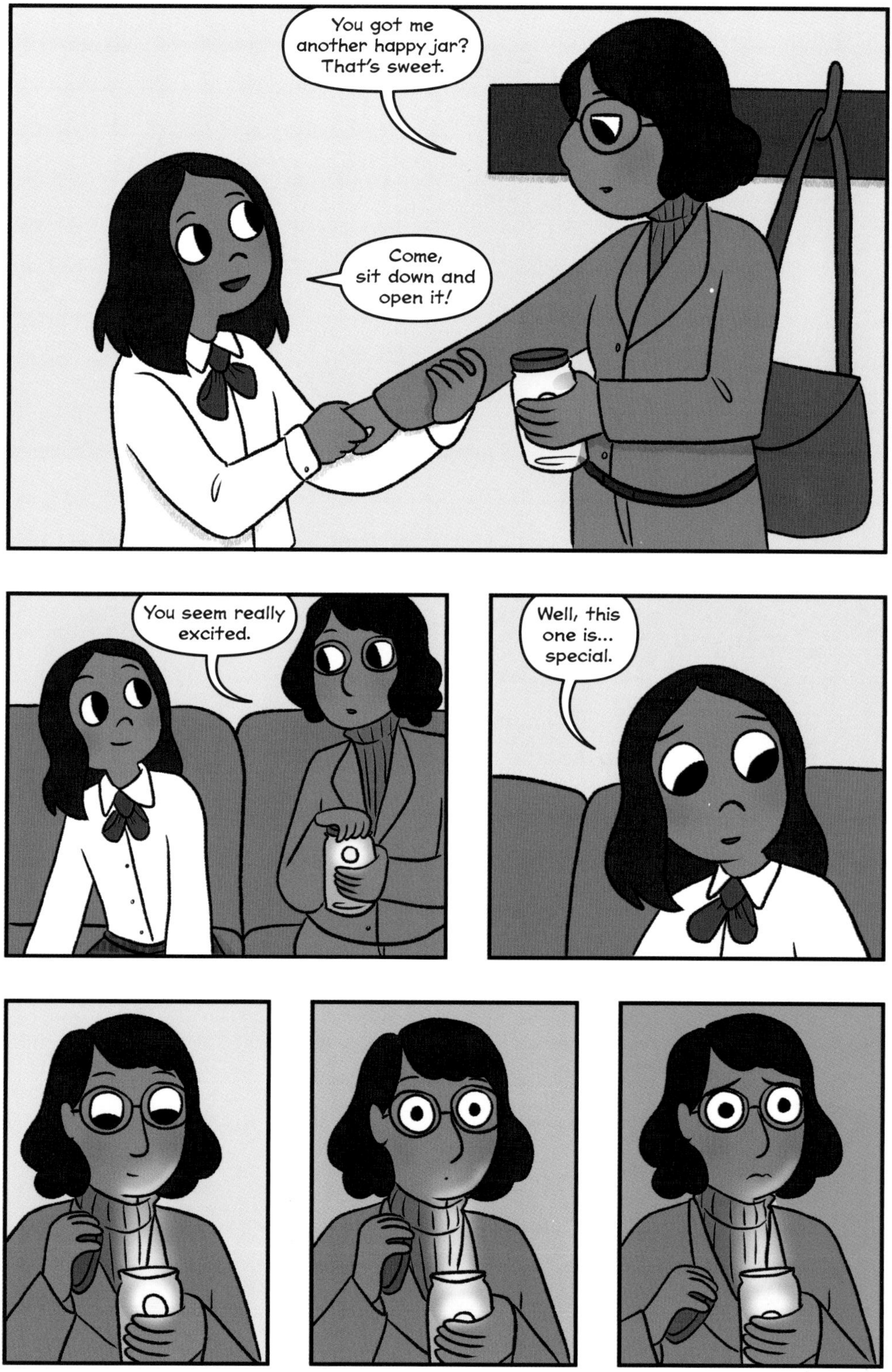
You got me another happy jar? That's sweet.
Come, sit down and open it!
You seem really excited.
Well, this one is... special.

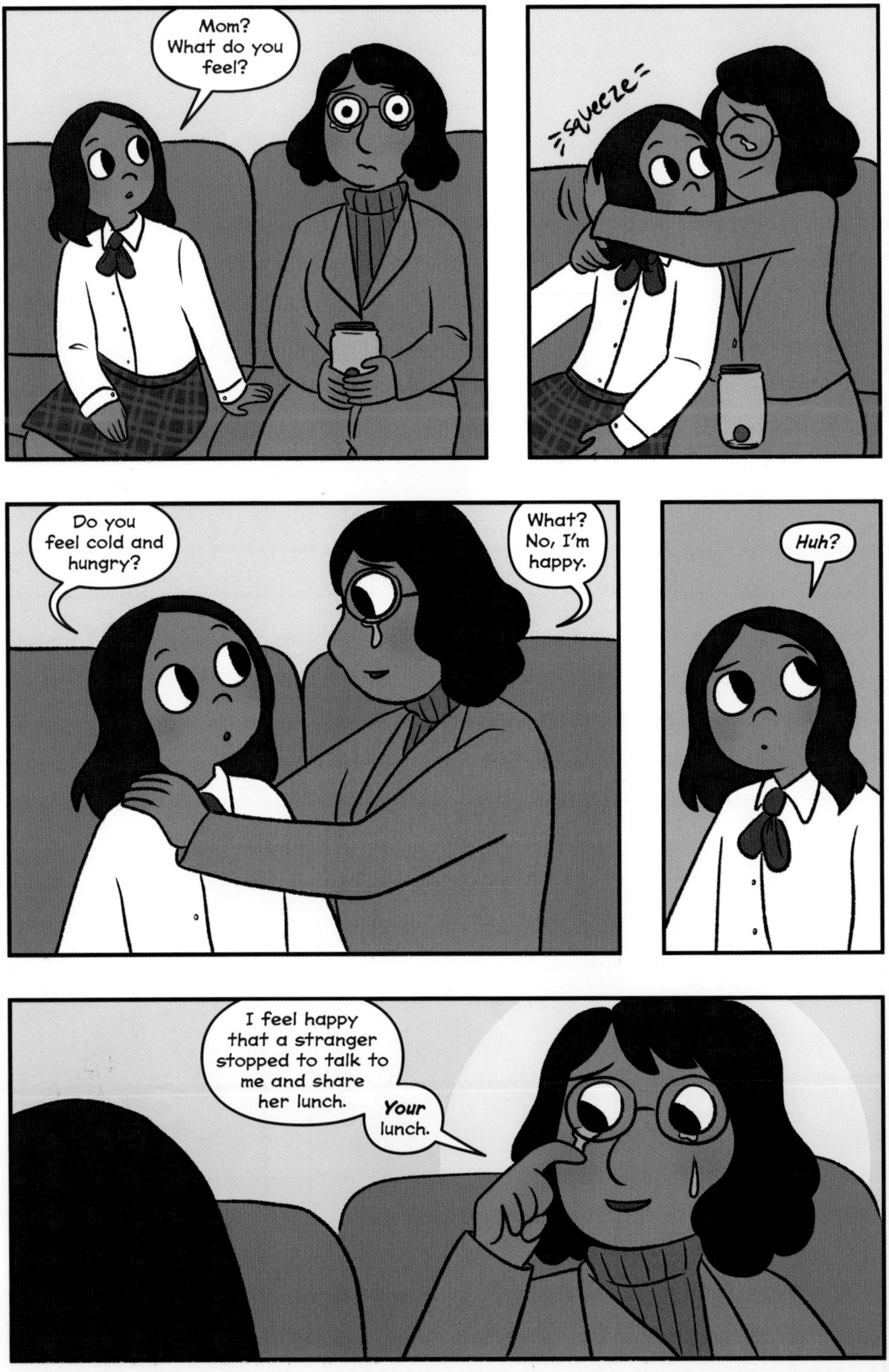
Mom? What do you feel?
SQUEEZE
Do you feel cold and hungry?
What? No, I'm happy.
Huh?
I feel happy that a stranger stopped to talk to me and share her lunch.
Your lunch.

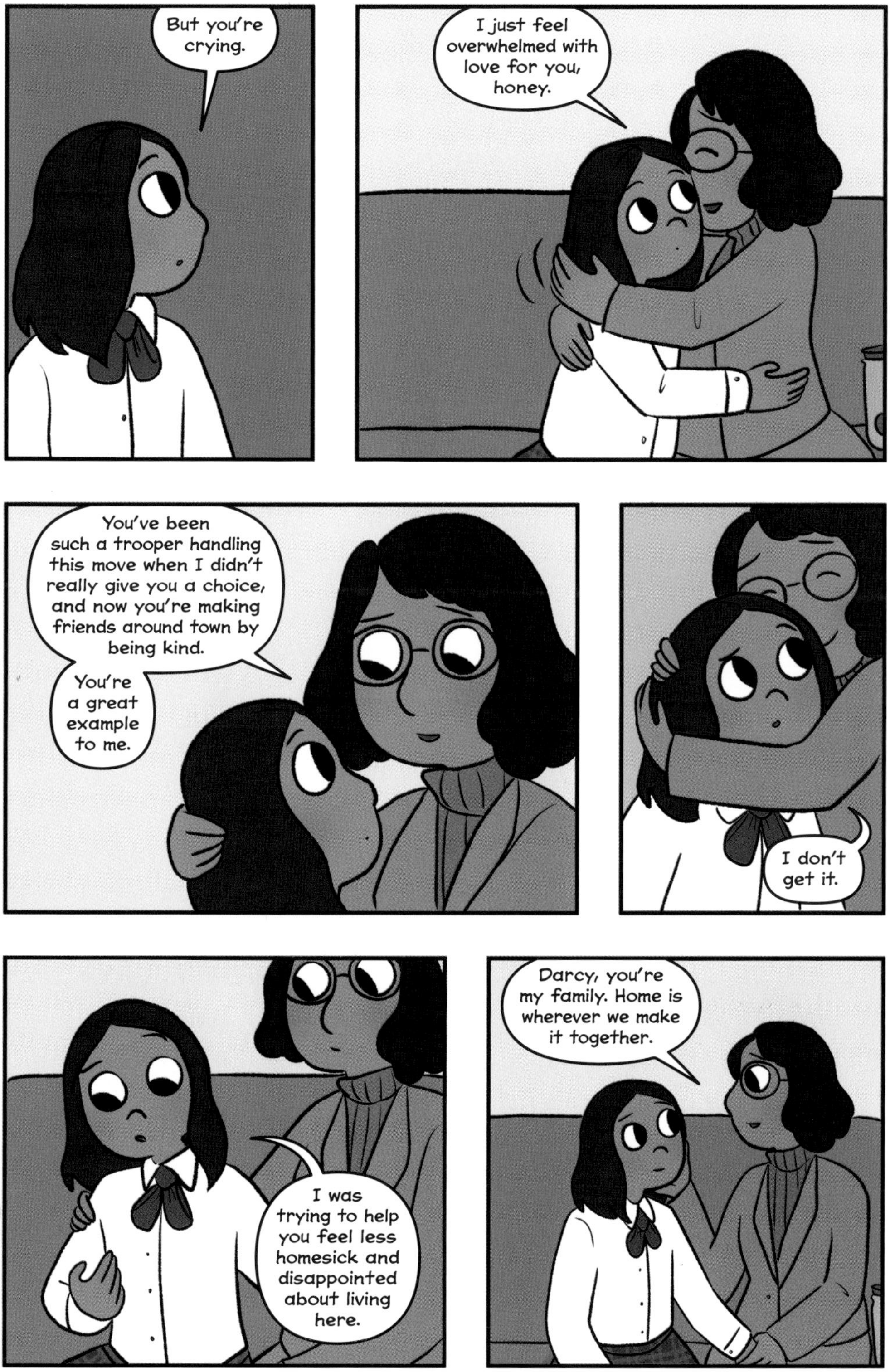

But you're crying.
I just feel overwhelmed with love for you, honey.
You've been such a trooper handling this move when I didn't really give you a choice, and now you're making friends around town by being kind.
You're a great example to me.
I don't get it.
I was trying to help you feel less homesick and disappointed about living here.
Darcy, you're my family. Home is wherever we make it together.

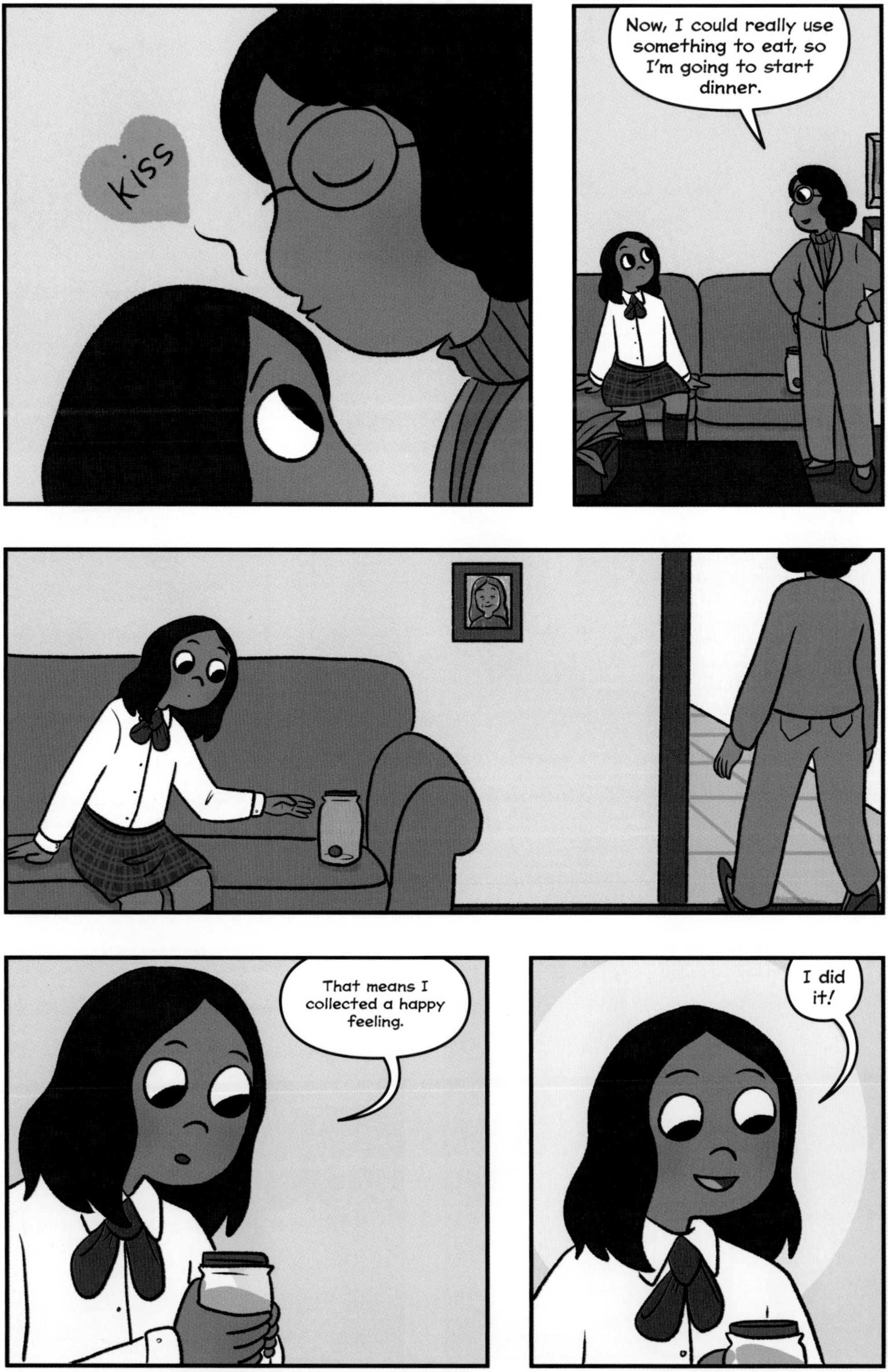
kiss
Now, I could really use something to eat, so I'm going to start dinner.
That means I collected a happy feeling.
I did it!

Chapter Eight

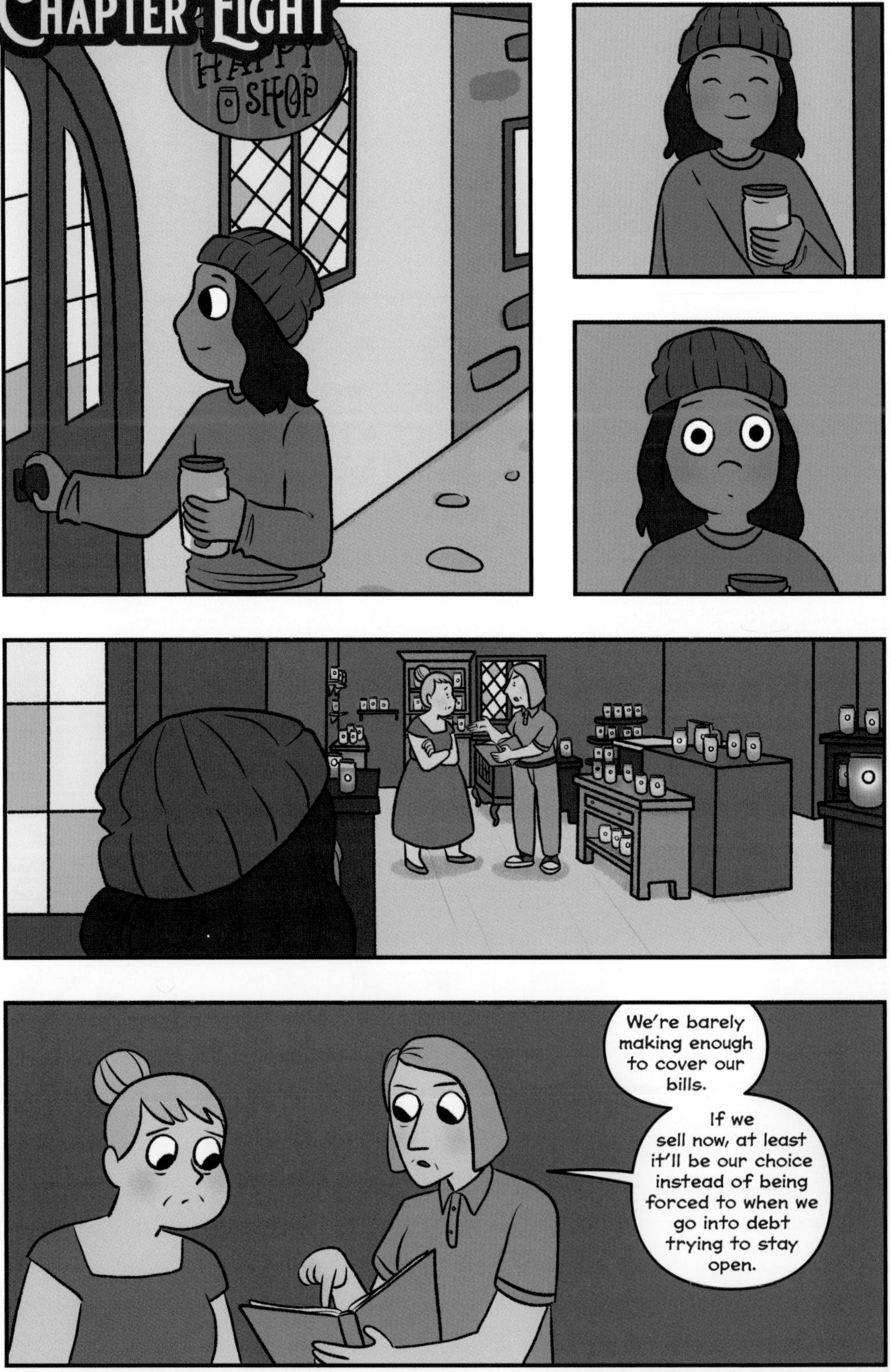
SHOP
We're barely making enough to cover our bills.
If we sell now, at least it'll be our choice instead of being forced to when we go into debt trying to stay open.

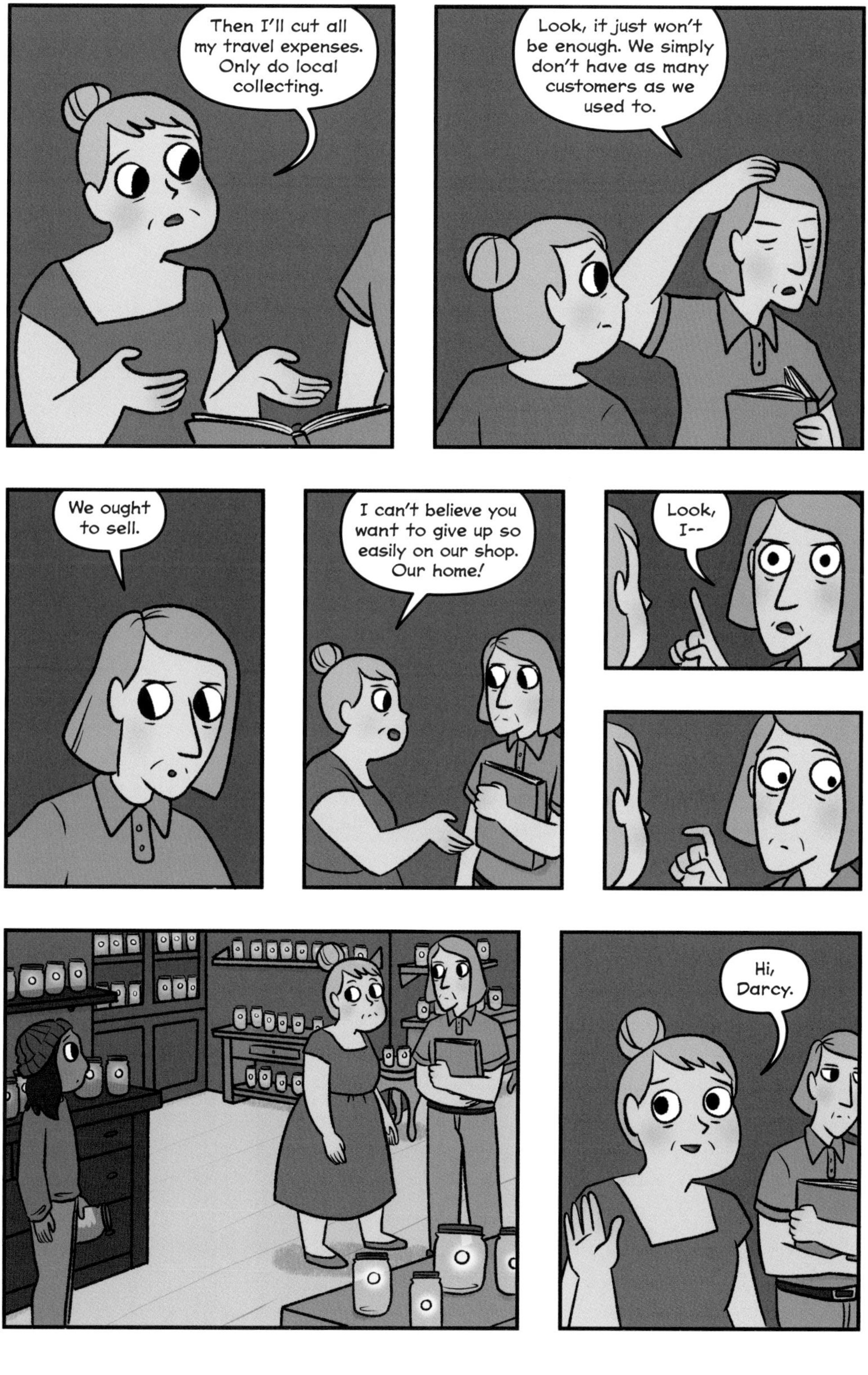
Then I'll cut all my travel expenses. Only do local collecting.
Look, it just won't be enough. We simply don't have as many customers as we used to.
We ought to sell.
I can't believe you want to give up so easily on our shop. Our home!
Look, I--
Hi, Darcy.

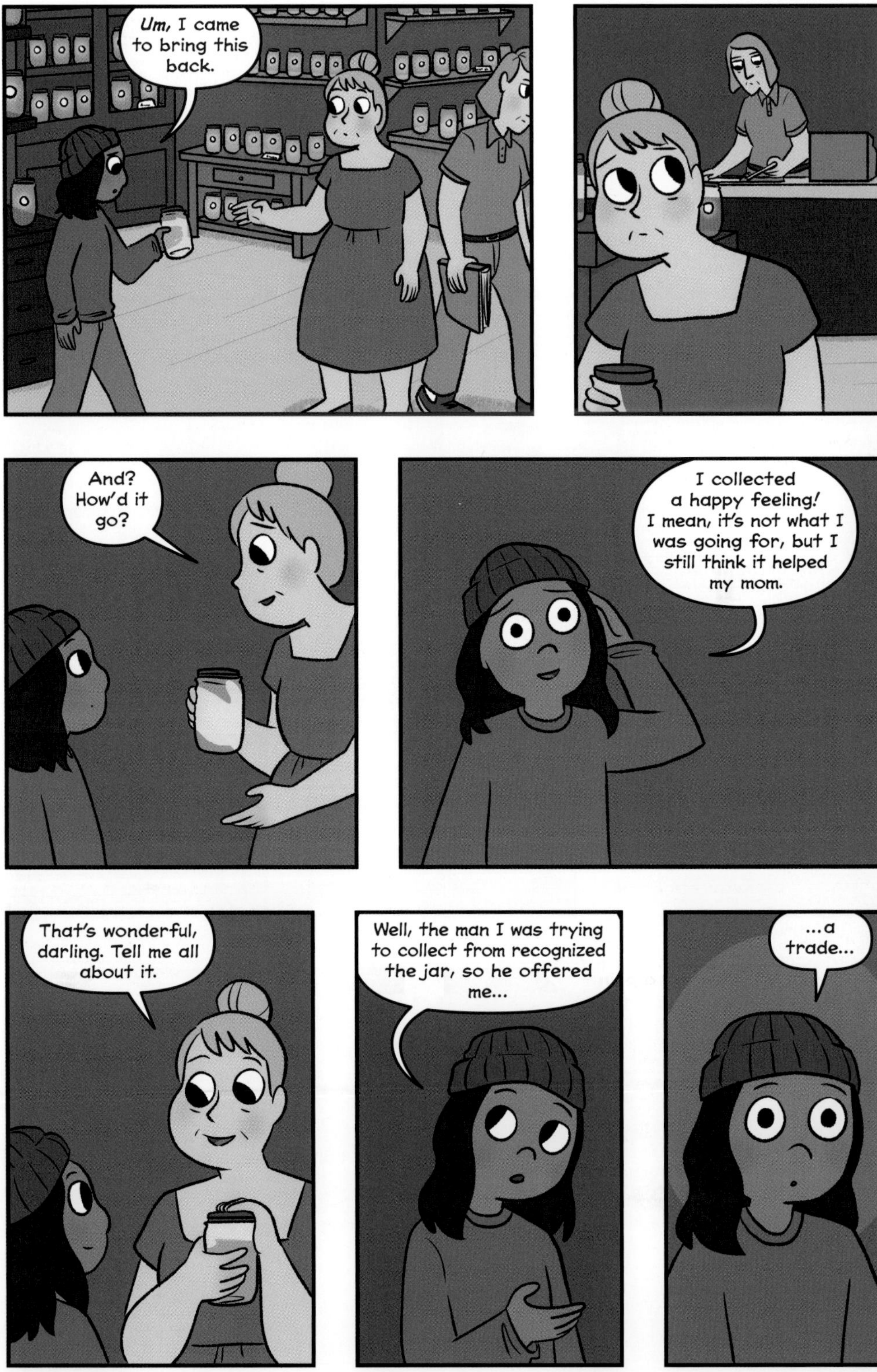
Um, I came to bring this back.
And? How'd it go?
I collected a happy feeling! I mean, it's not what I was going for, but I still think it helped my mom.
That's wonderful, darling. Tell me all about it.
Well, the man I was trying to collect from recognized the jar, so he offered me...
...a trade...

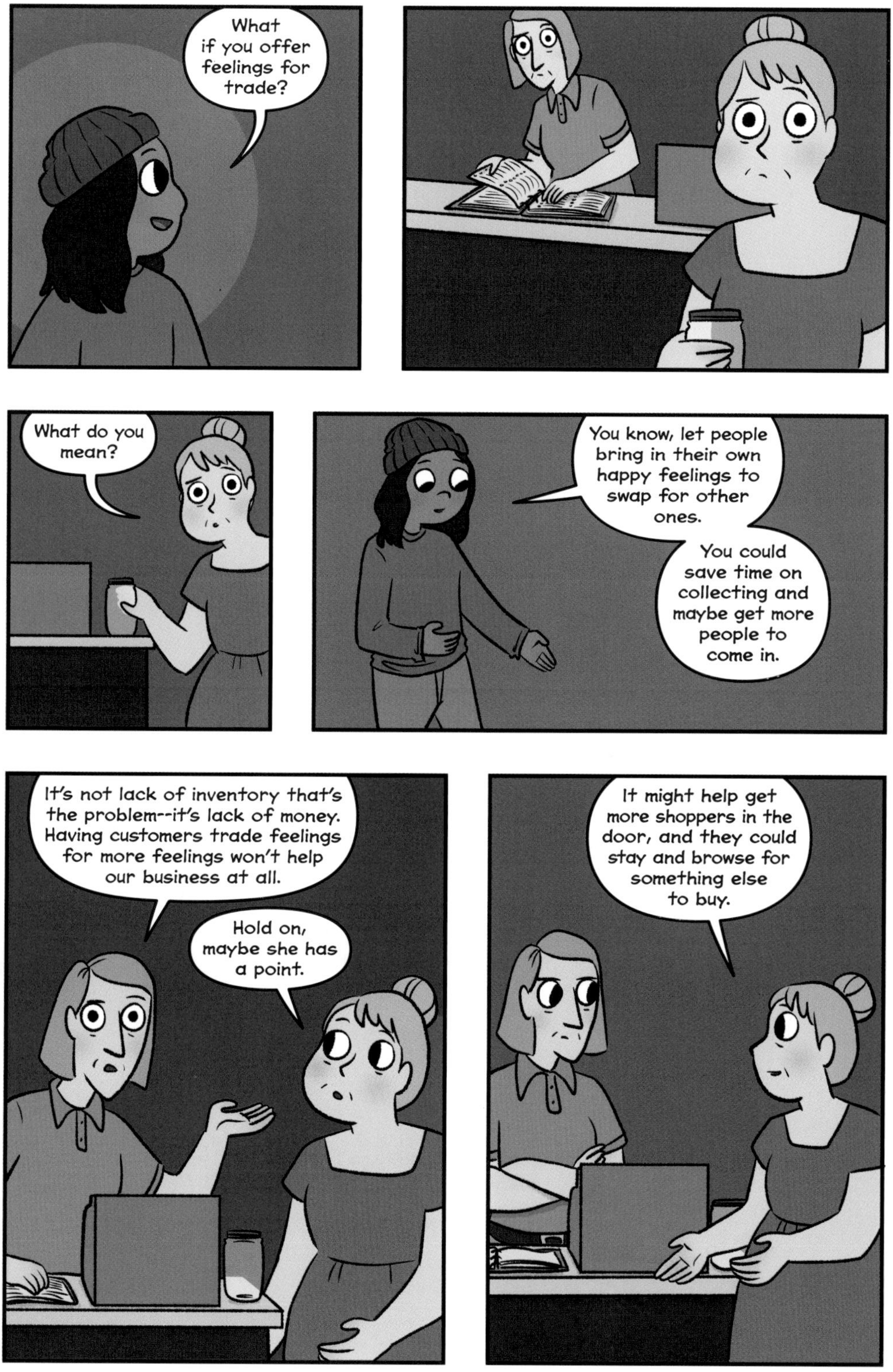
What if you offer feelings for trade?
What do you mean?
You know, let people bring in their own happy feelings to swap for other ones.
You could save time on collecting and maybe get more people to come in.
It's not lack of inventory that's the problem--it's lack of money. Having customers trade feelings for more feelings won't help our business at all.
Hold on, maybe she has a point.
It might help get more shoppers in the door, and they could stay and browse for something else to buy.

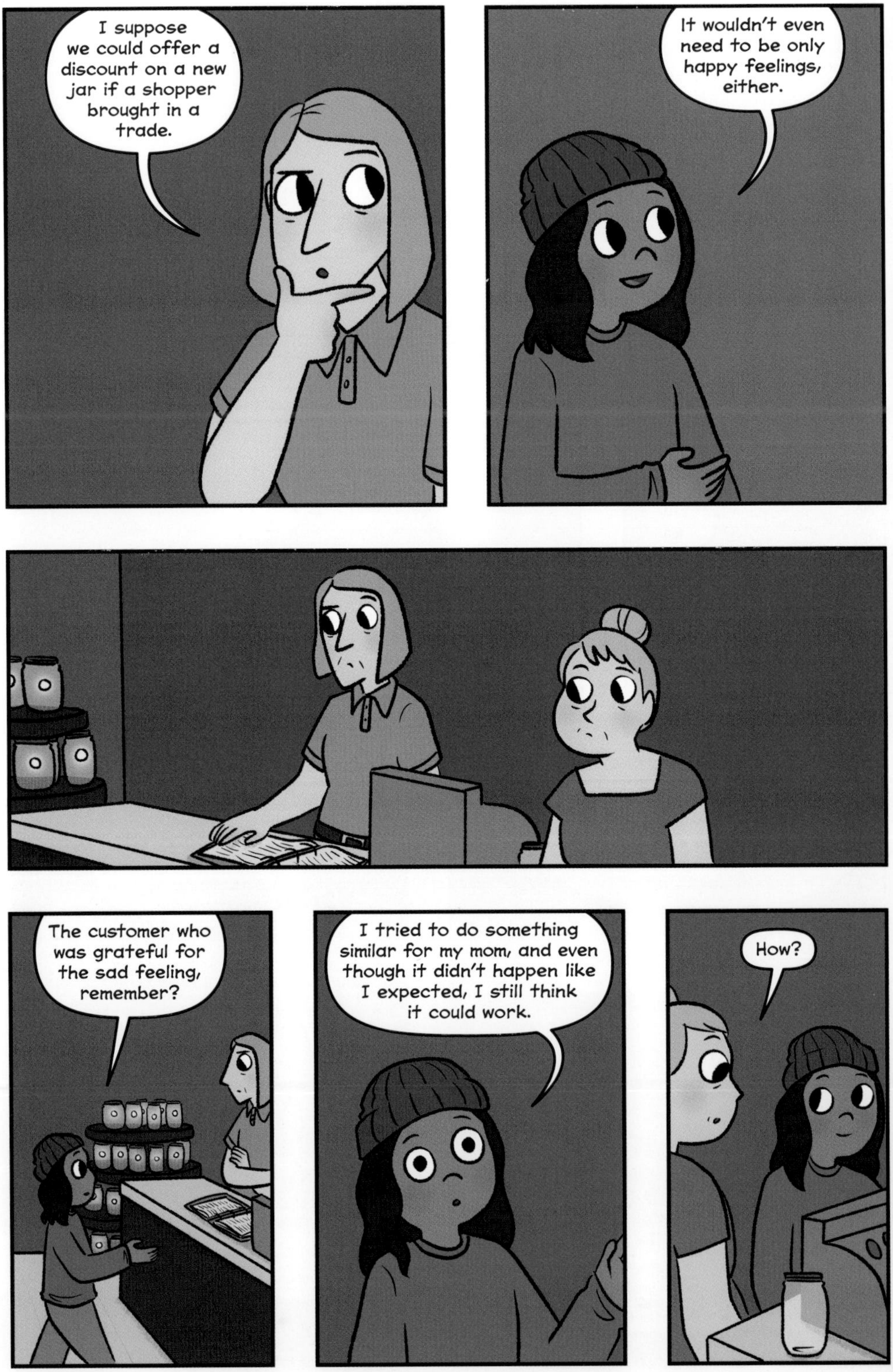
I suppose we could offer a discount on a new jar if a shopper brought in a trade.
It wouldn't even need to be only happy feelings, either.
The customer who was grateful for the sad feeling, remember?
I tried to do something similar for my mom, and even though it didn't happen like I expected, I still think it could work.
How?

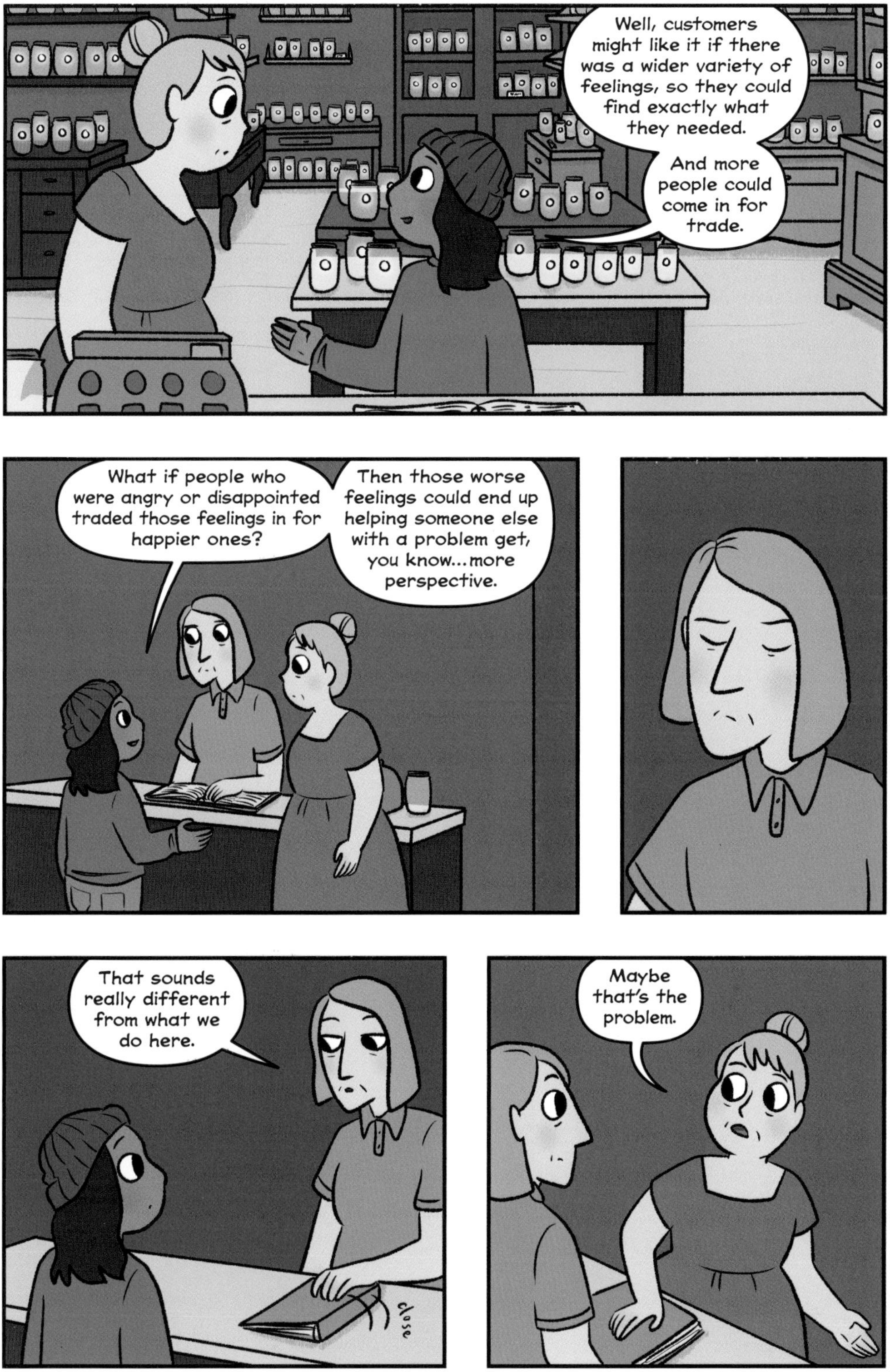
Well, customers might like it if there was a wider variety of feelings, so they could find exactly what they needed.
And more people could come in for trade.
What if people who were angry or disappointed traded those feelings in for happier ones?
Then those worse feelings could end up helping someone else with a problem get, you know...more perspective.
That sounds really different from what we do here.
close
Maybe that's the problem.

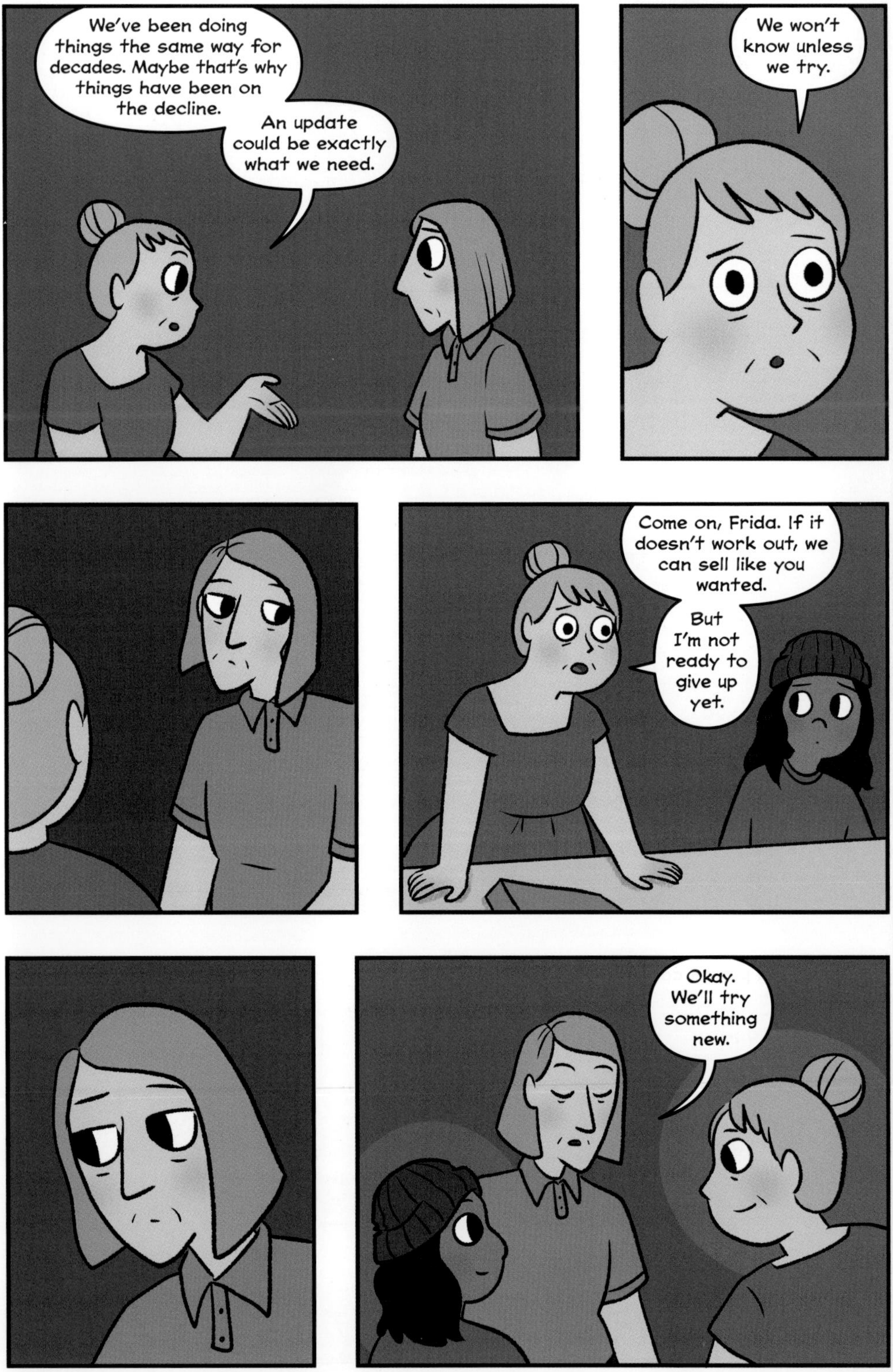

We've been doing things the same way for decades. Maybe that's why things have been on the decline.
An update could be exactly what we need.
We won't know unless we try.
Come on, Frida. If it doesn't work out, we can sell like you wanted.
But I'm not ready to give up yet.
Okay. We'll try something new.

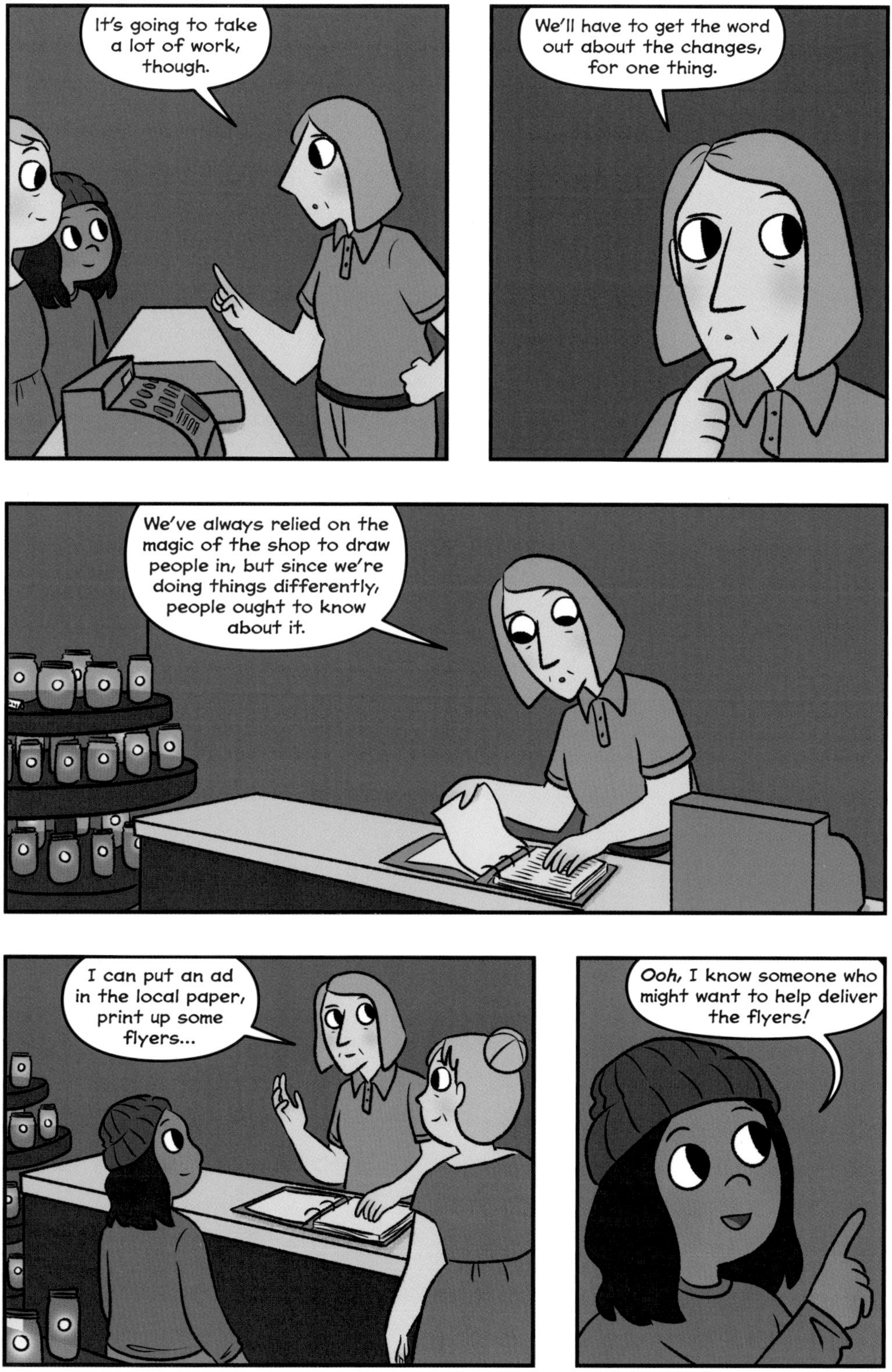
It's going to take a lot of work, though.
We'll have to get the word out about the changes, for one thing.
We've always relied on the magic of the shop to draw people in, but since we're doing things differently, people ought to know about it.
I can put an ad in the local paper, print up some flyers...
Ooh, I know someone who might want to help deliver the flyers!

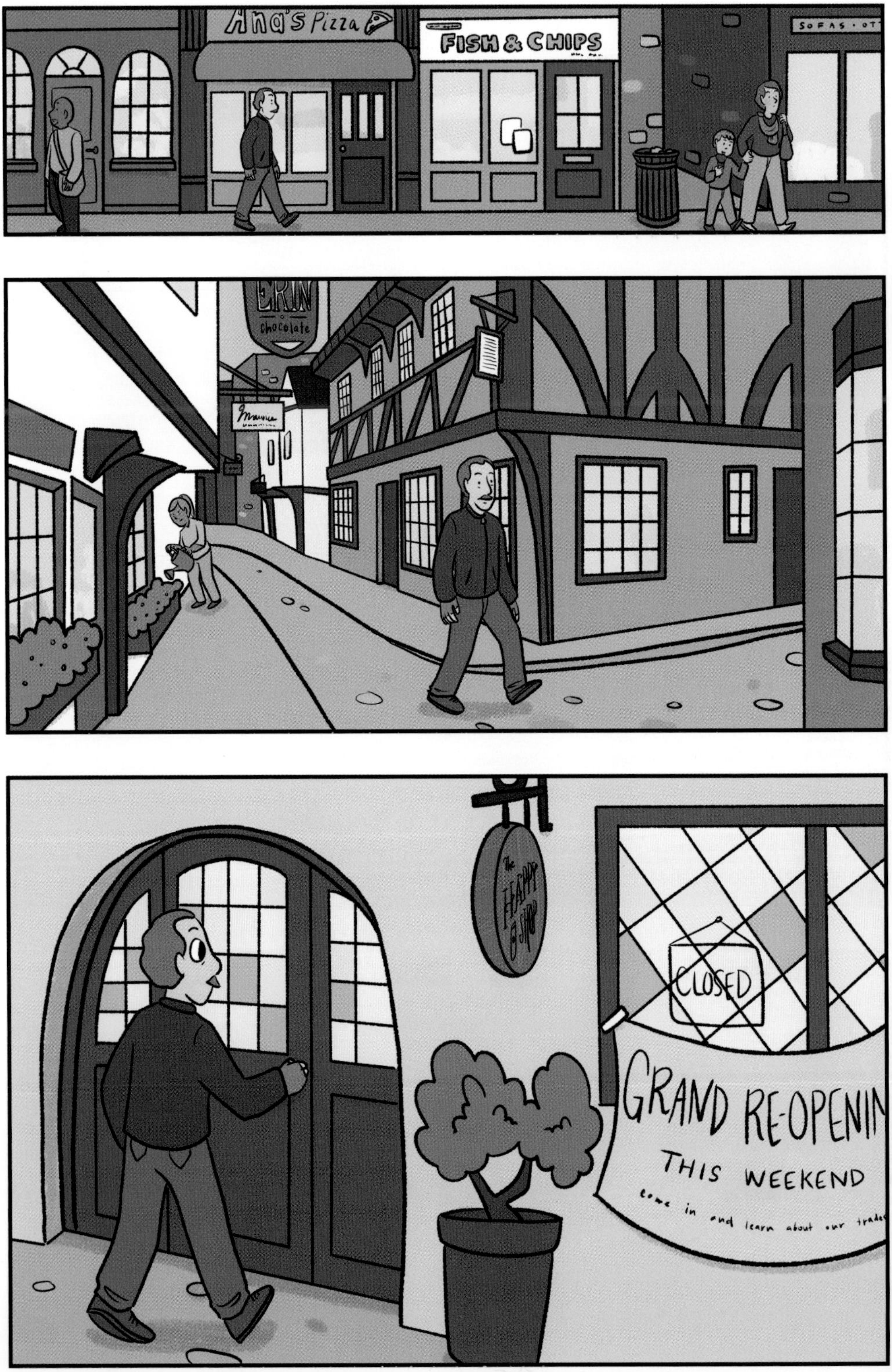
Ana's Pizza
FISH & CHIPS
SOFAS · OT
ERIN
chocolate
CLOSED
GRAND RE-OPENIN
THIS WEEKEND
come in and learn about our trade

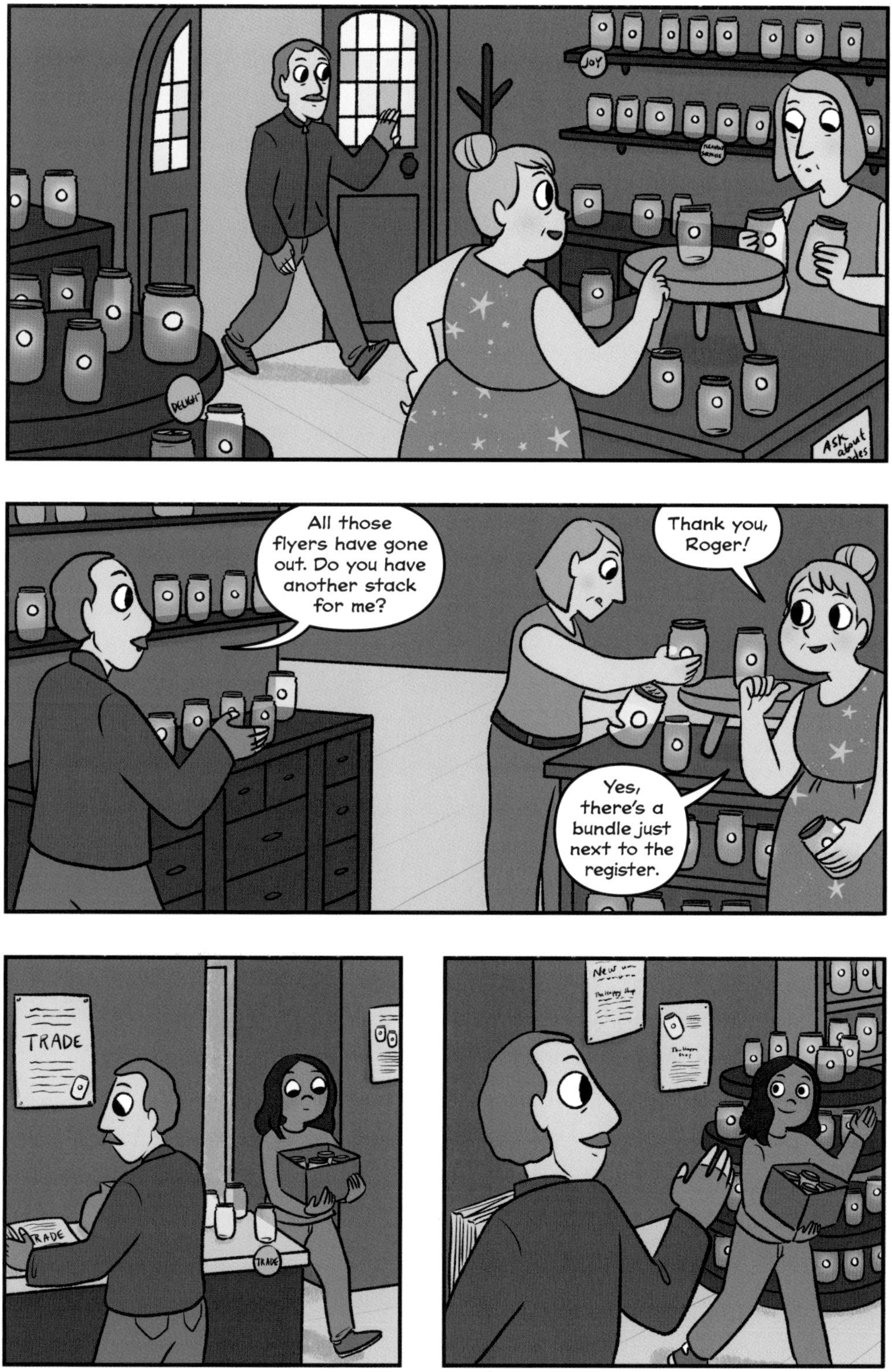
JOY
DELIGHT
All those flyers have gone out. Do you have another stack for me?
Thank you, Roger!
Yes, there's a bundle just next to the register.
TRADE
TRADE
TRADE

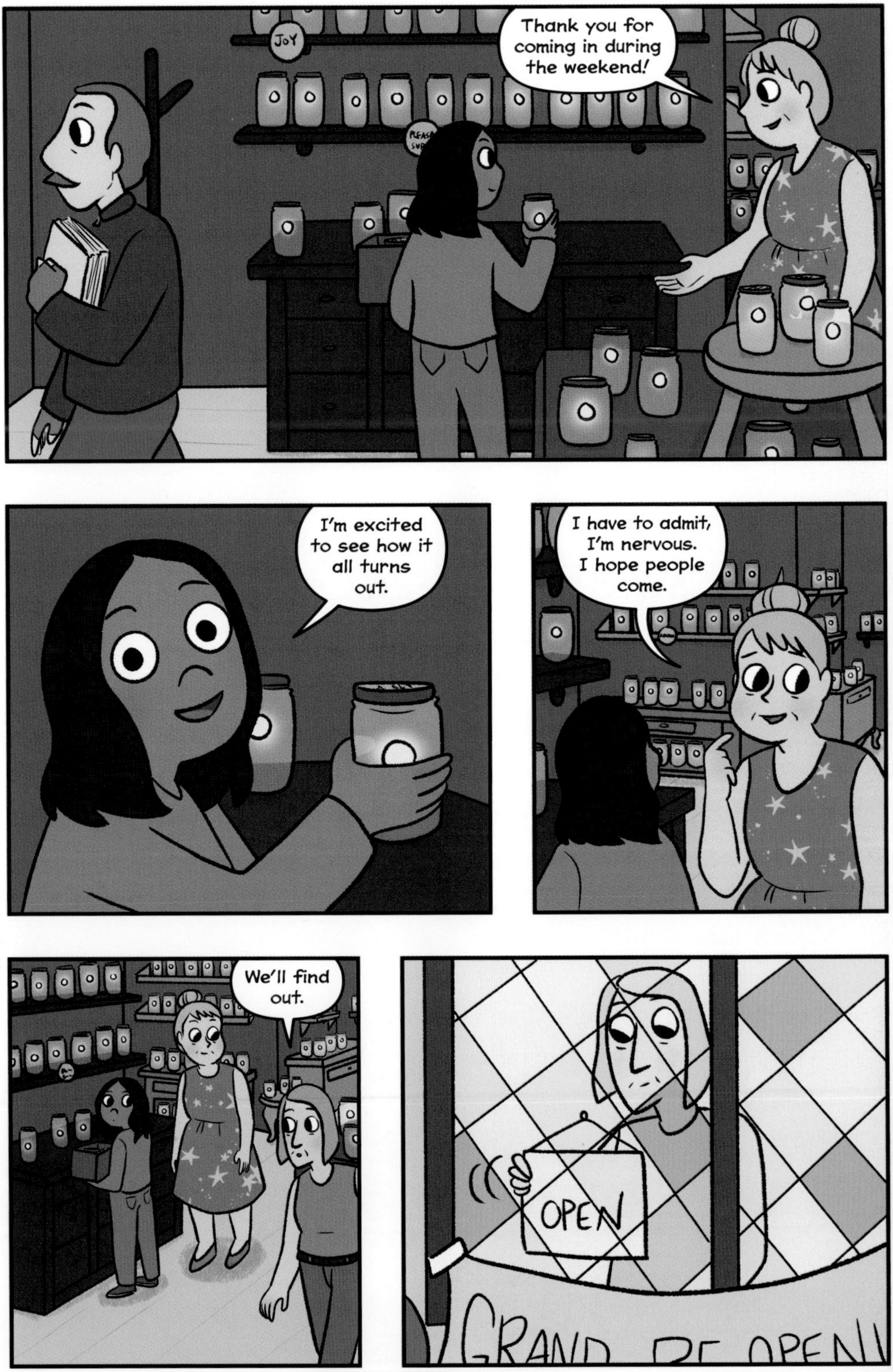
JOY
Thank you for coming in during the weekend!
I'm excited to see how it all turns out.
I have to admit, I'm nervous. I hope people come.
We'll find out.
OPEN

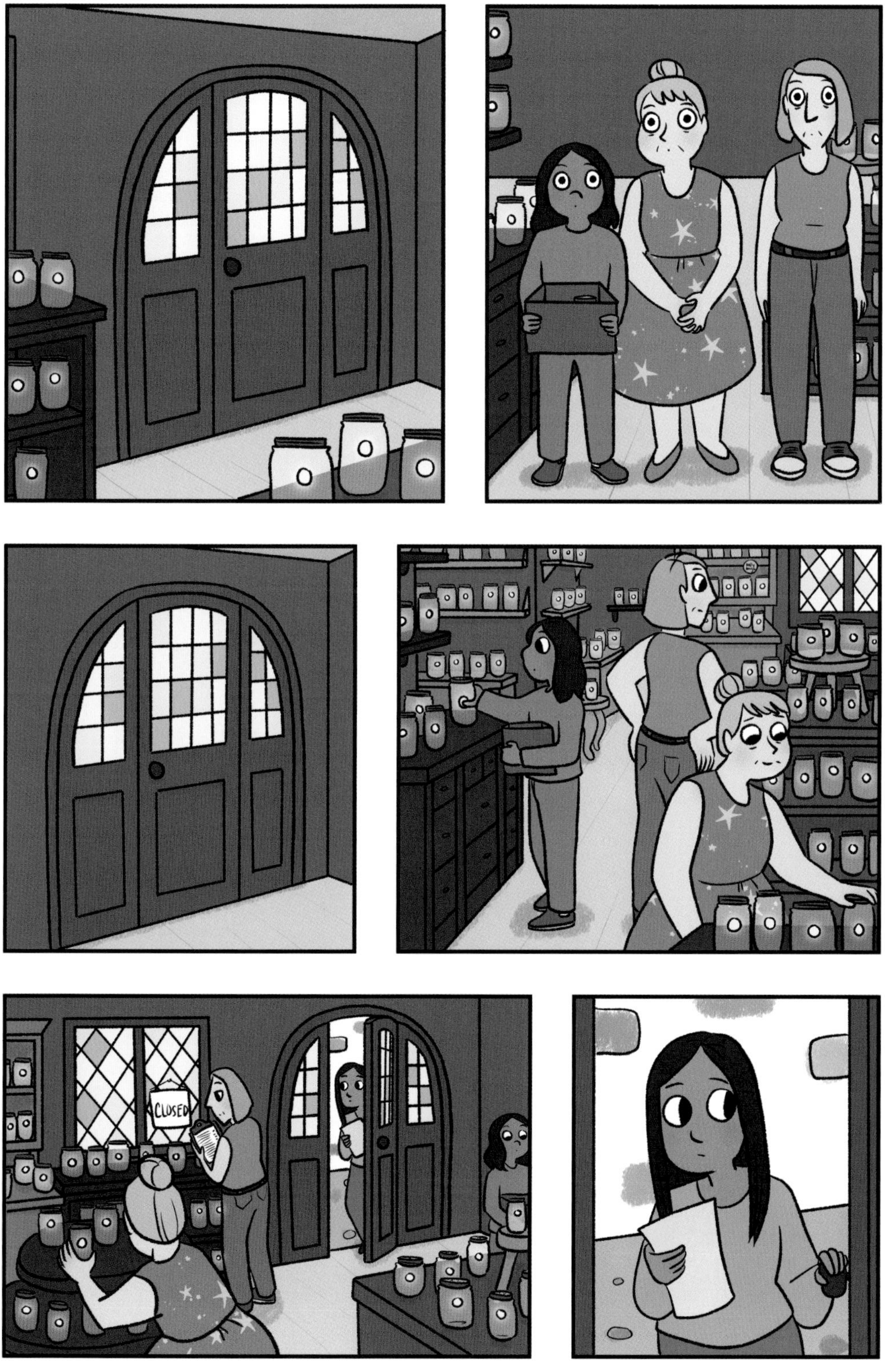
CLOSED

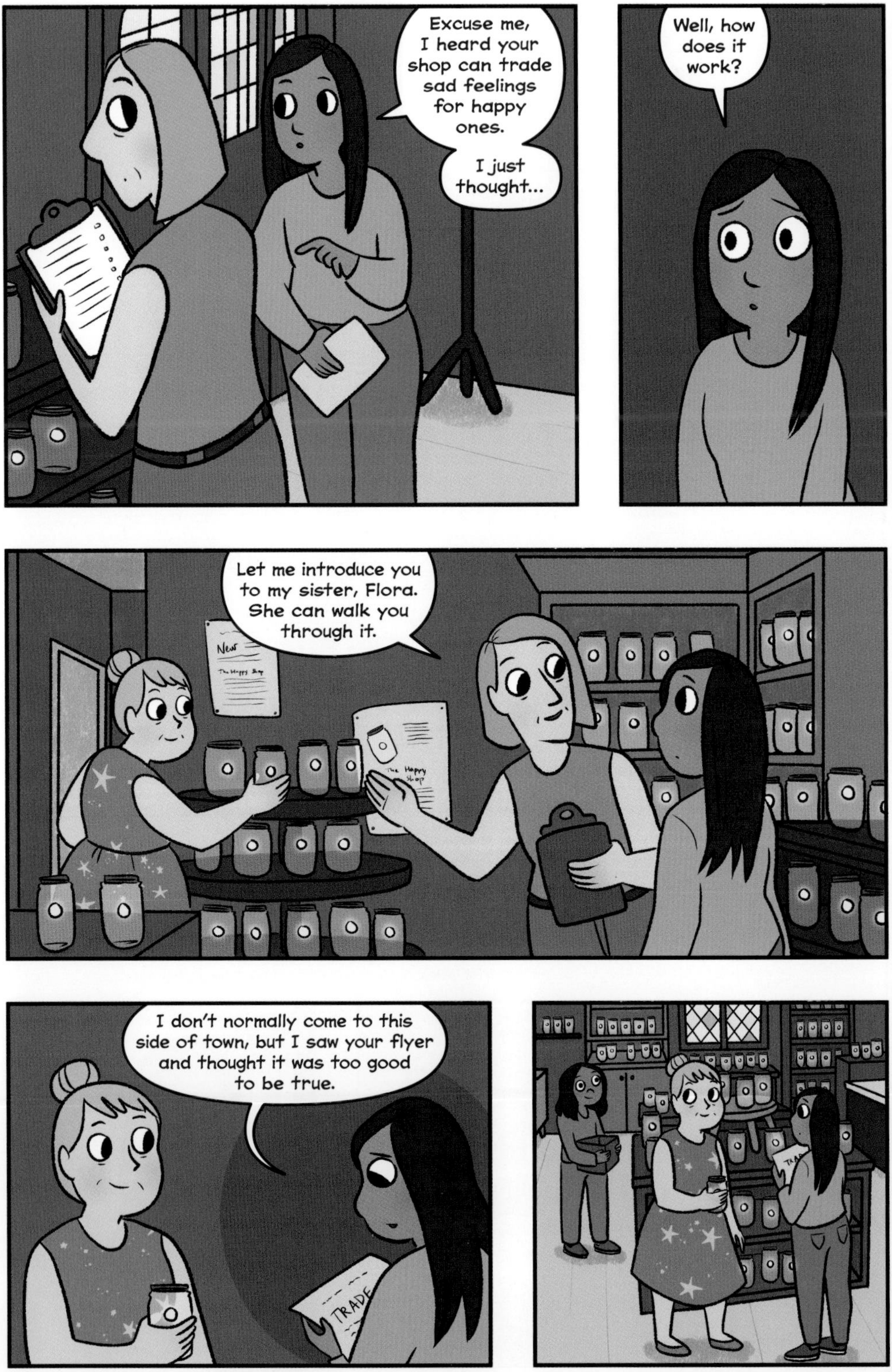
Excuse me, I heard your shop can trade sad feelings for happy ones.
I just thought...
Well, how does it work?
Let me introduce you to my sister, Flora. She can walk you through it.
I don't normally come to this side of town, but I saw your flyer and thought it was too good to be true.
TRADE

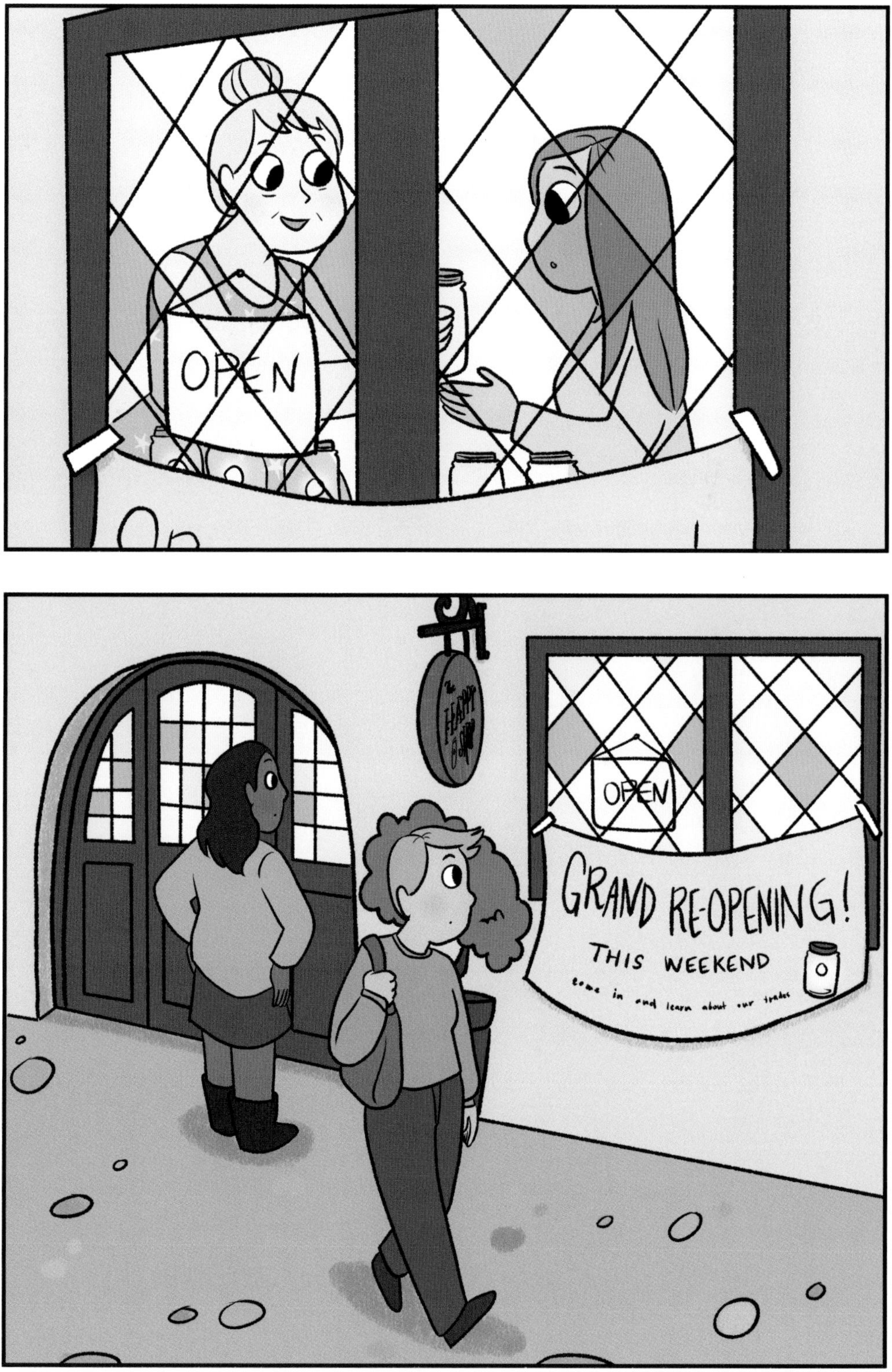
OPEN
OPEN
GRAND RE-OPENING!
THIS WEEKEND
come in and learn about our trades

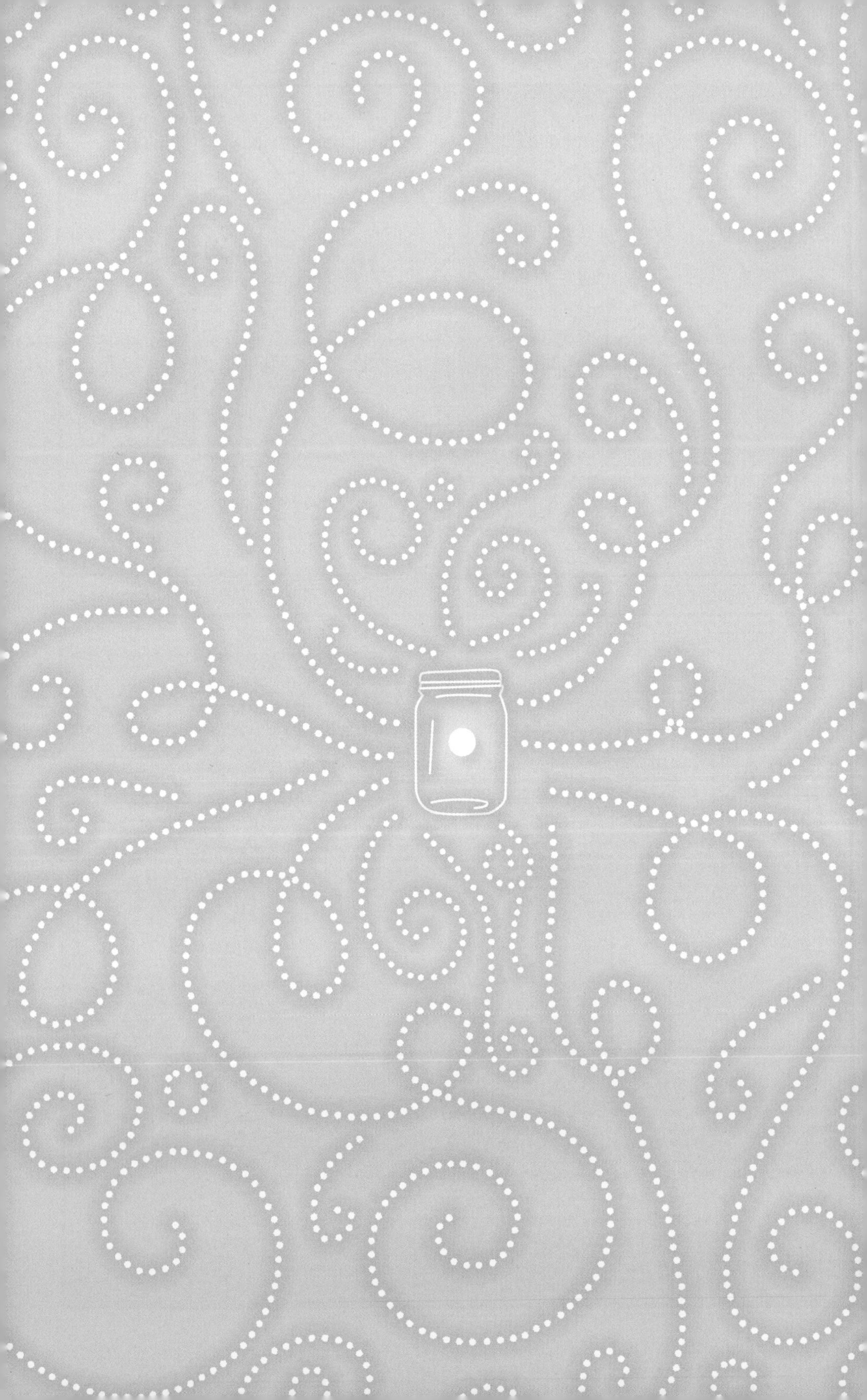

CHAPTER NINE

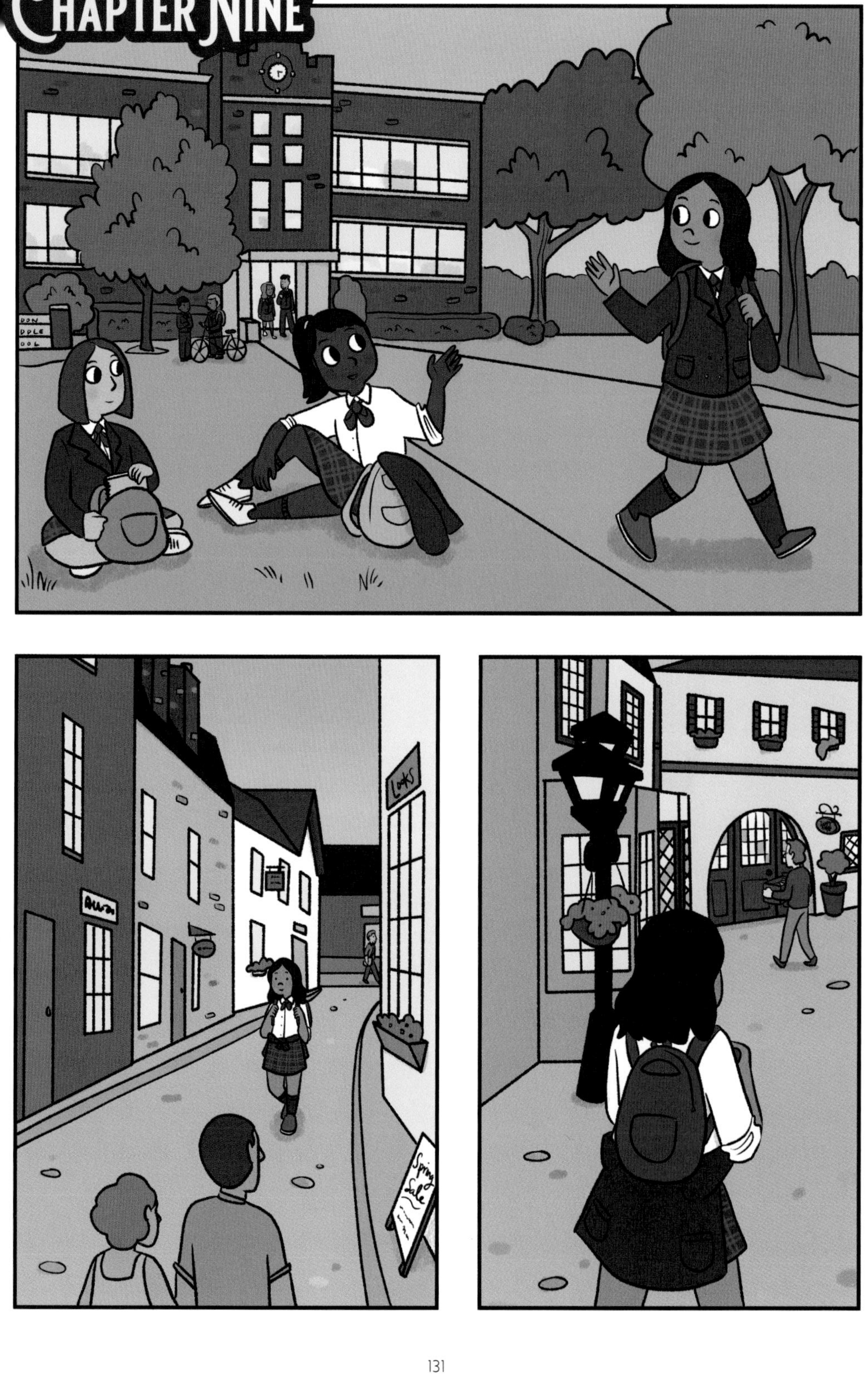
Looks
Spring Sale

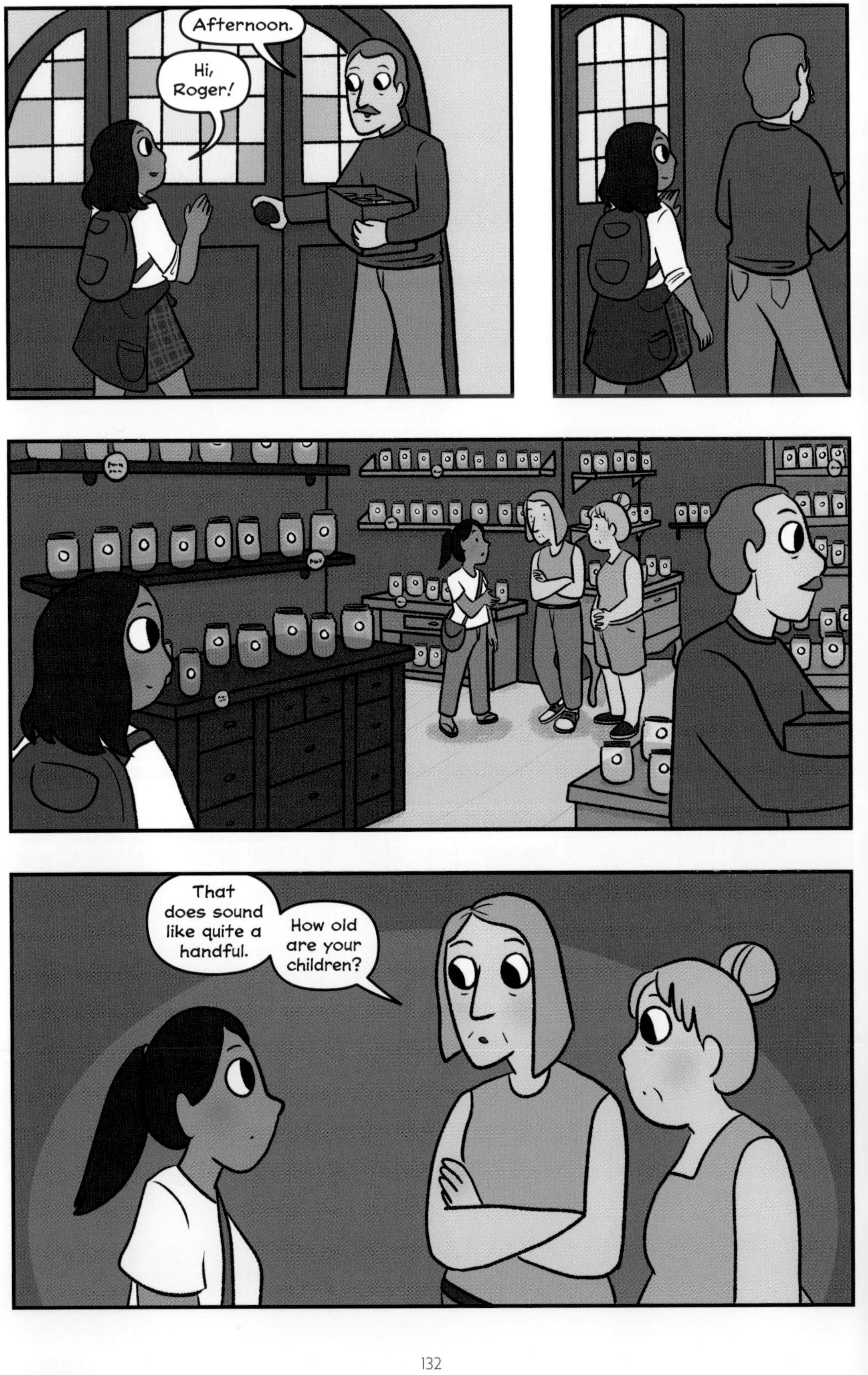
Afternoon.
Hi, Roger!
That does sound like quite a handful.
How old are your children?

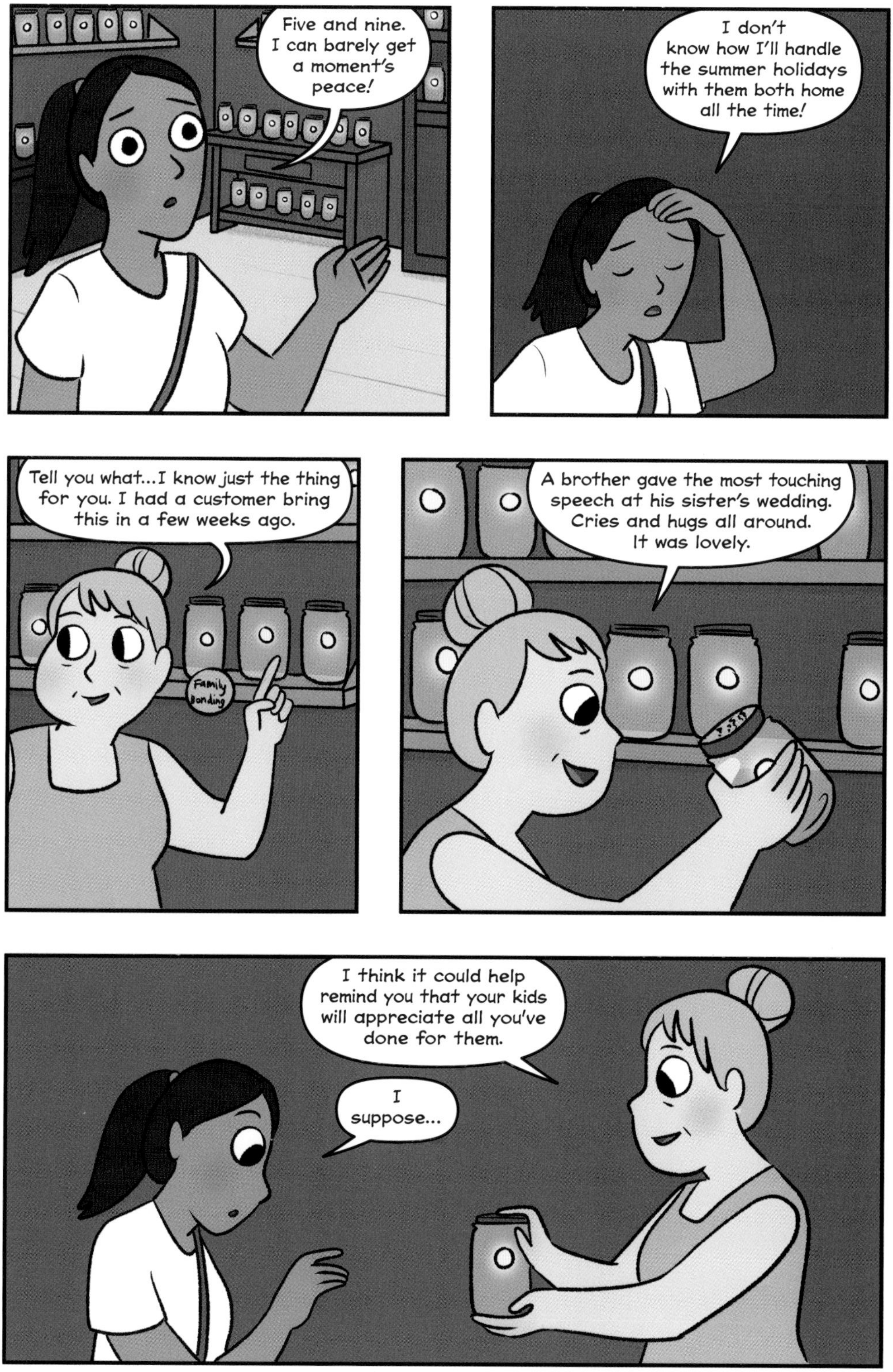
Five and nine. I can barely get a moment's peace!
I don't know how I'll handle the summer holidays with them both home all the time!
Tell you what...I know just the thing for you. I had a customer bring this in a few weeks ago.
Family Bonding
A brother gave the most touching speech at his sister's wedding. Cries and hugs all around. It was lovely.
I think it could help remind you that your kids will appreciate all you've done for them.
I suppose...

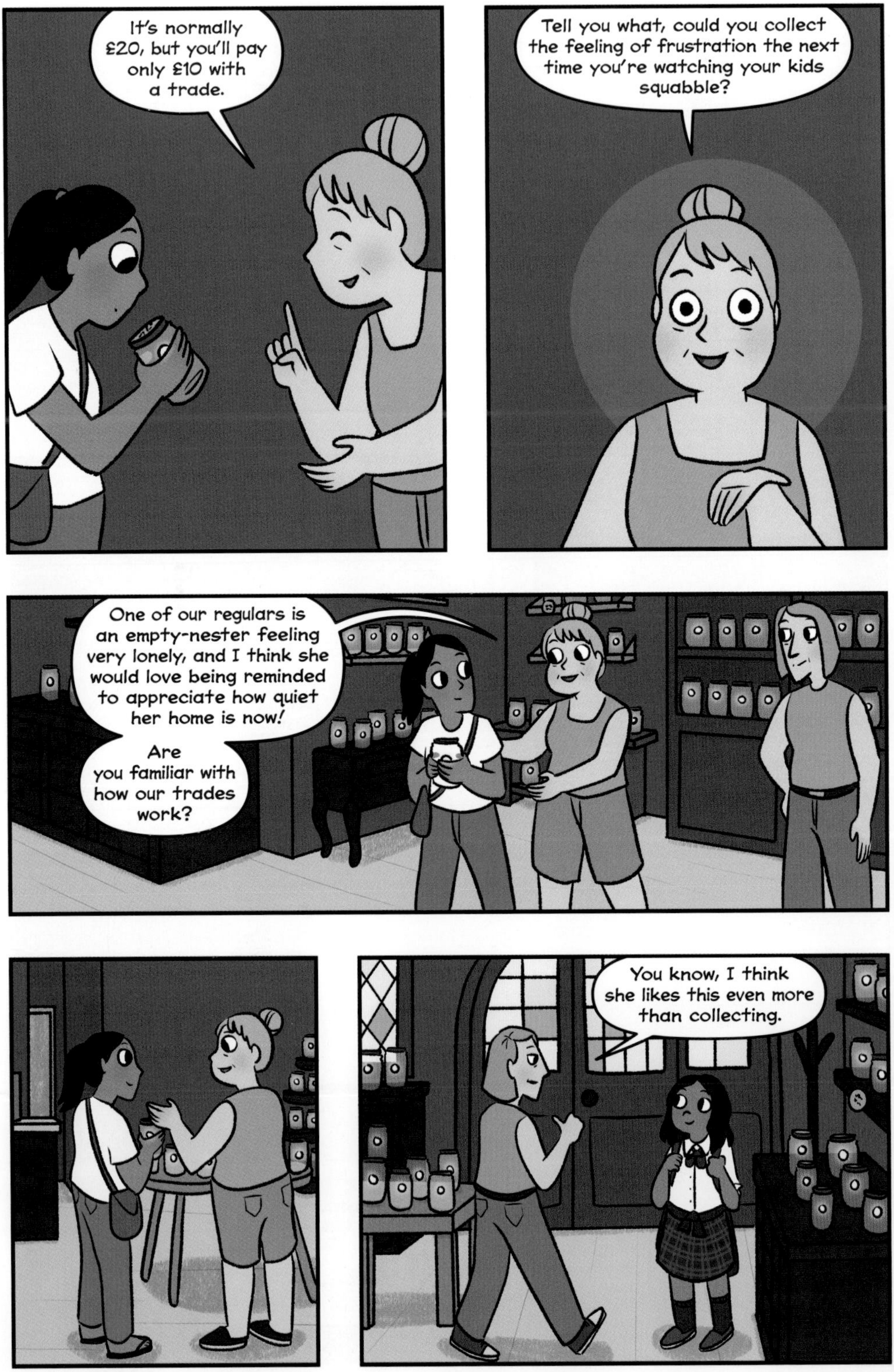
It's normally £20, but you'll pay only £10 with a trade.
Tell you what, could you collect the feeling of frustration the next time you're watching your kids squabble?
One of our regulars is an empty-nester feeling very lonely, and I think she would love being reminded to appreciate how quiet her home is now!
Are you familiar with how our trades work?
You know, I think she likes this even more than collecting.

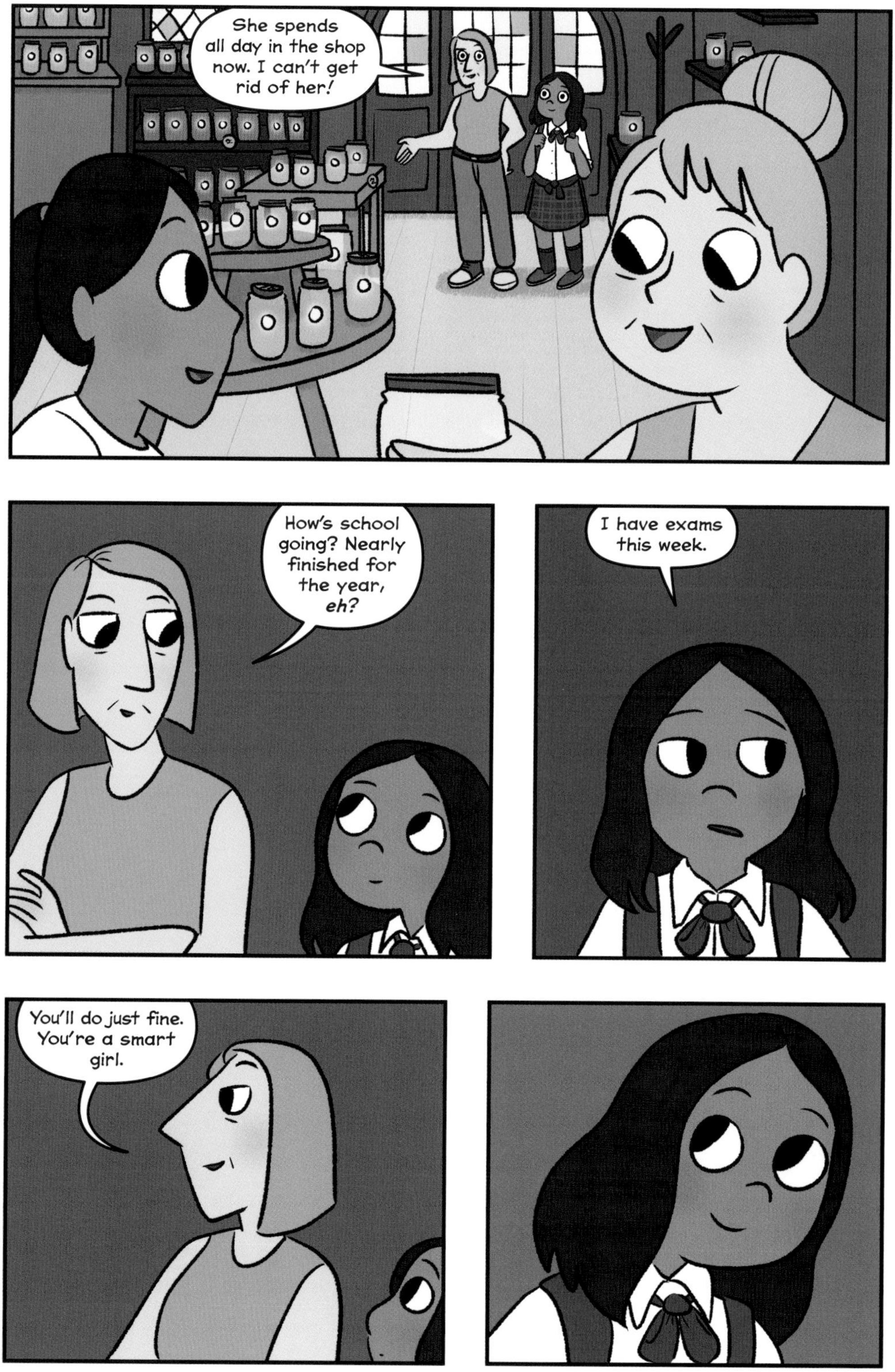
She spends all day in the shop now. I can't get rid of her!
How's school going? Nearly finished for the year, *eh?*
I have exams this week.
You'll do just fine. You're a smart girl.

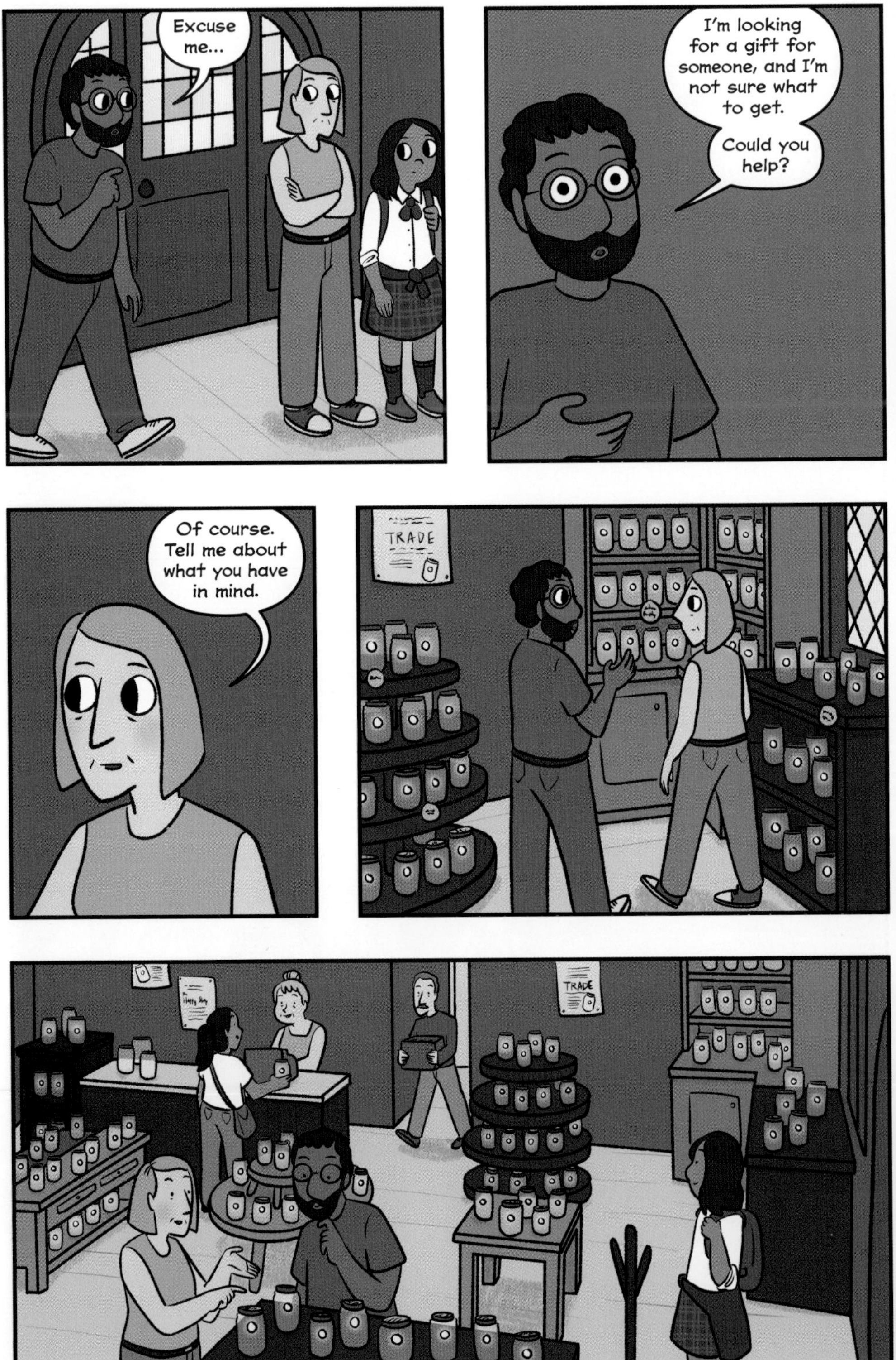
Excuse me...
I'm looking for a gift for someone, and I'm not sure what to get.
Could you help?
Of course. Tell me about what you have in mind.
TRADE
TRADE

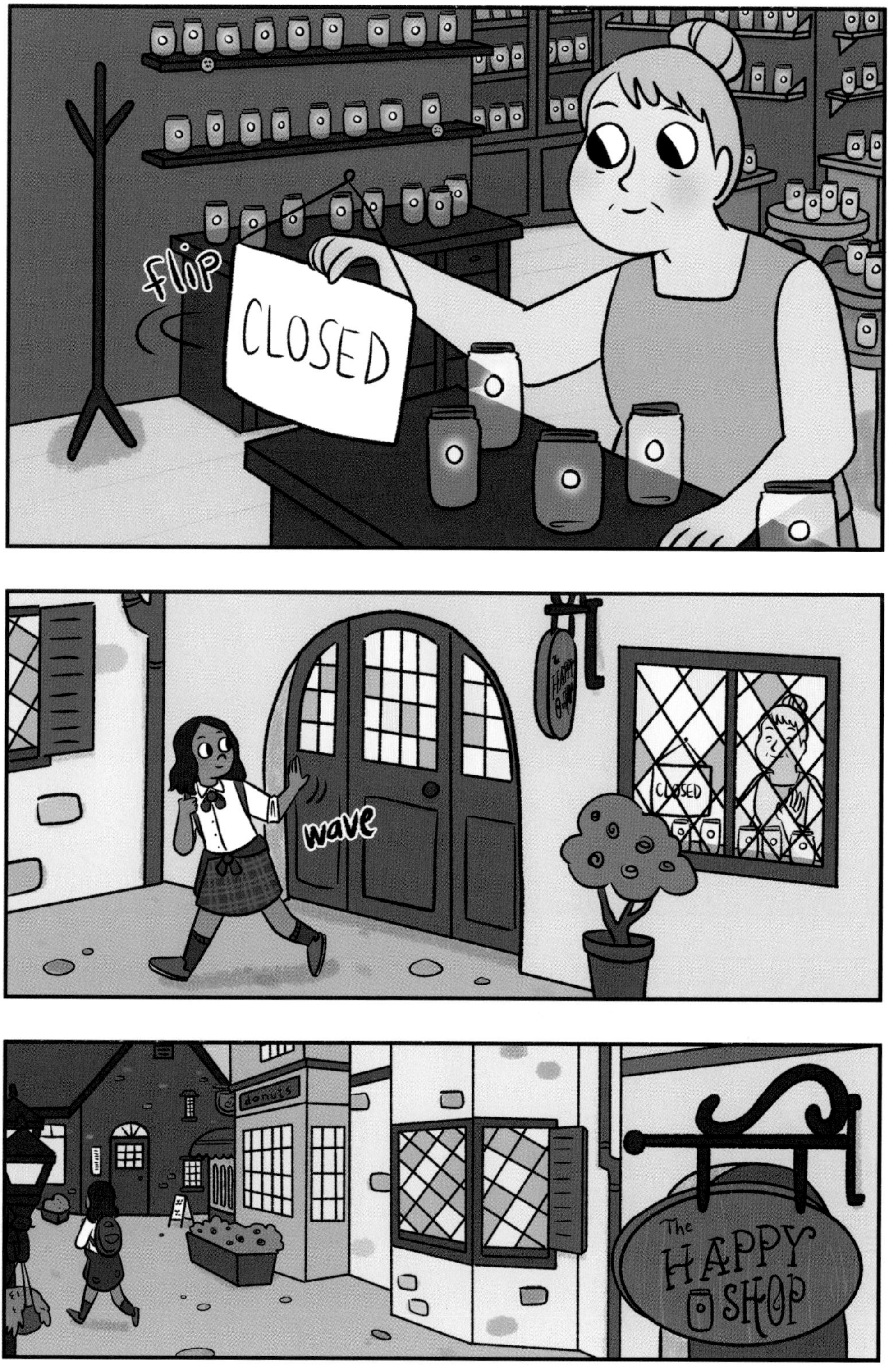
flip
CLOSED
wave
CLOSED
donuts
The HAPPY SHOP

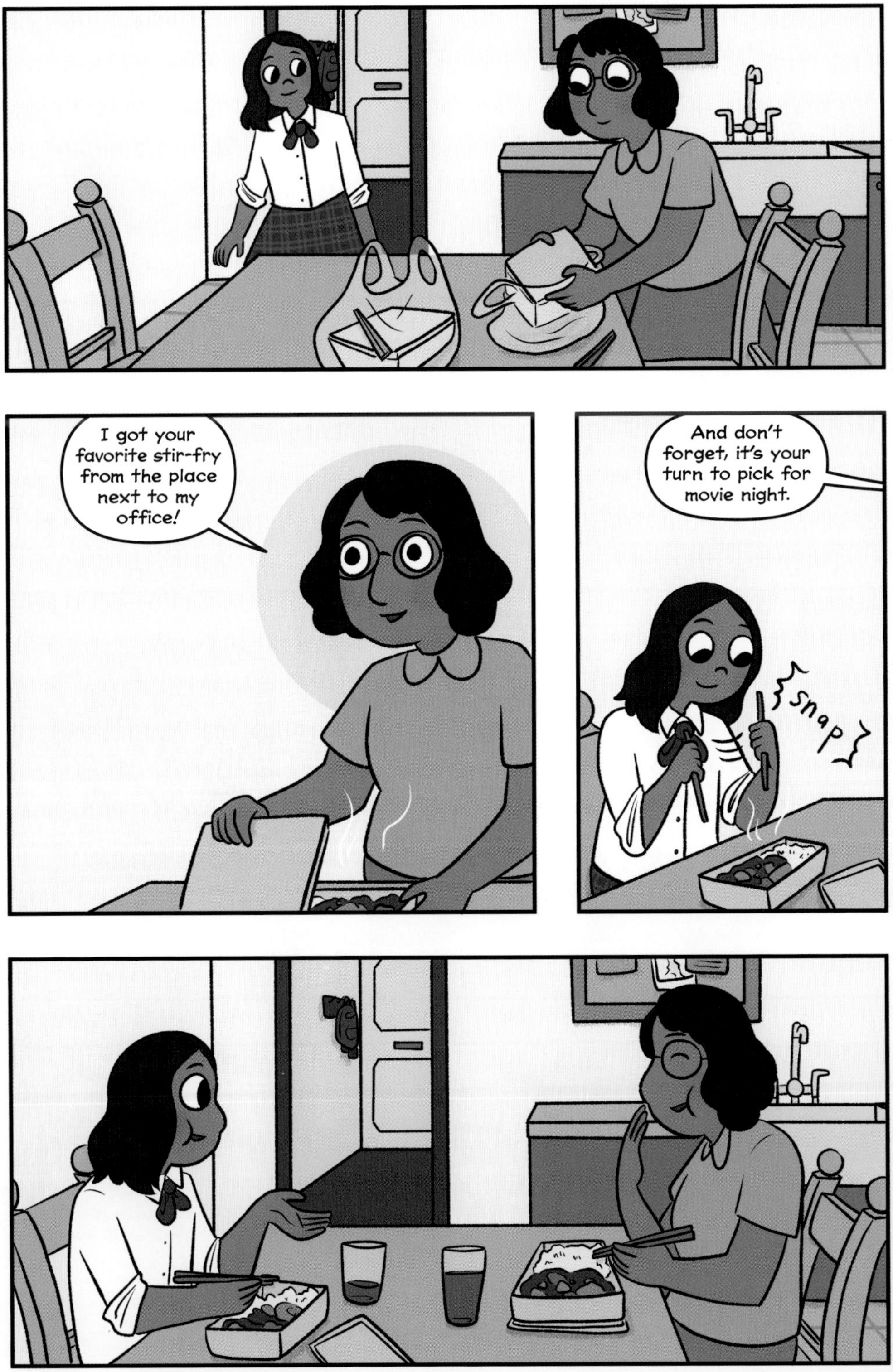
I got your favorite stir-fry from the place next to my office!
And don't forget, it's your turn to pick for movie night.
SNAP

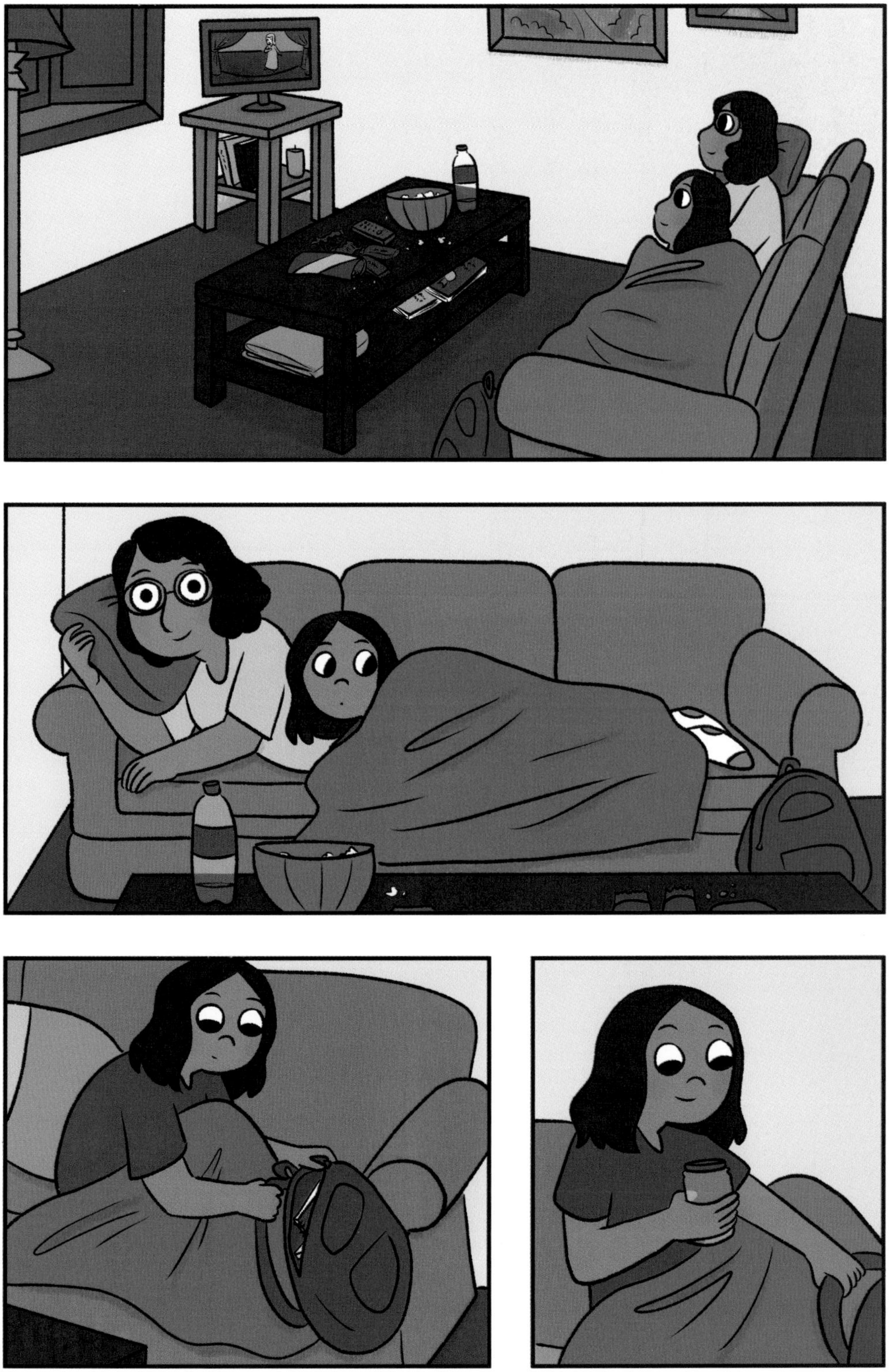

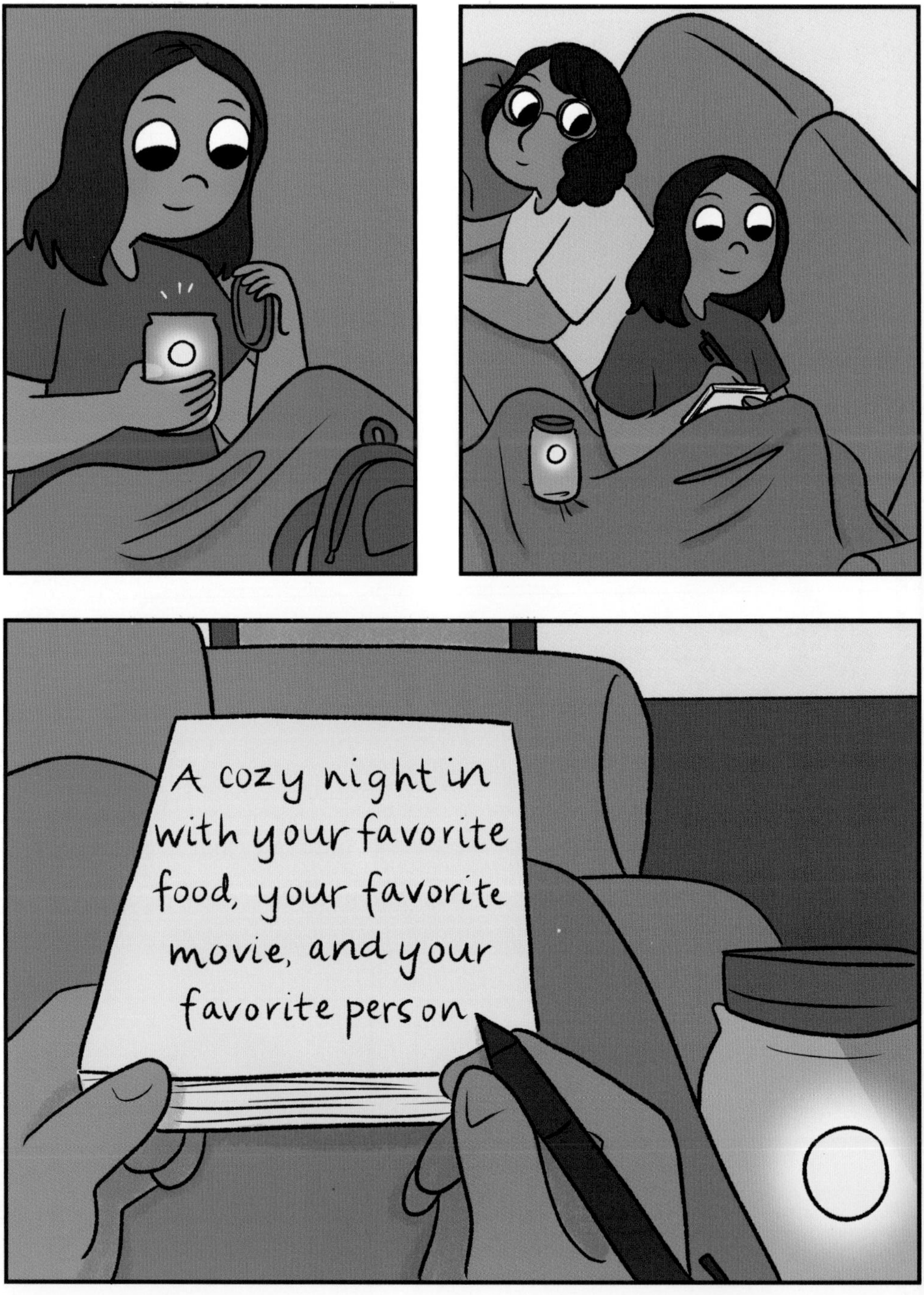
A cozy night in with your favorite food, your favorite movie, and your favorite person.

THE END

Character Sketches

DARCY

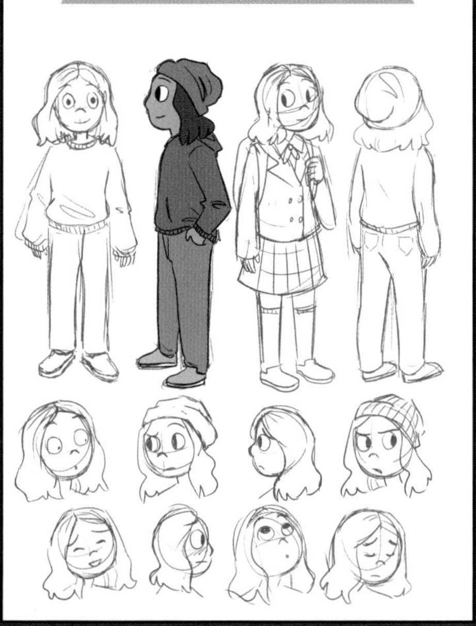

HELEN

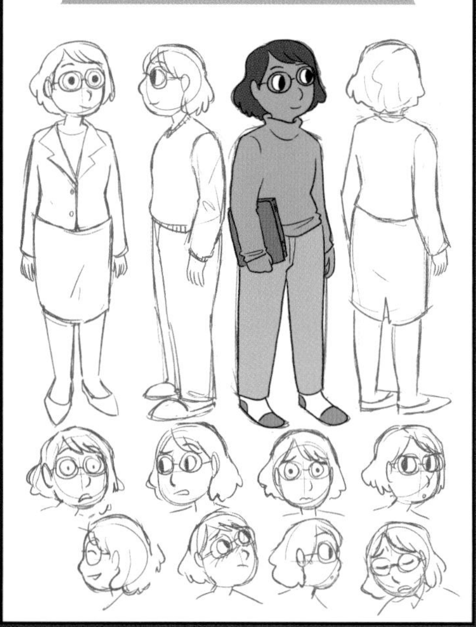

FRIDA

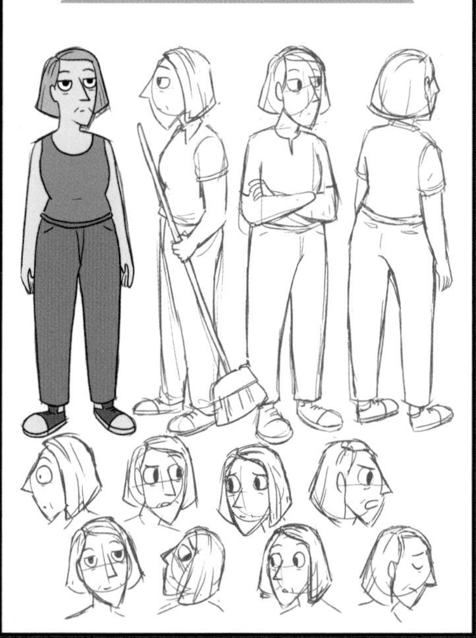

FLORA

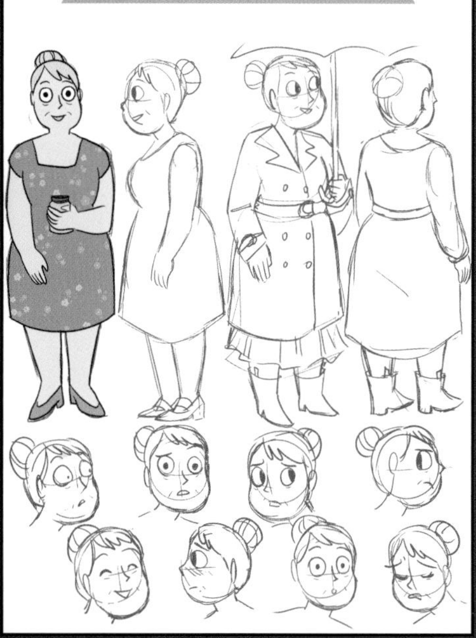

Sketches by Brittany Long Olsen

Process Pages

THUMBNAILS

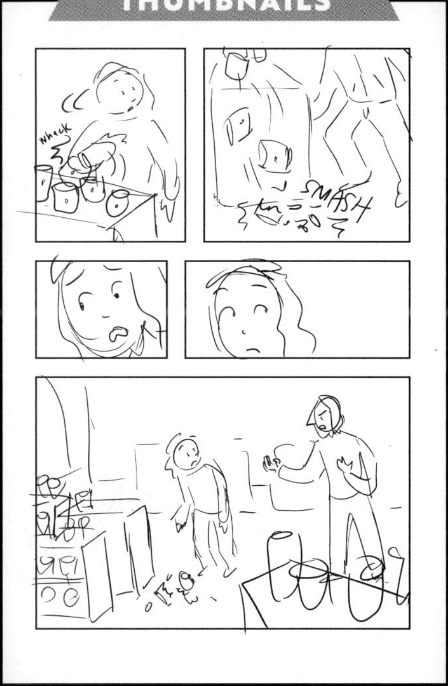
WHACK
SMASH

PENCILS

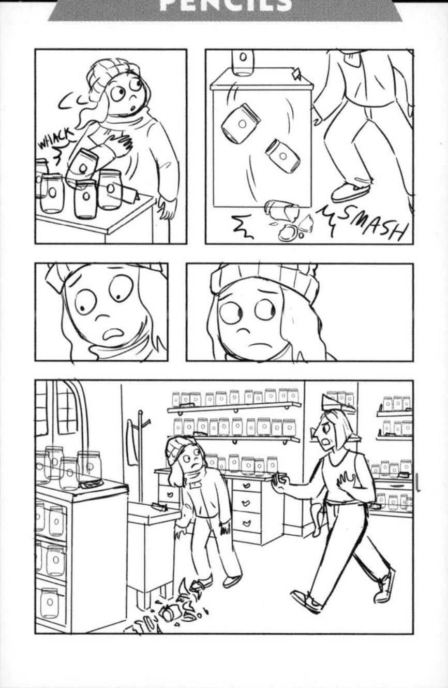
WHACK
SMASH

INKS

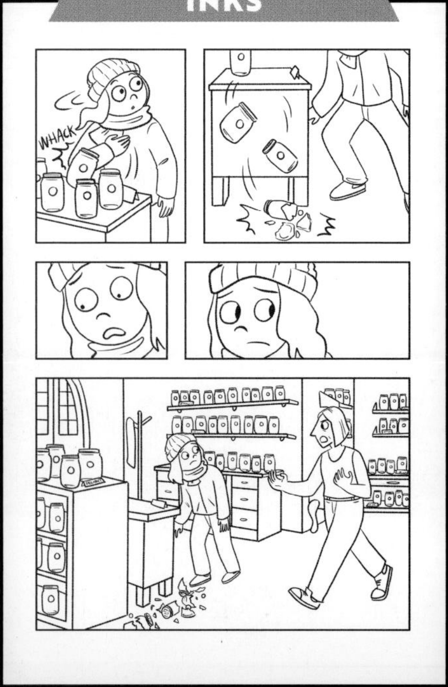
WHACK

COLORS

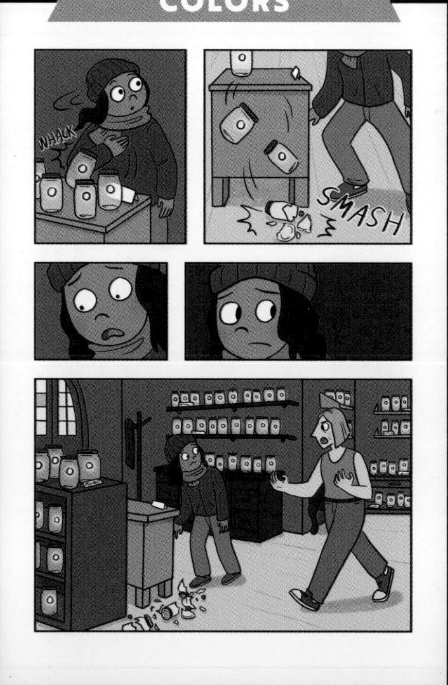
WHACK
SMASH

Process pages by Brittany Long Olsen

Brittany Long Olsen

is an author, illustrator, cartoonist, and editor. She has lived in three different countries over the past ten years and made comics about her adventures (and culture shock!) in each one. Her happy jar would contain videos of unlikely animal friends. She currently resides with her partner and their dog, Jetpack, near Portland, Oregon.

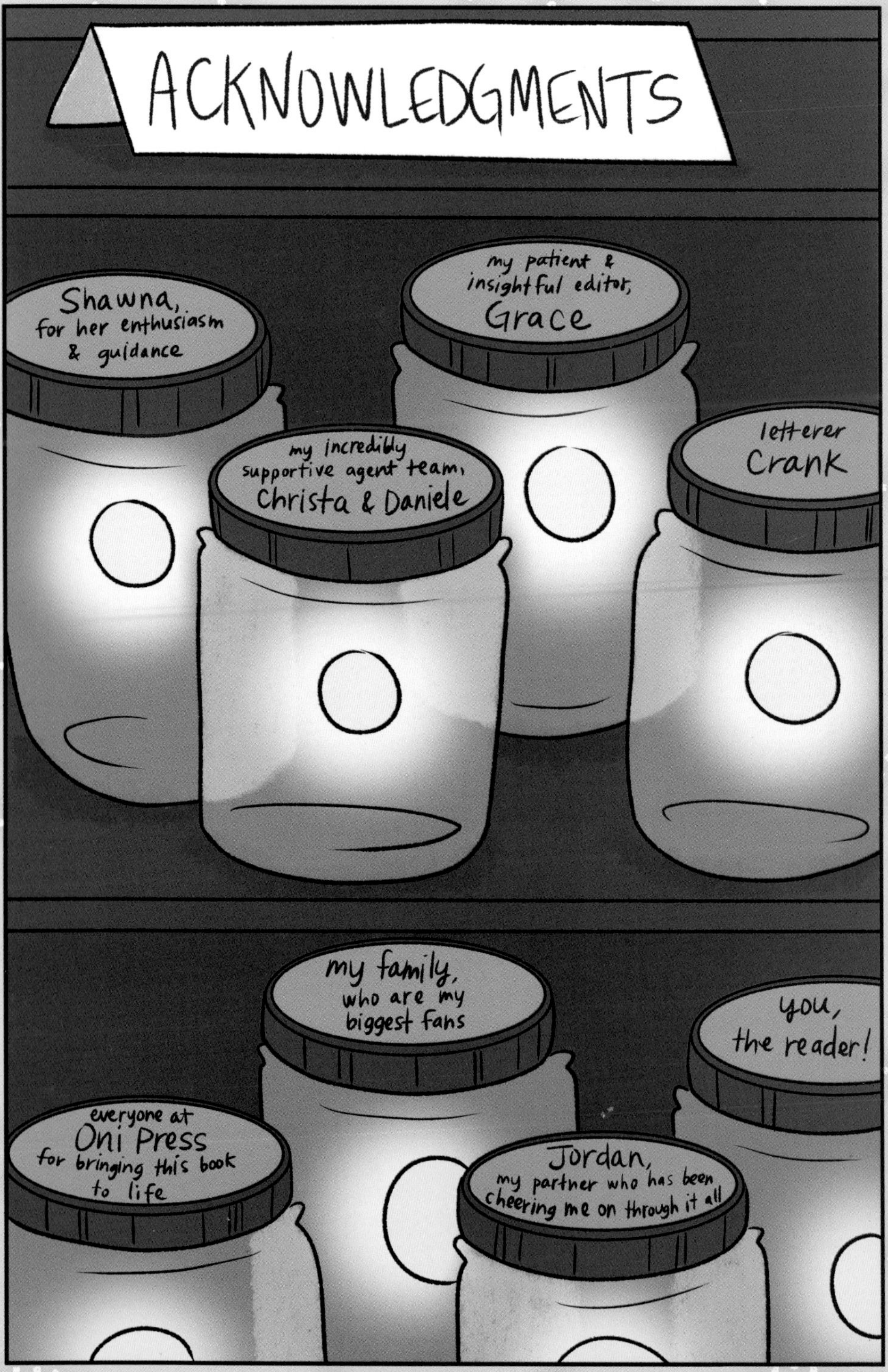
ACKNOWLEDGMENTS
Shawna, for her enthusiasm & guidance
my patient & insightful editor, Grace
my incredibly supportive agent team, Christa & Daniele
letterer Crank
my family, who are my biggest fans
you, the reader!
everyone at Oni Press for bringing this book to life
Jordan, my partner who has been cheering me on through it all